NO SMALL THING

by

Veronica Handover

Veronica
xx

First published 2018 by
49Knights
independent publishing house Edinburgh and Cambridge.

Text copyright © Veronica Handover, 2018

Typeset copyright © by 49Knights

ISBN 978-1-9993658-0-6

For more information please visit www.49Knights.com.

Printed and bound in Great Britain by Clays Ltd, Elcograf S.p.A

For Richard

Chapter One

In the end the words came quite easily. Rose blew on the ink, folded the letter and slipped it into the envelope that she had typed carefully at her desk.

Robert Unwin RIBA

She hoped that was right, frowned a little and ran a finger over the next line.

Angus & Latimer Architectural Services

The address was no problem; her mother had supplied it and she'd double-checked on the Internet, hoping in vain for some pictures. A first-class stamp and she was ready; she would post it on her way home. She allowed no doubts to creep in as she walked steadily, almost unaware of other pedestrians, her mind fixed on the post box at the end of the road near the tube station. She went straight up to it and shoved in the envelope so hard she heard it hit metal on the other side. *I've done it*, she told herself, gasping as if she'd been holding her breath. *At last, I've done it.*

The next day, miles away in a pretty country town, Rob and his colleagues walked back from Franco's, the restaurant at the other end of the market place, their usual haunt for celebrations and goodbyes and finally for this parting of the ways. An Indian summer, people were calling it; they carried their jackets over shoulders, hastening only a little, after a glance at their mobile phones.

'A damn good lunch. Thanks very much. I'll miss all this you know.' Rob allowed a little sentiment to creep in.

'Rubbish,' said Martin. 'You can't wait for the bright lights.'

'I'm not so sure about that.' They stood waiting at the edge of the pavement before crossing to the offices where he had spent the last twenty-five years, the latter part of which as one of the senior partners. There was not a great deal left for him to do in his last couple of days; he'd been assiduous in tying up loose ends, introducing his big clients to the other architects and writing some important thank-you emails to the various departments at County Hall. He'd rubbed along pretty well with the planners and the traffic officers who could easily put the dampers on any development. He would have a quick look at the small pile of letters and then make those last few calls on his list. He yawned as he swivelled a little in his chair, making himself comfortable at his desk.

The envelope looked innocuous enough. A photograph dropped from the folded sheet of paper and he did not need to read the words a second time. In the deepest recesses of his mind Rob had always feared this moment would arrive. You don't generally get away with much in life. Payback time; it is one of the hackneyed phrases, for good reason. His heart plummeted as the words reverberated. Then a second phrase began repeating itself. Please not now. Please, please not now.

He picked up the passport-sized photograph and studied it, his hands shaking. It could have been his daughter Gabrielle. Late twenties too, of course. Gabrielle's dark hair and wide mouth but the eyes were his. A definite likeness as they say. What the hell had got into the girl to try and make contact now, of all times? So much for the mother's promises of old.

'I need a father.' The words were obdurate.

He shoved the letter and the pictures back into the envelope. He began to put it in his pocket then changed his mind. The address was London. This caused another plummet of the heart as he remembered the imminent move to the capital. He should have told Carla long ago, as soon as the affair was over. Could he do it now? Carla would... he couldn't bear to think of it. She'd never had reason to doubt him. His mouth was dry with nerves. No matter that Gabrielle and Peter were grown up – they would be horrified. It would shatter their trust in him. Would they ever look at him the same again?

Stop panicking, he ordered himself. He needed to find out what the girl wanted. Work something out. It was nearly his last day in the practice; couldn't she have waited a week, he raged, as if his mail would not be forwarded to the new address? He swore and slid out the photograph again. After tearing it into tiny pieces and flinging them into the bin, he shoved the envelope deep into the middle of The Masters of Modernism from the pile of books he was packing to take with him. He threw on his jacket and paced around the office. He had to get out; he couldn't think straight in there.

From the very moment of waking and all day at work she'd been fizzing inside, trembling too with apprehension at daring to confront her father for the first time. How would he reply? She'd put her address, her mobile number and her email, covering all the bases but leaving her on tenterhooks, sensitive to every beep or whirr from the phones strewn over the desks in the office. It had been a relief when the usual Friday night exodus began, as early as they could get away with it, shouts and laughter as they pounded down the stairs, heightened by the excitement of a night out.

'Don't get too hammered!'

'I don't even drink!' that was Nazreen protesting.

'You not coming, Rose?'

'Not tonight. Promised I'd help out at the gig. But I hope he's cute,' Rose had called back, referring to Simone's blind date but her thoughts were stuck fast on all the reasons why her letter might not be answered. Could she have dropped him right in it? Her stomach curdled. She gathered up all the resentment of the past to weigh against the single act. It was too fucking bad.

'He'll have got it by now,' Rose blurted out, having raced up to Luke's flat on the floor beneath hers. Puffing a little from hurrying home she waited for his reaction but he remained hunched over a large black amplifier only looking up and giving her a grin that managed to convey some half-hearted encouragement. Nicknamed 'Baby' thanks to his cherubic features and rosy cheeks with mild hazel eyes under a floppy yellow fringe, he made her think of cream teas and tractors and not at all of the world of rock musicians he was part of. She preferred to call him by his proper name. It made her stand out from the crowd, she believed.

She knew it was no big deal to him, the quest that she'd embarked on. In general, parents sucked he had told her, warning that the letter was unlikely to deliver the results she was a fool to expect. She'd tried to downplay her feelings then, although her desperation was surely obvious. Still he had to have a go at her.

'You don't wanna get too hung up on him. God knows what you might get dragged into. You make your own luck in life; didn't I learn that the hard way?' He rocked back on his heels, shaking his head as if dismissing the thought and tightened the tiny screw in the amp circuit.

'What shall I do if he never writes back?' she regretted this at once. Luke was quick to scorn when a needy question was repeated for the umpteenth time. 'I know. I know. You think I'm a silly cow. Don't get my hopes up.'

'If he doesn't get in touch you could go down to that posh office and accost him. Ha, ha,' he laughed, 'you could do a citizen's arrest. I'm arresting you for neglect of one daughter for twenty-five years. See what he says to that.'

Rose didn't laugh; it was the kind of scenario she had toyed with for years. Not the arrest bit but the confrontation. What a coward she'd been. All the uncertainty could have been over long ago.

'If he got the letter today, I suppose I should give him a bit of time to decide,' she watched Luke's shoulders twitch at the tiresome words.

'Yeah. Give it time. You're bloody obsessing again. Let's have a joint, celebrate the weekend.' In fact, they both knew that Luke's work as a sound engineer was far more likely to keep him busy on Friday or Saturday nights when he did the honours for half a dozen bands that performed in the clubs and pubs of east London while midweek more often found him lazing in bed or tweaking the sensitive equipment that was so essential to his job.

'No, thanks, I'm going down the shop. D'you want like fruit or anything?' Rose made an occasional half-hearted attempt to encourage him into a better diet.

'Nah. I'll see you later. It's the Feathers tonight. Better be there by eight. You can sell tickets on the door.'

'Okay,' Rose answered, 'see you later.'

There had been a party on the ground floor not long after she'd had arrived. She and Luke had stumbled into bed together in the early hours but neither seemed to have much recollection of the night or intention to repeat the experience. Or so Rose told herself. They had become mates however, though mostly on his terms. She had gone along to the gigs with Luke from the start, enjoying being part of the vibe for which the area was renowned.

Ten minutes later, back from the corner shop, she pushed open the front door of the flats with an elbow, clutching a paper bag containing her supper: fish fingers, a tin of beans and a carton of strawberry yoghurt. Putting down the bag, she gathered up the neglected post that lay in heaps on the dull parquet floor, placing handfuls on the scuffed console table that stood against the wall. She liked to pat the piles into neater rectangles after flicking through them, the letters for old tenants, double glazing sales. There might have been a bill for her or a flyer about a new café opening, free Americanos on offer, you never knew. Nothing but rubbish. Tomorrow it might be different. She picked up her shopping and climbed the stairs, anticipation making her heart beat faster. All day, a bright image of the white envelope with the unfamiliar address had shone across her retina as she pictured it falling through a letterbox and an older man in his reading glasses, running a thumb along the fold and dare she imagine it? A look of such pleasure and surprise as if he'd won the lottery...

'Goodbye, goodbye,' was still ringing in the night air as Rob watched the last guests crunch their way down the gravel drive. He closed the front door with the usual heavy thud and lingered in the hall for a moment as Carla moved quickly into the kitchen. Following her, he began to line up a few bottles of wine that had been opened but not emptied.

'Bit of a waste, I don't remember opening all these.'

'Always happens. We can polish off one of them tomorrow. I'll chuck the rest or give them to Gaby and Pete.' Carla was in her efficient clear-up mode after the party, the farewell to friends from the village and the practice. He loaded the glasses carefully into the dishwasher, his mind on the evening's snippets of conversation. Months ago everyone appeared shocked at the decision to up-sticks but once the house was on the market they'd piped down with their disbelieving exclamations. Now people were used to the idea and if they thought the Unwins were mad, they weren't saying so to their faces. He and Carla had not rushed into it; though now he was beginning to wonder. He remembered the slow burn of excitement taking them over. As he'd repeated several times over the past year, they'd been seduced by the idea of fresh and stimulating surroundings. He didn't elaborate but not for them the slow decline of doing the same old thing year on year.

Rob, hunting dirty glasses, went back to the drawing room and looking through the door, was jarred by its abandoned air. This really was it. They were leaving, leaving everything safe and familiar. He stood in a dumb funk, stock-still.

Soon, clattering noises from behind stirred him to go across to blow out the candles they'd used to soften the emptiness, leaving a faint haze lingering over the worn green carpet. Much of the furniture had already gone to the auctioneers; in two days the rest of it would be packed by the removal men. He thought of the new owners inheriting a blank canvas, filling the space with their dreams, their aspirations no doubt exuding from every stitch of fabric and stick of antique furniture. They'd proclaimed their desire to take everything back to its origins. Good luck to them; he was not being patronising. They themselves might have done the same but his family had grown up with whatever they could afford at the time, a charming eclectic mix people called it. He and Carla had their dreams too for the new house, if they weren't about to be shattered. He just couldn't steel himself to show her the letter.

He put down the glasses on the worktop and took up a cloth.

'In a couple of days we probably wouldn't recognise the place. Doesn't that give you a strange feeling?' Never had he longed so much to turn back the clock.

Carla pulled on rubber gloves and ran the tap. 'I'm dreaming of bare walls and floors and the few decent pieces of furniture that we are going to buy.'

'I know. Clear the decks has been your mantra over the past few months.'

He saw her stiffen at his tone. Had he sounded sour? He got

13

on with putting out a boxful of empties by the back door, catching her eye as he came back in and doing his best to look cheerful. She had commented earlier on his long face. He had better say something.

'I suppose the party served a useful function.'

'Come on, it wasn't that bad. They're all sorry we're going.'

'I had the same conversation about twenty times. *How brave we are*, while giving me a doubtful look. Then saying they trust we won't forget them with all our new *London* friends,' he stressed the distasteful cadence.

Carla giggled, on a high from the party, 'Never fear, they will descend on us in droves, I predict. A free hotel when they fancy the theatre or a concert.'

'But we agreed that we want them to come,' he knew he sounded tired and defensive. 'This isn't about abandoning friends.'

'So long as everyone makes an effort, it will be fine. We do want them to come, of course. There will be plenty of room. And I'll want to show off the new house. Shall we leave the rest of the clearing up and get to bed? Roll on Monday.'

'So long as we don't live to regret it.' The words came out before he could stop them.

'Oh Rob, please. Not again. We'll have the time of our lives.' Her voice was teasing, cool, suppressing her excitement. 'Come up to bed.'

'Not like you to get wobbly about the move,' she was eyeing him in the mirror as he manoeuvred the electric toothbrush around his mouth.

'I'm just tired,' he snapped, sending froth into the air. 'They will insist on calling it retirement. Bloody annoying.'

'Never mind.'

Now lying in bed, her head heavy on his shoulder, he felt a shifty beat to his heart as she nestled close, adopting their familiar position, breathing in unison for a few minutes before the sleepy turn to the empty expanse of the bed, the drift down and down into nothingness. Tonight it did not come easy. Rob longed for oblivion; to be released from the torment that the letter had given rise to. What on earth had possessed him to embark on an affair only a few years into his marriage? How could he tell Carla? And what about replying to the girl? He thrashed about in bed, turning his pillow over again and again.

Chapter Two

In London, Gabrielle left the party when she came to the conclusion that no one very interesting was still likely to come through the door. She'd had the euphoria of heading out on a Saturday night in her newly single state, feeling the world was crammed with possibilities but by one a.m. disillusion had crept in. Really they were the same old faces: no one to get excited about. It was a bore extricating herself from the attentions of Curtis, an earnest American, who'd latched on some time before, delaying her escape by putting a finger to her lips that were probably stained with a surfeit of red wine and murmuring 'very sexy,' and ignoring her refusal to dance while ranting about the shortcomings of Obama. Just to put her straight, he claimed.

'You Brits all fell for his charisma but the economy is booming now. You wait and see,' he half turned, still prancing, to repeat it to a third party swaying to the beat nearby.

She slipped away, depositing on a table a half-full glass of Rioja among the bottles, stumps of candles and the oozing remains of a giant Brie and went quickly down the stairs and out. She walked along with her bag nestled across her chest. It was one of her tenets that marching purposefully with an air of entitlement to the midnight streets, you'd generally be safe. Anyhow, it was not far, not worth taking a taxi and there were plenty of people about. She stifled the urge to check her phone; no need to encourage some young mugger. Loud shouts rang out and she jerked around. Silence; keep going she told herself, striding on.

In the morning she would be heading to Berkshire for a last visit home. Of course, 'home' was her flat now, yet she was upset about never again being able to slink back to lick her wounds in the consoling familiarity of the old place or the village. She frowned, hiccoughed and corrected herself. Wounds were a fanciful idea: she didn't really do wounds (though she could deal them out;) rather it was a great place to bring friends for the weekend. Country walks and the pub were popular with flat-renting mates who had to content themselves with a park to see any greenery. It was stupid of her parents to sell; they'd never be happy in London. Dad might be okay but Mum? Where would she be without her interest in the shop, the ramblers, endless duties arranging the fete in the garden, the annual flower show and the meals-on-wheels she coordinated for the old folk? Oh, she would probably survive, Gaby conceded, her drive and organising personality would find her a new niche in the capital. She'd better not underestimate her mother: doing that in the past had led to some unforeseen consequences. Gaby grinned as she reached the entryway and held up her key fob to the electronic monitor.

Saturday morning had been set aside by the Unwins to dig up certain plants from the borders to transfer to the new garden. Rob paused as Carla, her hair pushed up under a sunhat, emerged with an armful of empty plastic pots.

'It's rather heart-breaking, remembering all the hard work,' she called out gaily, scanning the lawn and borders as she walked down to join him beside one of the dense flowerbeds.

'It's still looking good, though we need some rain,' she remarked.

'Bit different where we're going,' Rob offered, thinking of the tidy specimen plants in a formal pattern of gravel and grass. Carla had already talked about making a small wilderness beyond the pale blue summerhouse where several yards of orderly garden ran up to the back wall. He was more or less happy about that: it couldn't all be neat and trim.

With a vicious jab he speared a clump of purple leaves and then stood on the fork, balancing while the tines bit into the earth. He worked around the plant until it was loose and heaved it into a large container. He wiped a rolled-up sleeve over his brow as he stood in the warm September sunshine watching Carla patting a small clump of auricula into an old ice-cream carton.

'What are you going to tackle next? We could do with some of that euphorbia,' she prompted and they resumed digging here and there to remove the herbaceous favourites. Soon there was an untidy row of plants, all set for London. He looked over to the tennis court and paddock as memories surfaced of the arguments that had erupted during family games: Gabrielle stomping off in a sulk when riled by her brother's brutal attacking shots or an unexpected ace from her father. At once he felt sick at the thought of his children finding out about his misdeeds. Better to recollect the long Sunday lunches with friends, screams and laughter on the court and the white wine slipping down a treat.

'Hey, Mum, Dad,' Gabrielle, slim and graceful in a short summer dress was coming through the side gate. Something in her voice made him catch Carla's eye. What's up now? Rob wondered, quite used to some low-level friction between the women of the family.

He gave her a hug as she kissed him.

'A nice smacker for you, Dad,' she grinned. 'How's it going?'

Was she ignoring her mother? 'Look at that lot,' he gestured at the pots.

Carla straightened up and made a half-hearted attempt to brush soil off her hands before embracing Gabrielle with hands held clear.

'Sweetheart, hi. We've been sneaking some plants out of the border to take with us, but we're about done, I think. You can't really notice, can you? I just couldn't turn my back on them all.' She made a helpless gesture. 'The pub is booked for one so there's time for you to check your room again. Don't look like that. You said you'd cleared everything but there's still stuff in the drawers. Clothes, letters. You really should go through it all. There are cardboard boxes in the kitchen. I haven't got time to do it for you. Either take those old exam certificates and cups you won at swimming galas or—'

'I told you I've already taken everything I can fit in. We didn't expect to have to clear out every single memento of the past quite so abruptly,' she glared.

Here we go, Rob said to himself.

'But you left home years ago! How long did you expect us to store your old junk? If you don't want it in your place, that's too bad.'

'Carla, Gaby, we've been through this. No arguing. Moving is bound to be a bit of an upheaval for us all. We'll get over it, no doubt. It's a beautiful day and we're going out to lunch. Is Peter on his way?'

'I haven't a clue, Dad, but I'm sure he'll turn up for a free meal.'

He saw Carla bite back a defensive remark and change tack.

'We'd better go in and tidy up. We've got time for a coffee, anyway. How did the Milan presentation go, darling?'

Gabrielle at once became animated and beamed at them, in the familiar change of mood.

'Brilliant. According to Steve, I was at my persuasive best, if I'm allowed a little boast. There'll be a launch of the new brand just before Christmas.'

'That's my girl,' Rob said, 'you've been working bloody hard, I know.'

A few minutes later, they glanced out of the window at a

small blue Fiat pulling into the drive beside his sister's car.

'Here he is,' she said, watching her mother's face light up as she went to the door. 'It's about time he changed that old banger.'

'Ah, he's not fussed about having a smart car, you know Pete.' Rob watched him saunter across in the usual baggy sweatshirt, faded jeans and trainers.

'God. It's been stripped bare. Hardly recognise the place,' Peter's voice exclaimed from the hall.

'I hope you're not getting rid of that nice old desk,' he gestured behind him as he entered the kitchen.

'You were offered it, I seem to recall,' said Rob after they had embraced briefly, Rob looking up to his son who had inherited his maternal grandfather's height and fair good looks. 'We've promised some of this stuff to the new people. It's a bit late to decide you want it after all.'

'Where the hell would I put it? It's not as if you're moving to a tiny place. I can't believe there wasn't room for it and that lovely old sofa. I spent half my life lying on that to watch the telly.'

'That's forever etched on my memory. If you weren't kicking a ball you'd be prone in front of the box.' Rob had no intention of discussing furniture issues and sat down, drawing the Sunday paper towards him.

'Anyway, if you listened,' Carla interjected, 'you'd know we're having a whole new look. All this stuff simply won't fit in. You wait and see.'

'You know your mother. She's got a bee in her bonnet about change. Anyway, I'm all for it too. A completely different style,' Rob repeated, though he did not raise his eyes from the headlines. 'It's going to be —'

'I'm sure it is but it's hard for us to see our childhood vanishing into every cardboard box,' Gabrielle complained.

'Never mind, we'll get used to it,' Peter grinned, 'Mum's had this empty nest thing going on for the last few years. You'll have a new lease of life won't you?' he bent down to hug his mother as she wriggled away and shook her head in denial.

'What rubbish you talk. Let's go. And no squabbling over lunch. Please.'

After the meal in the pub, they walked home past a row of cottages and two 'executive style' houses, past the duck pond with its glossy drakes on the brown water and the substantial old properties built in Georgian and Victorian times, glancing through the lychgate at the long path to the church. They crunched across the gravel, laid in early summer to smarten up the place, ready for the market.

Rob was tired from the effort of acting normally, the one thing on his mind vying with the everyday reality of moving house. The others appeared to be taking stock of all that was to be left behind in two days time as they sat unusually quietly in the garden, chasing down memories, he supposed. He gazed with a slight smile at the house, its weathered bricks absorbing the sun, solidly unperturbed, denying the bitter draughts that the new owners would discover soon enough, as autumn stiffened into winter.

Peter and Gabrielle left at four o'clock in a spray of gravel and mournful shouts of goodbye and Rob went in to finish his packing.

Carla strolled back to the garden and dragged the old tartan rug to a sun-drenched patch of grass. She sat hugging her knees before stretching out and allowing her drowsy thoughts to skim over the years.

The rooks were arguing in the tops of the beech trees, way above her, disturbing the peace of late afternoon. On and on went the bossy cawing of the birds as they wheeled across the sky, joining the swallows and pigeons. The pink and red hollyhocks at the back of the border waved less flamboyantly today and the roses and petunias drooped, their dry roots aching for water. All that work over the years for the garden to be lost to her, someone else's responsibility or neglect. No point now in getting out the hose.

The lawn, tinged with yellow, stripes fading, would have other children wielding cricket bats or badminton racquets. On a scratchy rug, there would be a different teenage girl revising for an exam, getting brown in a bikini on bright, blustery afternoons like this. The ground gave off a scent, not of rich fertility but of repose, the lazy scent of an end of summer heat wave, plants wilting and everything signalling: it's over. Even the stone nymph, her shyness turned to sauciness, was brazenly gazing into the distance.

Soon the teak furniture on the grey sun baked terrace, its rough gnarled surface and legs mottled with lichen, would be stowed away in the damp shed for six months. (The cushions with their own washed out blooms given to the jumble sale last week.) Who would remember the al fresco dinners on humid nights festive with birthday candles, the idle dusk of the longest day or shivery, dank evenings when the weather would not observe the family's calendar of events?

In the orchard across the grass, apples lay on the ground beneath the trees, wasps busy around them. A few leaves had already turned golden like the pears hanging heavily, ripening in the sun above the long grass and the dandelion clocks drifting away. The yew trees she'd never liked formed a black backcloth, a brooding boundary to the graveyard beyond, throwing dark shadows like a second line of defence.

She rolled over, resting her cheek on her hand and shading eyes against the sun to see the herringbone pattern of old bricks, the tall sash windows and the heavy oak door with its large iron key: totems by which she had imprinted her life here. She'd always been aware that the house and grounds had been stolen for her identity, shoring her up with their solidity. Now they would be relinquished, scaffolding for someone else to wear.

Carla scrambled to her feet as the clouds rolled over the yews and the beech trees, her arms suddenly goose pimpled. She gave a last look round and went towards the house. Barefoot and linen dress crumpled, she padded in, a slight figure, trailing only a ribbon of regret, a loose binding to the past.

A mounting feeling of dread had been creeping over Rob as he continued to sort out his belongings. His innate tidiness was a bonus and made the job easier. Moving from room to room, he had been aware that Carla was giving him appraising looks. She knew something was up. You couldn't hide this level of anxiety from a wife of over thirty years. Not a chance. Had there been a threat in the letter? The words were a jumble now. He hadn't dared to look at it again.

The question of what to do had burrowed into every compartment of his mind. All through the false jollity of yesterday's leaving do and the last day in the practice, the knowledge of the entreaty from her, the girl, (he still couldn't say her name) had worried at him. Rejecting or accepting was his to choose but he knew only that he felt utterly at a loss.

He had played up the awkwardness of the final days at work and the fear of uselessness in the new life and was sick of Carla's reassurances.

'Everyone says it's quite an adjustment, retirement.' There he was, using the word he'd banned. 'It's not as if I was desperate to pack it in. After all, work has meant a lot of high points in my life. Remember how excited I used to get when something big was on the cards?'

'Too late to change our minds.'

'Obviously.'

'Besides, I've given up the shop too.'

'It's true though; I'd say our time here, apart from Peter being ill, gave us an excellent life,' he nodded.

'I'm not disagreeing.'

Yet how had it needed only the tiniest of aggravations barely registering as irritants, for the idea of pastures new to tip the scales into the decision to move on?

'You'll be fine. Anyway you're going to be project managing, looking for commissions. You're just tired.'

If you only fucking knew, he berated her silently, guilt making him angry.

The kitchen was bright, the lights bouncing off the unnaturally bare surfaces. Boxes littered the floor. The dishwasher hummed. Carla was clearing a shelf beneath the window. He didn't make a conscious decision to tell her at this particular moment. She had worn him down with her sideways glances, biting her lip, the enquiring frown driving him mad.

It isn't what you think he wanted to shout.

'For God's sake cheer up, Rob,' she continued tossing cookery books into a box.

He took two steps towards her and blurted out, 'you'd better sit down. I need to talk to you. No, it's not about the move. Can you just stop what you're doing? Please.' He closed his eyes for a moment, 'I haven't known how to tell you. Something awful, terrible has happened. Something from the past.'

'For Heaven's sake,' Carla moved across to hug him.

She didn't believe him. He felt sick.

'I made a terrible mistake. Years ago.'

'What? What on earth are you saying?' Incomprehension then wariness contorted her face. 'No, no. Please. Listen. I'd really rather not know. Don't tell me anything horrible. Keep it to yourself. I do not want to know. Please don't tell me something just to make yourself feel better,' she was backing away, her hands fending him off, shaking her head. The look in her eyes made him wince.

'I've got to tell you.' It sounded wrong. He took a breath, began again. 'I've had a letter. From a girl. She says she's mine. My daughter,' his voice was suddenly tremulous. 'I don't know what to do.'

'A letter? What letter? You never told me. When did it come? It's blackmail, I suppose. It's got to be. What girl? When?'

He cringed as she spat the words at him.

'Did you know about this?'

His pleading gesture gave it away.

'Are you telling me you've known about her all along? You've had another child? When? When did this happen? I don't believe it. It can't be true. Why are you telling me this?' she turned away and leaned over the worktop. 'Please tell me it's not true.'

He stood behind her and put his arms out helplessly, futile to try to comfort her. He'd never felt so wretched.

'I'm so, so sorry. I feel desperate about it, going through hell. I couldn't bear the thought of telling you, hurting you. It was all such a long time ago. Bloody years ago. There was a stupid momentary fling with someone at work, before we even moved here,' he was trying to convince the back of her head, talking too quickly. 'You know how these things happen. Someone threw herself at me. I was young, no thought for the consequences. Of course it was wrong. She was married but there were problems. Oh yes, she threw herself at me. She was desperate for a child, you know. She used me. That's not an excuse, of course not. But actually, that's what she did. She used me. We ended it almost as soon as it had begun. Then later, she couldn't hide it; she told me she was pregnant but she swore never to involve me. She never has. It was over just like that. We left London. I joined the practice here, in town. We've had a wonderful life, haven't we? Believe me, I never intended to hurt you.'

Carla turned slowly, a blank look on her face.

'I can't think of anything to say. I would never have dreamed of such a thing. There isn't anything I can say, really. I just haven't got the words.'

'Will you ever be able to forgive me?'

'All these years and years I've trusted you. Now you've ruined it,' her eyes brimmed, 'ruined it. Why didn't you tell me back then? How can anything ever be the same again?'

'I promise I won't let it make any difference. I'm in shock too. Look, we can deal with it—'

'Are you actually going to meet her? I can't take this in. What were you thinking of? Didn't you love me at all? It's been one big lie, has it? Our marriage. Our children. Didn't any of it mean anything to you?' Her voice rose. 'Gaby and Peter—they mustn't find out. Don't tell them. I can't bear it. Tell her to leave you alone. You can tell her to eff off. Oh, get out. I can't bear the sight of you. Just get out!'

She turned towards the sink, looking around, frantic to be occupied. He watched from the door; he knew her so well. She needed do something with her hands. She filled the kettle, trembling. He remembered a minor car crash that had made her shudder like this. She began to empty the dishwasher, knives, forks and spoons first. The mugs she hung on the familiar hooks, the plates clattering into a pile for the cupboard, the bowls to the back of the dresser, where the framed photographs of Gaby at her twenty-first and Peter, suntanned on a sailing boat, made her shut her eyes and clench her fists. Rob stood, uncertain what to do.

'Over my dead body,' she glared at him. He knew exactly what she meant. She was protective as ever for her children.

'I want them never to know, never to have to deal with this. Gaby would tear you apart.' Carla nearly smiled, a bitter look twisting her mouth. She lifted the kettle and dashed water into a cup, a few drops spilling on her fingers.

'Ouch,' she waved him away, 'don't.'

He could see the pain distracted her as she ran the cold tap over the burn. The water splashing on her hand seemed to ease the numbness on her face.

'Let it run for a bit,' he stood weakly beside her. She was strong: never going to pieces in family crises over the years, she would hang onto her dignity. Of course she would be protective of her family. He thought, if this girl puts a foot wrong, she won't know what hits her.

Rob made himself scarce for an hour. If only he could escape to his office. Never again would he be able to lean back in his revolving chair and shut out the world by closing his eyes and reclining in that pose recognised by everyone who'd ever worked at Angus and Latimer. He walked away from the village following a familiar footpath in the dusk, as if heading for the hills. How he wished... then he reminded himself how young he'd been, almost innocent in a way.

What irony, walking down the local lover's lane, he observed, shaking his head. The moon had risen above the treeline, the ruts of the track hiding in the shadows. In the distance the horizon deepened to purple. He walked until he began to worry about tripping over a stone and twisting his ankle, though he deserved punishment enough. He crept slowly home, stumbling here and there, nervous about the fall-out from Carla. He loathed himself for hurting her. At the same time he hoped the worst might be over.

Letting himself in at the kitchen door at the back of the house, he found her sitting bolt upright in an armchair watching the small television. He recognised the familiar jangling tune of a soap opera. Carla slowly turned her head to look at him. Relieved that her expression was composed, he squatted at her knees, as if seeking absolution. She put out an arm and rested it on his shoulder. Neither spoke for a long minute. To his horror, the characters on the TV were enacting a desperate breakup, the voices echoing the words they themselves had uttered earlier.

'Turn it off,' he begged. Slowly she reached for the control as the sob of despair was broadcast. 'You've destroyed every ounce of trust I ever had in you.' The words were cut off at the final accusing syllable and the kitchen went quiet. After an interminable awkward moment, Carla broke the silence. He'd never seen her look so plain.

'We'll have to deal with this as carefully as we can,' she stared at him, a hectic colour in her cheeks. 'It needs to be managed meticulously. We should do everything together. Find out what she wants. It'll be a damage limitation exercise. We've had a shock but we can cope with it,' she tried to smile, failed and shrugged. 'Just remember one thing. I never want to hear anything more about what led to all this, to her. Nothing. Do you understand?'

He stood up to get the circulation back into his legs and replaced the craven look with an abject expression. He knew he had to get it right.

'Will you ever forgive me?'

'That's completely irrelevant right now,' Carla moved away. 'Let's have a drink. God knows I need one.'

How quickly happiness drains away, she thought, waiting for him to collect bottle and glasses. Was it only yesterday they'd held a party to celebrate the future? He brought over the wine, sat opposite, all spaniel eyes, not Rob, her insouciant Rob at all. Over supper they both managed to speak quite calmly about the situation. Carla accepted that the girl's name was Rose and that she was a year younger than Gabrielle. Ladling out soup, making toast and putting cheese on a board were ordinary actions that could be done on automatic pilot. Beneath the rational pretence, she had the sensation of a deep and bloody wound slowly opening somewhere near her heart. She was conscious of waiting for the shock to pass; surely it should lessen hour by hour?

Somehow the meal was eaten; somehow they made their resolutions. Slowly the conversation turned to the first batch of removals that would be professionally packed on the morrow. It was a godsend that there was a great deal to do; she would concentrate on that. She cleared up briskly, no, she didn't need any help thanks, brushing aside his attempts to pick up plates and pans and prepared for bed quickly, longing to feign sleep, to be alone with her thoughts. Her face crumpled when Rob was in the bathroom and she allowed some tears to escape. Moments later, eyes dried on a corner of the duvet, she lay as if paralysed.

Rob was woken in the night by a vicious stab of fear. There had been no cataclysmic hailstorm of accusations or abuse thrown at him. Perhaps that was still in store. He would be punished one way or another, he was sure. The queasy feeling in the pit of his stomach was telling him so.

Chapter Three

It had been an emotional leave taking for them both he supposed, as they drove over the familiar bumps of the cattle grid for the last time. It would be strange returning to the village to see their friends. It was quiet in the car. She wasn't exactly freezing him out, but they seemed to have run out of things to say to each other. They soon overtook the removal van; he sped past with a toot on the horn. The car was packed with luggage including a cool-bag containing the scant remains of the contents of the fridge and a carton of milk. Tucked behind the seat were the kettle and a carrier bag of tea and coffee. Carla always took care to provide refreshment for themselves and the men. She looked over her shoulder; a black bin liner full of bedding had been squashed on top of everything.

'We'll survive if the removal men don't make it.' Was she attempting some light humour?

'You and your teabags.' After that the conversation hugged the safety of the traffic situation all the way into London. Fortunately it was all go once they had collected the keys from an inconvenient high street and the estate agent who was smug about the successful completion, a self-congratulatory air about him and only remembering after five minutes to wish them well in their new home. He drove slowly down the leafy street to the house, halfway along the terrace of tall brick Victorian houses. This time she did not pause with him to admire the façade with its gables and sash windows; she stepped inside the front door and hurried through to the back to open up and let the sun stream in.

'That's better,' she called.

Rob's professional eye surveyed the empty interior and his heart quickened. Perhaps everything would be all right.

Uneasiness had wrapped its paralysing tentacles around Rose as she waited for a response from her father. She felt as if someone had pressed the pause button at that very moment when she posted the letter. She found herself gazing unseeing out of windows, arriving at doors with no recollection of the journey as her flimsy hopes waxed and waned and she was unable to settle to anything, irritable with all and sundry and ignoring her mother's phone calls. It was late on Sunday evening when the text came. It was brief: he acknowledged receipt of her letter, would be in touch. Rose dropped her mobile onto the table and hugged herself with a strange feeling she found it hard to name. She sank into a chair and tried to visualise a thread linking the two of them, slinking away through London, stealing through the suburbs and slipping into her father's home. Would his wife know all about her and would his children accept her? She stared at the message absorbing the non-committal tone of the words. Her euphoria cut short, she composed a reply. She would be cool and dignified. Thank you. I will look forward to hearing from you. Love Rose. She sent it and jumped to her feet. This will show them, she thought, nodding to herself with absolutely no idea to whom she was referring.

Carla woke to new sounds, rolled gently over towards the window and watched the rectangle of lesser dark lighten. She listened; a surprising amount of birdsong. She wished she'd learnt the calls when she was young. No church bells but a very faint murmur of traffic. Rob breathed evenly beside her; his face tucked into the crook of an arm. Suddenly she remembered. Her habit of counting her blessings, the tally of good things in her life as an insurance against disaster seemed a risible practice now. Her rational mind prodded sharply at the drowsy misery. Keep it in proportion, she ordered. She pulled the duvet closer, analysing her reactions. There was shame. Shame that Rob did not feel he could talk to her; shame that nothing had flagged up a red exclamation mark over all the years. There was a bald assessment to be made. If she had known, would her marriage have survived? It would have led to a lifetime of distrust. Every time he had looked at a woman, every time he'd been late home, she would have wondered: suspicion tainting everything. Jealousy made so many marriages intolerable. She had been spared that. Could she turn it all around and view it as a kindness, giving her so many years of happiness? So much of her distress hinged on Rob's deception and his apparent ability to wipe the slate. Her resentment bubbled, boiled over. She had to get out of bed.

They had been a week in the new house. Carla was getting dressed in a hurry, pulling on jeans and a sweater. She was fired up with an all-consuming zeal to get the house straight knowing it was partly a displacement activity to subdue her fury with Rob. Their entire past felt undermined by this new edition of their shared history. It was incredible too, that she could feel the torment of sexual jealousy, so many years after the event. What fantasies had he been dreaming all these years, obliterating Carla? Maybe they still turned him on to this day.

Down she went to an unsorted pile of boxes and bags. She ran up the stairs with a bag full of shoes. Some of these she hadn't worn for quite some time. Perhaps she should have thrown them out but shoes had always been her weakness and these leopard-print high heels were glamorous accessories on evenings out. She associated them at once with stupid complacency and hurled them across the room. She would get rid of the damn things, put them in the dustbin.

No need to take it out on the shoes; think of the positives. She forced a switch from infidelity to champagne and celebrations in Rob's work, the architectural awards he had won and the long list of satisfied clients over the years. Emotion seesawed in an exhausting hectic turbulence.

Again she went back down the graceful staircase that lent the hall an elegance they had noted at the first viewing. They had been so excited that day. The sly gleeful looks they had exchanged as they were led around contrasted with their serious demeanour as they made their comments to the agent.

'The kitchen is in need of modernization. Rather dark too.' No need to get the agent overexcited if they were to negotiate the price down.

'Let the house rest on its laurels,' Rob had declared when their offer had been accepted. 'The bones of this house are so good. We'll keep everything pared back, no need for any frills.'

She was glad Rob was out of the house today. The exhilaration of being in their new home had not materialised. Rob's belated confession clouded everything; the very fact of Rose tripped her up at every turn. Carla made herself a cup of tea and a slice of toast. Where had she gone wrong? She thought back to the pert schoolgirl she'd been, growing up in the West Country and the compelling 'love at first sight' narrative of her marriage. She tried to reach that younger version of herself, recalling the familiar phrases ready on her lips if anyone asked. An account she'd had no reason to doubt before. Was it no longer valid?

Slowly, she scraped butter over the toast.

Leaving school to work for an airline had seemed a glamorous choice in the Upper Sixth; in those days only the real swots considered going for a degree. She pretended that she'd rebelled by turning her back on further education but it just hadn't figured in her imagination. It was only much later that she regretted it. Oh, not for learning's sake so much as for the confidence it would have given her. At the time, she'd felt envied, both for the travel and the British Airways outfit, navy with assertive flashes of red. She always felt good in the uniform, her hair in a sophisticated chignon, court shoes clacking merrily along the endless airport corridors in a posse of aircrew, the public hastening out of their way. And later, on board, bestowing the wide smile on her passengers, noticing the softening of their buttoned-up arrival, basking in their appreciation. She'd loved it all: the stop-overs where she would lie beside a swimming pool drinking rum and coke in a clique of bikini clad girls, giggling with gay stewards and flirting flight officers; evenings getting sloshed on duty-free in a crowded hotel room before venturing into the steamy night for a curry or paella.

At a family lunch, when Carla was well into the job, an aunt had used the term 'glorified waitress' and she'd been hurt by that, baffled by the sneer. That it was a common phrase to be bandied about was wounding and it brought her self-esteem down a few notches. Was that what people thought? Her defence was to be funny about the work, making it out to be a lark, which it was.

Rob had not been a passenger for her to look after. She'd met him in a pub in Richmond; tipsy on martini, she'd smiled first.

'Are you watching the match? Don't let me get in your way,' he'd responded at once.

She'd laughed, shaken her head but he kept glancing at her over his pint and soon she had turned her back on her friends and pretended to watch the rugby. He was seriously good-looking with even features under thick brown hair. He did not have the bulk of a rugby player; tennis was his game, he told her later. In the jubilation of an England win, they had exchanged numbers, had promised to 'have a drink sometime' and turned back to their friends.

She did not raise her hopes unduly; he was out of her league, she suspected. She'd had to wait only a day before the phone call came and she sat on the floor as they chatted; she didn't even know where he lived or what he was. They had nothing to go on; she was desperate to sound interesting. It seemed an odd way to go about things. They laid out their stalls in awkward sentences and jokey interrogations. The minutes passed. When would he ask her out? She hugged her knees while he quizzed about the airline, the next trip, west London; he got on to tube stations…tube stations! Finally like a dogged fisherman's very last cast of the lure the question came, 'When are you free? We could have dinner.' She affected nonchalance as she made the arrangements.

Things had moved swiftly and it was not many weeks before she booked tickets to Rome for the weekend, using her discount. They'd been dazzled by the place and by each other and they returned as a unit.

Rob could have had anyone: she'd always known she was lucky that someone with so many attributes (her cheeky mates in the airline, both male and female had, according to their usual method of evaluation, given him a high score. A point for looks, another for job and prospects, a point for sense of humour and personality, he was nearly off the grid.) His finicky ways, the perfectionism that developed later, might have knocked him down a bit. Had he been 'too good to be true' literally, and she a numbskull not to realise it?

'He obviously adores you,' her mother had remarked drily, with a touch of pride or perhaps surprise. Carla had adored him back for thirty years, not counting disagreements over children and minor skirmishes that were the stuff of everyday life. During that time she'd shed the bright schoolgirl and the fun loving yet efficient stewardess who was soon promoted to run the first class cabin then a desk at the terminal before Gabrielle had come along. It was Rob who'd pushed for the Old Manor when others were daunted by the cost of a new roof and the rising damp. They'd got it for a song in today's terms, between one boom and the next and quietly put things right, as and when they'd had the money.

How had she never seen the signs? At night now, she ground her teeth, asking the same questions over and over while Rob breathed and turned quietly beside her in untroubled slumber. Or so it seemed.

She finished her breakfast and put the plate in the dishwasher. Time to get on with her tasks. She went out into the hall, wondering which room to tackle. She frowned at a row of cardboard boxes, inconveniently near the back door. Rob was such a control freak, anything the removal men unloaded had to be placed just so. It had been embarrassing the way he had got them to put things here, then there, regardless of the impatient looks they'd given. Over the years, she'd always tried to make subtle changes to the position of this and that, tiny rebellions that were probably pointless. In the end he usually had his way; she couldn't deny he had a good eye. She remembered the hoo-ha when she'd bought that lovely table in the auction. It would not look right, Rob had insisted. She'd sold it at a loss in the end; she couldn't be bothered to make a fuss. Would it be different now, with the minimalist look they were aiming for?

She ran her hand over the smooth texture of the wall; she liked the neutral colour scheme here, mainly grey or white, the fashion at the moment. She walked across the wide oak floorboards of the hall; like all the fittings, they lent an opulence that was wholly tasteful. She bent down to pick up the post. These days every pile of mail had a faint malignant trace of Rose's bombshell.

Carla's imagination seethed with vivid and difficult

scenarios: court cases or a drug problem, demands for money or the girl's mother being dragged into everything. She clung to the lie that she could cope whatever happened.

Turning to the back door, she stood on the threshold to contemplate the garden. The orderly geometry would soon become a mud bath, full of builder's paraphernalia. For the time being it was a soothing sight with only a few fallen leaves contradicting its precise charm.

She'd better get on. The days were passing with little progress to show for her efforts. Tonight they would be gathering with some of the street at a Neighbourhood Watch meeting. It was odd to be an outsider after so long in the old village where their presence was a given at so many events.

It was a refreshing change, she told herself, sinking to her knees by a cardboard box. Tearing off the sticky tape and pulling back the flaps it was clear at once that she hadn't been nearly ruthless enough. She sat heavily on her heels. What were these old jugs and bowls doing? Had she imagined that the young would make use of them? Over several weeks there had been a well-trodden path to the charity shop. For now, things could be banished to the back of a cupboard. That was meant to be a thing of the past. In this brave new world clutter was forbidden. Never mind. Rules were made to be broken after all.

An hour later, not stopping to relax after her box emptying, she drove to the nearest supermarket. It would be fun finding the best shops as they became familiar with the area. She ran through a mental shopping list and headed down the first aisle: something for supper that wouldn't take long to get ready. They would eat after the meeting. She pressed on, from one job to the next, keeping occupied.

Chapter Four

In a small flat on the lower ground floor of an ex-council block, a thin pale girl bent her fair head towards a computer. It was eight o'clock in the morning. After a poor night Nina had crept out of bed to check her emails. Soon Peter's alarm sounded and he groaned and clambered out of bed. Ten minutes later, Nina looked up, hearing a snort from across the room.

'God,' Peter exclaimed, throwing down a letter onto the stained Formica table, 'that bastard Cossart is putting up the rent and implying we can like it or lump it. Nearly seven hundred a month for this shithole,' he glanced around the war zone, his name for the dim basement he had occupied for two years. Periodically, a good clear up almost restored order to the place, but housekeeping was not his forte. Basically, Nina had concluded long ago that he was contented enough and too lazy to look for anywhere better. She put up with the grubby ambiance when she stayed over but unlike her boyfriend had failed to become accustomed to the mess, the deep gloom and the appalling long drawn out *ting ting ting* from the doorbell of the corner shop next door. It was a loud jarring ring gradually diminishing in volume as the vibrations of the bell subsided. In the early days of excitement at being with Peter, this had got on her nerves in only the most minor of ways but the shop bell now scorched her consciousness both early and late. Opening hours were five a.m. until midnight and the harsh jangle rang out whenever anyone entered the shop for a late night pack of cigarettes or the morning papers. Peter was also oblivious of the regular yellow flash of the beacon on the crossing which lit up the room through the wide gap in the flimsy curtains, searing Nina's eyeballs beneath the ethereal violet lids he raved about. (Where he had got that from, she really did not know.) Oh yes, this place was a dump and sleep almost impossible as far as she was concerned. Peter could do a lot better. In spite of all this, she loved him, partly for the way he could banish her blues with his good natured matter-of-fact approach to life and partly because he was the best looking by a mile of all her boyfriends over the years.

She gave him a sympathetic look while calculating the fallout. Where would he go? She needed him near. It was a source of humiliation that he'd never asked her to move in. She had skirted round the subject but he never took a bite. He lifted his shoulders, sighed, rubbing his forehead and gave a vicious glare at the outside steps and wheels of vehicles passing the window. His legs were still tanned beneath the white shorts. How fit he looked in spite of the negative body language.

'You'll work something out.'

'I'd better,' he turned to grab a hefty racquet bag containing all he needed for his day. 'I'm off then. Can't keep a banker's wife waiting. Hayley, you know the one. Tell Mel to back off if she gets too much. See you later.' He did not stop to give her a kiss but she was used to that.

Nina picked up the letter and contemplated it without actually reading it. A germ of an idea stirred. She would have a little ponder at work today. If she mulled things over, solutions could creep up on her. She had a minute to weigh herself before heading out to the studio. Peter had watched like a hawk as she drank her detox smoothie. He was turning into another member of the food police, insisting she add some nuts to the blender. Now she felt revoltingly bloated. The needle on the old fashioned scales hovered just below forty-six kilos. She could have cried.

Nina, on a packed tube train after work, contemplated the long day spent sketching out alterations to wedding dresses designed by the 'sought after' Melanie Davies, as people tended to call her. The train clattered onwards bearing Nina and her preoccupations. She had been triumphant the day she was offered the job some three years earlier but now disillusion was beginning to set in. She kept reminding herself that the experience was invaluable but her boss was temperamentally unsuited to training anyone unless you counted being screamed at when her exacting standards weren't met. Lavish praise alternated with these outbursts; Nina had to admit that things probably balanced out. Melanie was just black and white and her bark, once you got used to it, a lot worse than her bite.

'I'm meant to be your protégée,' Nina had yelled, once, in self-defence.

'Not for long,' Mel had replied, icy with anger, 'if that happens again.' Children might have softened the edges but she was single-mindedly devoted to her successful business. Nina leaned back in her seat, recoiling from someone's armpit just above her and noted the figures of skinny girls hanging on the straps along the carriage.

After supper, when Peter would be watching the telly might be the best time for her to broach the subject.

In fact, the flat was a topic hanging heavily on Peter's mind too and he brought it up as soon as she arrived that evening. At night, the ceiling bulb cast a sickly glow over the room. She crossed at once to switch on the bedside light before filling the kettle.

'I've been thinking about that damn letter,' he lifted the newspaper off the table in a vague effort to locate it. 'It might be worth appealing to the landlord's better nature. He did tell me he wouldn't be likely to raise the rent at the end of the year. Now he's going back on his word.'

'Don't you think you could get somewhere better for that

sort of money? It's a complete rip off. He's only interested in making a killing on all his properties. Didn't he crow that he owns several in this building?'

'He's always boasting how he got them for a song. Pretty sickening. He's not giving me much notice either. A month, if I want it. I suppose that's in the contract,' Peter tossed the paper back on the table.

'You could have stayed with me if I wasn't already sharing with Becky.'

'You're sweet but I know that's not possible.'

'Your mum and dad would let you stay there while you looked for somewhere, wouldn't they? The new place would be really handy for your weeks at that Scimitar place. You've got a lot riding on that.' She gave him a look, 'A permanent post would be amazing.'

'I'm not holding my breath but it would be almost too good to be true. No more traipsing all over town for three or four hours coaching. I could triple what I'm making,' Peter pulled a bottle of beer from the fridge and hunted for the opener. 'Sure you won't? It's Friday night.'

'Why don't you pop over to your parent's tomorrow? Didn't your dad want a hand in the garden?'

'I could go after my ten o'clock session. Fancy coming?'

'It's my Saturday on tomorrow. More Bridezillas,' she pulled a face. Tantrums were a hazard of the job.

'When you have your own studio it will put a different complexion on it.'

'I know, I know. Roll on the day. Anyway, I've been thinking I might look for something else.' This familiar refrain was ignored. Peter was a funny mixture of off-hand and considerate. Now he was looking at her.

'I'm going for a take-away at the Turk's. What can I get you? You must have something.'

'Pete, stop fussing. I've already eaten.'

'What?'

'If you must know, I had an avocado salad with prawns. Very healthy.'

'Hmm. You're wasting away. Look at this skinny little arm.'

She slid her hand under his shirt. 'This little arm is going places. I wonder where it's going?'

He pulled her towards him.

It was their second weekend at Number 23 and a light drizzle was falling over the garden as Carla watched Peter and Rob heave the last urn onto its base. Then they both stood back, contemplating. Fine droplets of moisture shone on their hair.

'You're getting wet,' she called from the back door.

'They should be well out of the way of the building work, I think. I'm glad we brought them. They're a bit 'country house' but still. A reminder of the past,' Rob added with fake pomposity, turning to Carla. So much of what he said seemed fake to her these days.

Peter looked over asking, 'What's up Mum?'

She forced a smile at once, 'They look fine there, well done.'

'I might pop over to that garden centre and pick up some compost and bulbs,' Rob said.

'Pete, can you help me sort out the wifi? I don't know what Dad's done to it. There's no signal at all. It was working fine, last night.'

Peter gave his father a grin and followed her indoors, wiping his face with a sleeve.

'It is a bit damp out there. Dad wants to plant some stuff in the containers. It's a cool garden. He seems pretty happy here. Gaby and I did wonder.'

'It wasn't just me wanting to move, you know. It's a lovely house. He's in such a rush to get going on the extension, though. I keep saying 'what's the hurry?' but he's already found some builders who are just about to finish a job and can get cracking as soon as we want. Apparently, it's got to be finished before the party in March. You know. My famous sixtieth. He wants to be able to show off to everybody.' She put her laptop on the table, sat down and looked searchingly him. Was there something troubling him? 'Anyway, darling, tell me how you are?'

'Fine, Mum, fine,' he knelt on the floor and pulled out the plug to disconnect the wireless router and then pushed it firmly back. Settling down in a chair, he slid the laptop towards him, sipped his coffee and surveyed the room. She gazed around too. Three packing cases stood under the window and every surface had its share of miscellaneous items and papers. A corner was piled high with coats and boots awaiting a new home. Some pictures were propped against the wall just inside the door.

'Looking around, it strikes me you could do with another pair of hands. I could help, you know.'

'We haven't got the place as straight as we'd like,' she sighed. 'I can't believe it's taking so long. I'm always waiting in for deliveries. Oh and the electrician never turned up. All the plugs are in the wrong places and now the Internet is on the blink. It's incredibly frustrating. Nothing is simple any more. Your father is driving me insane. Nothing gets done because it has to be done 'properly'.

'He was always like that. Anyway, it's early days, Ma. Would it help if I spent a bit of time helping you with all the fiddly little things? I could fit it in next week, before running that course at the Scimitar Club. Whoa, what's the password? I think we've got a signal.'

'Um, Dawlish 1989 I think. Buckets and spades,' she gave another bright smile, 'nostalgia!' She gathered her wits, 'Really? Could you help a bit?'

Peter nodded, flashing the wide family grin.

'I've been hoping to see more of you and Gabrielle, now we're in London too.' She felt like hugging him.

'Here you go. Wifi up and running. I could test out that attic room for you. Let's go and have a look at it.'

Carla sensed what was coming but gave no sign. 'Some of the radiators aren't working. We need to get the boiler serviced, I suppose. I did have a name somewhere but I have no idea where anything is.'

'No problemo. We'll sort it.' On reaching the top landing, Peter confided, 'Actually Mum, there is a bit of an issue with my flat.'

'Oh?'

'It's just that they're putting up the rent and to be honest it's on the wrong side of town, what with you here and the possibility of a permanent job at the club. If I stayed with you for a night or three, I could suss out the rental market round here. What do you think?'

'Of course you can. You don't need to ask. This is a lovely big room.'

'Peter coming to help?' Rob could not keep the scepticism from his voice. 'First time ever.'

'I don't know why you have to be down on him all the time. He's offered and I've accepted. It will be fun to have him around for a few days. He'll bring his stuff over in a day or two. Get him away from that girl. I'm sure she's very sweet but much too skinny, if you ask me. I do wonder if she's got a problem.'

'She's thin all right but rather beautiful you must admit. Amazing eyes. You don't want to be down on her. You know it's counterproductive with Peter.' Rob looked at her in that way he had, 'He's a big lad now.'

Carla's hackles rose at the patronising tone. Carrying on as if nothing had happened: that was so typical. He sat with one leg over the arm of the chair reading the paper without a care in the world. Well, she wanted Peter to come and stay and that was that.

Whenever Rob vented his frustrations on the subject of their son, it made Carla fume. They had pulled together so hard during his years of illness. It was infuriating that he was so critical of Peter while she could not or would not switch off the unwavering support she gave to her boy. They had nearly lost him. It coloured everything for her, even as his teenage years had bloomed with good health.

Rob carried on peering at the paper, opposite her, emphasising his concentration by leaning forward. To think there had been another child all along. She considered how lightly he had worn that knowledge. Stop it. Don't let your mind wander there, she told herself.

'I know you think I'm too soft on Pete,' she gave a little in order to draw his attention back. Rob turned over the page and adjusted his reading glasses.

Carla gave up. She gazed morosely through the rain-spattered windows and a picture of Peter as an adorable cheeky toddler came into her mind. She could remember quite clearly the first of tens of visits to the consultant.

She was back there, the nerves knotting her stomach, the very words etched forever.

He sits at his desk, having ushered them in to the sanctum. His face is concerned, his fingers making a steeple as he breaks the news.

'I'm afraid Peter's blood test was positive. Of course we shall do all we can to help him make a full recovery. That is by no means impossible. We will begin treatment immediately. I must warn you it may be a lengthy process.' He pauses as if to assess their reaction. He is grave, practised at this. He is not expecting Carla and Rob to shout or scream and rail against fate. He expects dignity and that is what he gets.

Frozen, Carla accepts at once that life has changed irrevocably.

Rob rallies himself to ask a question. 'Tell us about the treatment.' He leans forward. The words roll over her; they have always been associated with old people before.

Now they walk in silence down the corridors into the hospital ward. Peter is in a cot. His two-year-old self had been indignant about this, earlier. A lifetime ago. At home he has recently graduated to a proper bed. He bounces upright.

'Mumma. Dadda.' He doesn't look ill at all.

'My precious,' is all Carla can say as she hauls him possessively over the bars to hug him tightly. She forces her facial muscles to soften.

'We have to stay here a little while longer, darling boy.' He clambers away from her into his father's arms.

'Swing, Dadda' he shouts, 'Swing Petey.'

The rain pattered loudly on the window as a squall passed over the house. Carla came back to the present, dismissing the scans and the drips and needles of so many years of their lives. A similar anxiety weighed her down today. Bad news moving like a toxin in the blood, sluggishly gaining ground.

Slings and arrows of outrageous fortune. The words tumbled into her head. At some point, she knew, they would have to meet Rob's secret daughter.

Her mind was jumping, making random connections. She needed to get busy. There was still plenty of unpacking to do.

'I'm going to have another look at those drawings. There's something niggling me,' Rob said, deftly folding the paper into the neatest rectangle and getting up from the chair in one economical movement. Where on earth did Peter get his expansive slouchy habits from? For a sportsman, he seemed to carry the air of a couch potato whenever he was at home, transforming his professional athleticism into a round shouldered, scruffy and amiable good for nothing. Carla smiled. She would defend Peter, be in his corner, whatever happened.

The boy had no malice in him. There was little doubt he would be the one to accept the altered status quo with equanimity. Carla winced at the thought of Gabrielle's stormy defensive reaction. It would be a fall from grace by her father that would undermine every aspect of their relationship.

Rob had insisted from the start that he would prepare his plans for a large rear extension and investigate the likelihood of planning permission before contracts were exchanged. He was adamant that his agreement to buy the house was dependent on being able to do exactly what he wanted, in spite of Carla's exasperation. She had huffed and nagged afraid they would lose the sale. Everything else about the place was what they wanted, not far from perfect. But Rob was emphatic, his dark eyebrows meeting over a forthright gaze.

'I must have a project to fill the gap that leaving the practice will make.'

She had gathered from the adjectives 'innovative and stylish, different,' that he wanted to make a statement of some kind.

'I fully intend to pick up some commissions from it, too. Full retirement is not an idea I relish, as you know.' She'd been given another look. She understood: he felt far too young for that.

She could see he was gratified when the plans were given the nod by the officers of an overworked planning department trying to keep up with a never-ending surge in applications. Later on, properly submitted, they were approved without major alteration and the work could begin.

It seemed hardly any time at all before the builders were descending on the house. Rob and Carla had barely settled into a new routine. That was the beauty of it, he told her, no routine to disrupt. Perhaps descending was not the right word. Carla stared out of the window at eight forty-five on a fine blustery autumn morning: still no sign of activity. She frowned at the faint hum of traffic from the main road a few streets away. A white van had been parked outside in the tree-lined street for at least twenty minutes. In contrast to its immobility, there had been a final scurrying and rearranging inside the house as the Unwins prepared for the invasion.

'You should get in Polish builders,' everyone had told them. This lot, (admittedly so far invisible) were from an established local firm recommended by a friend of a colleague of Rob's. They had provided a reasonable quotation and reluctantly agreed to a penalty clause on timing.

'What on earth are they waiting for?' she felt agitated, keen to get the work underway and yet scarcely ready for more upheaval. Two more impatient minutes passed as she stared out.

'Maybe Terry is giving them a pep talk before they begin,' Rob said with more than a trace of irony. Carla nudged him just as he turned away.

'Oh look. Another van has arrived. Ah, that's the boss. Look. That's him. Here they come. I'll let them in.'

She was greeted with Terry's unexpectedly engaging smile. A toughie, maybe an ex-soldier, Carla had wondered on first meeting him. The shaven-headed, bulky man in a navy donkey jacket stood in front of three less imposing figures. She smiled back and waved them in.

'Hello. Morning. How are you, Terry?'

'Hold it boys,' Terry stuck up an arm. 'Buster, the dust sheets.'

'Thanks, that's great.' Carla retreated to the bottom of the stairs, pleased to see a protective sheet laid all the way through. She followed as the four men trooped along, nodding to Rob as they emerged. He had taken up a position in the garden, the better to embark on the short address he had planned over breakfast, to lay down the law about timekeeping, tidiness of the site and a request to refer to him all the inevitable queries in order to have a perfect understanding of the project.

'It's great to see you all here. I'm sure we'll get on very well if we stick to a few ground rules,' he began. Carla hoped it was the best approach.

The youngest, barely out of his teens, looked about to roll his eyes but a cold stare from Terry put paid to that, she noted, relieved. Her chief concern was that although the early work would be done before the removal of the rear wall of the house, the access was right through the building itself. She stood in the doorway feeling in the way but wanting to make friendly overtures.

'You must tell me your names,' she smiled encouragingly at the lanky one in the colourful shirt first.

'Buster,' said red-shirt, looking at his boss. 'Well, that's my nickname, right?'

'Sean, that's me,' said the wiry one in a soft Irish accent.

'And this here's Jacko,' finished off the foreman, pointing his rolled set of plans at the kid who grinned at her.

'Let's make a start then, lads. We need to bring our tools and materials in, Mrs. Then you'll be able to shut the door and forget about us.'

'Oh yes, of course. Not a problem,' assured Carla, at once determined to be out as much as possible for the next few weeks. 'You can make your tea in the little utility room near the back door.'

The men gave a cheerful thumbs-up.

'Good idea,' said the boss. 'Get the kettle on Jacko me lad and we can make a start.'

Carla and Rob exchanged a glance, suggesting 'let's leave them to it now,' and went indoors.

'I do wonder what we've let ourselves in for?'

'They'll be fine. Don't worry about it.'

Heavy treads sounded as a barrow full of tools was trundled through the house and a robust voice sang about manning the barricades. Rob's eyebrows went up and his mouth twitched.

Carla studied the blackboard that stretched across one wall above the worktop. An essential requirement of their former lives, this was up on the wall before any paintings or prints. It read in a bold scrawl:

Monday BUILDERS!! 2 pm Arts Club, supper Pete
Tuesday Refugee Centre Play Wyndhams
Weds Electrician
Thurs Curtain Lady
Fri Hair/Nails Dinner Stefano's
Sat
Sun

'You've only put down one thing,' Carla looked over at Rob, 'you're going to get awfully bored if you don't get stuck in to things.'

'You worry about yourself. I'm supervising this lot. And I've got the refugee place tomorrow morning.' He raised an eyebrow as he looked towards the window, at the tableau in the garden. The four workmen sat on improvised chairs, a workbench, a sack of cement and two large upturned containers, Rob's precious stone planters. Each man was either smoking or reading, engrossed in the Daily Mirror.

'Christ. Just look at them. Good thing I haven't planted my bulbs yet.'

Terry noticed the abrupt movement in the window and barked something inaudible. Within a second the men were on their feet, active with measuring, putting pegs in the grass and spade wielding.

'A veritable hive of activity,' Rob gave his wife a sardonic look before picking up the chalk and adding to the list on the blackboard.

REMIND Terry about the PENALTY CLAUSE

Chapter Five

Carla's afternoon had driven away the usual dull listlessness. For days she had woken up feeling she was swimming against a strong tide before being borne along for a while by a raft of consoling lies and distractions. Enlivened now by a successful first encounter with the local association of The Arts Club her thoughts bubbled. She had been told, on applying, how fortunate she was to be accepted: there was nearly always a long waiting list. 'That's so lucky,' she had murmured respectfully down the phone.

She had found her way easily enough with her little fold-out map, explained that she was waiting for her membership card and slipped into a seat in the hall, feeling self-conscious and eager. The lecture, with slides, on 'Art of the Ming Dynasty' was especially well timed, for a new exhibition was opening at the British Museum. Marvelling at the exquisite illustrations and absorbing commentary, she felt sure the displays would mean so much more to her now. The urbane white-haired collector of Oriental works of art demonstrated the earlier and later styles in painting and ceramics, jade carving and lacquer work. Carla made a determined effort to take in and remember the facts. Repeating to herself, 'mid fourteenth century to mid seventeenth century.'

After a while it was very easy to drift into studying the people nearby as they wriggled to get comfortable on the shiny, hard plastic seats. Carla already had her ticket for the exhibition. Instead of chatting stiffly to Rob during the evenings she retreated into her own thoughts and scoured the papers to book up the certain-to-be popular events, determined to adhere to certain elements of the new life she'd aspired to: soaking up the culture and mixing with like-minded souls. She read the critics assiduously, noting the stars awarded to each play or film, the extravagant reviews of new novels, managing to laugh at herself and her quest; the essential reading list grew longer and longer. She would ask for books for Christmas, books, only books she hungered for. Yet she had fallen out of the habit of reading in bed, it was easier to pretend to be sleepy and turn off the light.

On the bus ride home from the talk, her reflections turned to her surroundings, both inside and out on the teeming streets of rush hour. She enjoyed her journeys, taking in all the little details. Dressed in a black hijab, a woman emerged from a chauffeur-driven car, under the impassive gaze of the wild-haired man propped up in a doorway, in his filthy sleeping bag. Three girls in patterned leggings pranced past, singing or chanting, arm in arm, giggling. So many faces, all of them riveting. She rang the bell and got off at her stop to walk home. It was so convenient, the final leg a pleasant stroll of barely a quarter of an hour. Similarly, the nearest underground station was in reasonable reach. Number 23 was gradually becoming home. She hadn't missed the Old Manor once in the last few days. Things she was cheerfully informed would bother her such as traffic (noise and amount) foreigners (the number of) and the unfriendliness of neighbours have not troubled her at all. True, it had not been an overwhelmingly warm welcome at the Neighbourhood Watch meeting the other night. People were polite but somewhat reserved in spite of the communal aims of the gathering but one couple had chatted agreeably and parted with a promise of drinks.

'Soon, very soon, I'll drop in an invitation. You'll get to know a few locals,' a beaming smile with perfect teeth from the attractive wife, (second wife?) Louise. The husband was older, charming too.

Carla rounded the corner by the monkey-puzzle tree and gazed down to the house. No vans. She supposed the builders must finish at five and she hurried along keen to see what had been achieved on day one.

She studied the houses before crossing over. How fortunate they had been to find such a desirable property in the right area. The people on the left had been round early on to welcome them and offering any help needed, 'you mustn't hesitate to ask.' She had hardly clapped eyes on them since. They were fund managers with barely teenage children at home, attending the nearby private day school. Some days the kids straggled by with their backpacks; usually they were bundled into the car as their mother drove to work.

Carla now peered at the other side, trying not to be too obvious. This lot had not made contact or been at the meeting. The curtains weren't closed against the dark and the streetlight shone into a long room with a big mirror above a fireplace and a row of abstract pictures on the wall. A Range Rover was parked outside but there was no sign of anyone. Perhaps she should apologise for any builder's noise; there was bound to be a racket at some point. She would pop round later and try to catch them at home. Back in the village… she stopped herself: that was not a phrase to be used too often but so hard to avoid it. In the country there would have been plenty of introductions by now. In a matter of days, any newcomers would have been assessed on their likelihood to play Bridge, join the Tennis Club, Bowls or Cricket Club and invited to add their names to the church flower rota or list of volunteers to mow the graveyard. It was bound to be different here. She turned in through the gate. This was London, anonymous and exciting.

'Hello,' she called. No one answered. She breathed in the

quiet, kicking off her shoes and padding along the hall. She was holding on to a pragmatic calm that she had decided, walking along the road home, would be fitting along with an uneasy truce with Rob in spite of her instinct to punish him. So long as the girl did not cause trouble ... In a couple of days they would see how the land lay.

Rob must be out. In the kitchen, she went straight to the window and was buoyed up by the sight of the trenches dug in the dark brown earth and a winding indentation in the grass from the barrow that trailed round the summerhouse to the back of the plot. Day by day there would be visible measures of progress; suddenly the building work seemed less daunting. It would be got through; it was a finite period of turmoil. She peeped into the utility room to see all the mugs upturned on the draining board, the surfaces wiped clean and a tea towel hanging neatly from its hook. Good. They were not messy buggers anyway.

Pete was coming this evening. She'd better get going on the meal. She turned on several lamps for a welcoming effect to negate the lack of furniture and returning to the kitchen took the meat and vegetables from the fridge. He hadn't said anything about Nina so with luck they'd have him to themselves. He was bringing over some of his stuff to leave upstairs: mostly clothes, he had promised. She was sceptical about that. Rob would be more than irritated when the ball machine, the bike and the speakers and familiar paraphernalia of Peter's life were lugged through the front door. A few thumps sounded from the hall. Good, he had arrived.

'Pete, let me take something off you,' she went to grab an armful of tennis racquets, but he held tight.

'No. I'm fine. Hi Ma,' he bent to kiss her on the cheek and went straight up the stairs.

'I may as well dump everything in my room,' he called over his shoulder as he clumped up in his size twelve trainers, his blonde hair slick and dark from the shower.

Carla looked out of the front door at the car. Good God. The seats appeared to be stacked high with pillows and duvets and the passenger seat had some kind of office chair folded into it. Behind her Pete was thundering back down.

'Let's get it all up before Dad gets back,' Carla urged. 'He'll go berserk if sees this lot. I haven't a clue how long he'll be, incidentally. Have you got all your stuff here?'

'Just a bit more to go,' he replied tactfully. 'Anyway it will be out of sight, out of mind.'

'Yes, yes,' she stared at a box of LPs. 'Haven't you got rid of all these old things?'

'They're back in now, Ma. Don't worry, if I get the job, I shall be out of your hair in no time.'

"Don't be silly. It will be lovely to have you under my wing for a little while. Come on, give me that, you take the heavy things.'

Peter sat down clumsily on the bed to survey his new domain. He gave a little whistle of pleasure as he took in the gable window with a narrow table in front of it and the spacious area around the large bed. He had stacked his possessions in an untidy pile against a wall; books and CDs, vintage records and rolled up posters and clothes spilled from Tesco bags, he would sort them out at some point. He searched on his mobile for a favourite playlist and turned up the volume. He lay back on the pillow with his eyes closed, a hint of a serene smile about the corners of his mouth.

Carla peeled potatoes and sliced them up to be cooked in the oven with cheese and cream, her son's favourite. She was glad to think of him up there in the large room at the top of the house, plugging in his equipment and unpacking his things. She went to the door and listened to the music drifting down, reminding her of the racket that used to accompany him always. He should have learned an instrument, she thought for the umpteenth time. She frowned, recalling some piano lessons, or was that Gaby? Anyhow, neither of them had stuck at it. She slid the dish into the oven below the sizzling roasting tin and looked at her watch. Where was Rob? Had he mentioned a meeting?

She took a brush out of her bag and slowly ran it through her hair, brushing it straight back from her forehead. She would have to find a new hairdresser. She made a list: doctor, dentist, plumber, electrician. She could always ask the neighbours, of course. She took out a small mirror and a lipstick and deftly stroked it over her top lip, then over the bottom and pressed them together. Her mouth turned down at the corners these days, an ugly new development. She tried half-smiling then let the droop return. Her face looked pale between the dark wings of her hair, her eyes had deep shadows. She hoped it was only the light; she needed to keep up the cheerful pretence since the pleasure she had taken in looking nice had evaporated. She would perk up when the house was straight, she was sure. The sofas were due any day. It would be good to sit in the front room; she had become rather tired of living in the kitchen. At that moment she heard the front door open and Rob came in.

'I see he's arrived.'

'Hello, how are you, too?'

'Sorry but I saw Pete's car. What sort of day have you had?' he was making the effort to be nice. He put his briefcase in its designated corner and looked about the room. Before she could answer, he headed for the back door.

'Anything to report? How did it go with the builders?'

'Okay, I think but I was out all afternoon. No word about the sofas, though. I did try to ring. I'm sure they said this week.'

'All in good time. The guys seem to have got on quite well today.'

A cold draught blew through the house.

'Can you shut the door? It's freezing.'

'I'll pop up to see Pete.'

'He'll be down in a minute. Why don't you open a bottle of wine?' she gestured towards the window and tried to sound positive. 'They're pretty tidy, I'm glad to see. The boss-man is a bit of a character. We had a good chat this morning.'

'Hum. I've been thinking. There'll be quite a break over Christmas and New Year I suppose. I must talk to Terry about that.'

She heard the hint of frustration in his voice.

'Give them a chance. At least we can get Christmas done and dusted before the impact on this room.'

'True. Have you talked to your mother yet?'

'She's worried it will be a bit much, descending on us when there's all this going on.'

'But there won't be so much going on over the Christmas week. We should persuade them. And it will save us going there.'

'Oh, typical.'

'Why? What have I said?'

'Anything for an easy life—'

'Rubbish. What's got into you?

'Shush. Pete will hear us. I just can't stand the way you carry on as if nothing has changed. *Let's make plans as usual...*' The singsong sarcasm slipped out and then the anger. 'You haven't got the imagination to even conceive of how difficult it is for me, coming to terms. If I ever do.'

'For God's sake. How many times do you expect me to apologise? I've grovelled, oh yes, I have. Don't shake your head. D'you think I wanted this to happen? You've no idea the dread I've lived with.'

'If you expect me to believe that—'

'Believe what you like but I've had enough of the constant

aggression.' Rob stalked out as she stood rigid with anger. There were footsteps running down the stairs and a thump at the bottom.

'Pete, how's life?'

'Hey, Dad, the prodigal returns. Building work started I see.'

They came in together, all smiles.

'Shall we have a beer?'

'There's some in the fridge. Help yourself and pour me one too.' Rob looked at her. 'Carla, vino?'

She breathed out. 'Please.'

Chapter Six

Rose carried the heavy tin of pale greeny-grey paint and the roller up to her flat. She was careful not to thump past Luke's door, he would no doubt criticise the bourgeois impulse to tart up her room, just in case the absent parent deigned to call. She wished he could be a little less uncompromising. She would simply turn it into a joke if he got on his high horse.

She avoided the worn hole on the landing carpet for fear of tripping and put down the burden outside her door. She had braved a call to the agent to request permission to paint the living room and undeterred by the admonition to use only a bland colour had nipped round to the nearest B&Q. Entering the room she surveyed the bare walls and furniture dragged towards the middle. She had saved a week's worth of the Metro from the tube and deciding to begin with the shortest wall, she spread out the sheets of newspaper to protect the floor. She bent a spoon trying to open the tin but was soon at work, hair tied back, the magnolia obliterated satisfyingly quickly by broad sweeps of the foam roller.

Beneath the concentration an uncomfortable awareness nagged at edge of her focus. Her father, Robert Unwin was not falling at her feet rejoicing in his new-found daughter. 'You're my girl, Rose,' she'd dreamed of him saying, putting an arm round her pliable shoulders leaning in to his warmth. Again, she reread his reply to her letter. It was unfathomable, the words seemed to have been measured like rare drops of something priceless, nothing exuberant, nothing to say he was thrilled to hear from her, at most accepting that she existed. Be satisfied. He has not rejected you, she told herself, playing the waiting game once more. Only her mother's sceptical look as she exaggerated his answer chilled Rose somewhat. Was there a possibility that Angie would be *jealous* of her daughter?

'Collateral damage,' Rose said aloud, remembering the phrase used by a school counsellor trying to understand her, in one of those sessions that peeled away the protective layers that Rose had wrapped around.

'Side effects. You must foresee the consequences of what you do. You're losing friends; your mother's at her wits end.' Bore on, she'd muttered under her breath, unrepentant. That was a long time ago and she'd grown up. Soon all the loose ends would be tied and Rose would put the past behind her.

She stood on tiptoe with the roller and drew it down to the skirting board. She had reached the corner and stood back, careful not to drip the paint everywhere, satisfied. In time, when Rob came to visit, the room would look really nice. Ready for him, fresh and fashionable, a backdrop to her dreams.

It was Monday morning. Terry pulled his woolly hat down over his ears. Was he growing soft? He'd shaved his head for years but the sharp gusts of wind were bitter. He cradled the mug as the lads joked about their weekend. Pints down the boozer and a take-away Chinese.

'What d'you reckon to this set up then?' Buster tilted his head towards the house.

'Nice family. Nice family,' Terry nodded slowly. 'His Lordship's a very reasonable guy for an architect; you should see some I've had the pleasure of dealing with. Time will tell, of course, but early impressions are extremely positive. We are in the land of milk and honey, providing we do a good job and stay on schedule.' He looked around at them. 'And that's largely up to you.'

'I can smell money,' said Jacko with a smirk and they laughed in spite of Terry's frown.

'Since when did you get familiar with the smell of money?' chuckled Sean.

'You know what I mean. Excavating a wine cellar and all those deliveries. Fancy names on the boxes, Bosch this and Heals that.'

The others creased up again and Terry said, 'I'm glad that work is not interfering too much with your appreciation of the material things in life.'

'I'm just saying,' Jacko continued with his theme, 'there's hardly anything that isn't brand new in the place. Look at that front room. Classy even if it is only half furnished.'

'Half furnished? Don't be daft. That's the minimalist look, you dummy,' Buster raised his eyes.

Jacko deflected the jibe and spoke in an undertone to the lads, 'I think the Mrs is all right. Yup, she's okay but he's a bit of a nob, a bit of a know-all, know what I mean?'

'What's that?' Terry turned back, 'did I hear right? You better watch it. He's fine, Mr Yoo. Just fine. Take a good look. That's what a successful professional looks like. You could all take a leaf out of his book. Now, let's crack on. We'll see if we can get a smile off him before the day's out.'

The following morning, Rob woke with a start as the alarm on the bedside table shrieked. How had he put up with that noise every morning for God knows how many years of his working life? He'd got out of the habit of setting it, but today he needed to be out early. He'd better get a move on. Ten to six and hardly a glimmer of light at this hour. He hurried to get ready for his first morning of volunteering.

He and Carla had been pleasantly surprised when a 'welcome' drinks party was held in their honour, just a week earlier. The friendly couple from the meeting they'd attended had been as good as their word and dropped by with an informal invitation.

They were introduced to a dozen or so locals at the party. Red or white was offered and tasty mouthfuls of homemade nibbles. The guests were cosmopolitan, a French couple, two diminutive Chinese and a towering white-blond Swede among the usual types. Rob enjoyed this kind of thing. He knew he could charm and amuse with no effort after a lifetime of dealing with difficult clients. Anyway, he generally liked people, took them as he found them. A newcomer, he was an object of interest. Now and then he glimpsed Carla in the corner of his vision, listening intently as someone talked on and on. He contemplated his wife for a moment, her petite figure in its dark red sheath. Even in heels she had to tilt her head to the tall Scandinavian and her expression looked unlike herself, fragile, somewhat brittle. She'd always been good at putting people at ease and drawing them out but this guy seemed to be delivering a monologue. Should he rescue her?

'Rob, I want to make sure you've met simply everyone,' he was whisked away towards a couple coming through the door.

Towards the end of the evening, Rob had his arm well and truly twisted. He never even saw it coming. Much taken with his hostess, a woman with the svelte looks of a past in modelling, he listened fascinated as she gave him the lowdown on the neighbourhood. Then she launched into a tale of setting up a breakfast club and advice centre for refugees and asylum seekers. It had been operating for a year in an adjacent but run-down part of the city. Louise was articulate and perfectly used to getting her own way. He was polite, surprised; he wouldn't have put her down as a do-gooder. Before he knew it, he had agreed to help out. All it took was a further chat on the telephone the next morning and he was well and truly lumbered. Carla had looked sceptical on the walk home.

'I always said I wanted to do something,' he reminded her.

'Yes, something like using your professional expertise,' she said. Was there a faint hint of antipathy to Louise with her long blonde hair and statuesque figure?

Even this early the streets were busy as he strode happily along, a jacket over his shoulder, bathed in the special glow that 'paying back to society' was meant to give. It was a little soon; after all, he reminded himself, he hadn't actually done anything yet.

He was getting a kick from being up and out in the nipping air and keeping fit was all part of the new regime. His parents had popped their clogs as he put it, far too young. All part of the reason to pack in the daily grind with Angus and Latimer. That wasn't quite accurate; he had mostly loved it; crises apart, it was not a grind. And he'd had the privilege of working on some inspiring schemes. They may have been based in the provinces but there was nothing provincial about their most ambitious projects.

From now on, he would walk as much as he could. It was a brisk forty-minute journey and instead of muddy fields and dripping woods there were buildings to look at, shop fronts, a multitude of people and not a Barbour in sight, thank God. He had a bounce in his stride, a fresh experience ahead of him. Nothing to do with Louise, he reminded himself. Three tower blocks loomed up ahead. The area became seedier; not much sign of gentrification here, the names above the shops written in Arabic or Urdu, he wasn't sure.

A building that had done time as a Pentecostal church was set back from the street. There was a notice board full of posters: Jumble Sale this Saturday. Toddlers Mondays and Wednesdays at ten. Bingo, Friday Night. This must be it. He was early. The hall doors were closed and locked. Perhaps there was a side entrance. He'd just turned down an alley to the side of the building when he spotted Louise unloading her car. She gave him a wave and came towards him, smiling, weighed down by several bags.

'Rob. Sorry. Have you been here long?'

'Just got here,' he grinned. 'All ready for the fray. Let me take those.' Louise lowered the bags to the ground and proceeded to unlock the door.

'Here we are. Just plonk them in the kitchen would you?'

Tables and chairs filled the middle of the hall. She went across with the key to a small room where half a dozen computers stood on trestles along one side, large boxes of colourful toys and books on the other.

'These all come out,' she gestured to the toys. 'The play area is over there. The other helpers will be here in a tick. We've got about twenty minutes before we open.'

Rob hauled out the colourful containers.

'Thanks. Now, if you could be in charge of the scrambled eggs. Jan can take over the kid's stuff. Here's the pan. Use two-dozen eggs for starters. Utensils in that drawer. Bowl. Salt and pepper,' her voice was brisk as she pointed. There was no time to waste, as packets of beef sausages were ripped open and put under a large grill. She pulled sliced white loaves out of the bags and started on the toast. Rob cracked eggs, concentrating on the task. A grey haired man and a large fair woman in her forties hurried in and were introduced quickly before they set to work, laying out plates and cutlery. The smell of sizzling fat was making Rob hungry. Would he even get a cup of tea, he wondered? The eggs were beginning to firm as he stirred energetically.

'Five minutes,' someone said.

'Better beat up the next lot. Same again, please Rob.' Louise gave him an encouraging smile. Rob hopped from stirring to whisking as the door to the hall was opened. The scrambled eggs looked perfect. His mouth watered as he put them on the counter. He hoped Louise would notice but she was busy. Wouldn't the eggs go cold? He stood feeling at a loss, watching the people coming in: the women in long robes and headscarves, while the men tended towards casual western dress. Louise moved to the counter now, greeting the clients by name as they came to collect a hot drink and a plateful of food. She addressed a personal remark to most of them, enquiring after a baby's health or how the family were faring at the bed and breakfast. There was genuine concern he noted admiringly. She was looking quite ordinary today in jeans and a baggy shirt, a striped apron folded at the waist. Not at all the glamour-puss from the party. A noisy drunk tottered affably loudly towards the serving hatch.

'Take over, Rob, could you?' Louise said, moving out into the body of the hall. Rob smiled and said good morning to each person in the queue, asking 'tea, coffee?' and spooning the scrambled eggs onto plates.

'You know the rules, Gordon. Come back tomorrow,' Louise insisted as the man held her arm, rocked a little on his feet. 'No, you can't come in today. Yes, you have. You know you have. Better luck tomorrow.' Rob was impressed; the drunk was turned and shown the door in a way that brooked no argument.

Before long, a hubbub of voices rose amid the rattle of cutlery yet children were unusually quiet, Rob noticed, glancing around the room. No running around creating havoc as his would have done at that age. Three small children played with a cracked pink plastic palace; babies were in their mothers' arms. Cooking duties over, Louise asked him to check for anyone needing help with the computers. He went towards a young Somali who was applying for a driving licence, frowning as he attempted to fill in the form.

'How are you doing?'

'I need English licence,' he looked up, 'then I get work more easy.'

'What sort of work are you hoping for?'

'Maybe delivery,' his expression was resigned, far from

hopeful.

'Can you manage okay?' asked Rob before moving on to the next person, a middle-aged man, frizzy hair in a halo around his head and bloodshot eyes that flicked over Rob. He was emailing his family in South Sudan, he shrugged and his shoulders slumped. Rob commiserated on the situation, affected by the difficulties people had to face, picturing his own comfortable home.

At nine fifteen an efficient clear up began and the door was opened to let everyone drift out. Equipment was collected and put away or washed, dried and stored in kitchen cupboards as the hall was to be vacated by nine thirty. Two hours had passed in a flash.

Louise stood wearing yellow rubber gloves, brushing a strand of hair from a shiny face and effusive in her thanks.

'Marvellous. It's great to have you here. We have only just been coping with the numbers. Another pair of hands makes all the difference,' she bestowed a look on Rob that would ensure his return, peeling off the gloves and apron.

'Let me email you the rota and you can see which sessions we need you.'

She was assuming he was committed, he realised, bemused. All the helpers left together, calling out, 'See you tomorrow.'

Rob answered and shook his head as if to clear it. How had he got involved so quickly? He set off on the walk home, not quite so briskly now.

It was a sunny morning, two weeks later and Rob was sauntering along, gazing at his surroundings with a benign eye, full of the satisfaction of another session at the centre, volunteering alongside the delightful Louise (as he thought of her). The twice-weekly experience was now very much a part of his new life. He stepped nimbly between a group of office workers and deliverymen who clogged the pavement outside a restaurant. Having banished suits from his life, he wore expensive jeans, a light blue cable knit sweater under a soft woollen jacket and black Italian trainers that enabled him to lope along.

He really did feel athletic, he considered, in spite of the fact that he hadn't played squash for years and the tennis had fallen by the wayside since the move. There was something rejuvenating in the air. He caught sight of himself, reflected in a shop window. Not bad for his age. He nearly did a hop, skip and a jump. And thank God he still had his hair. He raked the fringe off his forehead and thought about the morning's work. He seemed to be turning into the resident IT expert. It was good to be part of a team, even if Louise was the only one he wanted to impress. Weren't the others a bit sad really? Worthy, yes, but a bundle of laughs, he thought not. Louise was inspiring; that's what it was. She made everyone feel that anything was possible. And she knew just when to drop her voice and say something to make one feel special, on the same wavelength. He was picturing her as he'd seen her at the party when his mobile vibrated in his pocket. Gabrielle.

'Hello, Gaby.'

'Dad, you won't believe this.'

Rob's heart missed a beat. He stopped walking. 'What's happened?'

'I can't believe it. They called us all in at nine o'clock. The company's been sold without any of us being told a thing. My job's going...' her voice wobbled, 'the whole marketing department are getting the bullet. Just three month's pay and get lost. No longer needed. What on earth am I going to do?'

'Calm down a minute. Are you absolutely sure about all this?'

'I told you. They just called us in to tell us. We're all in shock. Nobody saw it coming.'

'That's bloody disgraceful. Unbelievable. Look, come over

later. We'll talk. And don't worry; you'll get another job. After all, you've got a fantastic track record. You'll be okay.'

'I hope so, Dad. I can't afford to be out of work with the flat and everything. All of us in the same boat too. Anna and Claire were crying,' she gulped. 'Okay, I'll see you later.'

He slipped his mobile into a pocket and walked on no longer seeing the people ahead or the cracked pavement under his feet. Redundancy would be a big blow to Gabrielle's self-esteem; she'd always been top of the class, a high flyer with an excellent degree. This was bad luck but he was sure she should have no trouble finding something else. Hell. It was a distraction he could well do without. He scowled recognising the selfishness of the thought. Carla's resistance to the very idea of Rose had preoccupied him since the move. Surely she realised that he was going to have to meet the girl soon. His brief acknowledgement of her letter had returned a composed reply. A couple of cautious messages later had gently postponed any meeting. Now the silence from Rose had become unmistakeably expectant. He frowned again. It was all very difficult for him to manage. And in the end he would have to brace himself for Gabrielle's hostile recriminations. That was not going to be a lot of fun.

Chapter Seven

'Let's get there early so that we're in position, as it were,' said Rob with little trace of the agitation she supposed he must be feeling. At that moment, he seemed a million miles away from Carla. He had ditched his first fearful reactions and spoke of 'dealing with the fallout' as if a minor family row had taken place rather than the shock of a grown up child springing out to capsize them. She too was trying to be matter of fact about this meeting that had been hanging over them for the past weeks with neither of them inclined to broach the subject.

'Are you talking to her?' she had demanded, breaking the stalemate at last.

'Not exactly.' Rob admitted that he had exchanged some text messages with the girl, adding that meeting her was inevitable.

'It may be inevitable but I don't have to like it and if it's taken her this long I can't see what's the hurry. I fear she'll be a leech once she gets her hooks into you.'

Rob just looked at her. Carla concluded he had spoken to Rose. It was like being cheated on. How they would break it to the children...she recoiled from the idea for the hundredth time.

'I'll fix it up. We'll just do it. Then at least we'll have a clearer idea of what's going on. I can't ignore her forever. Okay? Are we agreed?'

Going along in the car, her bag tucked between her feet, her mobile already on silent, she held her hands tightly in her lap.

She flicked her eyes to the right. The familiar profile sickened her. That Rob's handsome open features had concealed a secret for so long... She stared ahead wondering if he would have preferred to be going alone. He had never intimated that he would. Somehow it seemed important to present a unified front, calm acceptance was to be their attitude or so Carla had ruled. It would set the tone and prevent the emotional outburst they had better be prepared for, just in case.

'We must keep our cool, whatever she says,' she told Rob for the third time, pursing her lips, as they drove around looking for a parking space. His face was impassive, only a hint of apprehension now betraying itself as he tapped insistently on the steering wheel with his elegant thumbs. Neither of them had gone on playing the 'what if' game; it was pointless to give in to flights of fancy, Rob insisted, claiming to have put Rose out of his mind as they waited.

'Here we are, thank God,' he said reversing capably between a large silver Mercedes and a white Mini. Carla ran a comb through her hair, glancing nervously in the mirror and running a finger over her lipstick while he put coins in the meter.

As they remembered, the restaurant was unassuming, not overly large and fairly quiet. They had lunched there once when house hunting. Carla had suggested it was better not to be too close to home. As far as she knew, Rose was ignorant of their new address although it would not take a genius to discover it. They sat bolt upright, eyes on the entrance.

They ordered a bottle of white wine, the waiter hovering for the tasting but Rob gestured for him to pour Carla a glass. They drank too fast and Rob gave her a top-up as the door opened. His hand shook, making a tinkling waterfall of sound. No. It was an elderly couple. Two other tables were occupied not far away; a man entertained three women at the nearest one, holding forth, bathing in their attention and two men in business suits had their heads together over a laptop at the far end. Rob looked at his watch again then poured himself a glass. They studied the small vase of yellow and purple freesias on the table and Carla bent forward for the scent.

A dark haired girl burst through the door, looking about with big anxious eyes. She glanced at the older couple and then as the waiter was taking her jacket, let her gaze rest on Rob. Carla clutched her chest, a pang of distress shooting through her from top to bottom. Rob was halfway to the girl, embracing her now, laughing as she laughed and holding on to each other's arms and leaning back to stare. Carla felt miserably de trop, standing as if to attention by her chair. She shouldn't have come. She rearranged her face into the dignified expression she had planned and stood up to hold out a hand to the girl who was all gleaming teeth and Gabrielle's eyes and hair, Gabrielle's sister, no doubt about it at all. The proffered hand was ignored as Rose dived around it hugging her.

'Oh, I'm so glad to meet you,' she cried.

They sat, suddenly subdued while the orders were taken. Then Rose's excitement bubbled over. She disarmed them by declaring that she wanted for nothing. She'd had a funny old upbringing, but she'd survived, she announced cheerfully.

'Everything's going well for me,' she told them. 'I've been working as a graphic designer for a small ad agency. My boss is pretty okay. I'm renting this little flat, you know, in the East End, really cool, been there forever, long before it became all fashionable,' she sat back, her eyes sparkling. 'Sorry, I'm talking too much. Your turn.' She took a forkful of lasagne and looked from Rob to Carla and back. So life was wonderful, Carla repeated to herself. What could he do in the face of this endearing onslaught? With a swift glance at Carla, Rob began.

'Well. We've got two children, Gabrielle and Peter.'

At this Rose was almost out of her seat with delight as if she hadn't known.

'I was hoping there would be.'

Carla butted in. 'They don't know about you.'

'Yet,' added Rob, softening everything with a gesture that Carla recognised as give us time.

'I don't want to make things difficult. That's the last thing I want.'

'What do you want?' Carla gave her an intent look.

Rose took a breath and looked down at the table.

'I don't really know. I've wanted to find out about you,' she looked up at Rob, 'for ages. My first dad pushed off when I was two. I've always known that Adrian was my stepfather: it never made any difference. Wanting to know about you was something I had to do. Mum told me to wait until I was older so I did. She said I'd better be prepared for rejection. If you never want to see me again, I'll accept it.'

The dark eyes began to well and her expression was so tragic that Rob shook his head at once and even Carla found herself protesting.

'No, no.'

'Don't be daft. Of course we'll meet again. Anyway you must meet Gabrielle; you're the image of her. And Peter,' Rob nodded at her plate. 'Come on. Eat up.' They obediently picked up their forks and resumed pushing the food into little piles. Only Rose tucked in with enthusiasm.

'I don't even know where you live,' she said after a minute.

'We've recently moved to London,' Carla answered first, avoiding giving the actual address. 'Everything's in chaos, builders wreaking havoc. You know how it is. When we're straight, perhaps we could organise something with our young.'

'That would be so wonderful. I can't wait.' Something, a slight wobble betrayed an underlying nervousness. Had she blown it? Carla could read the girl's thoughts.

'So you're an architect?' Rose changed tack.

'Yes...sort of retired but hoping to work on some new projects. Tell us about a bit more about yourself. Did you get a degree?'

'I did but I lived at home. It wasn't that much fun. There's a lot of technical stuff with design software.' There was a silence as Carla and Rob came to the same conclusion. Rose had inherited his aptitudes. She chattered on, giving an account of her life and avoiding any mention of her mother. Finally she sat back, beaming. 'That's about it.'

'Peter is a talented tennis player: a coach, in fact. Gabrielle's in marketing.' Carla gave this information reluctantly.

Rose leant forwards with a rapt expression, hoping for more but Carla moved to pick up her bag, placed it on her lap in a signal that lunch was over.

'I'll get the bill.' Rob waved at the waiter. 'Did you come by car?'

They stood in an awkward threesome on the pavement to say goodbye. Carla watched as Rob gave Rose a fierce hug. It was obvious that he was entranced. From now on, Rose would have to be taken into account.

Neither said a word as they walked back to the car. They looked at each other once they were sitting side by side. Both sighed but for different reasons.

'Well, well, well,' said Rob, 'I'm not at all sure what's hit me.'

'Don't you think she's a bit too good to be true?' Carla caught his affronted eye. 'All that "I'm so happy" and "I want nothing from you." Maybe we should take it with a pinch of salt.'

Rob said nothing but his lips made a thin line. He put the key into the ignition and looking in the wing mirror, pulled out into the traffic. Let's be normal for a bit, she wanted to say.

'Can you take me up the King's Rd? There's some shopping I want to do.'

'When shall we tell the children?'

'For God's sake, give it a break. We've met her. Shall we

digest that first? We don't have to rush headlong into anything.' Carla knew what a sour look she had on her face. Shut up!

'All in good time,' she forced a pleasanter note into her voice.

Rob reached over and squeezed her knee. He was happy, damn it. He nodded, relief obvious.

'It will be okay. I've got a gut feeling. But you're right. There's no rush. She's waited this long, she can wait a bit longer. You liked her though, didn't you?'

They crawled along in slow traffic. He was able to take his eyes off the road and look at her for her answer. The appeal was infuriating.

'She was fine,' Carla snapped. 'It's too early to tell. You can't judge a person on an hour's acquaintance.' This was dishonest of her. He had always valued the accuracy of her split second judgement on people. She glanced over but Rob had chosen to keep quiet.

Rose danced along the pavement as soon as she was out of their sight. Oh, it had gone so well; she'd played her part to perfection. She'd known instinctively what qualities would win them over. Winsome, endearing, open, she'd had them all down to a T. She felt high as a kite. She'd done it. Her fears had been unfounded. So what if he'd never wanted to get in touch. Now, he'd seen her; he'd hugged her. She ran down the steps to the Tube and as it was her lucky day there was a train about to go. She dived through the doors just in time, swinging into a seat, her face flushed with excitement and two glasses of wine. She took a deep breath as if she'd been holding it for the past couple of hours.

It was going to be all right. Yes, she was almost sure of it. Robert, HER FATHER, she added several mental exclamation marks, had liked her. Her feet did a drum roll of triumph on the floor.

'Sorry.' She had jogged the man next to her, a plump businessman with a tan leather briefcase between his feet and a copy of The Times in arms spread wide, encroaching on her space. Never mind! For once the sodding world had done her a favour. She was owed it all right. Never had she felt so pleased with herself. All the bad times dumped in the trash. Her eyes shone then her face fell. If Rob was a pushover, what about the wife? Rose pictured a vixen, sniffing the air for what? Danger? Predators? She is wary of me, didn't invite me to the house. Not yet. But soon, her father has promised.

'We need time to tell them and the children need time to come to terms with it,' Carla had spoken with an air of finality.

We mustn't give the poor darlings too much of a shock, Rose thought.

'Of course! The last thing I want to do is impose. I'm so grateful that you've come today.' She had given her sweetest smile, making sure to look a little anxious, too. She had better win Carla over or she'd never get to meet her siblings. A son and daughter she'd noted when looking up her father on Google. No other detail but she'd pictured them looking ultra conservative with neat haircuts and good teeth. They might react badly at first but would soon see she was, how could she put it? A positive in their lives – why not? The idea of them poured now like warm treacle into her mind. Oh the joy of having a half sister and brother. One of each, she crowed. Gabrielle and Peter. Peter and Gabrielle. Meet my brother. Well, half brother, she would say, introducing him to people.

The train jolted and braked. Oxford Circus. When the passengers settled themselves, she smiled at her wavy reflection in the window musing that Rob was not only good- looking, he was actually very fit. She'd pictured an older, grey haired man, severe and intelligent. She imagined him thinking, what an adorable girl. Oh, she would soon wangle her way in; get what she deserved. Such luck the family had moved to London. She mustn't push it, though. Just be patient, she told herself. Her expression was resolute. After all, it had taken her years and years to get this far.

Chapter Eight

The noise of metal grating on concrete, crashing and shovelling outside competed with Peter scraping his spoon around a bowl of cereal. Rob could just hear Terry's voice lecturing the lads. He strained to hear.

'Hush a minute, Pete.'

'Struggle, workers, chains...' Good grief, did he have a Marxist on site? He leaned closer to the window but a quick look showed Terry was now answering his mobile.

'Hard-core, something, something...' The builder turned away and Rob moved back. He doodled on the back of a white envelope from a pile of mail and sipped his tea while the crunching noises resumed opposite; Peter had shaken another helping from the cereal box. Perhaps he should be worrying less about the project and more about his children. Carla had been adamant this morning, her voice low, in the safety of their bathroom, that having met Rose, they should plan their usual Christmas and then break the news to the children.

'It's bound to cause ructions and I can't imagine what Mum will think. She'll probably die of shock.'

'That's rubbish. Your mother's always had her feet on the ground. She's the least of our worries.'

'Shush. Not too loud. I agree but let's have a peaceful Christmas first. It's not asking for much. Gaby moving in with us when she lets the flat is going to be a bit of a trial.'

'I thought you wanted to see more of the kids. Now's your opportunity. Don't complain.'

'I thought you might have noticed that my complaints have been minimal, considering.'

Having delivered a crisp parting shot, she disappeared to give instructions to Uldis, the Hungarian cleaner they had acquired through Louise. Then she would be off as usual, he supposed. He was damned if he was going to ask her where. The chilly atmosphere could return with a single acerbic remark from either of them. Frankly, he was getting utterly sick of the tight-lipped look she resorted to when any uncomfortable subject arose. Only in other people's company was she playful, her old self. The rest of the time she was an automaton, supervising the household, cooking meals, taking an interest in the builders, wearing a mask over the wound he had inflicted. Christ, he'd apologised hadn't he, sworn bitter regrets, calmed her fears? He ground his teeth and gulped down some cold coffee. Ugh.

Rob contemplated his son lounging at the table, still chewing cornflakes and flicking through the colour supplement, his hair sticking up all anyhow, the polo shirt with Scimitar picked out in red embroidered letters. Neither of them had had ambitious dreams for Peter in the early days, only gratitude that he was healthy and astonishment at his bean-pole rise to well over six feet. Besides, he was completely resistant to pressure of an academic kind.

'Will the job be full-time over Christmas?'

Peter had begun his month as a replacement to the Head coach at the Scimitar Club, (romantically named by an early patron, an escapee from the Ayatollah) thanks to a good word put in for him by one of his clients who knew someone who knew someone. It was a stroke of luck that the man would be off for months, enduring the pain and indignity of a torn Achilles tendon. On his first day, Peter had been tipped the wink that a job might become permanent if his face fitted. That had raised Rob's expectations.

'Over the holidays?' At last Rob had his attention. Yes, he was swallowing and blinking to make the effort to keep his father sweet. Really, he could read Peter like a book. A cool unwavering eye might elicit a response from the boy.

'Yeah, well, there are loads of courses for kids. Keeps them out of the parents' hair when the au pairs all go home for Christmas.'

'Keep hard at it. That's the way to make an impression,' Rob bit back any more. Peter loathed that kind of encouragement.

'There's a big demand for coaching. Could be good news for me, Dad.'

This was a pleasant surprise: a faint hint of purpose from one who refused to show any concern about the future. If only he could find favour with the people in charge. Rob had a vision of his son forever knocking balls outside the sort of ramshackle pavilions of second-rate tennis clubs that he himself had belonged to in his younger days. One thing was certain; Peter would be popular enough with his new clients. No need to worry on that score: he got along with everyone.

'So, you're enjoying it and staying here at home is working out for now?' Did he have to sound so stiff?

His son gave a non-committal shrug and looked out of the window where the youngest labourer was playfully clouting another on the backside with a shovel. Rob gave up waiting for an answer, as Peter appeared lost in thought, hardly registering the antics outside. Surely it was an agreeable novelty to coach in an exclusive venue with all those courts, indoors and outdoors, the bar and the swimming pool? If only he would show some enthusiasm. Still, he must be getting to know the ropes and the clientele. He pictured Peter with the irrepressible youngsters in the after school sessions and especially the pre-teens who had yet to become blasé and listless. In a rare comment he'd described those hours as the most enjoyable.

As for Peter's thoughts on the arrangements at home, they

appeared to be non-existent. It was unlikely that domestic considerations ever entered his head. Home was comfortable and convenient and he could look forward to seeing Nina in the evenings when he was not coaching. His doting mother would cook his supper, his girlfriend hover around him like a moth. What's not to like? Rob wondered. Nina had begun to stay over much of the time, as Carla had pointed out. Would they ever prise him out of the nest? He continued to stare as Peter scraped butter and Marmite onto a slice of toast.

Over the next couple of weeks Rob managed to put delicate matters familial entirely out of mind while setting up his venture into design consultancy, visiting his financial adviser and a website guru and meeting former clients at their London apartment. A possible project was exciting stuff and it had suited him to be out and about. Drawing the preliminary sketches had occupied him fully; his study door had remained closed for many afternoons. Then there was a lull over a week and he rallied himself only for his volunteering.

On the dot of four one evening, the workmen had packed in when a cold fog descended over the garden and even the voluble Terry had given a brief farewell.

'Season of mists and mellow fruitfulness,' he intoned as he passed through the house on his way out, turning up the collar of his navy jacket.

It had been a rather unsatisfying day, Rob concluded as he sat on the edge of his desk, mercifully alone in the house for once. He remembered with a small pang the little catnaps he used to enjoy, a chance to re-order his thoughts during the switch off. Since the kids had moved in, the place seemed half the size and overrun with people. Outside his office his longing for order was denied in a thousand ways. Gabrielle pleased herself, rolling up at all hours, oblivious of their requests for considerate behaviour. She had commandeered the larger of the spare bedrooms; her stuff was everywhere. He fervently hoped it would not take her long to find some new employment. They had helped her move her personal possessions from the flat: a familiar task from university days though with fewer empty beer cans and carrier bags full of who knew what, jollying her along as she relinquished her independence, declaring herself 'the most pissed-off' she'd ever been. Privately, Rob considered her lucky to have found tenants ready to pay a decent rent, keeping her going for the moment.

In the new house a slow creep of clutter was gaining the upper hand, no matter how often it was rerouted back to the bedrooms. Even Carla was beginning to sigh as she gathered up jumpers from chair backs and mugs and glasses from any convenient surface.

Rob relished the quiet moment and moved back to his chair, gliding it silently towards him. He sat down and half-closed his eyes. Beneath heavy lids he gazed through the window; dusk was falling and the streetlights had come on. Intermittently, cars went by. Minutes passed, yet he did not sleep. He sat bathed in the faint green glow from the Internet router on his desk. In the past he'd been motivated by clear-cut goals but that purpose in life had suddenly deserted him. Recently, he'd been too passive, adrift on a slow tide of events. Studying Peter at close quarters, he'd become aware of his preconceptions, the standard responses to the boy's nature. Still, Carla was too soft with him. It wouldn't do to have both of them pandering to him.

Carla accused him of being unruffled by the consequences of welcoming Rose to the family. That really wasn't true; the very idea of her induced longing and apprehension in equal measure. He could not understand how he had closed his mind to her existence for decades: fear, he supposed and too late now to rewrite history. Light footsteps pattered on the floor outside. The door handle turned slowly, tentatively and he sensed an eye peeking through the crack before a diffident voice sounded.

'Can I make you some tea, Rob?' It was Nina, venturing down now that the place was quiet.

'Lovely. I didn't know you were in. Black for me,' he smiled, relieved at the interruption. 'I'll come and join you.' Somehow, Nina's delicacy called for politeness. He could find some thinking time later and he liked talking to the shy girl with her appealing air of innocence. Peter could do a lot worse.

She perched awkwardly on the edge of the elm rocker until the kettle boiled and she sprang up lightly to pour water in the mugs.

'I've done you ordinary tea, is that okay?'

'Sure. Always builder's for me. Thanks. Been in long?'

'A little while. I'm just waiting for Pete. We're seeing some friends later.'

'How's the designing going?'

'Designing?' Nina shrugged her narrow shoulders. 'I've got a sketchpad full of ideas. My dream is to set up on my own but getting noticed is very hard. The fashion world is all about knowing the right people and if you don't get spotted at college then it's really tough. It was lucky that Melanie gave me a chance. She liked my stuff in the end of year show. If no one will take a gamble on you and set you up, working for a designer is the next best thing, however frustrating it is to see your drawings nicked by someone else.'

'That's not good. But you mustn't give up. Your chance will come, I'm sure,' he blew on his tea for a moment and gave her a querying look. 'Peter was saying the job at the Scimitar may turn into a permanent thing. Have you got any idea how he's getting on? He tends to keep us in the dark.' He made a dismissive gesture.

Nina swung her legs down and curled them up the other way.

'I think it's going quite well. He's very keen. Actually, he's been putting in quite a lot of extra time. He teases me about the yummy mummies collecting the kids at the end of the day.'

'Don't be silly. He despises them really,' Rob grinned. What a little ninny. Pete was besotted with her as far as he could see. 'You should show Carla and Gabrielle your sketches. They'd love to see them. I'd love to see them. Perhaps you could design something for Carla. Now that's an idea.'

'D'you think so? Maybe. If she'd like it,' Nina got to her feet as she heard the front door open.

'I'd better get on. See you later, Rob,' she darted a smile as she slipped away.

'Hello.'

'Hi, Nina.'

Gabrielle's purposeful footsteps clacked towards the kitchen and an icy blast swept in with her.

'Have you got a tenner I could borrow, Dad? The taxi is waiting. I didn't get a chance to go to the bank. Thanks,' she grabbed the note and hurried out.

A minute later, she was back, giving Rob a peck on the cheek as he raised his eyebrows.

'Don't look like that,' she had a humorous glint in her eyes, 'you know I'll pay you back. Where's Mum?' Without waiting for an answer, she almost bounced up and down, 'I should get the deposit from the tenants tomorrow. Hey, rent coming in for the next six months. You won't know I'm here Dad. I shall be quiet as a mouse. That will make two mice,' and she glanced up at the ceiling. 'She was vanishing up the stairs as I came in.'

'Pete's happy.'

'I promise you I shall be out of here before he is. It won't take me long to find another job though I still can't believe the way they've treated me.'

Before she could launch into the customary tirade, Rob sprang up and switched on a floodlight in the garden, 'Here, have a look at this.' A pale mist hung over the site; the summerhouse a ghostly shape beyond. He put an arm round her shoulders as they stood by the window. 'I'm excited now.'

'Can't see much. The fog's come down. Are they getting on well?' Gabrielle craned her neck. 'Terry is a good bloke don't you think? The things he comes out with.'

'I call him our cement-laying philosopher. He's got a quotation for every eventuality. We had the Ode to Autumn earlier.'

'Appropriate. That new guy is extremely dishy, by the way. What's he called, Aidan or Adonis perhaps?'

'For God's sake, Gaby, behave. No flirting with the builders.'

'Course not. Just appreciating the finer things in life. Mum agrees with me anyway.'

Rob shook his head in mock despair.

'Where is your mother? I haven't seen her all day.'

'When I asked her, all she would say was, places to go etcetera, etcetera. What's she put on the calendar? Hum, not very illuminating. I expect she'll be back soon. Is she okay, do you think? She's been a bit remote recently.'

'She's probably coming to terms with her nice quiet life being invaded by her offspring and hangers on,' the last words were regretted at once.

Gabrielle folded her arms defensively then glanced up at the ceiling again, 'I know what you mean,'

'I shouldn't be unkind. But she does seem to be here rather a lot.'

"Well I can promise you that I for one will be out of here the minute my finances recover.' She laughed, 'As far as Pete goes, I dare say you'll have to kick him out.'

'Oh, it won't come to that. In spite of appearances he's keen to get on in the big wide world, I'm sure.'

'I'll leave you with your illusions. I need to make some calls. Can I use your office, Dad?'

'Good idea. Get some privacy. And check some of those

websites. Grafting will pay off in the job hunt, you know.'

'Okay. Okay. I wouldn't mind some tea if you're making a cup.'

'Get on with the calls then. Mum and Peter should be in soon. Mum's been escaping as much as she can while the builders are working. She's exploring everywhere, you know, walking for bloody miles, clutching her A-Z and a map of the bus routes.'

Chapter Nine

Shivering a little in her pink jacket, but knowing the shops would be overheated, Carla set off for Sloane Square armed with a shopping list. She went slowly along looking in the Christmas windows, admiring their originality. Once inside Peter Jones, she consulted her list. There were plenty of things she needed to buy on almost every floor of the store. She went up the stairs first to look at the shoes; after the miles she'd covered in the past weeks, her most comfortable pair was nearly worn out. She dithered before making up her mind on some flat tan boots with rubber soles that were perfect for winter and then continued to meander through 'Occasion wear'. The over-embellished dresses and jumpers, beaded and sequinned for the season, did not appeal. The styles she had picked for her little boutique had reflected her own taste: pared down, well cut and hardly a pattern in sight. Flattering to most shapes and sizes. She'd always loved clothes, using them as a bulwark against the world. Looking 'nice' gave her confidence, overcoming that feeling of not being quite good enough, ridiculous though it probably was. The shop had been both hard work and fun, it was no easy matter running a business and keeping in profit; Gabrielle helped out sometimes in the university holidays, getting on well with Carla's assistant, Bridget, who became a sort-of confidant to the impetuous student forever inclined to antagonise her mother.

In the hi-tech surroundings of the electrical department, all dazzling primary colours against the white background, Carla concentrated on the task in hand. She stared at the long row of irons; Uldis had made a negative comment about the one they used. She read a few words on some of the packaging and decided, market research completed in a perfunctory way, that it would be better to shop for one online. Perhaps get Uldis to have a look too. Besides she was in someone's way and she headed to the upper floor, clutching her bag of new boots and wondering who would ever go to the shops in the future. Yet here it seemed as busy as ever.

She fingered the heavy linen, enticed by the subtle geometric print. The muted shades of green and turquoise would suit the last remaining room since Gabrielle moved in. Carla was ambivalent about the homecoming; she'd always been susceptible to the moods of a happy Gabrielle who enchanted but a grumpy girl irritated the hell out of her. Of course it was a joy to have her near, she told herself. She moved on along the stands, roll after roll of fabric in luscious colours and textures. No grubby little hands of grandchildren for a few years yet, no dogs or cats, though she would miss Topper always. If ever there was a time for pale luxurious furnishings, she longed for cream linen, soft grey wool, eau de nil velvet, it was now.

She would ask for just a sample of the print; she pulled out the heavy roll and carried it awkwardly to a counter. She unfailingly wished she were taller, feeling dumpy in spite of her slim figure. The assistants paid her no attention and were busy and slow, methodically measuring metre after metre for some vast windows while she stood beginning to seethe.

In the end she waited so long she decided she might as well buy the three metres required for the blinds. Doubts struck as she inserted her card into the reader. The assistant had a semi-smile on his lips as he slid the bag across the counter.

'Thank you, madame.'

She was gracious in return, moving away and juggling the

carriers, still questioning her own judgement as so often these days, agonising over the tiniest thing. Perhaps living with Rob and his precise ideas had stunted her imagination, there was no doubt she was plagued by too much choice. She remembered the app. that Gabrielle had downloaded for her.

'You take a pic of anything you like. I'll be able to see what you're looking at. You want my approval, don't you?'

It was too late for that. Carla began to compose a few witty comments about consumerism to accompany any future pictures and make Gabrielle smile. Capturing the Dream or Slave to Style she might call it.

'Carla. It is you.'

She turned, recognising the distinctive voice. A friend from her Parish Council days beamed in triumph as if snaring an elusive prey. Carla smiled back noting the perfectly arched brows above immaculately made–up eyes, the copper-tinted hair.

'Janet, hi. How nice to see a friendly face,' she laid it on a little. 'What are you doing up here?'

'Oh, just a spot of shopping, then meeting Steven later. You got time for a cuppa?'

'Why not? Let's go up to the café. Actually,' Carla went on as they went towards the escalator, 'I'm escaping the new cleaner. Hungarian, you know. Rather terrifying. She has a stern unflinching gaze. I showed her round the other day; her English isn't bad. "I must to tell you the i-ron is not good." Cappuccino? There's a bit of a circus going on at the new place. Builders,' she raised her eyebrows to indicate the awfulness; decided she was babbling and shut up.

'How's Rob?'

'Fine. How is Steven?'

'He's okay. Fine, I mean. You know. Grumpy because of the knee. It's still not right.'

They sat down at a small square table and Janet began a tale of her own renovations from years before. Carla did her best to look interested; it was hardly relevant now.

'Actually, Rob is going spare,' she interrupted. 'You know what a perfectionist he is. They're doing their best though, the builders.'

'When are we going to get an invite?'

'Gosh. Soon. When things calm down a bit. We're in such a muddle.' Janet was looking amused. 'Really, you've no idea. We do miss everyone, obviously. How are the Welbys and the Morton-Smeatons?'

'Oh, fine. Just the same as ever.' Janet gave an account of the prominent families in the village. 'Have you heard the latest about the Andersons?' she continued. 'Apparently, they're splitting up. It doesn't altogether surprise me. He's always had a roving eye. Awfully sad for the children, though. But don't breathe a word; it may not be true. Poor Olivia, you must have heard from her. Her sister is refusing to have the mother so she and John are completely lumbered. She's marvellous, though, not a word of complaint. Of course, the main topic,' the arch look returned, 'getting absolutely everybody agitated is the proposed housing development, on your old land, opposite the Manor.' There was a glint in her direct gaze. 'Ooh, your name is mud! Selling that field to the farmer and then scarpering, you must have known you were asking for trouble.'

Carla sagged under the accusation then sat up. 'We didn't seriously think that it would get planning. You can't blame us for cashing in if someone was fool enough to buy.'

'People think Rob must have had the inside track, selling when you did.'

'Absolutely not.' She heard herself sounding shrill, injected a note of calm. 'On the contrary, it never came up. It enabled us to buy a decent house up here, that's all. The Johnsons made us a silly offer for the field. If we hadn't sold it, then the next owners would have. Blame the Planning department not us, if it goes through. We don't know anything about any development.'

'I'm only saying. It was lucky for you. It slipped under the radar at the time, the farmer buying it. He's being treated as a pariah. Your buyers are up in arms that their solicitor didn't pick it up. Anyway, it might not go through. The opposition is mounting as we speak. It's quite near the church and only just outside the conservation area. The locals are giving the Parish Council a hard time. But, tell me, how are the kids? Rufus and Giselle are flying high though I do say so myself,' she gave a smirk. 'Peter still doing the tennis coaching?'

Carla blew on her coffee and took a sip. Insufferable woman, she remembered now.

'They're fine, thank you. Doing very well. Now, I'm on a quest for curtain material.' Should she risk showing her the piece in her carrier bag? No, the wretched woman was banging on again.

'My interior design chappie took me down to Chelsea Harbour once. A revelation. Dreadfully extravagant but these guys are so much cleverer than you and me. It's all too easy to make an expensive mistake and then you've got to live with it!' Janet gave a little scream. 'Remember Monica and that ghastly wallpaper. Nightmare. We all had to lie about how much we liked it.'

'It wasn't that bad,' Carla said feebly, then rallying, 'we don't want to lose our individuality. Rob and I are definitely going to make our own decisions. Now, I must get on. Give my love to Steven. It's nice to see you and I'll be in touch. You must come over for lunch one Sunday. As soon as the builders have gone.'

'Oh, so lovely to see you too. I'll tell them at church that I bumped in to you. You do look a teensy bit tired,' she raised one of the well-plucked eyebrows, 'I hope all this work on the new house isn't wearing you out.'

'Not at all. I've never had so much energy. Everyday there's some new excitement. It's all marvellously exhilarating,' she bent to brush Janet's cheek. 'Places to go, people to see, ha-ha,' Carla strode away, round the tables, escaping with relief.

Down the wide staircase she went and out into the square, busy with noisy traffic, pigeons almost under her feet. What a waste of time. She peeped into the shopping bag to look at the material in daylight. She'd made a good decision. Now, on to that wonderful shop that sold tassels and trims. The voice in her head sounded doggedly positive. She stood for a moment at the crossing, waiting for the cars and taxis to stop, conscious of her appearance and Janet's unkind comment: 'looking tired' indeed. She wished she hadn't bumped into her; the comments made her cringe. It was a shock to think they were in the firing line with people in the village complaining about them. She put a hand to her mouth, blinked back a tear and swallowed.

Reaching the other side, she buttoned up the pink jacket, its bright hue a rebuff to the snide remarks and regained her composure by picturing the spare room nearly finished and the first guests arriving. If only Olivia could get away from looking after her mother. Her old friend was struggling to get outside help for the eighty-five year old who'd had a bad stroke. Carla was missing the phone calls and Olivia's ironic comments on life.

'Rob, listen, I saw Janet today. She was bitching about a huge new development going for planning in Johnson's paddocks and our old field, across from the Old Manor,' she had gone straight into Rob's office, blurting it out. 'You never knew anything about it did you?'

'Course not. Oh, there may have been the odd rumour but name me a village that hasn't got those.' He stared into the distance, not catching her eye, his hands still hovering over the keyboard.

'You never told me.'

'There wasn't anything concrete.' He bent his head again, away from her stare, tap-tapping his sentence. 'Why, are our buyers complaining?'

'Janet said major grumbles. It wasn't why you agreed to sell?'

'Don't sound so vindictive. Of course not. It made a hell of a difference to what we could afford here. You weren't bellyaching then. Their solicitor did the appropriate searches, I'm quite sure. Don't worry about it. Not our problem,' Rob pursed his lips, his chin set: end of discussion.

'I don't like to think of people assuming we'd been given the nod. Don't you care about our reputation?'

'For God's sake, Carla, give it a rest. No one can accuse us of anything. If a new application goes through it's their bad luck. Nothing to do with us. We got a fair price at the time, which they were quite happy to pay. We'll put the record straight if anyone asks. Now, don't lose any sleep over it.'

'Okay. We'll tell them what's what when we go back for the dinner at the Mayhews. Anyway it may never happen. There's bound to be a hell of an outcry from everyone in the village. But it would be awful if the Old Manor lost its lovely view. Still, look at us. You can never guarantee there won't be change.'

He did not rise to the bait, 'Too right. You can't plan for every eventuality. Fingers crossed anyway,' he changed the subject, pointing to his drawing on the screen. 'Look.'

'Something else to worry about now. Can you show me later? By the by, Mum and Gillian would like to come for Christmas. I thought the day before Christmas Eve.'

'You decide. I don't mind driving down to collect them.'

'She said the train. It will be nice for them to see the kids. I'll give them a ring tomorrow, warn them it's total chaos here.'

Chapter Ten

They had become used to the presence of Terry and his Merry Men as christened by Peter. Each day, Rob held a detailed discussion with the builder as the outer elevations rose.

'He's pretty clued up,' was the verdict on Terry, the burly, poetry quoting theorist who had developed a habit of stopping by the kitchen with a commentary on current affairs, both a greeting and introduction to the day. He would lean his head around the door and make a pronouncement. Sentence by sentence, he gained ground until he was leaning against the worktop or holding on to the back of a chair. Soon a vigorous exchange with Rob, Gabrielle or Peter would take place. Carla would lean against the stove, an amused bystander who might be slowly drawn in. This allowed time for Jacko in the small room next door, to make the tea, a prerequisite for the morning's labours. When Rob had gone out early and Peter and Nina had left for work, Carla began to enjoy trading observations about Brexit, the Congestion Charge, the corruption of MPs, global warming and so on. Some days Terry was for believing that CO2 was the culprit and other days expressed a spirited revoke in favour of the deniers. The subject varied by the day. The disgrace of house prices was a topic to which he often returned. Predictably, immigrants taking the work from poor beleaguered Brits also featured. He shook his head over the number of builders who had gone bust since the influx of Poles and made a point of praising the patriotism of the Unwins. 'Pity more people haven't discouraged all these foreigners. I haven't anything against them but.'

'They say we need the extra workers, if you think of the NHS for instance.'

'A lot of these builders are swanning off to their own country now things are so uncertain. They've made a packet, can set themselves up at home, no doubt leaving all sorts of problems behind. How is anyone going to be able to chase them for shoddy work? Mr Yoo, he's a decent bloke sticking with the English. And a few Irish,' he glanced through the window, barked a laugh, 'but they're more or less English give or take a few centuries. Yes, Sean's one of us.'

On arriving today, he'd posed a question for Carla as he leaned with his big hands on the back of the chair, fixing his level blue gaze on her.

'Have you any idea how many council leaders are paid more than a hundred grand a year?' he nodded at the newspaper on the table, then reinforced that by tapping an accusing finger on The Times, 'It's all in here. One of these exclusives. Over a third of them are paid more than the Prime Minister and half are getting over a hundred grand.' He shook his head sorrowfully at her, throwing up his big hands in bemusement.

'We've got it all wrong, somehow. All wrong. And don't get me started on bungs and brown envelopes.' He withdrew from the kitchen and made his way to the rear of the house. Carla had been let off the hook. She hadn't needed to say a word. Had he really read The Times this morning? The wide scope of his conversation was stimulating, she had to admit, but sometimes at eight thirty in the morning she found herself lacking a cogent argument. On the days when Peter was having breakfast late, due to a cancelled lesson, he encouraged Terry to linger, drawing out a strongly held hotchpotch of both reactionary and revolutionary stances, the former culled from recent news and the latter a throw back to his early days as a maintenance engineer on the Underground. It kept her on her toes, Carla reflected as she sat at the table, a mug of tea in front of her, watching the men through the window.

The walls of the extension were rising inexorably, Buster's head bobbing up and down on the far side. What on earth was he doing? Within the palisade, as she called it, a small wine cellar had been excavated and concrete laid over the hard-core. Sean and Jacko walked the plank to reach the wide gap into the garden. Only a sea of mud remained of the grass but the rain had stopped.

A slight noise made her turn. Nina hovered apologetically on the threshold of the room.

'Coffee, or would you prefer tea?' Carla smiled in welcome, wondering if staying over was becoming a habit. Nina approached the table and held out a packet.

'Could I make myself some green tea?'

'Of course. Help yourself. What about breakfast?'

'Thank you,' she gave a little wriggle, 'but I can't eat first thing. I'll have something later.'

'Aren't you working today?' The query sounded brutal.

Nina's enormous grey eyes held hers for a moment. 'Oh yes, but I don't have to be there till ten. Is it okay if I carry on leaving my stuff in Pete's room? I know it's been rather a long time. Actually, there's a bit of a problem with my flat,' she looked down at the kettle.

'Oh dear, I did wonder,' said Carla, concerned for several reasons. 'What's happened? You're over in Shepherd's Bush, aren't you?'

'Becky, my flatmate, has got her sister moving in. Basically, she's kicking me out now that little sis has come to London to go to college. Actually, I was on the on the sofa for weeks before coming here.'

'Good heavens, didn't she give you any notice? That's very poor. Why don't you sit down? Are you sure you I can't tempt you to some muesli or something?'

'Oh no, thank you. I usually grab a bite on my way,' she turned to the window. 'The builders seem to be getting on.'

Carla got up to put plates in the dishwasher. 'Organised chaos, I hope. Rob's in charge, though. I'm under strict instructions not to interfere but I do get a bulletin from Terry every now and again. He's a hoot. The fun will start when this wall has to go.' She turned back. 'What is it, Nina?'

'You seem to take everything in your stride.'

'On the outside, maybe. One just has to get on with things and hope for the best. I'm sure you'll find another place in no time.' Feeling guilty at this automatic platitude, Carla made for the door. How difficult it was to get a moment's peace: the girl was perfectly sweet but what on earth was Peter doing lumbering himself with someone who had the makings of an eating disorder? God forbid she should move in with him to any new place. Not that he was actually looking yet. She glanced at her watch as Nina gave a little wave.

'I'm off now, Carla. Have fun.'

Was that all she was doing these days? It had an empty ring about it.

'Have a good day at work.'

It was a shame Rob didn't care for Rubens: the critics had praised a wonderful collection. She looked into his office to tell him where she was going.

'I only ordered the one ticket,' she told him. 'I know you're not mad about Rubens.'

'You might have asked me, though. I suppose you'd rather go on your own.'

'It's hardly a pleasure spending time with you. You're always pre-occupied.'

'The other way round you mean. You're the one who's always in a shitty mood.'

'Well, are you surprised? You drop a bombshell on me and

expect me to feel nothing? Have you the faintest idea what it feels like to have thirty-five years of love and respect and everything thrown back in your face? To feel worthless, duped, deceived— '

'Don't be ridiculous. Nothing's been thrown back. How many fucking times do you expect me to grovel? I can't do anything about the fact of Rose now. She exists; get over it.'

Tears sprang to Carla's eyes. 'You… you just don't care do you?'

'For God's sake. I can't talk to you any more. It's pointless. You may as well go to your bloody exhibition. I've got work to do.'

'Oh, bury yourself in work. Good for you.'

She could see he had bitten back his response. She hated herself for losing it. Today had raised their animosity to a new level. They had hardly talked recently, with constant bustle around the house, the kids there in the evenings. Had Nina left? Carla prayed she hadn't heard anything. She walked to the front door, her anger burning. Let him suffer a bit more, if he were suffering. It was hard to tell. Every time she thought of him a hard nugget of disapproval made her stiffen. She had never doubted her feelings for him but since the night of his revelation she had seen something weasel-like in his face. Rose would never know what she had destroyed.

Carla switched the blame in the endless turn and turn about that her mind was prey to. She went briskly along the street, still niggled by Nina's harmless *'have fun'*. Rob had started seeing clients, had got stuck in with his refugees, was doing something for others. She felt a compulsion to do something too, not to compete but to lend her some gravitas. Oh, she was preposterous. She'd done plenty in the past. Let her get on with life without thinking of the effect.

Chapter Eleven

'Thanks, Mum,' Gabrielle patted her stomach, knowing her mother liked nothing better than filling them up with a traditional roast dinner. Of course, Nina had to draw the attention to herself by insisting on a tiny helping to be eaten in oh so dainty mouthfuls. Gaby did not have much sympathy; she had a suspicion that Nina raided the fridge when they were all out and refused to believe there was a serious problem. Gabrielle had observed everyone carefully over lunch while joining in the pleasantries and good humour, ordering herself to go with the flow. Tricky subjects were avoided and she could see that her mother was relaxed, her guard down. A silence fell over the table as Rob put his knife and fork together decisively, ready in paterfamilias style to address them. He leaned back in his chair and waited. Peter was wiping his plate with a piece of bread. After popping it into his mouth, he began to fiddle with his phone.

'No mobiles at the table.'

Sighing and slowly, very slowly, Peter put down the mobile while staring at the screen. 'I'm not fourteen, Dad.'

'Just good manners.'

'I wouldn't mind a walk, I haven't been out today,' diversionary tactics from Carla who saw that Rob was determined to engage with Peter and had forgotten whatever pronouncement he'd been about to make.

'Your probationary period at work should surely be up by now. Aren't you going to tell us how you're getting on?'

'What do you mean?'

'No need to look like that; I only asked.'

'It's a simple enough query,' Gaby could not help putting her oar in. Peter was so irritating; why could he never give a simple answer?

'No, it isn't; it never is. It's a loaded question.' The usually mild blue eyes flashed towards his mother, 'There's always a sub-text with you, Dad.'

'For God's sake, I literally wondered if you were enjoying the job,' Rob took a deep breath and looked at the ceiling.

'You're wondering if I'm managing the job; if I'm going to stick at it. That's what you always want to know.'

'Don't be so bloody touchy,' Gaby chipped in again. Rob looked meaningfully at her. Butt out, Gaby. All right, she would button it for once.

'You're being silly, darling,' her mother looked at Peter, 'you're over-reacting. I'm sure he's enjoying it,' she told Rob. 'You are, aren't you?'

'The manager is a bit stressy, you said.'

'Thank you, Nina. I can answer for myself.'

Gabrielle watched his eyes circle the room. Now her mother would intervene again: Carla was trying to look encouraging, a tentative smile hovering, as if to say, it's all right, don't lose your rag. Gabrielle raised the usual challenging eyebrow, waiting for the outburst that was sure to come. Nina, feelings hurt, looked down at the table. Rob affected bafflement.

'I'm not sure why my wellbeing is of such interest to you, all of a sudden,' Peter protested. 'But if you must know, in all the weeks I've been at the club, I've had precisely no feedback from the manager. At the beginning he told me I would have to sink or swim and I can only presume I am swimming.'

'Bravo little brother. That's the spirit. Whereas I was praised from the rooftops and then had the rug pulled out from under me. The ways of management are mysterious indeed.'

'You'll get a job soon,' Carla insisted, putting a hand on her daughter's arm. 'Fingers crossed for the interview next week. Now, who's for blackberry and apple crumble?'

Gabrielle sighed and stared out at the garden, holding her tongue for once.

'If you're not happy with what I'm doing, just say so, Dad.' Peter had definitely taken umbrage.

'That's nonsense. I'm simply interested. What are the members like? It's a very expensive place.' This was an effort to move the conversation onto a more equable plane.

'They're okay, I suppose. I've hardly got to know anyone. They probably think I'm still a temporary fill-in. Well, I'm sure that in time I'll find out if they want me to stay. The other guy will be off for at least three months, possibly even six with his injury, so I wait to see.'

'The same job for six months? That will be a turn-up for the books.' Gabrielle looked around at her audience. 'Well, it's true.'

'I'm sure they'll want you to,' Carla glared at her daughter, crossing her fingers under the table.

Was Peter pacified? He reached over for the last of the roast potatoes and crunching it in his teeth went out into the garden.

'Did you have to?' Carla asked.

Bugger them, thought Peter as he lit up a cigarette and inhaled deeply. He closed his eyes, allowing a slow stream of smoke to drift away and told himself to cool it. He didn't usually let them get under his skin. It riled him to see his mother always rooting for him. He didn't need it; he was quite capable of standing up for himself. He walked over and looked back at the house. That wall would soon be gone. He tried to imagine the finished space for a moment then pictured their old house with its familiar dimensions and furniture, the dog lying in a warm patch, head on paws, eyes following one around the room in case of a titbit. Peter stubbed out the cigarette on the wall and threw the end into the nearest bush. Going back inside, a few minutes later, it was obvious his mother had been talking about him. She moved the pepper mill from one spot to another. Gabrielle's expression was scornful, not in the least repentant. His father wagged a finger at him.

'You'll never go far if you can't even manage to give up smoking. Call yourself a sportsman? Where's your will power, my boy?'

'I hardly smoke at all. You know that. Get off my back, Dad,' a smile softened his words. 'Anyway, I more than make up for it with all the exercise I do.'

'You certainly put me to shame,' said Gabrielle, 'but then you stole most of the family sporting ability. It's not fair, bro,' she pouted cheerfully at him now, appeasing him for the earlier stabs. Peter rewarded her with a fraternal grin.

Carla was serving the crumble and looking as if she was searching for a neutral topic of conversation, that artificial blandness on her face.

'I've got two tickets for The Dog in the Night Time, you know that marvellous play, on Saturday afternoon. Any of you like to come with me?'

'Not really my cup of tea, I don't think,' his father shook his head.

'Sorry, Ma, I'm coaching,' Peter gave his usual excuse but sod it. His sister made the effort for once.

'If you're desperate, I will, if I can get out of lunch with the lot from work. Work that was, I mean.'

'Don't be silly. That would be a shame,' Carla hurried to answer. 'I can easily ask someone. Not to worry.'

'It wouldn't do any harm to go online and check out the jobs market again, Gaby. Just in case.'

'Dad, give it a rest.'

'It would be nice if everyone resisted jumping down my throat every time I suggest anything. Not you, Nina, of course.'

'It's frustrating looking for work and equally frustrating being in work,' Nina's quiet voice dropped even more. 'My boss is not a bundle of laughs these days, either. The atmosphere used to be fun. I think she must be having marital problems.'

Carla at once began to gather up the plates.

'Nina,' she said, reproachfully, looking at the food on the girl's plate.

'Sorry, I'm full but it was delicious.'

Peter pushed back his chair as his mother brought over the fruit bowl.

'Come on, Neen, let's go.'

'Have a piece of fruit. It's good for you,' his mother said.

'I will later. Thanks for lunch, Ma. We're going round to see Ben.'

'You could put your plates in the dishwasher,' said Gabrielle.

'Oh, sorry,' Nina jerked back, 'I was just going to.'

'Not you Nina, you did the potatoes. We're still trying to housetrain Peter, aren't we darling?'

The plates crashed into the machine as he bit back a retort; it was lucky they did not break.

'There you are, that didn't take a second. See you later.' Carla rested her forehead in her hand and stared at the table for a moment. Gabrielle peeled a satsuma, wondering how long she could stick being with the family.

'He's rather touchy today,' Rob looked after them as the kitchen door closed.

'Perhaps, he's worried he won't get the job. You have to let him open up when he's ready to tell you something, you know how it is, with Peter; you can never rush him. Anyway, I'm sure he's giving it his best shot. He's leaving very punctually every morning.'

'Let's hope so,' Rob looked out through the window. 'If he

doesn't get offered it we could put him to work with Terry. Humping bricks for a few weeks wouldn't do him any— '

'And are you going to put me to work too?' asked Gabrielle.

'You could clean alongside Uldis— '

'You're hateful.'

'Learn a thing or two about housekeeping.'

'The salary for that job next week is in the region of fifty grand. That'll change your tune Father, dear.'

'It certainly will, and I sincerely hope you get it. You deserve a bit of luck and it would get you out of our hair.'

'Thanks. I just— '

'Look the sun's out. Who'd like a walk?' interrupted her mother.

'Good idea. It gets dark so early now. Come on, Gaby, keep the old folks happy.'

They put their boots in the car and set off. Parking was easy for once and they were soon walking briskly along the path, skirting the wide sandy area known as 'the beach' and following the perimeter of the park towards the silhouette of the football ground at the far end. Then they cut across the grass towards the river walk. Overhead and under their feet the foliage was a rich russet and gold. They paused to lean on the railing, watching an 'eight' rowing powerfully along, scything through the brownish-grey water leaving curls of pale froth. Two joggers pounded by in bright red trainers. Carla breathed in the scent of mud, remembering the walks they used to take out of the village towards the hills. This was more interesting with the boathouses across the wide indolent river, the motor yachts cruising along and an avenue of trees to walk through. Rob stared at the new blocks of flats going up. London was a building site. He would be part of it.

'We must look at the memorial,' Gabrielle insisted and they set off to see the memorial to the volunteers in the Spanish civil war. She paused in front of it with a dreamy look.

'Respect,' she nodded. 'Amazing to have such conviction and I don't think they were brainwashed into it. Not like the jihadis.'

When would the time be right to tell her about Rose? Not now with all the uncertainty about work and her precious flat being rented out. Carla was convinced that Gaby would react badly. Daddy's darling would find it a bitter blow to share him with a half-sister. She would come round eventually, wouldn't she? Carla fretted while her daughter's laugh rang out and she tucked her arm into the crook of her father's. They had always got on, those two. As a teenager she'd been a nightmare, against her principles to agree with anything her mother said. Ah well, she'd more or less grown out of it. It was odd that neither Peter nor Gabrielle seemed to notice the coolness between their parents; she was sure it must be evident. Better that way. Try as she might she could not stir herself out of the antipathy he aroused in her. Look at him…full of the joys of spring. It was infuriating. She nearly tripped over them as they halted suddenly.

'Lookout.'

'Speed up, Mum,' Gabrielle grabbed one arm and Rob the other, making her run for a few yards as they laughed in their exuberance. 'We'll get you fit too.'

Now she was the jerky little marionette between two taller figures; Carla remembered how she and Rob would swing Gabrielle into the air as they held her hands and she shrieked for more.

'Don't be grumpy, Pete,' Nina told him as they walked up the main road, 'it's just the usual brother/sister thing. I always longed for a sister. Matt was so foul to me when we were growing up. You wouldn't believe the teasing I had to put up with. Even so I miss him dreadfully since he went away. I suppose he wasn't to know that Mum and George would end up abroad too.' She glanced at his face, 'I know Gaby is a bit cutting but deep down she dotes on you.'

'Funny way of showing it. She and Dad are never satisfied. He can be such a nob. They both like to get in a dig whenever they can. I should be used to it after all this time.' He held Nina's hand as they went down the steps into the Tube. On the train he grabbed a seat for her and then stood near the doors trying to shake off the exasperation.

As a young child he had always worshipped Gaby. He was her messenger, her bag carrier, errand boy and the butt of her acerbic wit. He had often puzzled over why he rubbed her up the wrong way. What if his illness had demanded all the attention? That was a long time ago. *Get over it, Gaby*. Now her comments to him over lunch had hurt. He usually dismissed the caustic asides, letting them wash over him. Perhaps he should retaliate, God, he could come up with some withering comments of his own. Still, years of defusing situations had become a habit.

She could be such a bitch. A memory struck him as he rocked with the movement of the train.

He has come home early from school. Mum has sent him up for a bath to wash off the mud from a game of football. For once his eleven-year-old self is luxuriating in the warmth. He can picture it still, the water swirling up over his bony white chest.

He hears giggles, footsteps running up the stairs. Instantly, he knows he has forgotten to lock the door. Before he can move, it crashes open and Gabrielle and a cohort of her friends look in, screaming out a jeering burst of nonsense. His hands are ludicrous, hovering to cover himself, the towel impossibly out of reach. The girls turn, crying with mirth and thunder down to Gabrielle's room. Climbing out, he is trembling with shame and fury. He catches sight of his face in the misted mirror. Scarlet and anguished, it looks hideously babyish to him.

Their catcalls resound in his ears, although all he can hear is the loud music of Westlife. He knows the girls are sniggering about him, his dick an object of ridicule.

He creeps past their door. His room is no sanctuary this afternoon; it's been invaded by the scene inside his head: his sister's face lit by a cruel hilarity, the taunting merriment a mirror of the others.

He plays on his Xbox and the murderous sequence of violence takes him over. After a while, the humiliation is buried deep. He has always known how to act as if nothing mattered.

He shook off the wretched memory as he shifted to make room for four teenage girls who scarcely took their eyes from their mobiles as they entered the train. They, poor sods had social media to contend with. He glanced over at Nina who sat demurely, a faint smile on her lips, her little feet neatly side by side.

Chapter Twelve

If only she'd taken a photograph of him. Rose flipped through the paltry text messages from Rob as she sat hunched in a chair, her face cloudy with misery. She could not believe that nothing had come about since that lunch weeks before. What a let-down. She was certain he'd promised to be there for her now; hadn't his eyes told her that? Yet she felt more alone than ever. What could she do to impress him? She must seem so negligible, so not worth knowing. Perhaps she wasn't good enough to meet his posh children with their private school accents, their arrogant ways. She knew the type. She gritted her teeth in frustration. Soon it would be Christmas. Her unloved guitar gathered dust against the wall; learning through YouTube was unlikely to make her a budding rock star. She winced, remembering how she and Luke had agreed to turn themselves into the next big thing on that first drunken evening. She had a few blokes after her this year but she was still hoping that Luke would show a bit more interest. A couple of cringe-worthy dates arranged on Tinder had put her off for life. Laughter filtered up from the hall. She might pop out to the shop, there was always a chance she'd bump into one of the others from the flats, go down the pub, rescue the evening.

A modest sprinkling of fairy lights twinkled in tiny front gardens all over London and a few tasteful garlands and decorations of pinecones appeared on doors along the streets in the Unwin's borough. In early December, Nina appeared, cheeks flushed from hurrying through the cold, holding up a garland of ivy leaves and twisted branches of red berries.

'Carla, a little present for you. To thank you for having me to stay.' She added hurriedly, 'you don't have to put it up if you don't like it. It's all natural though, nothing artificial.'

'Oh, it's gorgeous. How lovely, so pretty. You look like a little wood sprite in your velvet coat,' Carla gushed her thanks, hoping the red berries would not drop on the doorstep and be trodden through the whole house. Footsteps sounded in the hall.

'Terry, before you go, be a dear and bang a tiny nail in the front door for this pretty wreath.'

Outside in the dark, the little task completed, Terry looked back at the house. He packed some tools carefully in the van. Only three weeks and then the break. The lads couldn't wait but he wasn't too excited. It would be quiet at home in the time off. This year his son would be at the in-laws, up north. Terry thought of Christmas day with his sister and her family. His brother-in-law wasn't a bad bloke; they always had a couple pints down the pub together and the nephews might be able to keep their noses out of their phones this year. He should be grateful. Next year though, he'd take a month off, go to Oz to see Mandy and the grandkids, do a spot of travelling. He'd seen the sights of Melbourne the last time. He climbed into the van and set off for home. He began to hum, giving full voice when he reached the chorus.

'*Waltzing Matilda, waltzing Matilda, who'll come a-waltzing Matilda with me,*' he filled the van with sound, hanging on to good cheer, tapping out the rhythm on the steering wheel. He'd email them tonight.

Chapter Thirteen

It had been a strange Christmas, Carla decided. Her mother and her aunt valiantly shared the spare room for three nights, politely vying with each other to offer first use of the bathroom. They made all the right noises about the house and professed excitement about the extension. Rob was fond of them both and went out of his way to entertain them with teasing remarks, crossword puzzles and a vast jigsaw of Constable's *Cornfield* that crept across his desk like an octopus. Gales of chatter and laughter invaded the house, yet in spite of days fuelled by generous quantities of whisky, wine and beer, something was missing. Carla had tried and failed to enter wholeheartedly into the spirit of it all, though her pretence was convincing. No one appeared to notice a distance between her and the rest of the family. She could engage fully with outsiders: Laura on the committee with her, would be a kindred spirit, given a bit more time to get to know one another and the builder, Terry, surprisingly the two of them could chortle like a pair of school kids.

In the run up to the festivities, she went through the motions to compensate for her indifference. At the Old Manor, a carol concert, log fires, cards strung from corner to corner and a huge tree in the hall would set the scene. Here, all her efforts looked merely artificial. Not that she yearned for those details, in fact the thought of them made her shrug dismissively. How very conventional they had been. She wrote her cards in front of the television over several evenings, making sure to sound upbeat in her news.

Mad about the new house! Builders here en masse. Peter's landed on his feet! Gabrielle and the rest of us well.

She opened the Christmas cards from old friends with a frown. Often there was only a hasty scrawl of names under the printed greeting, lacking the warmth of a *fondest regards* or *lots of love*. No one claimed to be missing the Unwins.

The workmen downed tools for ten days but the unfinished project inevitably caused some disruption. No, Carla's heart just wasn't in it. Beneath the smiles an ache remained. Christmas drinks with the Farleighs, two doors down, had lifted her for a couple of hours. Somehow the days went by, as she made sure the elements were in place, drinking too much with the rest of them, jollying everyone along to ensure they had a good time. A few well-chosen presents and an abundance of food gave rise to the usual exaggerated cries of astonishment and gratitude.

Surprisingly, Nina had been the most helpful. Turning down her mother's offer of a flight to join the couple in Tenerife had seemed wilful to Carla, but frankly the girl had outshone her own children. Gabrielle had a knack of being out with friends whenever a pair of hands was needed or someone to sit and chat to the 'oldies' and on the 24th Peter had gone down with a heavy cold and hacking cough rendering it necessary to lie on the new sofa watching films or rallying bravely to sit up and play computer games. Wires trailing all over the floor, half empty mugs of lemon cold cures and sticky cereal bowls were hazards spread around him. Rob was annoyed by the mess and seemed on edge. His usual festive bonhomie had an absent minded air at times. The old ladies dismissed Peter's germs, although loud gargling could be heard through the bathroom door at bedtime. They insisted on helping with the food preparation, getting under Carla's feet in the kitchen until she drove them out to play Scrabble. Much discussion centred on the question of attending midnight mass or giving in to the secular position that Rob and Peter subscribed to. In the end, no one made the effort. Christmas Day unfolded around the invalid's languishing form. Traditional silly games that harked back generations made them giggle and straggling crocodiles set off on walks to pass the time between meals and by the day after Boxing Day, life was back to normal. Soon the young would move out again and the project could reassert itself. For now however, there was no sign of a job for Gabrielle and although Peter had been taken onto the permanent staff at the Scimitar amidst much rejoicing, he had no energy for flat hunting but claimed to be saving up for a such a move. Much to his outrage, hostile wrangling with his old landlord about the return of his deposit was taking place by email and telephone.

Carla thought his feathers might need smoothing after the remarks that Rob had made earlier.

'For God's sake get off your backside. You'll be surprised how much better you'll feel,' Rob only just stopped short of using the word 'malingering'. He had gone then to sit at his desk, pointedly bowing his head over a neat pile of papers.

Typical. Rob was never one to dole out much sympathy to Peter. Just wait till you get flu, she thought. But he probably wouldn't, he never did. She pushed open the door of the front room.

'Oh, Gaby you're in here too.'

'I'm about to give little brother a pep talk,' she pointed the mug she was holding at Peter.

'Aargh, I'm feeling too rough for one of your little chats, Gaby.' Still in his pyjamas, he looked flushed and unshaven. He groaned again and pointed the remote control at the wide TV screen before adjusting the cushion behind his head. Racing cars hurtled noisily around a track.

'Darling, you must drink plenty. What would you like?'

'A hot orange squash might help my throat. Thanks, Ma.'

'You can see he's not feeling well,' Carla said.

Gabrielle snatched the remote and turned off the set. She closed the door quietly and perched on the glass coffee table not two feet from Peter, weighing him up.

'I'm not sure it's a good idea…' Carla remonstrated.

'What?' he asked, his eyes heavy and disinterested. He rubbed a hand over the stubble on his face then a bout of coughing overwhelmed him. His sister waited. He unwrapped a throat lozenge, holding it in his palm until the fit was over. He sniffed. Carla slowly collected the debris of mugs and magazines, curious. Gabrielle's incisive voice, though lowered a notch or two, went straight to the point as usual.

'What's going on with Nina?'

'What d'you mean?' he croaked.

'Don't be stupid. She's living with you in case you hadn't noticed. Does she think it's a permanent arrangement?'

'Shush. She'll hear you. I haven't got a clue. No, of course not. It's just till she finds somewhere.'

'But she's not looking,' Gabrielle still fixed him with her perceptive stare. 'What's more, I think she seems quite comfortable right here. I find that a little worrying, don't you?'

'What's worrying?' Carla turned back with her hands full, affecting an airy tone.

'Gaby's poking her nose in where it's not wanted. Give me that remote.'

'Tell me how keen you are,' Gabrielle challenged him, 'because she's looking very settled indeed and if you don't reciprocate her feelings, you should dump her now. You're not ready to get serious. Admit it Pete, you are just being lazy really. I'm sure you don't mean any harm but Nina will get her hooks into you if you're not careful. She's a bit needy I reckon. Mum agrees with me.'

'Whoa,' Carla said, ' we haven't discussed it.'

Peter dragged himself to a sitting position. He looked

disconsolate, threw off the rug and thumped the cushion.

'That's such rubbish. You're talking crap. I like Nina. I hoped you did too—'

'Never said we didn't.'

'Anyhow, she needs a few friendly faces around when her parents have dumped on her the way they have. But she's okay. In some ways she's as tough as old boots. She'll be all right, I promise you. She takes me as I am. You worry too much. Now can I watch my Formula 1?'

'Just be careful, my love.' Carla wanted to have her say. 'It's too easy to let her get the wrong idea. I can't think how she has ended up staying here with you. You must have encouraged it. You're taking a big risk if you're not serious about her and you don't want to be unfair to the poor girl. Concentrate on where you are going to live and think about whether or not you want her with you. It's certainly nothing to do with your father and me. We can see she's got a lot going for her. She must be very talented. But you're too young. Plenty of fish in the sea remember. And I do worry about her eating habits. Aren't there some nice girls at that club of yours?'

'Please,' groaned Peter, holding a cushion over his eyes to block them out.

'Don't say I didn't warn you,' Gabrielle was relentless. 'Plus it's hard to talk to you when she's always there. You never asked us if she could move in.'

'Okay, okay, okay,' his voice rose as he held out his hand for the channel changer.

Gabrielle and Carla went into the kitchen. Peter resumed watching the TV. In a few minutes Carla returned with a hot drink steaming in a mug. Only the biting of his bottom lip gave away the undercurrent of emotion that his sister had provoked.

'I'll get some more cough mixture when I go out. Poor old thing. When are they expecting you back at work?'

'Tomorrow, but I might ring them if I have another bad

night.'

'I should. Now, before I go is there anything else you need?'

'Can you get me some of that fizzy vitamin C?' he tore his eyes away from the screen for a second. 'Thanks Mum,' he sounded extremely sorry for himself.

Carla reflected that she'd been doing this sort of thing for a very long time.

Chapter Fourteen

Dear Grandpa,

Thank you very much for the card and the £25. I wont waste it and think I might put it towards a new jacket. Keep the snow off!! I saw a nice one in Topshop and the sale starts next week.

Work has been going quite well and I'm keeping my fingers crossed for a pay rise soon! They might be sending me on a course, one day a week, to learn more about design. It will make a change from the office and the same four walls, you know what it's like.

I expect it's really snowy up where you are.

Best wishes for the New Year to you both. Keep well.

Much Love

Rose

It was nice that HE hadn't forgotten her at Christmas. Angie had delivered the card belatedly after a long train journey to see her father in a village outside York.

'The old bugger's in clover,' she had reported. 'Hannah is surrounded by her ever expanding family and they all seem to dote on your grandpa. He is certainly looking good on it. They're planning to come down for a visit in the summer; mind you we've heard that before, haven't we?'

Rose just shrugged.

'We could go to a film, have supper together tonight. What d'you think?'

'Look, I'm quite capable of entertaining myself. In fact I'm out tonight.'

'Any word from you know who?'

'I'm not expecting anything yet. I knew you'd start.'

'It seems odd to be so backwards in coming forwards.'

'Leave it, Mum.'

'Just don't let it get you down. Don't forget to thank Grandpa. You could ring him up, have a chat.'

'I'll see. Thanks for the cushions; they look nice. Cheery.'

'That's what I thought. A lovely bright colour to cheer you up.'

'Mum.'

'Okay. Okay. I'm off.'

Rose fished out the book of stamps from a drawer and looked at the square that was missing. It really hadn't got her very far, had it?

'I wonder how formal it will be?' The Unwins were getting ready for bed the night before the dinner at the Millers. Rob pulled a shirt over his head.

'I'm happy to wear a jacket but there's no way I'm wearing a tie.'

'I'll wear my black dress. You know the one. Yes, you do. I wore it practically every time we went out last winter. You can't really go wrong with black.'

'Buy yourself a new one if you wore it to death last year. I think we can run to a new outfit now and then.'

'No one here's seen it but if you're bored with it?'

'I'm not sure I even remember it,' Rob said.

Time to change the subject. 'So, a united front tomorrow evening,' the words had just popped out before she could edit them.

'We are united. What are you on about?'

'I don't want another fight but I don't always feel very united. Since we got here we've done even less together. It's not what I imagined.'

She sat down heavily on the bed. Sitting down beside her, his arm drawing her close, he made soothing noises.

'Don't be silly. We're fine. The odd row doesn't mean anything. I'm sure we both say things we regret afterwards. Look, it's just hectic at the moment.' He smoothed his hand over her hair and gently massaged the knot at the top of her spine with his thumb. 'We're in a kind of limbo. You've said so yourself. And the kids: everyone all over the place, literally. Now Nina. The builders. You know. It's not us; it's the situation. Come here,' he took her face between his hands, turning her to him.

A long slow kiss, the first proper one since the Rose bombshell, made her cling to him.

Carla relived the tender moments of the night before as she made her way through the quiet streets the next day. She couldn't deny it had been good. Yet, today, she thought, she felt no different. Whatever walls had been breached, they seemed to have risen up again. Her body might have overlooked her grievance but her mind had not yet reached acceptance. Rob will think it has, though, she concluded.

She reached the florist's and stood outside, trying to make up her mind. Chocolates or flowers? she asked herself. A delicious scent filled the air and a longing for summer, for the garden at the Old Manor washed over her.

'Um, maybe half a dozen lilies,' she asked the assistant, pointing to the pale pods. The flowers were carefully wrapped in pastel tissue and raffia. Carla held them with both hands; there had not been much change from her £20 note. She made her way home, thinking of the evening ahead. They'd met the couple at Louise's party back in September and had warmed to them. In the run up to Christmas, a few invitations for drinks in the neighbourhood to their delight had landed on the doormat and now a summons to drive the January blues away.

Carla, with freshly trimmed and blow-dried hair, wore the black dress: a safe and sophisticated choice. It felt good to be going out within walking distance again. They had always enjoyed the brisk march from home and back after evenings out, entertaining each other with a humorous post-mortem. They might have walked arm in arm tonight but the lilies and the bottle of wine were in the way. Carla had argued that the wine was unnecessary but Rob had chosen a good bottle and was determined to present it to his host.

Carla still bristled when she thought about their recent return to the village and the pointed remarks, scarcely disguising the vitriol, about the proposed development near the Old Manor. The plans had not yet been approved but the Unwins were criticised obliquely while rapturous remarks in praise of the new owners of the Old Manor seemed excessive and rather rude. The evening had grated on Carla; she could hardly wait for midnight and the uncomfortable bed in a chilly spare room with dripping taps at the basin and pipes that burped and thumped when anyone used the water. In contrast to that well-oiled, fairly raucous New Year's Eve, the dinner party this evening was quite formal.

'Sparkling or still?' Daniel murmured over her shoulder.

'Oh, sparkling, please. That's lovely, thank you,' she tilted her head towards her host as he filled the crystal glass and moved on to the next guest. On Esther's instruction they had left the drawing room and entered a dining room. Elaborate candelabra flared at each end of the table, casting shadows onto the deep green walls and lighting up the gilt on the antique French furniture. Daniel in his black collarless shirt had stood at the end of the table and peered through his reading glasses at a sheet of paper.

'Now let me see. No, this won't do,' he chuckled as they stood waiting and the seating plan for the party of eight was ditched as he continued theatrically, 'I want Carla next to me.

Sorry, Soulange but I saw you the other night.' Amid titters and protests from the other women, Esther rearranged them and the starter, a twice-baked cheese soufflé, puffed and savoury, was rushed out from the kitchen. Once seated, Daniel's confidential manner took over as he put his head close to Carla's and seemed determined to give her every ounce of his attention like a parcel wrapped and tied with ribbon.

'I want to hear all about you. I insist you start from square one. Go on. Tell me, where were you brought up?' his large brown eyes fastened on hers.

'I'll bore you to death. Maybe I should make up something unusual and fascinating…really I'm awfully dull.' She made a neat incision and watched the soufflé sinking.

'Nonsense. Let's compare. I'm a North London boy. Now you,' he forked a mouthful and chewed slowly.

'Originally from the West Country, my father was a grain dealer. Down near Exeter. Sadly he's no longer with us but my mother lives with my aunt near Taunton. That works surprisingly well. They have the odd spat but basically it's been a huge success. They were with us for Christmas, actually. Enough about me before you nod off,' she looked into his eyes again and began to eat. Dan embarked on a tale of his upbringing while Carla tried not to be distracted by a conversation across the table. The grey haired woman was complaining about the scourge of basements being excavated all over London.

'The whole street was shaking,' she complained. 'Unstable… walls pinned… too much foreign money…' Carla gathered the gist of it. The woman looked across at her and made a gesture of appeal. Carla sympathised, turning down her mouth and shaking her head.

'Our street seems to have escaped that so far,' Daniel gave way to the continuing grievance.

'It sounds awful.'

Rob was head bent, serious and quietly describing what? She strained to hear. It was probably that refugee centre or no, their building project it must be. She had heard the word planners.

Plates were passed up to Esther at the end. Rob insisted on carrying them out for her and appeared to be helping her dish out the main course. He winked at Carla in the old way as he came through with two laden plates.

The evening passed pleasantly and Dan continued to be a good host, taking care to listen as well as talk, while the man on her left, (a keen fisherman, name dropping rivers whose occupants he had appeared to have decimated, all over Scotland and Wales not to mention Iceland, Russia and the Caribbean) was agreeable enough. Now and then laughter erupted. It was infectious even if she hadn't always caught the punch line.

'That was nice. Did you enjoy it? Now we can claim to know three more couples,' she said on the walk home.

'That's good. Yes, very enjoyable. Very decent wine, Daniel served,' Rob said. 'He mentioned a temperature controlled cellar and I'm afraid I couldn't resist telling him about the one we are putting in. Talk about keeping up with the Jones— '

'I hope he didn't think that.'

'I should have kept quiet, I suppose. We didn't have much chance to talk over dinner but he seems a good sort. Esther is nice. I liked her. Intelligent. I think you would get on well with her. She likes plays and things. You know, art galleries, concerts. Just up your street.'

'She mentioned a book group. There's a meeting coming up soon. I'll have to read the new Margaret Atwood. You know, we're soon going to meet lots of people,' she forgot her usual distance to give his arm a slight squeeze. 'Just what we hoped would happen.'

'It takes a bit of time but then things snowball.'

Their footsteps rang out in the near silent streets. It was bitterly cold, their breath pale clouds under the amber lights. Hardly a car passed and most of the houses were in darkness. It was still exciting to be walking through night-time London with its unfamiliar scents and noises, the faint hum of traffic beyond the rows of houses and the orange glow that hid the stars.

'Are you missing the old place?' she wanted to know.

'No. Why, are you?'

'Honestly?'

'I've hardly thought about it. Too busy,' Rob insisted, 'but what about you?'

'Oh, not really. I get a tiny nostalgic twinge now and again. But definitely not missing it.'

Now Rob squeezed back. 'Good,' he said. 'Onward and upward,' an unusual elation making him chuckle. He thinks I'm thawing, she told herself. Well, I've got news for him. I'm not.

It was another Saturday night and Rose was sitting on a wobbly bar stool in the venue, at the bottom of a steep uncarpeted flight of stairs, a pint glass half full of coins on a table beside her. The wide room consisted of a bar where a small crowd stood with their drinks, a few chairs against the other wall beneath fly-spotted framed photographs of some of the greats and a pair of hefty speakers on either side of the low stage. She nodded and tapped a foot in time to the beat as the singer, in a green embroidered mini-dress, belted out a song. *My damaged heart* went the lyrics; join the club, thought Rose. It was a good voice and worth being on the door for a couple of hours. Besides, another group, the main act, were due on when the dismantling and setting up were completed; then there would be a stampede down from the pub above for the last performers. They were popular locally and Rose had seen them twice before. The lead guitarist had long dark hair and pop idol looks: deep-set eyes smouldered on the posters advertising the gig.

She banged her knuckles on the table, applauding as the girl in the emerald dress thanked the thin crowd for supporting her and stepped down to be lost in a group of friends. She caught Luke's eye across the room and wondered whether to buy him a drink. A voice called out 'yo! Baby' and he was accosted by a band member pointing to the mike. She pulled her mobile from her bag and reread every text that Rob had sent. It did not take long. Each time she felt an urge to contact him she looked at the messages that were depressing in their skimpiness of emotion. As usual the effect was to discourage any pleading she was tempted to make. She put the mobile away. Perhaps he would contact her soon; every day she told herself the same thing.

The lead singer came past, touching her on the shoulder and nodding at the money in the glass. It was unlikely to pay much more than their travel costs, she knew.

'Ta, love.'

'No problem!' she called to his back view as he headed for the stage, gratified that she'd had some recognition. She would tell the girls in the office about him. Make it a bit more elaborate. She folded the promotional flyer into her bag as loud footsteps began to thunder down from the bar and the sound check commenced with a crackly repetitive chord and the drummer and guitarists began to tune up.

Chapter Fifteen

'You must let me buy you a drink, afterwards.'

Peter hadn't imagined it. She had been a little too interested in him last week. This was her fourth coaching session. Edwina finished collecting the balls at the far end of the court, her tiny skirt only just decent as she bent down. Peter tossed the last few balls into the container and came up to the net. She stood with her head tilted to one side, her figure all too evident in the clinging outfit. He smiled, avoiding her eyes.

'More drills first,' he ordered, 'back to the T.' He'd been warned about the older married women, shamelessly chatting up the male staff. Tristan, the swimming instructor had not gone into detail but had told him about what the staff called 'self service.'

'There's plenty up for grabs, you can just help yourself. Some of them are sexy as hell. Make sure the boss doesn't get wind of it, though. He would not approve. Just remember you'll be playing with fire.'

'I've got a girlfriend,' Peter said to shut him up.

'Yeah, yeah,' Tristan had replied, smirking as he wolfed down his macaroni cheese.

God, he could be irritating. Anyone would think that Peter was wet behind the ears. Hadn't he been chatted up by his clients often enough? Women might be predatory but he was well aware there was always a tiny bit of room for doubt. No, he would not rush in where angels fear to tread. He had his head screwed on.

He ran across court to chase down the wild return and sent it gently back. A rally began. In fact, he considered, Edwina had the makings of a fine player. The ball bounced near the back line and he employed some fancy footwork to return it, taking a little off the pace. She admitted she should have kept up the tennis after school but had been picked for a netball team at university. The tennis had lapsed. Now she was keen to improve. She was enthusiastic, working harder than anyone, jogging on the spot between shots, trying again and again when she had got it wrong. And her wonderful laugh would ring out, like now. He heard a gurgle of mirth as she missed the ball altogether. Not something that happened very often.

'Did you see that?' she giggled, repeating the poor shot in an exaggerated way. Oh, she was fun to teach all right. He couldn't help smiling.

'Think low to high,' he demonstrated.

'I could do with a nice cold drink,' she said when the hour was up. 'Can I get you something?'

'Thanks, but I've got another lesson now. I'll grab some water from the fountain.'

'Maybe next time,' she grinned at him before pulling on her sweatshirt, tugging it down when it snagged halfway. 'Thanks, Peter, that was brilliant. See you on Friday,' she gave his arm a little touch and waved her fingers at him as she turned.

He bent over the water dispenser and took some gulps to quench his thirst. There'd been something in her eye, he was sure. No harm in a little bit of flirting if it kept the ladies booking up the sessions.

Here was his twelve o'clock; a retired gentleman with shorts painfully fastened beneath a considerable paunch, had begun a series of warm-up exercises at the side of the court. Peter was glad he'd been shown how to work the defibrillator.

'Mr Palmer, how are you doing?'

'Call me Neil, Peter. I'm fine thanks.'

'Let's get cracking with the warm up then, Neil.'

One morning, Carla had woken at the sound of Rob's alarm and lay listening to the rain pattering across the window, reminding her of mice running behind the skirting board in their old home. When he went downstairs, she kept her eyes closed and tried to get back to sleep, feeling unwilling to face the day. Gradually she became aware that her joints ached and her throat was sore. In spite of her usual resilience, she had caught Peter's cold. She heard footsteps and voices on the stairs but did not call out. Soon all went quiet. Before the men arrived, she struggled down to open the curtains, something that Rob never bothered to do when he left in a hurry. The rain still streamed down causing a small flood in the road. After a meagre bowl of cereal and a coffee she rang her mother and aunt to see if they were all right.

'Darling, we're fine. Oh, dear, you sound dreadfully husky, though. Poor you. You seemed a little peaky over Christmas. Annette was saying you weren't quite your usual self and wondered if you were having second thoughts, pining for The Old Manor.'

'Absolutely not. That's ridiculous. We will be thrilled when the extension is finished. We always knew it would cause a certain upheaval. I don't know what she's on about. I just wondered if you'd picked up Peter's cold. I seem to be going down with—'

'Oh, we're fit as fleas. Not a sniffle between us. You know we never put the heating on in the daytime. It's so much healthier to have a window open, some nice fresh air. I expect you've let yourself get a little run-down.'

'Rubbish.'

'You looked after us so well at Christmas, don't get me wrong. It was lovely but maybe you overdid it.'

'I didn't overdo it; no one can help getting the odd cold.

131

Well, if you two are quite all right, I need to get on.'

In fact, she had decided to stay at home for the day, pampering herself with hot drinks and keeping out of everyone's way. She had gone back upstairs with a hot water bottle after a very brief word with Terry. She did not want to waft about in view of the men, unable to settle to anything, croaking when they came to the door. Better to stay out of sight. She climbed back into bed, piqued by her mother's words. *Second thoughts* made her frown and left her disheartened. Usually, she banished any negative feelings as quickly as possible by projecting herself into the completed alterations, the halcyon time, nearly in reach. Today her cold and the dismal outlook lowered her mood. She had not yet found new friends; her children were out of sorts; the house was cold, not in temperature but in atmosphere with little that was cosy and familiar. The comfy old sofa with the dog's head on her knee and the warmth from the fire would not be replicated here, all hard edges and spotless furnishings. Which you wanted, she accused herself. Yes, she missed the old place when she was feeling ill. Here, she was alone in the midst of her family. They abandoned her to her own devices. Of course they did; it was a long time since they had needed her. She halted that train of thought; it was only her throat and the weather and the thought of Rose, edging ever nearer. She pulled up the throw and turned on the bedside light; the day was so dark. Perhaps Gabrielle or Rob would appear, make her a cup of tea, dash through the downpour to the chemist's and bring up the paper.

She remembered now that Gabrielle had said she would stay over with a friend. That might have been a euphemism. There had been quite a few nights when Gabrielle did not come home.

'If you live here you must conform,' Rob had snapped the first time, 'you could have been murdered for all we know. At 'least have the courtesy to ring us if you're not coming home.'

'I was being considerate, not wanting to wake anyone up at two in the—'

'You can creep in. You did it often enough when you were younger.'

'If I creep in, you won't know if I'm in or not, so what's the problem?'

'Just do as we say,' Rob was determined to have the last word.

Reliving the argument was wearying. Hoping Gaby would be careful was an old refrain. Carla blew her nose on a damp tissue and tried to get back to sleep. No one came home.

Poor Carla, Terry had thought earlier as she gave him a crestfallen smile and pointed to her throat.

'Better keep clear, Terry. Cold alert. I'll see you later.'

In spite of the husky voice, she looked young with the lack of make-up, defenceless, the poise absent.

'Bad luck. Spoil yourself for a day or two.' And he'd gone outside.

Standing legs wide and arms folded, he watched the men: another day, another load of bricks. The walls were now several feet high. Terry mused on his conversation with Peter. Since the big lad had moved in with his parents, the family dynamics were interesting to observe. Sharp remarks would fly between brother and sister, more in habit than in spite, he surmised. Not surprising they had moved home given today's rents. Peter was an affable fellow, much more laid back than his dad, not at all a chip off the old block. Gabrielle was the one who took after her father, an attractive girl even if she did think she was the bee's knees. Sharp too. Gift of the gab, definitely. Peter was a different proposition. Still, he had his head switched on more or less. How had they got on to the subject of tube fares yesterday? Somehow that had led to the industrial action threatened next week by the drivers. Terry had tried to explain it to Peter but he feared it had fallen on deaf ears. As it usually did on the privileged, let's face it. Terry shrugged, he was well out of that world and his ideas had shifted a bit. Inevitable with his own business to run these days. One of the bosses. He barked a caustic laugh at himself. Never mind, it had been a lively five minutes and Carla listening away to them both. The lad's off at that job of his, a pretty cushy number if you ask me, Terry said to himself, shaking his head. Playing tennis all day? What kind of work is that? Still if he'd been a football coach Terry wouldn't have thought twice about it. He'd better beware hypocrisy. The young were good at pointing that out.

He'd checked the kitchen a few times to see if she'd re-appeared but she hadn't. He'd get the lads going then pop over to give that quote to the lady in Brook Green. It would be a serious job all right: a complete refurb, then on to the suppliers to sort out that invoice.

He had a word with the lads and went back through the house. Still no one about. As he drove up the road he noted the white vans parked here and there. Not many of the names were familiar; they looked unpronounceable in fact. *Wojcit, Nowak, Wisniewski*. He'd heard that some of the Poles were going home having saved a fortune but they'd be replaced by others, Terry was sure, Brexit or not.

Chapter Sixteen

She sat up straight, scarcely grazing the back of the chair. Attentive, yet relaxed, arms resting lightly beside her notepad and pen. She'd bounced back after a couple of days of feeling off-colour, her cold disappearing in time for the January meeting. Carla looked around the table at three men and six women: par for the course on the average committee, especially for anything connected to the arts. Not wholly comfortable with her new position, she kept wondering how she had been promoted so quickly: only a couple of weeks as a member and then the AGM and the surprising election. It might have been a case of 'better the devil they didn't know' as one or two other candidates had been overridden in favour of the newcomer. Rob said it stank of skulduggery but how was she to know? It had been a sort of whirlwind romance, the coercion more flattery than force, the arguments for her inclusion delivered in a charm offensive by the chairman. There must have been someone they were desperate to keep out. No doubt she would find out in time. She was mostly keeping her head below the parapet, concentrating on listening and jotting down the odd note. So far she had written only: Sir John Soane Museum March 18th then a doodle around the capital letters. The planning of the summer programme was in progress; the discussion as to what, where and how was still going on. It was a pity that the young Italian wasn't here today. He looked as if he'd liven things up.

'Very astute,' someone remarked a little later when she had

volunteered an opinion. She stopped a grateful smile from spreading at that tiny acknowledgment. She needed to be sensitive to all the nuances, guessing there might be factions. A new group had started up not far away, causing waves of consternation. The meeting moved to item number four on the agenda. It was becoming clear that this particular organisation took considerable pride in their reputation for the many 'coups' they had claimed when a famous yet reluctant worthy had been persuaded to perform.

'To be accurate,' a fellow committee member on her left, leaned over to whisper, 'that means a tired lecture to a rapturous hall full of old people who can boast about it afterwards.' Carla suppressed a smile while he continued murmuring into her ear in a funny high voice. 'My dear, he was marvellous. Have you ever heard him speak? No? Ah, but he was riveting, so insightful, absolutely charming to talk to.' Carla wished he would be quiet; it wouldn't do to get the giggles. She concentrated on surveying her surroundings, the old rehearsal room of a theatre. Harsh lighting from a hundred watt bulb under the elderly pendant shade was uncomfortable directly underneath its blaze and left dim and cavernous depths elsewhere. Carla fancied she could smell the grease paint and the musty odour of old costumes. Suddenly there was excitement around the table and people sat up. An experimental theatre group were to perform. Several of the committee, in a desire to escape the commercial conformity of current West End productions as they put it, agreed to attend together one evening. Safety in numbers, they laughed.

Mark Rylance, Simon Russell Beale, Rachel Weitz, Carla daydreamed about all the actors in plays she would go to this year. Hearing her name mentioned, her daydream abruptly shattered, she listened to comments about an administrative matter, nodding to show she was paying attention, feeling a fraud and wondering if she would be of any use at all to the group.

'Let's see. Item number seven on the Agenda,' the chair, a woman carrying off the look of a nineteen fifties secretary, with winged frames to her spectacles, announced disapprovingly, 'Committee Room fees. Discuss proposal to negotiate with landlord or possible alternative venues.' She stared around, daring them to give their views.

Carla waited. This place was convenient for home; she hoped they would not move too far. Voices rose. It seemed nearly everyone wanted to air an opinion, even if they simply repeated another's point of view. Why couldn't people just say 'I agree'? She caught her neighbour's glance. Had he raised his eyebrow a fraction of an inch?

Half an hour later, the meeting broke up as coffee and biscuits were served. They gathered round and included her as they chatted, at ease with each other. Carla told the story of the move to the area, where they had come from, what and who they had been. That was important it appeared. People liked the sound of an architect; she knew that of old. A professional: they approved. As for herself, she made no mention of the former air stewardess; there was no need to go back that far.

'Oh, I dabbled in the rag trade, you know, running a little boutique,' her answer was ready, letting them make of it what they liked. She'd done more than dabble; her tiny shop had been popular with women of all ages. Often at this point, she'd receive glances at her clothes and compliments. She was not surprised how frank they were today.

' You can tell. Your clothes have lovely tailoring.'

'Thank you.'

'You could be French, you know?'

'You look effortlessly chic.'

She smiled at that notion and asked a question to change the subject.

It seemed she was now 'one of them.' Plans were being made to meet at a pub for a quick drink before the play in a few days time. Some spoke in a droll way of bracing themselves for a potentially gruesome evening.

'Harry is a terror for walking out at the interval,' the speaker nodded towards the man who had sat next to Carla. She had a better view of him, saw that he was late fifties or early sixties, with a face that had been handsome. Taller than Rob, his short grey hair was neatly cut, the rimless reading glasses pushed onto his forehead above slightly hooded eyes etched around with laughter lines.

'My motto has always been enough is enough. Suffering in the cause of art is only all right up to a point,' he defended himself in a voice with a pleasant timbre.

'Just don't embarrass us, Harry,' called out black spectacles whose name Carla had momentarily forgotten. 'I'll never get over The Donmar,' she shook a finger at him. With that they broke up and went off their separate ways.

Carla found herself at the entrance beside the subversive Harry.

'What happened at the Donmar?'

'Too embarrassing,' he pulled a face. 'Tell me. First impressions?' he lifted an eyebrow.

'Interesting. Yes. Good…fun.'

'That's the spirit,' he replied, 'it should be fun. Some people have a tendency to forget that.'

'See you at the play?' she asked.

'Oh yes. Looking forward to it,' he insisted as if to negate the earlier comments. 'See you there.' They smiled a farewell and she slipped into the crowd on the pavement, walking as if she had a purpose. Where now, to take stock of whether she had been saddled with an onerous chore or a satisfying commitment? It was a toe dipped into a new pool and she was going to the play with them: her involvement might lead to all sorts of interesting expeditions. She felt a surge of elation. London was waiting for her: museums, galleries, concerts, the Eye, the Shard, endless possibilities rose before her. But not endlessly on her own, she prayed. The thrill dipped, dimmed in an echo from her childhood; *can I bring a friend? Pleeese*. She'd nagged for a sister or brother, disputing the perks of being an only child. *It's boring.*

She paused; she had little desire to go home. She pulled out the battered A-Z she always carried. If she continued walking along here, she would pick up a bus to the Royal Academy. She was now a 'friend' of the gallery. She swung her bag onto the other shoulder and stepped out again. Later she might walk up Regent's Street to browse the shops. They had always been a temptation; taking a professional interest was only half a joke yet she prided herself on being reasonably thrifty. 'Reasonable' meant she could splash out when the occasion demanded and having the pick of the stock at her shop had been a bonus. For the present, she was cautious. Let their finances settle down after the move and the building works. Figures from the pension plan revolved in her head but as yet life here was an unknown expense. They had offset the extra cost of living in the city by owning a single car and using public transport. It had been one of the selling points of the move, although sharing a car for the first time was an adjustment. She felt wistful about her lovely Audi, driven now by the local garage mechanic's wife. It seemed that nostalgia could sidle through the barriers all too easily.

A fine drizzle and the sound of tyres on a wet road made her hesitate again; she raised a hand to her hair, catching her reflection in a shop window. She looked spruce, organised, a woman who knew where she was heading. She shook her head slowly as if to say, 'you couldn't be more wrong.' Here she was again, beset by doubts.

She moved slowly past the pictures. *Twilight Royan* reminded her of place in Somerset where she'd spent a holiday as a child. It struck her that Gabrielle would have liked this show. Why hadn't she thought of suggesting it? The exhibition of Scottish Colourists struck her somewhat poignantly as good family stuff, something for everyone. Accessible was the word. That they had been overlooked for decades was shameful. The vibrant hues in Cadell's *The Blue Fan* were gorgeous. She could relate to these paintings. She stood back to let others peer. The Peploes were wonderful. Some, familiar from postcards, looked homely with their approachable subject matter. She liked the fact that you didn't have to work too hard. She was really dreadfully ignorant. Perhaps she might do an art appreciation course and learn the proper language to use.

Chapter Seventeen

Over the weeks as the extension began to take shape, Rob allowed himself to become excited. The steel beams of the frame soared into the sky and an enormous quantity of glass had been ordered. It would be as magnificent as he had planned. The new member of the team, a dark eyed, serious young man with the face of a poet according to his daughter, was frequently on site.

'We can rely on Aidan,' Terry assured Rob, 'he's passed all the exams. Structural engineering and whatnot.' He nodded sagely, adding possibly unnecessarily, 'he's used to dealing with architects.'

Rob had to agree that Aidan knew his stuff. Things were looking up and he could stop worrying about the extension being completed on time. They had been right to think Carla's birthday would be the perfect occasion to celebrate the new house.

Within days however, the temperature had dropped and a leaden sky foretold snow. A heavy fall blanketed the streets overnight. A vast cream tarpaulin was spread over the building works and the lads allocated to an indoor job elsewhere. Rob did his best to distract himself from the vision of an abandoned site by working hard on the design for a new house, an idea that had been on the back burner for some time, pushed aside by commissions at the practice. He spent hours in the office emerging now and then to make a hot drink and glower at the weather. Whether anyone would ever build his house was a moot point, he acknowledged but at least it kept him occupied. He gazed through the window at streets grubby with churned snow, the pavements a lethal skating rink. He recalled schools closing when the children were young and sledging parties tramping in wellingtons up the hills beyond the farm to congregate at the best spot for a fast run down. He thought of Carla, putting most of the other mothers to shame, as they declined the thrill with a shudder; she would hurtle down the steep slope first, to please the children, pretending bravado while he had his heart in his mouth waiting for a painful tumble: the old Carla, steady, strong and brave.

She'd been nagging him to be sanguine about the snow, 'what's the hurry? It's only a minor hold up.' She seemed to be focused on planning the bedrooms. No hurry there, he pointed out, what with the dust from cement blowing in every time a door opened. Yet mood boards with samples of fabric and pictures of chairs and curtain styles proliferated around the house. There was little warmth in their exchanges and Rob vowed to himself that he would be sweetness and light from now on. No more ranting about the snow.

The work had been halted for a week and Carla woke to the instant knowledge of another snowfall. The light was more penetrating, the silence profound. The abnormal quiet of muffled streets did not last long. By breakfast time the black tarmac tainted the creamy slush on the busier roads. In the garden at Number 23 the urns were stocky snowmen and the builder's mess a puzzle of white humps. The young people tramped extravagantly through the house every evening, scattering ice across the polished floor, shedding coats and scarves, dumping backpacks all over the hall.

On this particular morning Carla decided to stay put and enjoy the tranquillity of the house instead of trudging through the snow on a pointless errand. By ten thirty with several small tasks completed, the restlessness returned. She sat at the computer and looked up the website for her old shop. She was pleased to see no particular transformations to disturb her. She had promised to be a sounding board but Bridget had not yet taken up the offer. It had meant a great deal of paperwork to change the lease and the bank account, to inform the suppliers and the auditor. In the end, it was mostly relief she'd felt as she relinquished the business, back in the summer. Now she was feeling the pain of surrender: it had been her baby. She left the website and opened her photograph album, scanning back a few years, the pictures a kaleidoscope of the past. She smiled, a tear in her eye as she enlarged the one of Gabrielle at five on long-suffering Mischief, the Shetland pony; how fearless she was, the hard-hat with its jockey's blue silk swamping the tiny imperious figure. Here was Peter, his head between Mischief's ears, as he hugged the pony round its neck, stirrups dangling. Windy holidays in Cornwall, one much like another, their jackets billowing and hair streaming, the sand, grey from the rain, beneath their feet, picnics under an umbrella. And some bright days where the water glinted behind comical figures in goggles and snorkels, the dog with a ball, racing across the beach. The pictures blurred as she whisked through them, parties spilling into each other, anniversaries, fancy-dress, Gabrielle in cap and gown, Peter's county trophy for the under eighteens held high. She shook off the malaise by deciding to go out and face the weather after all. Only a few flakes were drifting past the window. Carla had an idea; she would buy Seville oranges and make marmalade.

'Another bad forecast,' Rob shook his head in disbelief, the following morning, dressed in a thick fleece, ear cocked.

'Heavy snowfalls are expected over the South East.' Even the voice of the man on the radio held a touch of dismay. How much longer could this go on? What had happened to global warming, the tabloids asked? For nearly two weeks the weather had been holding up the works. He could see that Carla was over her Christmas blues, resolutely cheerful. She told him that one person fuming and railing against the weather was quite enough.

'Lucky Terry and the men working in the warmth of a block of flats,' he grumbled. 'Such rotten timing, this bloody snow. Another couple of weeks and it wouldn't have mattered.' He glowered from the window.

'What's that?' asked Carla, busy with the marmalade, running the slicing attachment of the mixer.

'The snow. God, that noise.'

'Sorry,' Carla took her finger off the button and looked anxiously at the oranges.

'I do hope they're fine enough. I should have done them by hand. You'll all complain that the slices are too thick.'

'Another couple of weeks and it wouldn't have mattered,' Rob repeated.

'Never mind. I'm sure they will speed things up as soon as they're back.'

'Let's hope so or it won't be finished for your birthday.'

'Rob, listen. I've been thinking. I really don't want a party. What is there to celebrate about being sixty? I'd much rather forget it. Then the pressure to finish the extension will be off. We can all relax and— '

'Don't be ridiculous. The whole point has been to showcase the project on your birthday. We said we would invite all the old crowd up for your big day.'

'But I have no desire for a big day. If you want some fancy do, you carry on. Just don't centre it all round me.'

'For heaven's sake, let's drop the subject. Things will look different when the builders have gone. Anyway, the kids are looking forward to it.'

He watched her running the machine, feeding in the rest of

the halved fruit, the fragrant juice leaking over the worktop. He got up to pass over a cloth, scowling at the unnecessary mess.

'Damn the children. Does everything have to revolve around them all the time?' she made a show of the wiping, overly thorough.

'You've changed your tune,' he snapped. She threw the cloth towards the sink and proceeded to bang a wooden spoon around a large pot.

Rob marched out. If only she would drop the injured wife stance. It was always there not far under the surface and the slightest thing could trigger the hostility. Not a good time to bring up the subject of Rose and introducing her to her siblings. When would it be a good time, he wondered? He needed to get out of the house, get some fresh air. It was claustrophobic in there, a snowy cocoon. He would head over to that café he liked and read the first copy of the weekly journal Carla had ordered for his Christmas present. He was already falling behind with it. That would be civilised urban behaviour; being part of the café society appealed to him. He pictured Les Deux Magots, Simone de Beauvoir and Sartre. He could lose himself in philosophical reflections; rise above his petty concerns. It would take the aggravation away for a while. He changed into a pair of shoes with a decent tread.

'I'm going up to the shops, might have a coffee,' he remembered his vow to be pleasant, accommodating. 'Do you need anything?'

'I'll take the car later, stock up a bit.'

'Sure you don't want me to?'

'You never look at the sell-by dates.'

'Huh,' he protested, 'I'll see you later then.'

So far the issue of one car hadn't been a problem. That was the beauty of living in London. He closed the front door behind him and pulled up his collar. The roads were clear but the pavements still slippery with packed snow. In places it had been swept into grey heaps, crunching under his feet. He trod with care, the journal tucked in his pocket. He patted the other pocket; he might drop a brief text to Rose. Perhaps not, not until he had something concrete to offer, it was pointless to get in touch. Anyway, he seemed to have forgotten his mobile.

Carla did something she had never done before. Rob's phone lay forgotten on the table. She picked it up and weighed it in her hand for a moment. Then she began to scan the record, first of his phone calls and then his emails. Did she know what she was looking for? Perhaps she needed some evidence to justify her continuing animosity: another woman's name or a series of calls to Rose. She'd often held his phone, answered it in the car or used it to send a text when they were out together. This was different. She was snooping, delving into corners that might give something away: the lists of contacts, emails, texts and apps. How sickening she was; she disgusted herself. She stopped. There was nothing besides a phone number for Rose. That was no surprise. The record of calls had been thoroughly deleted. But this was Rob: a neat freak. The sort of thing he'd always done. She closed the mobile down and polished away her fingerprints. She sat down and closed her eyes for a long minute. She had never known this bitter killjoy streak in her. She hadn't understood the fragility of a marriage, the hairline cracks that could give way without warning. She acknowledged only one thing: his silence had afforded them a unity for all that time. If she had never had to know, she would be happy still. Instead, she lived with a panicky feeling that foretold an earthquake or a volcanic eruption. She gave a start as a quiet knock sounded on the front door. No one was expected but a familiar figure stood there, the white van at the kerb.

'Oh, Terry, it's you. Come on in,' suddenly she was cheerful.
'Not disturbing you?'

'Of course not, I'm only making marmalade. Don't be silly. It's a pleasure to see you,' idiotically, she had almost said she'd missed him. 'Come in. Let's put the kettle on.' She smoothed her hair, hoped some lipstick remained.

'All right then?' he stood just inside the door, bundled up in his donkey jacket. Was it only builders who still wore them? She beamed at him and turned quickly to the sink.

'Fine, thanks. And you?'

'Smashing. I'm just going to pop out the back, have a look at something, if that's okay?'

'Course. I'll make the tea.'

Before the snowy weather, in the late afternoons as dusk deepened into darkness, the lads would pile into their van, revving the engine as they drove off and Terry would be invited in by whoever happened to be in the kitchen, for a final cup of tea. He would sit at the table with Rob and Carla to go over the plans, complain about suppliers and chew the fat. The bluff persona was left aside with his jacket and woolly hat on the banisters. The literary allusions peppering his speech hinted at a sharp intelligence and he was an articulate conversationalist. Carla watched as they discussed building matters. She joined in when the talk moved on as it usually did, to topical issues; it was a pleasant forum for voicing one's opinions. Over the weeks, long before the bad weather, it had become a mutually enjoyable half hour. Missing her circle in the country and Rob the companionship of office colleagues, Terry had become a friendly sounding board. Giving away enough titbits about himself for them to trust him, they became quite frank (without mentioning Rose) in their talk of past lives and family matters. He commiserated daily with Gabrielle over her setbacks: the applications ignored or rejected and teased Nina in an avuncular way until she turned pink. He had become quite part of the family. Carla was enormously pleased to see him back again.

'Here you are. Grab a chair.'

'Very nice of you. A cuppa is just the ticket. Love the smell of those oranges,' he drew a deep breath in through his nose. 'Popped in to say we should be back on site next week. Just wanted to let you know. I guess Mr Yoo is a mite frustrated. Whatever the weather, tell him, we'll be back. They're reckoning on one last heavy dump and then the thaw.'

'Well, Rob has an impatient nature,' she confided, sitting down opposite him, placing Rob's mobile onto a small pile of mail and the newspapers she was gathering at the end of the table, automatically tidying up. 'Besides, it means so much to him, professionally, you know, to get it finished. At the moment he doesn't know what problems may be lurking further down the road, in the construction, I mean,' she was gushing.

'Here's yours,' she pushed the mug closer to Terry and looked at him properly for the first time. 'Is the other job nearly finished then?'

'I can put my second team on to it. Yours is the priority. This extension will be top of the Premier League when it's done.'

They a exchanged a smile.

'All quiet today?'

'Thank heavens. What a weekend. Too many of us cooped up here. The foul weather and everything. They all begin to bicker. Gabrielle does need a job; she's rather on edge. There's another interview coming up, so we're hoping. And we're a bit worried about Nina. Have you seen how thin she is? She's rather latched on to Peter, I fear. Don't get me wrong; I adore her, but. Did you have a good weekend?'

'Very good. Sunday lunch at my son's in Ealing.'

'Is he married?'

'He is indeed. Ant's his name. He's a chef. You get fed very well, round theirs. I can see you're busy. That smells good.'

'Thanks for letting me know about next week. Marvellous. Now, I'd better get on with my marmalade.'

'So you had. Until Monday then,' Terry rose to let himself out.

Carla measured out the sugar, sprinkling each tablespoon over the pan, watching it dissolve in the bubbling froth, like her mood, lifting, knowing that some things could move forward again.

Chapter Eighteen

Four people sat at computers in a compact, overheated office. Flurries of snow obliterated the usual view of bricks and windows. An open door revealed the boss, his backside propped on his desk, talking to his secretary, somewhere out of sight. Rose gave him a quick resentful glance. He had spoken contemptuously about her designs for marketing a new brand of baby food.

'Derivative,' he had dismissed it. She glowered at the rudeness. If he considered it unoriginal, he should not be so free with the 'too wacky' comments she was more accustomed to hearing. She glared at the items she'd been charged with promoting: the tins and cartons on her desk decorated with sickly smiling infants in cute poses. Ugh. She would never have a child. It wasn't worth it. And if she did, she would avoid commercial products like the plague. Make everything herself: organic, fresh. Any child of hers would be better looked after than she had ever been. Resentment about her childhood swelled alongside her annoyance with work. Her mother had been a self-indulgent cow, had prevented Rob from being a part of their lives. Her mother had a warped personality, punishing him for not being there by refusing to let him be there.

'Be an angel, Rose and have another go at that,' Hugo her boss waved airily from his office towards her drawings illuminated on the white board. So he had noticed her stiff back and arms folded in mutiny.

'Will do,' she relented, removing the image. How she longed

for something less prosaic to work on. She looked around at the team. Not necessarily the bright sparks Hugo believed they were. Rose was sure she did not get the acknowledgement her work deserved; her ideas were definitely the most creative in the daily brainstorming sessions.

'Off the wall,' they would giggle at her daring, glancing at each other.

'Honestly, you're brilliant, Rose.'

Give me some credit, she felt like shouting at her boss.

She closed her eyes and waited for inspiration. Nothing came so she wasted time doodling on a pad and gazing around the office. Finally, her scribbles morphed into another brief and she lost herself in creating a scheme for a fashion house. By five-thirty she was ready to pack it in, relatively satisfied. Perhaps inspiration for the baby food advertisements would strike in the night.

She waited and waited for a bus, shoulders hunched against the cold and her head tortoise-like under the hood of her anorak. A sleety rain seeped through a worn seam and ran down her neck. She'd never got round to buying a new one. She reached in with chilled fingers and yanked at her collar, pulling it tight. She hated winter. People stood under umbrellas, complaining and sniffing until a packed bus rumbled up at last. She edged along and held onto a rail as the bus lurched forward. The man squashed in beside her in the aisle coughed continuously in the moist heat. Rose turned her head away and tried not to rock into anyone. She was sure Carla and Rob would be driving around in an expensive car, the effective air conditioning system keeping them toasty. It was a relief to get off. She walked doggedly along to the flat in boots soggy from the slush, her toes unpleasantly cold and slippery.

It was a week later and Gaby, still in bed at nine thirty in the morning, was looking at Instagram and Facebook. Of course, it was a compulsive habit that made her view the latest posts but how often did the activity leave her with a bit of a sour taste in the mouth? Sulky faced, she scrolled through the pictures: grinning wankers, the usual glasses of beer or wine held aloft, silly selfies in idiotic poses. Advertisements. Suddenly there was her ex-boyfriend in a photograph. She frowned, wondering whether her indifference was absolute. No emotion apart from a mild regret that it hadn't worked out. He was kind and funny but she'd never really fancied him. Not like the engineer who might, just might come today. He was the best looking man she'd clapped eyes on in ages. She sighed. No doubt he had girls after him all the time. She'd do better to think about the presentation she had to give on Wednesday. She closed her laptop with a sudden snap and leaned back against the headboard. She had slept for hours but still felt tired. She pushed her hair out of her eyes and tried to summon the energy for a shower.

Since she had lost her job, Gabrielle's problems were accumulating. A list of them ran through her mind with heartfelt expletives: *fucking* redundancy, *fucking* endless job hunting, *fucking* living at home at twenty-eight. In the past, academic work, sport, friends and jobs had all come easy even if she had slogged over revision at times and put in long hours of graft, the ensuing success was reward enough. She'd thrown herself into every promotion, zipping up the pay ladder, her self-confidence matching the salary but now look at her. She'd been junked. Gabrielle threw back the duvet to force herself out of bed, yet still lay there. She knew she was frittering the weeks away, getting up late, dropping in to noisy bars to spend the evenings drinking with friends who fled from their offices at six o'clock. She'd always relished that raucous atmosphere, the end of the working day downtime with its letting go of inhibition in the crowded bars of the city. The hilarity, chat-up lines, confidences and indiscretions fuelled by oversize glasses of wine were heady ingredients. In those surroundings she could still feel one of the gang. So much was depending on the next interview. It would be frustrating to fail again. She pulled up the bedclothes, wriggled to get comfortable, thumped the pillows behind her back and opened the laptop again.

Half an hour later she was downstairs helping herself to a bowl of muesli and watching the men working on a task above her view: ladders and legs. No Terry today and disappointingly, no Aidan. The kitchen had become a goldfish bowl where everyone studiously avoided eye contact while covertly observing all the comings and goings of each other. Now the men appeared, in their blue denim and check shirts under padded jackets, climbing down onto the concrete base. No builder's bum on view. She smiled at the ridiculous observation. It still looked bloody cold out there. She considered her bare shoulders and looked down at the tops of her boobs visible above the skimpy outfit she slept in. It was a good thing Dad was out: he had criticised her for appearing in her nightclothes.

'For God's sake, Gaby. You'll have all the men letching after you. Have some sense.'

But today nobody was looking anyway.

'Darling, still here?' Her mother appeared at the kitchen door.

'I've had a go at my presentation. I'm so bored. There's nothing to do.'

'You sound about fourteen. Where's your dressing gown? You should go for a walk; get a bit of colour in those cheeks. Hanging about here is pointless. You were late again last night. Another evening out drinking?'

'Perhaps I'll go for a run.' Gabrielle continued gazing into the garden. 'I shouldn't have let my gym membership lapse. I used to be quite fit.'

'Go on then, get some exercise. It'll do you good. The

weather is going to be improving, apparently. Maybe the sun will even come out.'

'D'you know where my trainers are? I might have to borrow yours.'

'No. Find your own. They're under your bed I think. And take care, it's still slippery out there.'

Slowly, reluctantly, Gabrielle stirred herself. She pulled on the tight leggings and a yellow top, feeling a vestige of her former pride in being fit. She checked the mirror critically; flabby but if she held her stomach in, she might pass. She would run every day, she resolved. Before long she would have another job and her old routines could resume. She plotted her route as she ran downstairs and did some perfunctory stretches outside the house. A cold wind whipped her hair around her face as she set off in the direction of the park, skidding over the icy patches and just avoiding an elderly man in a thick overcoat, hat and mittens. They both apologised and she crossed the road, gulping the freezing air and breathing it out in white clouds. Reaching the park gates, she set off at a steady trot along the path. Then she flew over the crisp grass to test herself, carelessly sliding, enjoying the country scent of damp ferns and rotten timber under the remains of the snow. Along the embankment, she watched the pale mist on the river and alternated the jogging with medium paced walking to get her breath back, slowing only when a golden retriever with a stick in its mouth took an interest in her. She cut back, running beside a narrow winding path with trees dripping overhead. At the memorial, she bent to recover, her hands on her thighs, panting raggedly. Half an hour was quite enough, she decided. No need to go mad on the first outing. Arriving back, she was still gasping but proud of herself.

'Oh my God. You've been running,' Nina couldn't help stating the obvious as she came to a halt on the bottom stair. It was the following morning and she felt a sharp contrast between her dress with its long sleeves, caught in a frill at the wrist and Gabrielle's athletic appearance, oozing vigour. She was aware of Gabrielle's eyebrows lifting a fraction.

'Very sixties. Hey, you could join me next time.'

'Oh, I'm totally unsporty. I was hopeless at games. Never got picked for a team at school.'

'That's just feeble. Any one can go jogging. Though it's hardly as if you need to lose weight. Still, it's good for muscle tone. I'm trying to stick to my New Year's resolution, a run every day. I'm going up to shower.'

Gabrielle bounded upstairs as Nina shrank back against the banisters feeling she had come out of the attic bedroom five minutes too early. The force-field round Gabrielle somehow diminished her. At least SHE had a job to go to, she reminded herself, the word 'feeble' still chiming in her ears. Her indignation mounted as she thought of all the time she had to spend altering wedding dresses for brides who tended to lose weight at the eleventh hour. *It just fell off them* Melanie had a habit of repeating. Why oh why, did it take Nina weeks to lose a pound? It wasn't fair. And besides, she did spend quite a lot of time exercising. No one knew about that either. There was a lot you could do quietly in your bedroom with the radio on. But she was still just a big fat blob. If she wasn't careful, Pete would notice she had put on weight, would tire of her. He seemed to be spending more and more time at the club. The job was working out well for him but thinking about it stirred up her insecurities. The 'club' conjured visions of a clique of muscular, beautiful girls with long glossy manes of hair, skin-tight tennis outfits and legs up to there. How on earth could she compete?

Nina shrugged on a thick cardigan from a hook in the back hall, topping it with a jade velvet coat that had seen better days and a pompom hat she'd knitted. She let herself out and hurried along, a fringed bag over one shoulder. On her mind were the two dresses she was working on, her drawings approved and the fabric pinned to the paper patterns. They would soon be cut out ready to sew unless the boss had other ideas. Melanie seemed more critical of late. Nina almost skipped along, sliding through the crowd, getting into the slipstream of a tall city bloke in a dark suit powering his way past the lower orders. She mustn't be late.

Her mobile rang and she fumbled for it as she pattered down the steps to the tube.

'Hi, Pete.'

'Just wanted to catch you before you got to the shop. Thought you and Gaby might like to come over to see the joint, have a swim maybe, later on, after work. What do you think?'

'I could do. Have you spoken to Gaby? It would be nice to see the place. I haven't got a swimsuit though.'

'You can buy them here,' Peter spoke breezily, 'or borrow off Gabs. She won't mind. I'll ask her to bring a spare. Come over about six thirty.'

Now Nina's mood veered between anxiety that she would look enormous in a bikini and pleasure that Pete had suggested the visit. All the way to work she imagined herself in an ill fitting swimsuit, her tentative descent into the water while Gabrielle would be certain to make a perfect dive and demonstrate a fast crawl to the shallow end, leaving Nina clinging to the steps, showing her up as a *feeble* person who couldn't cut the mustard.

Nina pressed the bell outside the shop. It was five to ten. The first appointment wasn't until ten thirty. Then a constant stream of girls and their mothers would be there with their overwrought faces, trying on dresses for the first rapturous time or having an anxious fitting, deciding on veils or shoes. The stock consisted of four sizes of a dozen designs and every dress would be custom made to order with individual additions. She could see Melanie approaching through the glass.

'Good. You're here. We've got to squeeze in that wretched de Vere woman and her precious daughter before the ten thirty appointment. They'll be arriving any minute.'

'What's the problem?'

'A change of mind, altering half the dress, I don't doubt. Well, it will cost them. I sometimes wish I'd gone in for designing teapots or cushion covers.'

'You still could.'

'Thanks for the comforting thought.'

Nina was already removing the unfinished dress from its silk cover and placing it in the dressing area.

'It's beautiful. What's the panic?'

'Here they are. Open up would you and lay on the charm? You're good at that.'

Am I? Nina wondered, returning Melanie's sudden grin.

So this was where Pete did his coaching. The impressive glass-fronted building was intimidating. Would she be asked for a membership card? Two women stood chatting loudly just inside the door, car keys twirling in their fingers.

'Must dash. I'm collecting Orlando from his violin lesson.'

Nina skirted round them. Women of her age, taking it all for granted. Thankfully there was Peter, laughing with the receptionist. He caught sight of her at once and beamed. Nina's heart lifted.

'Come and meet Lucia.'

The girl at the desk tossed her shoulder length black hair; electric blue glasses gave her a forceful gaze and a smart, body-hugging trouser suit came into view as she stepped out with a professional smile. Gabrielle came striding across the reception area as they were saying hello.

'Lucia, meet Gaby. My sister. We'll do a quick tour and then the swim. You must have seen the outdoor courts as you came in.'

He led them through the building and along a wide corridor. 'These are pretty cool.' They looked through glass to a row of indoor tennis courts, busy with games in progress.

'At this time of year most of the coaching is inside which is great. No freezing my bollocks off in the drizzle. When you're back on a fat salary you should become a member here, Gaby.'

'When, being the operative word.'

So this was what you got for an annual membership of several thousand pounds, Nina's internal commentary continued. He led them past the bar.

'We'll have a drink later.' He waved airily towards the squash courts and the gym. 'Cutting edge equipment, of course,' and they arrived at the almost deserted pool. Nina stared, imagining the long sliding doors open in summer, a row of teak loungers occupied by recumbent forms along the wide sun drenched terrace. How the other half lived.

'Not bad eh?'

'Come on,' Gabrielle urged.

In the changing room, Nina looked doubtfully at the proffered bikini.

'I'm not sure it will fit.'

'Just do the strings up tight,' said Gaby, whipping off her clothes carelessly and putting on a red and white striped bikini. 'It'll be fine.'

Gingerly, with her back half turned, Nina stepped into the bottom half, pulled it up and began to fiddle with fastenings that were complicated by small wooden bobbles.

'God, you are skinny. Let me,' Gabrielle bent to adjust the ties for Nina. 'In fact you look amazing,' she added, watching as Nina pulled on the top, 'straight out of a magazine. Come on, let's go.'

Nina warmed to her but she had been right about the

diving. Gabrielle leapt from the edge in a flash of legs and pointed toes, entering the water with barely a splash while Peter wallowed in the middle of the pool. Nina hurried down the nearest ladder and swam breaststroke towards him as he grinned, his hair plastering his head and water streaming over his face. They wrapped legs round each other, began to sink and parted to fool about in the water, avoiding two serious swimmers doing lengths.

'The temperature is perfect. You could get used to this,' Nina called out as Peter came to rest after a bout of thrashing along in a version of butterfly stroke. He trod water as he put his arms round her waist. 'It's cool, isn't it. I'm pretty chuffed they've kept me on.'

Nina hugged him and then tried to sink him, pushing on his shoulders while he fought back shaking water out of his eyes.

'No chance.'

Gabrielle was swooping seal-like, over and under the water before alternating crawl and backstroke for a few lengths. Half an hour later, a group of teenagers splashed into the pool, ignoring the rules by dive-bombing into the deep end.

'Enough of that,' Peter remonstrated.

'Let's go for a drink,' he told the girls, swimming to the side and pulling himself out in one graceful movement. Gabrielle followed suit, hitching down the bikini bottoms with her thumbs. Nina swam to the steps opposite, aware that Peter's eyes were on her, emerging like a water sprite she hoped with her hair streaming down between her shoulder blades and at the same time worried about the size of her bottom in the tiny triangle of fabric.

'Tell me about this job you're going for.' Nina tried not to look at the bowl of crisps on the table as they sat in the bar with a view over the tennis courts. Gabrielle put down a glass of white wine and pushed damp strands of hair behind her ears.

'You've heard of Endicott Bailes?'

'Yeah, the ads are all over the place.'

'They're after someone to develop the label. The job is to do with brand strength management. You know, Pete, marketing capability development stuff, like I did before.' She rattled on, 'Creative strategies and using technology to build the label and whatnot. Sorry, jargon.'

'I totally get it. Mel could do with a bit of that.' Nina's eyes returned to the crisps. Perhaps she would have just one.

'It's not as senior as my last job but actually better paid. I'm working on a presentation so I've had to do some research. There's quite a lot on their website. It should be interesting, if I can land it,' she frowned, 'it knocks the old confidence a bit when you get turned down.'

'Third time lucky,' her brother encouraged. 'I have a feeling.'

'So you're clairvoyant now are you? Let's go home and eat. Mum was going to get supper for us. I'm starving. I've had a lot of exercise today.'

Chapter Nineteen

If only she would shut up. Rose was exasperated with her mother. How stupid to go looking for some kind of sympathy. She should have known better.

'Give it a rest, Mum,' she ordered, rubbing her forehead before abandoning the newspaper and staring across at Angie who lounged, feet up on the flowery chesterfield in a bright lime-green kaftan. The combination was enough to start a pounding behind her eyes.

'I only want to know what you found out. You've hardly told me a thing. You can't blame me for being curious. Don't keep saying the past is the past. It is still very real to me,' she took her eyes off the television for a few moments. 'There was a lot at stake at one time. It could have been enormously difficult but I got round it. You imagine it was easy for me, I suppose? I'm just incapable of being dishonest and Rob was all too keen to slam the door in my face.'

'Oh yes? It was mutually agreed I seem to remember.'

'Well, that was convenient for him, wasn't it?'

'You can't have it both ways, Mum.'

'That's beside the point. All I wondered, all I am fascinated by, is what sort of a life he leads. Does he look happy and prosperous? Where exactly does he live? That sort of thing: nothing to get worked up about, just a little natural curiosity. No need to jump down my throat,' she waved her hands airily but the nonchalant pose did not fool Rose who waited for the sharp eyes, half hidden beneath a long fringe (a remnant of the style Angie favoured in her twenties) to circle the room and settle on her.

'If I ever get the chance to find out, I will be sure to pass on the information,' she threw herself back in the chair and folded her arms.

'I warned you it might be a tricky situation. Don't say I didn't warn you,' Angie returned to an earlier theme. The faded russet hair and lines around her mouth were a far cry from the dimpled allure of her youth. Rose glanced up at the portrait painted by an art school friend of the young Angie and compared the familiar well-worn features. Rob may have recognised the eyes, which could still hold a lazy coquettishness in their hazel depths but the rest of the package was quite different. Rose glared, felt like kicking the chairs.

'Is this an 'I told you so'? It doesn't help, Mum. Can we just drop the subject until I have something concrete to report?'

Angie sighed. Her mother's sighs had been the background noise for much of Rose's life along with repetitive anxious queries.

'Why aren't you out with some friends? It is the weekend you know. You should be having a pub lunch, going to the cinema at least. At your age I was out every night.' Angie shifted into a more comfortable position on the sofa.

'Good on you. I haven't seen any friends recently. I may as well go back to the flat and sit on my own.'

'Now you are being ridiculous. I just hope all this business about your father is not going to knock you off your even keel. You've been so much better the last couple of years. What's happened to that nice Luke? Have a cup of tea before you go, my love. And stop worrying. You mustn't let things get you down.' The look was surprisingly severe. 'You're taking it all too much to heart. I've been worried about that. It's not good for you. I can see you're all on edge these days. You've lost weight and I never think you look your best in those grungy colours.

Perhaps you should make an appointment with the doc.'

'No way. Forget that. I'm fine. It's just frustrating, waiting for him to make a move.'

'What will be will be.'

'I suppose that was your philosophy when you had me,' Rose seethed. How her mother got on her nerves.

'Make us a cuppa,' replied Angie evenly, already looking back at the television.

Rose went through to the rear of the Edwardian terraced house, her jaw clenched. The later years of her childhood had been spent here; the comprehensive school a twenty-minute walk away. This place had always been shabby, long before it became fashionable. Now the raffish air and painted furniture was a look reproduced time and again on the high street. Not many of her friends remained in the area but at Christmas she had seen a few of them, home for the festivities. Their lives seemed to be panning out well. She recognised the familiar resentment in a moment of self-awareness sparked by her mother's warning. As she ran the tap, she berated herself for becoming obsessed with the Unwins. They did not deserve such attention, the way they were behaving. That first and only meeting with her father and Carla had raised her hopes far too high. Day by day, like an unrequited lover sinking into despair, she was watching her dreams crumble. She gave the tap a further vicious twist in vain. No one was likely to change the washer these days. She fished out the teabags, dumped them in the bin, splashed in a drop of semi-skimmed and carried the mugs through to the living room.

'Switch on the fire while you're up,' Angie said. 'Don't you want to watch this? It's such a nasty cold afternoon. We can be blissfully idle in front of the box.'

'I've seen it. There's nothing else worth watching. I might as well go, after my tea. No. Leave it on. You can watch it. I know you want to,' she added petulantly. She knew she sounded like a spoilt child but she didn't care. She sat in the chair, resting her mug on the old linen cover with its shiny arms nearly worn through. If only Rob would get in touch again. It must be Carla stopping him. She had been certain that at Christmas he would acknowledge her. The season of goodwill and all that. What a downer. Waiting all day for a message that never came; all through sickly mulled wine with the neighbours and dinner with her Mum's friends, Rosemary and Ian, feeling like a lame duck among their married daughter's family. Charades and daft games spoilt by the two young brats being overindulged by their parents. It can't be hard to send a text, she had reasoned.

She sipped her tea and tuned in to the film on the telly. What rubbish. Darker conjectures about Carla crept back. She hadn't been taken in by those vague assurances, those pert bird-like mannerisms. Rob's wife had been uneasy; Rose could tell. She shrugged, it was what she had expected: just another hurdle to overcome. No big deal.

One afternoon she left work early, pleading a headache. She'd thought she might scream if she didn't get out into fresh air, if you could call it fresh. Her frustration was mounting.

She walked across London Fields keeping a watchful eye on several dogs loping away from their owners like determined pit bulls: Staffordshire terriers in studded collars and thickset muscular dogs with uncertain intentions. Her eyes lingered on the playground full of small children on the climbing frame and toddlers running around the equipment, mums and dads watching from the side. Her father had never even seen her as a child. When had she become conscious that she lacked a proper dad? Of course Adrian had stood in for a time but it wasn't the same. Cute in a tutu at the ballet show, chosen for the A team at netball, passing all those exams: she'd wanted to make him proud, in case he turned up. Some hope. But he'd missed the lot. That was sad for both of them, wasn't it? They'd had him though, all those years. Peter and Gabrielle had been able to take him for granted. If it hadn't been for Carla he might have had a place in her childhood. A few minutes from home the idea ambushed her. She knew it had been creeping up on her for weeks. She would find the Unwins' address and check out the house. She'd take only a tiny peek from a distance and be very, very careful not to let anyone catch sight of her. Just to satisfy her curiosity a little. If he couldn't care less about her, she had nothing to lose anyway.

She hurried up the stairs to the flat, determined to avoid Luke's mocking smile. His comments had annoyed her.

'I told you not to rely on any latent paternal instincts. He's far too comfortable in his middle-class niche to let you disturb the status quo. Who are you kidding? Okay. Okay. Hang in there if you want. Play your cards right, it might be a nice little earner for you.'

Rose scowled as she unlocked her door and went straight to the computer. In a moment she Googled Angus and Latimer the architectural practice and before she had time for her nerve to fail her, dialled the number.

'I'm a friend of Gabrielle Unwin. Stupidly, I've lost my mobile with all her details and their new address. I just wondered if you might be able to give me their new phone number or address?'

'Oh sorry, love, data protection and all that. If you'd like to drop off a letter we can send it on for you?'

'Oh, okay, thanks. I'll probably do that. Thanks very much. Yeah. Thanks a lot.'

She was an idiot. She should have known they wouldn't hand out private information to strangers.

It struck her then: the phone directory. The obvious place to look and it might have saved that stupid call. So long as they weren't ex-directory.

She opened the BT website and within a couple of minutes, bingo. She'd found him, address and all. She copied it into her mobile and sat back. Rose looked at her watch. Too late now but she could set off early tomorrow. Change at Oxford Circus and just a few stops beyond that. In a few hours she would walk up his street, look at his house, breathe the same air. She felt invigorated, jumped up and walked around. The colours were saturated as if the room with its second-hand Ikea furniture had had an instant makeover.

Chapter Twenty

Carla stood wrapped in a towel, deciding what to wear. She envied the young who looked good in anything. She had no idea what suited her any more. Staring at the mirror, rejecting her unadventurous option of dark jeans, white shirt and a cardigan, she pulled apart the hangers, looking from one end of the wardrobe to the other. The leather skirt over knee high boots and a chunky pullover felt about right. It was lucky that she had not thrown them out years before. She went back into the bathroom and after wiping away the steam, leaned towards the mirror and drew a narrow black line along her lower lashes and brushed grey powder shadow onto the lids. An eyebrow pencil hovered in her hand before being rejected. A few strokes of mascara followed and Carla completed her makeup. She puzzled over her reflection. 'You look well,' her friends used to tell her but she wasn't confident about that any more. She had had her face 'done' on a recent visit to the cosmetics department of one of Oxford Street's department stores. She had always drifted past the beautifully packaged wares in the perfume hall, occasionally making a purchase, confident that she neither needed nor wanted advice. This time, she had succumbed unexpectedly; her confidence in her looks had been going down in direct proportion to her age mounting. She must have reached a tipping point. The over-painted face of the assistant should have put her off. Instead, balanced on a spindly stool like a idiot, right in front of the world going by, she submitted to the deft fingers smoothing and tapping her face and applying several layers of expensive primer, foundation, powder and blusher.

'Just to emphasise the contours,' she was told and the girl put a restraining hand on Carla's shoulder as she sensed a break for freedom coming. The eyes of customers passing by glided unseeing over her newly defined features. Under the shop lights her face had looked striking and youthful. She took possession of a tasteful little carrier bag full of the new brands and extra free samples, excited at her vibrant appearance. Somewhere between walking out and arriving home the magic had faded. Soon she had given up the little sponge, the shimmering palette and the fat brush that was meant to enhance the apples of her cheeks. Was she desirable still? Rob had resumed a tactful distance from her, while she 'got over' things, she assumed. Had that woman been the only one?

Perhaps she should initiate the sex but since the sole occasion weeks ago, on getting into bed each night her limbs grew heavy, her mind drowsy and her libido sank to rock bottom. They were getting by with momentary handholding now and again and a ritual peck when one or other of them left the house; they seemed a parody of the chaste 'older couple'.

She'd better go down, the builders would be arriving. She applied a light slick of lipstick and turned away. In spite of the continuing disruption, Carla looked forward to the distraction of their arrival every morning and to measuring their progress every evening. She hurried down the stairs.

Rob was out with his refugees and she'd heard Peter clumping past her bedroom door on his way to the sports club. Gabrielle had gone out early for her run and Nina had probably slipped off to work. Carla ate her cereal while she waited for the men, one eye on the window. They had taken to putting a cone in the road to keep a space free. Good, here was the van. She ran her fingers through her hair and brushed crumbs from her mouth.

There was a noise in the hall, footsteps going past, then a voice and a quizzical eye falling on her.

'Good morrow, dear lady. Your serfs pay homage,' he bowed his smooth head, the skin gleaming for a second. His large frame filled the doorway.

'Oh, Terry, hi. Good morning. How's the team?'

'Wonderfully well, I thank you. We are all rejoicing that the snow has gone and shall take up arms against any further inclement weather. Progress is the name of the game. Effort will be redoubled and Mr Yoo will gaze favourably once more upon your humble servant,' his eyes were mischievous. Carla could not help smiling.

'Can you really catch up after all the time lost?'

Terry's features arranged themselves into mock severity.

'We shall endeavour to do so.' He reversed out of the kitchen to reappear beyond the plastic sheet that had been erected in place of the original wall. The three young ones looked briefly at him and continued with their separate tasks. No Aidan today, it seemed, or not yet. Terry climbed a ladder and disappeared from view. How old was he, wondered Carla again? He reminded her of the tough guy in a detective series she watched occasionally. Beside him the others looked like striplings. She smiled at the word. Terry's language was catching. He often seemed to be quoting from Shakespeare but that would be unlikely surely? She knew he'd been in the union back in the day but where on earth had he picked up this ridiculous delivery? The ironical nuance and tilted eyebrow saved it from being irritating. Thankfully the freezing weather had gone. It had been frustrating to see everything abandoned on the site, Rob tense, wondering each day if anyone would turn up. Now they could get on. She looked at her watch; he was usually home by ten. Gabrielle's run now took the best part of an hour; she claimed it helped her to focus. On what exactly, they all wondered? No one liked to ask and Gabrielle wasn't volunteering. Job-hunting was still a permitted conversation topic but exasperation was setting in. Carla sympathised. Gabrielle had always been on the crest of a wave, riding high. Soon something must come up trumps. She had given her mother a scathing look for suggesting that a period of temping might be a good idea but had eventually agreed to look at the job advertisements in the local paper.

Carla checked the time. She was ready to leave for the British Museum; that was her plan for the day. She often spent hours in a solitary way, 'pleasing herself' was the spin she put on it, walking for miles, browsing should she pass an interesting shop or doing a detour into a park. In fact she felt adrift. Day after day, she repeated her own little pep talks. If her old friends from the village insisted on being judgemental and resentful, it was their loss. For the first time she was free of the obligations she'd acquired over the years. Here there were few expectations and demands from outside; no one was fussed if she came or went. If lonely, it was liberating too. She was perfectly self-sufficient, after all. If she wanted company she should just pick up the phone, not feel victimised if someone said no. She could have asked Bella today, mild Bella who'd shared the school run and would have popped on a train to meet up. It was easy enough to suggest an exhibition, lunch in a little bistro, a spot of shopping. Keeping busy kept her out of Rob's way, too. Since Christmas he had been dropping hints that it was time to do something about Rose. Before long the diffident allusions would become demands. The very thought was a reminder that he had gone to bed with some else. *Don't think about it*, had become her mantra.

She spent a few minutes tidying the kitchen, all too aware of the figures moving about in the extension. She took care not to catch anyone's eye. Her kitchen was a stage set with a front row full of critics and her movements became stiff and mechanical. She wanted to look active, vital not a frumpy old hausfrau pottering about with plates and dishcloths.

The telephone rang.

'Hi, it's Rob.'

'Hi.'

'Look, I won't be back for a bit. Forgot to say we're having a strategy meeting.'

'Okay. I shall be off soon anyway. I'll see you later on.' Carla glanced out at the workmen. She gave Terry a little wave, turning before he could respond. Why did she feel so foolish all the time?

A few minutes later she was hurrying along, glad that the ice was melting. She didn't notice a girl slinking back round the corner and crossing the road quickly. Carla turned right. She would enjoy walking up the King's Rd; there was absolutely no rush.

They must be stupid, Rose concluded, not to think how easily she could find them. Not telling her the address was tantamount to inviting her to look them up in some directory. Oh, the impatience she was feeling. They had no idea. She was tortured by the thought of them living their cosy lives just across London. Did her brother and sister even know of her existence yet? She doubted it. It made her so angry, she could weep. All she wanted was a glimpse of them. The street was too open though. Nice tall terraced houses, an expensive neighbourhood, smart cars. She'd taken in that much but catching sight of Carla had given her a hell of a shock. It wouldn't do her cause any good if she got caught hanging around outside the house. She'd better clear off, come back another time, maybe. Taking a last look, she almost collided with a runner who dodged round her, a dark-haired girl in neon Lycra, tinny music coming from the wire in her ear. Rose looked back as the girl rounded the corner and was gone. The temptation was immense. She followed about fifty metres behind. Watching carefully, her heartbeat almost stalled, she noted the place where a glossy laurel hung over the railings. The girl stood, stretching her arms above her head, leaning this way and that before opening the door. Crossing the road, and losing sight of the house numbers, Rose counted the gateways opposite. It was the one. 23. She hurried on. It must have been Gabrielle, her half sister. Her pulse was thudding now as she turned down another road. God, she'd almost touched her. Gradually hopelessness stole over her. Would they simply shut her out? She needed to talk to Rob. Something was holding him back, stopping him from making contact again. That ferretty wife. After all this time, he owed her something, surely. She wasn't going to wait much longer. She tightened the scarf viciously round her neck and felt for her gloves in the pocket. A bitter wind gusted around her as she reached a street that was busier with cars and pedestrians. Now she could relax. No one would notice her here; yet the smug houses mocked her as she walked past their smartly painted fronts with window boxes showing the tips of spring bulbs. She brooded on a single question. Just how much longer was she prepared to wait before Rob contacted her? The exhilarating glimpse of Gabrielle, surely that was Gabrielle, made her even more impatient. She walked on quickly, driven by thwarted hopes and remembered work for the first time. She'd better ring in, make an excuse for her lateness. She'd tell Hugo there had been a line closure on the Underground.

Edwina too was running late. Peter had booked one of the out of the way courts for the lesson, far from prying eyes. Not that there was anything to see, he reminded himself. And yet. He was finding himself beckoned by a little finger of temptation, becoming entangled in the silky threads of Edwina's web. He had little doubt that she was spinning him into something: exactly what, he hardly dared contemplate for fear of making it real. Nevertheless an undercurrent had been fizzing away during the times he was alone on court with her. Her teasing remarks had become more personal and were accompanied by gulps of laughter that almost admitted how naughty she was. He imagined she must be pushing forty but in great shape and the way she gathered her hair into an untidy topknot for tennis made her seem ten years younger. She was extraordinarily attractive, unlike some of the others: the over-made up, Botox smooth and trying too hard types. Generally, Edwina avoided looking as if she was flirting. It was as if she knew you fancied her but let you get away with it, he told himself. Somehow it put the onus on him. He noticed that he had begun to look forward to Wednesdays and Fridays and was annoyed with himself at how disappointed he was if she cancelled the lesson. 'Cat and mouse' had occurred to him more than once. Then he felt guilty about Nina, adorable Nina who had burrowed her way further into his life than anyone before.

They were essentially living together, as Gabrielle had pointed out. He hardly knew how it had happened. And in his parents' house. It was absurd. It could never be permanent: just until he'd saved a bit more and he could go flat hunting again. The best thing to do would be to move in with one of his mates. If only Nina had a functioning parent instead of that waste of space of a mother. In fact, she was rapidly adopting his parents. It was an unusual flash of intuition. Troublesome reflections tended to be an anathema to Peter. He shook them off at once and went to reception to see what had happened to Edwina. The spacious foyer was the bustling hub of the Scimitar, thronged with members. He edged round them with friendly looks seeking his gregarious pupil.

Beyond the glass entrance, a small Mercedes sports car was going too fast round the car park. That would be her, he was certain.

Today, the backhand was going well.

'I think you've been practising,' he called out.

'You noticed! I'm playing with a friend every Monday evening.' She returned a nearly flawless shot that had him chasing to the tramlines and at the same time deftly informed him of her presence at the club after work. No, he was imagining it. His mind scampered off in a daydream of being offered a lift in the sexy car…

He sent the next ball into a lob and made some small jumps on the spot as Edwina ran towards the back of the court. He was back to the lesson and reality. He grinned at her.

'Right. Let's have a look at that serve of yours,' he commanded, walking round to join her at the other end of the court.

It was the closest to her he had stood. The faint scent of citrus and ferns was delicious. He moved her hand on the racquet to demonstrate a different grip. The current jumped between them. It was almost a magnetic force. He stood back, alarmed at how close he had been to touching her again. The warning about inappropriate behaviour came back to rattle him. Christ, he'd better be careful. A false move could cost him his job, not to mention accusations of harassment. Now he was in a cold sweat and concentrated on the technique he was teaching. Edwina appeared oblivious. Enthusiastic about her tennis, she was earnest and funny. It was very appealing. He just had to watch his step. Nothing could be allowed to happen yet the promise was in her eyes, glinting, provoking in their faux-innocence.

Chapter Twenty-One

'Where do you go to, my lovely?'

Gabrielle gave an acknowledging wave in the air as Terry's voice rang out in his tuneful baritone with the old song on an unexpectedly sunny Saturday. After undoing the padlock on the bike, she hitched up her dress to the very tops of her thighs and wriggled her backside onto the saddle, planting the red high heels on the pedals and she cycled hard to the junction. A passing lorry driver gave a toot on his horn. She grinned and clung to the handlebars catching the slipstream whooshing by.

The weekend traffic was atrocious but least on two wheels one could coast past the queues and creep up to the lights while drivers could merely glare. She was glad she had retrieved her bicycle from a friend's back yard. In her new keep fit mode she would pedal everywhere (within reason) she told herself. She shivered at a crossroads; the bright sunshine had misled her. Lucky for the bride, though.

She was on her way to Winchester; her friend Lily was to meet her train. Before the ceremony they would join everyone for a drink in the village pub. At the station, Gabrielle struggled to fix the chain to the metal bar of the cycle rack; it kept slipping out of her numb fingers and she banged her head twice on the saddle. Finally she'd locked it. Now, a dash for a ticket. Announcements over the loudspeaker were making her anxious and she glanced at her watch. Only a few minutes left. She yanked down her dress and hurried as best as she could, wobbling a little on her heels past WH Smith and the crowds of people pulling wheelie bags. At the ticket machine she discovered she was empty handed. Where the hell was her handbag? Dismayed, she pictured it in the basket of the bike. She kicked off her shoes and ran in her tights back along the concourse and out of the station, praying no one had noticed it: her expensive designer handbag with her wallet, her make-up and phone. Everything.

It was nestling in the bottom of the basket. She had no time to enjoy the enormous relief of finding it still there but snatched it up and dashed back inside the station, her bare feet slapping at the concrete. A crowd was swarming off the escalator; she sidestepped and swerved past. She came to a halt, suddenly, bursting into giggles at the sight of her shoes being held aloft by a tall young man beside the ticket machine. He was peering in every direction until noticing her bare feet he lowered the shoes and held them out to her with a bemused smile.

'Did you forget them?'

She shook her head. 'Course not. Thanks, but I'm going to miss my train. Oh no,' the announcement of the imminent departure made her jab at the screen in furious haste as she keyed in her destination, muttering, 'Not Single, Return, you stupid machine,' and attempting to feed two twenty pound notes into the slot. She clutched the ticket as it emerged and looked up, taking him in properly for the first time. She noticed a rather big nose, reddish hair and freckles. Not her sort at all. She stood, dejected now, watching a train pulling away from the platform. She put one foot then the other slowly into the shoes. Now they were nearly the same height.

'I've missed it. God knows when there will be another one. How idiotic I am.'

'Bad luck,' his expression was anxious. 'I do hope I didn't delay you?' He picked up a holdall and swung it onto his shoulder.

'No, of course not. You rescued my shoes. I'd forgotten my bag, you see.' They looked at each other. 'It was in my bicycle basket.'

'If you check when the next train leaves, there might be time for me to buy you a coffee. Mine's not for half an hour.'

'Well, I'll see when it goes. Won't be a minute,' she walked towards the information desk as he stood waiting. He was quite fit, she concluded, looking back at him. In a moment she gave him a thumbs-up; she had plenty of time. She waved towards the café. As she joined him he lowered his bag onto a chair.

'Grab a seat and I'll get them. What would you like?'

'A large cappuccino, please. I'd better ring the friend who's meeting me.'

'I'm being chatted up by some random bloke and I've missed the train. Sorry. I'm getting the eleven oh four instead. We'll be okay for time won't we?'

'Yeah, no worries. Random strangers at stations, could be interesting.' Gabrielle strained to hear over the over the announcements and rumbling of trains.

'Got to go. See you at twelve thirty. Byeee.'

A cup of coffee was placed in front of her.

'There you go.' He folded his long legs under the small round table to sit opposite her.

'Thanks. That's really kind.' There was a moment's silence while she looked at him.

'I'm Gabrielle, by the way. Cheers,' she raised the cup.

'Algie,' he shook his head, 'no need to comment. My parents have a lot to answer for.'

'Don't all parents?'

'Too right. One way or another. Where is this wedding? Will you be in time?'

'An old school friend is picking me up me in Winchester. I've told her I'll be an hour late but we should make it in plenty

179

of time. Everyone is meeting at a village pub for a drink.'

'I'm glad you didn't go without your shoes.'

'I was never going without my shoes. I had merely jumped out of them to dash for my bag. I was so worried it might be stolen. I'm out of work at the moment,' she confided, her mouth turning down at the corners.

'Well, it's good that it wasn't lost. You were lucky,' he gave her a cheerful grin. 'What sort of work do you do, anyway?'

She sipped the froth off the coffee. 'Mm. Marketing. Branding is my speciality. What about you?'

'I'm involved with 3D printing. It's a whole new world. Very exciting.'

'I don't know a lot about it, actually.'

'It would take too long to explain it all now. Perhaps we could have a drink one evening if you don't think I'm being too pushy?'

'Tell you what, give me your number and I'll think about it,' her voice was playful. 'Anyhow I owe you a coffee.'

'Put it in your phone then because I need to get my train in a minute. I'll be back in London after the weekend. I live in Clapham, by the way. Okay? 07705 576 298.'

'Got it.'

'Have fun at the wedding.'

She watched him walk away, tickled by the encounter. He was nice, different yet nice. But Algie, really.

While his sister was enjoying the wedding speeches and raising a glass of champagne to the bridesmaids, Peter strode along the streets near the Scimitar Club, nodding his head to the tune on his earpiece. He had needed to walk home after a day that had consisted of nothing but standing, standing, standing, feeding balls to people, hundreds of balls if anyone had counted. A static sort of Saturday, breathing for hours the warm moist, faintly chlorine scented air of the indoor courts. Out at last, his pace was as brisk as it could be in the packed streets at this hour. He accepted an evening paper from the outstretched hand of the newsboy.

'Thanks, mate.' Some days he could be physically knackered, fit for nothing but food and the telly. Right now, he felt pent up, ready to run a race or have three gruelling sets of singles with one of the other coaches. Tonight, though, he was expected home: dinner with Nina and his parents.

'It's not exactly relaxing to have you all taking over my kitchen every evening,' Carla had complained, 'so many different meals being prepared as you trail in any old time.'

Peter thought of Gabrielle with her chilled ready meals, Nina's pea-shoot salads and his own dull standbys, pasta with tuna and Spanish omelette. Mum loved cooking, so it made sense. He wasn't complaining.

Several girls looked boldly at him as they came along the pavement, eyes grazing his. He vaguely acknowledged that his height and blonde hair gave him a certain something; girls tended to look. He adjusted the racquet bag over a shoulder, put his hands in his pockets as he walked on. It was a quarter to six, the lit-up shop fronts still had tired Christmas decorations in the window; it amused him, the non-Christian cultures paying lip service to the season with a few gaudy bits of tissue paper and fairy lights. He skirted a trio of swaggering boys who seemed bent on mischief, a reckless look in their eyes. He held on to his mobile in his pocket. At that moment he felt the vibration and a beep of an alert.

Fancy a drink? Am nr Club. Edwina

She wasn't wasting any time. He'd only given her his number the other day when she'd made an excuse about being able to cancel more easily. Some instinct told him to play hard to get.

Sorry, rain check, nearly home, Peter

Another time. No worries. x The answer was immediate.

Food for thought, he raised his eyebrows. What did he want? Really, she was shameless. He decided to keep his cool, be friendly but not a pushover. At least, not for now.

He was grinning as he went on. He'd known something like this would happen. Well, he would let her do the running. He was happily in a relationship, no desire to rock the boat.

That evening he couldn't keep his hands off Nina. They were late down to dinner.

Two weeks on, all thoughts of his girlfriend were a long way from Peter's mind. After a couple of drinks in a pub, he and Edwina were in an uncomfortable clinch. Her car, parked down a quiet side street where the glow of the streetlamps was muted and the trees offered pools of darkness, was far too small and the bucket seats another obstruction. How could he tell her he had nowhere they could go? It would sound so lame.

'Anyone at your place?' he moved his head back to see her face. She pouted.

'Too risky at this time of day. Perhaps when my husband goes to Milan next week. He'll be away two nights,' she pulled his head back to kiss him.

'Your children?' in a corner of his conscience Peter hoped for escape.

'Prep school. Can you get away?'

'For a while. I'll try. Let you know next week.' He slid his hand back inside her shirt. 'I'd better go. Text or ring me in the day. Look. I've got to go now.'

The reluctance with which he moved belied his words. Finally, she turned the key in the engine and continued with the lift she had offered. He kept his hand on her thigh. She moved it between her legs and squeezed. Peter pulled it back and sat up. His mouth felt swollen with kissing. He needed to stop somewhere and have a beer. He shrank back in the seat as they neared home turf.

'Here, okay?' she flicked her eyes at him as she pulled up behind a car. She looked back again, caught his eye.

'Soon,' she told him.

'Better get going. I'll see you.' He climbed out trying not to look guilty, rehearsing a few words in case any one spotted him.

Yeah. Someone kindly dropped me off. Nice car. Edwina blew him a kiss before driving away. He wished she hadn't done that.

He might walk up to that pub on the main road. He couldn't just walk in the door at home. A quick pint was what he needed. He stood at the bar wondering what foolishness he was embarking on. He should pack it in before anything really happened. But shit, she was hot stuff. He looked at his watch and downed the rest of the beer. He had better get going. As he neared the house, he rearranged his mind to accommodate family and girlfriend, trying to convince himself he would never cheat on Nina and certainly not with a married woman with two children. Not with anyone, was what he meant.

'Peter, hello.' Terry gave him a genial look as he materialised behind the white van carrying a load of scaffolding poles that landed on the pavement with a heavy clang.

'Oh, hi Terry, how goes it?'

'Very well, thank you. How's the job?'

'Marvellous. Thank you. Marvellous.'

Terry's expression grew sombre. Was there a problem with the building work, Peter wondered?

'Carpe diem,' the voice was grave, 'I trust you remember that Peter. Terrible that plane going down. Did you hear how many died? Dreadful tragedy. You just never know.'

'Dreadful. Yeah, live for the moment. As you say, you never know. Carpe diem and all that. I'm running a bit late. Better get on in, I think.'

'Well, I'll be off now. Until tomorrow.'

'See you later.'

There was no sign of his mother in the kitchen and no smell

of cooking to make his mouth water. He was starving. On the way up to see Nina, he paused outside Carla's door. It would give him a few more minutes to compose himself.

'Mum?'

'Come in. What's up? Good day? Blue skies this afternoon.'

No matter how many times he had told her that the weather was immaterial, she insisted on believing that his coaching would be curtailed by rain. Maybe she should see the indoor courts for herself. It struck him that many of her attitudes had been fixed during his childhood and would never change. She still asked, 'Have you got your anorak?' when he left the house. Carla was lying on the bed, hefty paperback in hand. She wriggled to sit up against the padded headboard as he plonked himself down beside her.

'Yup. Fine, thanks. How's you? Feeling tired or something?'

'No, no, I've joined a book group. Thought I'd better make a start. Dad and I met this woman, Georgie, when we had dinner with the Millers up the road. She asked me join,' she frowned at the book, held it up for him to see the title. 'Rather a tome.'

'I don't suppose they read the bonkbusters in book groups. It might lead the worthies astray.'

'You are an idiot. Anyway, Nina has read this. She's going to give me a few pointers when I get further in.'

'She's quite a smart cookie under that 'I'm such a little dimwit' façade. She's a lot cleverer than me, though that's not saying much.'

"Don't be silly, darling, of course you're clever. You just missed rather a lot of school at a vital time.'

He shook off the fond gaze. 'We know perfectly well that Gaby got the brains of the family. She can run rings round me. She has had some dicks for boyfriends though. Didn't use her brains there. Is she out on the pull again tonight?'

'Don't call it that. It sounds horrible. She's having a drink with the girls from her old hockey team. Jenny, Tamsin, you know, the old gang.'

Peter swung off his feet to the floor. 'Oh yeah. I'm going up. See you in a bit. Are you still cooking tonight?'

'It won't take long. Don't panic.'

The music of Coldplay was drifting down to the landing. His footsteps slowed. In the room a joss stick burned.

'What's that pong?'

'Don't you mean hello, Nina, how are you?'

He dropped his racquet bag on the floor and collapsed on the bed, his feet hanging off the end, arms cradling his head. Nina, at a table under the window, leant over a laptop, not looking at him at all. He had feared scrutiny.

'God what a boring day. Never thought I'd say that, but sometimes the futility of what I'm doing really gets to me,' he groaned and eased off each trainer with a big toe. They landed with two thuds on the floor. 'I long for someone to coach with an iota of talent. Not oodles, just an iota.'

'Of course, I've had such a delightful day. No self-centred brides and their vampire-like mothers at all. And definitely not from ten until five-o'clock non-stop, with a pre-menstrual Melanie being sweetness and light all day long. Oh, yes, what a lovely day I've had.'

'Okay. Okay. We're both feeling like shit,' he lifted his head to look at her instead of the ceiling. 'Did something particularly bad happen or was it just the usual bollocks?'

'Just an accumulation of aggravations as Terry put it, just now. That man has empathy. He could tell I'd had it up to here; even made me this cup of tea. Sweet.'

'Come over here, Neen.'

Nina finished the sentence, wrote 'Love you xxx' to her old flatmate and tapped send. She turned and he edged across the mattress making room for her. Her skirt was a mass of red knife-edge pleats. He smoothed the fabric that spilled over his legs.

'Nice.'

'You smell of beer.'

'Just a quick one in the bar. Lie down,' he pushed gently at her shoulder but she wriggled to her feet.

'Can't. I've promised to help with the meal. You could come down too.'

'I will, in a minute,' he picked up the remote to turn on the small television that Nina had brought with her to the house. 'Just going to watch the footie for a bit.' He rolled into a more comfortable position.

Nina met Carla on the landing and was gratified to receive a warm smile.

'Hi, Nina.'

'Give me a job to do.'

'Let's go and have a look. I've planned a pork stir-fry. There isn't a great deal of preparation but I'm not about to turn down an offer of help. Perhaps you could slice the vegetables for me while I chop onions.'

In the kitchen Carla put vegetables on the worktop and reached for the chopping board.

'The beans and the courgettes?'

'Yes, please and those mushrooms, if you would. Here's a knife. Pete seemed to be looking rather pleased with himself this evening. I do hope he's settled in that job. Does he say much about it? All we get is a shrug if we ask.'

'He seems to like it. He's certainly putting in the hours.' She wiped the mushrooms with a paper towel, trying to sound upbeat. She looked up feeling Carla's eyes on her.

'Everything okay?'

'I think so.'

'Well you're both very young, far too young to be serious. Rob and I didn't get together until he was nearly thirty. A sensible age I think. Can you see the soy sauce anywhere? And I expect we need some chillies, don't we?'

'If you're fed up with me, Carla, I'll move out tomorrow. You know I didn't intend to be here all this time.'

'Don't be silly. I didn't mean that at all. Course we're not fed up with you. I said stay as long as you like and I meant it.' She touched Nina lightly on her back as she bent to the task of cutting beans into careful lengths. 'And I want to see you tucking in tonight.'

Nina straightened up, yanking down the short Fair Isle cardigan over her stomach.

'I get really bloated if I eat too much,' she rubbed her waistline. 'But I'm sure this will be delicious.'

'Now, lets get organised. The pork won't take long. Rob and Gabrielle are in the office putting some email together. She keeps rewriting her CV. I expect she's applying for another job. It's certainly taking its time. Do you want to do the stirring or lay the table? The noodles only take four minutes. I hope you're feeling hungry. You must eat you know. We don't want you fading away.'

Chapter Twenty-Two

It was a pity Rob grumbled to himself, that Louise's house was just too far along the road to get a view of it. Standing at the bay window as he had become accustomed to doing before setting off for the charity, he craned his neck again to peer in that direction, just in case. Damn. No sign of her. Steps sounded in the hall and he moved back. It was early, not yet six-thirty. Probably Gabrielle going out for a jog. She was showing some determination in this latest resolution; that was a good sign. Gabrielle and apathy were uneasy bedfellows. He poked his head into the kitchen where she was tying her shoelace, a blue trainer up on the table.

'Morning, darling girl,' he gave the back of her head a peck. 'I'm off to the Centre. See you later.'

'Just doing ma stretches then I'm outtahere,' she responded in an American accent, tossing her ponytail.

Rob slipped on his leather jacket and ran a hand through hair he had allowed to grow a little longer than usual, glancing for an acceptable moment into the hall mirror before leaving the house. Hurtfully, someone had once accused him of vanity. He darted a look to the right as he went down the steps. A few times, he'd been lucky enough to be offered a lift by Louise as she drove up to the main road on her way to the breakfast club. She always made sure to drive the old mini to the centre, leaving the Jaguar to Charles. It wiped out the exercise Rob enjoyed but it was irresistible to have her to himself, to sit side by side as neighbours and friends before she switched on her business-like persona in the drab surroundings of the hall, the refugees and homeless naturally commanding her attention. No sign of her this morning. He allowed himself a pair of gloves, pulling them on with deft hands but continued bareheaded in the chill, his breath condensing in white puffs. A low misty sky hung over London, streaked with pink in the east. No more snow, please, he prayed. The noise of aeroplanes heading for Heathrow droned loudly today. He turned up his collar and put an athletic bounce into his stride. There was still a chance she might overtake him. You are pathetic, he told himself. She would take him for the fool he was if she ever got an inkling of his admiration. A vivid memory of Angie, the mother of Rose made him cringe. Those days were well and truly over. Lesson learned a long, long time ago and the recent reminder a kick in the teeth. No, he just happened to like Louise. Besides, it was surprisingly rewarding helping out at the centre. He had found his feet at once and not only did he give practical assistance and advice on the computers with visa or job applications, he seemed to have become a sort of mentor to some of them. Not the smelly old vagrants who tried their luck with the place but the displaced families, young men with hunted looks in their eyes, bearing visible and invisible scars of a traumatic past in a faraway land. Several of the clients had opened up to him. It was humbling how they trusted him. Even Louise had commented.

'You're a good listener, Rob. It isn't easy for them to tell their stories, sometimes with very little English, not to mention the fear of being sent back. You're doing okay. Well done.'

Yes, there was something about her personality as well as her looks. She managed to be full of certainties and could defend them all right. No woolly thinking from her: she had her feet on the ground. In spite of her beauty she'd never have been taken for an airhead, the serious streak shone too strongly for that. He pulled his shoulders back: head up, best foot forward he told himself. Onward he strolled. Not many people about at this hour but always plenty of traffic. He admired the Audi R8 that purred at the lights as he crossed. Beautiful piece of engineering. He half-smiled at the driver. Lucky sod. The silver haired man reclining in his seat twitched his mouth in acknowledgement and revved the engine just a touch as the signal turned to amber. Rob watched its slow motion acceleration as the driver held back the power. Now that was a car if money was no object. He looked at his phone. Ten to seven. He would be there in five minutes.

Thank you for holding.

Rob glared at his phone then shrugged his shoulders up to his ears and released them, hoping his impatience would be replaced by calm mindfulness.

The breakfast session was nearly over and a group of women sat in a circle around the children who played quietly on the floor. Rob leaned an elbow on the table as he continued to listen to the recorded voice.

We're sorry for the delay. We will be with you shortly. It was the usual maddening experience, dealing with statutory bodies.

Why not visit us at www.thehomeoffice.org.uk?

Waiting endlessly for his telephone call to resume, Rob allowed his mind to wander.

We're sorry for the delay. We will be with you shortly.

His eyes were drawn to the only figure upright and unoccupied. He had tried to describe Dirik to Carla; he could tell from her face that there was nothing to surprise her in the account. He hadn't made her feel he was a real person, just another cardboard cut-out refugee. Nina would understand perhaps. He took the phone away from his ear, looked at it yet again, put it back to his ear and studied the young man's face, musing.

Today Dirik's cheerful smile is absent. He kicks listlessly at a child's toy dumper truck that has migrated from the play mat into the middle of the hall.

'What's up? You okay?' Rob's expression is asking a question that is ignored. He will talk to him later. He's developed a respect and a liking for the young Eritrean. His claim that al Shabaab has targeted him seems genuine. No one doubts that life in that country is a desperate affair. His journey to London has taken months. He has traversed Europe in the backs of lorries. Hidden in cramped corners, thirsty and hungry he has survived and entered Britain illegally.

At the Centre, Louise and the volunteers discuss the moral questions raised by the presence of these immigrants. Not many illegals will dare to access a place like this, where they might be reported to the authorities. So far unprocessed by the British system, (Louise and her team deliberately don't ask too many questions nor do they turn anyone away,) he has been driven here by the need for food and assistance.

Dirik's troubled eyes rest on a distant horizon when he speaks of his difficulties. His education is basic but his intelligence is obvious from a manner that is both proud and anxious. He found some manual labour for a month but that job has finished. He can't afford the rent for his share of a dormitory at a nearby hostel and Louise's pleas and pledges have been insufficient for him to retain his bed there. He has avoided the job centre because of his status but Rob is investigating a possible application for asylum. What proof does he have of persecution? he is asked. Dirik shakes his black curls once in negation. They have taken him to a lawyer to discuss his case. The man is not optimistic. The only hope at present is for him to find a manual job on the quiet and to keep out of sight of the authorities.

He catches Rob's eye. Dirik's English has come on well but he is beginning to look unkempt after a few nights of sleeping rough.

'Next week, maybe job,' he says.

'But where will you sleep?'

'Shelter, maybe,' he gives a shrug. Rob has found out that the shelters are bursting at the seams. It's a vicious circle and Dirik's grubby clothes will not endear him to employers. Rob resolves to bring in some jeans and sweatshirts from home. Peter will hardly miss them. Also, the charity shops are said to pass on unpopular items that remain on the rails for too long. The refuge is due an allocation soon. Getting him into some clean clothes will help with the job hunting. Even if Dirik is clothed decently, he needs to get a good night's sleep before long. Rob can't help comparing Peter with Dirik. All the advantages are on one side. The two young men should try swopping places for a week.

Rob shifted his phone to the other ear and watched the young man now slumped in a chair, warming his hands on a mug of tea. At last his call resumed. A harassed woman back at her desk, apologetic. He sat up, made his request and sighed as he disconnected the phone. Louise came near and he caught her eye.

'What'll happen to him do you suppose?' he looked across the room.

'He'll probably disappear off the face of the earth. They go to ground, you know: find others from the same place, rub along somehow. It's not so hard in London. There's a lot of casual work. Most employers don't ask questions. Like many of the undocumented migrants he'll scrape by on a pittance for a while and maybe get a lucky break. Worse case scenario, he'll be deported. There's an endless stream of Diriks, I'm afraid.'

Rob glanced across the tables where some of the regulars were still eating. He had noticed that they did not rush this free meal but chewed thoroughly and made it last. The amount of food his family threw away at home disgusted him. It would do his offspring good to come and help out. It might open their eyes to how spoilt they are. He too could do more to help and with the extension nearly completed he would soon have more time. He was filled by a desire to do something for these people. Back at Number 23 they have had power connected and a toilet added to the summerhouse at the bottom of the garden. That's where Dirik could stay for a few nights, until he sorted himself out.

'Louise,' impulsively he turned to her, 'would it be against regulations or anything to offer that young man a bed for a couple of nights? We've got a summerhouse in the garden going spare at the moment. Just till he gets work?'

'That's an incredibly generous thought, Rob, but really tricky without going through quite a few legal hoops. If he registers as an asylum seeker, it could actually be more straightforward but the responsibility would be considerable until his case is heard. No, it's not a good idea, I'm afraid. It would be too much to ask of you. To be honest, he's probably better off under the radar for the time being, sad though it is to admit it.'

'Stupid of me,' Rob shook his head. 'It just seems daft for some of us to have so much and at the other end of the scale there are the Diriks of this world. And so many in the same plight.'

Louise shrugged in a resigned way and turned to give her attention to a new family shyly entering the hall. Rob was frustrated. He hadn't anticipated that 'doing his bit' would stir up such a sense of the unfairness of life. He'd been so blinkered before. He adored his children of course but really they should be standing on their own two feet by now. If only Gabrielle could nail the job she was going for. And Rose. He sighed. That was another problem he couldn't keep pushing aside.

'Mr Rob. Please, I need translator.' A middle-aged man with an interview coming up: this was one of the services the Centre provided. Rob checked out the dates and put the request online.

He looked over to a newish helper in the hall, head ducked over a monitor just along from him. Much younger than any of the others and from her dark good looks her family must originate from India or Sri Lanka, somewhere like that. It took time to get to know the volunteers. He admitted he'd underestimated them at first; now he admired their lack of ostentation. It's different here, he mused, you wait for the stories. At home, people poke their noses in much more and there's no reticence. The young woman seems rather serious, doesn't smile a lot. Perhaps she's had immigration problems once. Of course her family might have been here for generations, probably as English as he is. He should be more careful about his assumptions. It wouldn't do to put his foot in it. She seems to be a bit of an IT specialist, already busy sorting out one of the vital computers. She won't usurp his role will she? Rob quashed that petty reaction and hoped for a chat later on, if he got the chance.

It seemed no time at all before he was on his way home again. The session had passed in a flash. He was pretty sure the hours in his office never sped by quite like it. Cooking, computing and counselling, the three C's he called them. That young Somali family had been in quite a state. Rob planned to go on a course to learn more about how to access help for the asylum seekers. Louise talked of 'pathways' but he still didn't have a clue. To be absolutely honest he'd never given a monkey's. Not his problem. Others would help them or kick them out: it was all the same to him. Now that he came face to face with them, got to know them, something had changed. He saw the refugees as people, not just labels used on the news. He caught the self-congratulatory note and pulled himself up. What he should be doing was listening to his conscience. He needed to speak to Rose. He shouldn't have let the last few weeks go by without a word. It wouldn't have killed him to send a brief text now and again. There was a lot of time to make up. She would be feeling shut out or forgotten and besides he was impatient to see her again. It gave him a fluttery feeling to think of her waiting for him to make a move. Her eyes had held a mute appeal when they'd parted after that lunch with Carla. Poor girl, they had kept her waiting far too long. He would have a chat, explain the situation.

He decided to stop at the nearby café on the long stretch of main road. He'd always turned up his nose at the look of it, preferring to walk on to the halfway point where the smell of freshly ground coffee at the Costa often enticed him in. He swallowed the first mouthful, grimacing. The double espresso tasted bitter. He would have done better to order a Nescafe in a place like this. He took in the downmarket décor, the tawdry lights and plastic fittings and with his index finger drew the rings that stained the table, wondering what to say. Better get on with it. He searched for the number.

'Rose. It's Rob, hi,' he put a smile into his voice.

'Dad. Rob. What should I call you?' she was excited. Hopes up.

'I think Rob? How's everything?'

'Everything's okay, thanks. And you?'

'Fine, thanks. Sorry I haven't rung before. Where do the weeks go? Still trying to overcome builder's muddle, you know. We're just waiting for the right moment to introduce you to the family. As I'm sure you understand, it's a little bit sensitive and Carla thinks it needs a careful approach. It's been rather tricky for various reasons, but we're beginning to see the wood for the trees.' (How evasive he was.) 'Of course, I'm sure that we can see more of each other in the future. Absolutely. Let's make a date very soon. In the meantime is there anything you need?'

Her voice was flat, disappointed, what he had expected.

'Not really, no. I was just hoping you know... perhaps by now. But of course I understand completely. No problem. Good to hear from you. Thanks for ringing. Take care.'

He finished his coffee, pensive, drumming a foot lightly under the table. He was sorry to hurt her, of course he was and he should have chatted for longer. She sounded slightly desperate but that was understandable. It would be put right soon, with luck. He downed his coffee with another grimace. Introduce her then integrate her, gradually. He was ready to work hard at that. He'd been hoping for Carla to come to it herself in her own good time. Nevertheless he felt uncomfortable. To be perfectly honest, he felt like a complete shit.

Rose felt tears pricking the back of her eyelids. Sod him. She clenched her jaw and sagged in the chair. Why couldn't he suggest meeting for a cup of tea or ask how she was feeling? He was just making excuses.

The extension. The builders. The children. Blah, blah, blah. Would this tune ever change? She turned back to her computer after glancing around the office at the other girls. She'd checked out their Facebook postings at the weekend. What a lovely time they had all been having. It was a rubbish feeling when you couldn't show a single photo of some fun event with your mates. Self-pity took hold of her in the familiar way. Flicking through the family gatherings on the screen had made her well up with envy. Who did she have after all? A useless mother and a stepfather who'd gone AWOL. That was how Angie always put it. Gone AWOL, as if he'd be back shortly. Only he wouldn't.

It was only ten; she had a whole day of office tedium to endure. Life wasn't fair. She closed her eyes and sat back again. No boyfriend unless you counted Luke. She had to be honest: Luke was hardly a boyfriend. There hadn't been anyone much since Ben and look how that had turned out. Her lip curled in disgust. He'd used her; that was the only word for it. And she'd begged as if she had no self-respect at all.

An email alert on the monitor changed her mood in an instant and she leaned forward. The confirmation of her place on a course on Aesthetics and Visibility in Design was exciting. It would get her away from the humdrum routine on a regular basis. As *investors in people* she had reminded her boss of the pledge in the leaflet for new personnel, *staff are encouraged to attend training programmes*. Hugo had looked annoyed then laughed.

'Hoist by my own petard.'

She put the start date in her online diary as second thoughts assailed her: she'd only applied to impress Rob but would he care? She had to believe that he would; she couldn't bear it if he didn't. Anyway, he'd rung. He'd been thinking of her and he'd rung. The classes would be inspiring and perhaps by then she might be part of a new family. Gabrielle and Peter weren't very familiar with east London: she could show them the cool pubs, the markets, some of the trendy galleries. They would be impressed. She could treat them to a meal at the Lebanese place. If only.

'Coming out at dinnertime?' Nazreen called across to her. She turned with a delighted smile.

'Yeah, sure,' Rose returned to the images she'd been manipulating. Better get it done quickly.

Chapter Twenty-Three

Each member of the Unwin family had become accustomed to sharing their lives with cocky Jacko, smiling Sean with his charming lilt and Buster with his ponytail and roll-ups, becoming familiar with them in the unbalanced relationship of employers and the workforce.

With Terry it was different; he was a larger than life character who amused them with his spouting of quotations and the daily bandying of ideas. They often asked, 'Did you hear what Terry said about the North Koreans?' Terry's obsession with current affairs revealed itself in every exchange. He brought in articles cut out of newspapers to illustrate a point that Rob and Carla were expected to consider. They shook their heads over him while admitting it was stimulating. Recently, he had asked Gabrielle to help him improve the branding of his company.

'You've made me think about it. I could do with a logo and everything.'

At first she had laughed but he was dead serious, he told her, his index finger jabbing the financial pages that lay open on the table.

'I need to move ahead of the game,' the good-natured features adopted a worried frown. 'The Poles who muscled in on the building trade look like staying so there's far more competition these days. I've got to stand out from the crowd somehow.'

'I know just what you mean,' Gabrielle told him, 'it's no

different from the big corporates. I'll have a think about it; do you a mission statement. Seriously, I will. Just let me get this job nailed first.'

On the day of a much-heralded interview, Gabrielle woke up feeling sluggish, head pounding, aching in every limb, convinced that flu had struck: typical of her luck, recently.

'Where's Mum? I don't feel very good, Dad,' she complained, hanging on to the kitchen door in her pyjamas, glum-faced. 'I'm going down with something. Some bug. I just know I won't perform well. Oh, it's sod's law that this would happen.'

'Take some cold remedy. You'll be all right. It's probably psychological; you've been building this up in your mind. Have your shower and I'll get something out for you. Is it ten thirty you've to be there?'

'But I feel awful.'

'Look it can't be helped. Get your glad rags on and you'll feel better. How are you getting there?'

'I'm driving. I know where to park and everything.'

'Here. Take this,' Rob was pouring hot water into a mug. 'Miracle-cure. There you are,' he shook the contents of a sachet into the mug and gave it a stir.

Gabrielle dragged herself back upstairs. Psychological? What rubbish. It was a cold at least but more likely flu. Her legs were lead weights and a film of sweat had sprung out on her forehead. No, she prayed, she couldn't be ill today of all days when she had a chance to land a decent job, a sought after one in fact. There were bound to be umpteen applicants.

She stood staring at the contents of the wardrobe, biting her lip. The choice she'd made earlier now seemed absurd. That red jacket would make her look like a traffic light. The dark grey suit was neat and flattering but where was her white shirt? Somehow she showered and got dressed. She piled on the make-up, sweeping on blusher to give herself some cheekbones in the puffy blur of her face. Now she looked feverish. She wiped off most of it and made do with the lightest of touches.

Just two streets away from home she was caught in a jam and the first tendrils of nerves took hold of her. She craned her neck to look beyond the line of traffic but could see no obvious cause. She peered at a street map on her phone and wondered if she dare risk a detour. She sat back, telling herself to relax. She had allowed plenty of time, calculating and recalculating when she should set off but now she began to suspect that she might be late. It was the ultimate sin; she would hardly recover from that. For ten agonising minutes she merely inched forwards. Tapping fingers on the steering wheel in consternation at the blockage, gritting her teeth and messing up her hair, doubts about her presentation began to torment her. She should have worked harder to perfect it. Her thoughts were disjointed as she struggled to remember the opening part that she'd chosen for its incisiveness. Cut to the heart of it, she had told herself.

'Please let it all come back to me,' she pleaded. Just then the queue drifted forward slowly and she snatched at the gearstick. A black cab shot past, appearing from nowhere to cut in to the line of traffic. She pressed down angrily on the horn.

'Fucking idiot,' she gestured for him to get a move on. At junction after junction, red lights were against her. What was wrong with the world this morning? Finally she could see the Endicott Bailes building up ahead. The public car park would be just beyond it. Deliverance. She indicated just as the red digital letters on the sign lit up. CAR PARK FULL. Gabrielle swore. She could feel the sweat under her arms. She opened the window and drove on with her elbows lifted. What a way to turn up. Shit, shit, shit. She revved the car, receiving the blast of a horn from behind and shot to the next set of lights before going around the block wondering why she had not foreseen all these difficulties. She looked at her watch for the twentieth time. She could just do it if she could only find somewhere. Hurray, another car park. Round and round the ramp she wound, wheels squealing, in maddening slow circles to an upper level. Who designed these places? She breathed a sigh of relief at finding an empty space. Five minutes to get there: almost impossible unless she ran. She held tight to her briefcase and went for it, clattering dangerously down the stairs and emerging at a fast trot on the pavement. She arrived in the foyer perspiring freely and out of breath.

'Mr Johnson's office please.'

Looking at her reflection in the mirrored wall of the lift she nearly despaired. Cool, calm and collected she was not but she was there, she told herself. Quickly she combed her hair and wiped away the smudged mascara and as the lift door glided open took a deep breath and stepped confidently into a large, bustling, open plan workspace. She took in faces at desks, tall windows and a girl coming towards her.

'Gabrielle Unwin?'

'That's me,' she smiled, hoping her high colour had subsided.

'I'll take you through to the boardroom. If you'd like to come along.'

She followed down an aisle between workstations, trying to compose herself. At the door the adrenaline subsided. *I know my stuff. Sock it to them.*

Three men stood waiting to greet her and she was offered a chair before they sat down in a row. The phrase three wise monkeys she dismissed at once to concentrate. She passed over some charts and launched into her presentation.

Almost at once the questions began aggressively, interrupting her spiel and thwarting her from relaxing into any kind of comfort zone. She thought scornfully that the young directors, although English, seemed to ooze American strategy from every pore. Too many bloody MBAs between them, she decided. Their comments insinuated that her methods were clunky, old fashioned: too British for the global market. She ploughed on with her pitch, justifying her position as it had been at the old company, claiming credit for successes unrecognised by the new owners. The trio of suits seemed to sneer at the examples she had chosen to illustrate her penetrating insight into the unmet needs and opportunities relating to the Endicott brand and market.

She went off at a tangent, growing desperate for some nods of appreciation, defining the purpose, identity and role of the company while its executives sat with bored expressions. One man was on her side now, playing 'good cop' as she tried not to flounder, his, the only kindly face in view.

'Give us some practical details of how you would build the strength of social engagement, build up our corporate citizenship?' he smiled encouragingly.

This Gabrielle could answer. She developed the theme with confidence and laid out her programme. Her poise was maintained but she could already smell failure as the interview was quickly wrapped up and she was charmingly dismissed.

'Thank you very much indeed for coming to see us. We will be in touch.'

Her stomach resumed its churning as she gracefully made her farewells. She knew the smiles would vanish when she turned her back. The same escort rose cheerfully from a desk to see her out. 'I hope it went well.'

'Not too bad, thanks,' she held her head up, feeling sick walking back through the main office, breathing in that buzzing atmosphere she so craved. Yet, for all she knew, they were over-worked and disillusioned. The girl was pleasant enough and Gabrielle continued to chat away full of counterfeit optimism.

What had gone wrong? The whole tone of her punchy presentation had fallen flat. Through it all, she had felt she was in a runaway car heading for a precipice. On and on she had pressed even though the faces were radiating negative vibes.

Back at the car she rested her head on the steering while she waited for the disappointment to subside. Phrases of self-justification began making a commentary. She rang Rob.

'Hello, sweetheart, how did it—'

'Dad. I messed up.'

'What do you mean? Have they told you so?'

'They didn't need to. I could tell. I wasn't on my best game. Oh Dad, I was depending on this one. I really wanted it badly.'

'Hey, don't get upset. Look on the bright side. Even if you didn't get the job, put it down to experience. Another one is bound to come up. Maybe something better and you'll be free to apply for it. I shouldn't worry about—'

'But I liked the look of it.'

'You on your way home? Why don't we go out for lunch? We can talk it all through. What do you think?'

'Thanks, Dad. I'd like that. I'll see you at home.'

Terry was keeping a lookout for Gabrielle's return. All the builders had admired the capable looking young woman twirling for them in the doorway to show off her outfit and agreed that she would be successful in the job hunt.

'Wish me luck.'

'Knock 'em dead.'

'I'd give you the job.'

'To be sure you'll get it. It's a cert.'

'Not so good?' Terry enquired. There was a wry smile in response.

'I don't know for certain yet but somehow I could tell I just wasn't what they wanted. It was demoralizing, having to go on, knowing they were not exactly in raptures about me. Never mind,' Gabrielle shrugged determined not to sound miserable, a failure. 'Something will come up. It was terribly American too, which was ghastly. I probably wouldn't have liked it anyway.'

'You're better off out of it, it sounds like,' said Terry as the work mates nodded in agreement.

'Yes, the Yanks always want their pound of flesh,' Gabrielle told them. 'It might have been the job from hell. I'm putting the kettle on. Coffee anyone?'

'Thanks. Bad luck but you must put it behind you.'

'Thanks Buster, I'll try to.'

'A Caesar salad, please.' The waitress in the little Italian restaurant in the High Street wrote down the order. Gabrielle gave her father a glum look. 'I'm definitely going down with something, Dad, my head aches horribly.'

'Well, don't give it to me. Seafood spaghetti, please,' Rob told the waiter. 'Keep plugging away; you'll survive. Now tell me about the interview.'

Father and daughter sipped their sparkling water and gazed at each other, one morose, the other with raised eyebrows inquiring.

'Oh Dad. They were horrible.'

'Come on, Gaby. Nil carburundum etc. The world is full of arseholes. What do you think went wrong? Don't feel you've got to rehash the whole thing if you don't want to. Give me a brief resumé.'

'In a word, I was rubbish.'

'Hang on. Think positive. Maybe you just didn't fit their idea of the person they wanted.'

'No. My presentation fell flat and then I found myself sounding horribly defensive when they queried things. It was awful. They were looking down their noses at me. They really weren't very nice, kept mentioning the 'American Business Ethos' whatever that means. A sort of put-down. I obviously need to do an MBA.' A baleful note crept in.

'Something else will come up. Silver linings and all that. The next company might sponsor you. Forget about the dreadful Endicotts.'

Gabrielle's mouth twitched. She extracted some tablets from a foil pack, tossed them cheerfully into her mouth and began to smile.

'Fuck them. It's their loss.'

'That's the spirit if not the language. Now, about Mum's birthday.'

'Yes we need to get organised. Have you finished the guest list? You were going to add any new London people.'

'Mm. It is more or less complete. I think I've got all the ones she'd like to have. What about the invitations?' Rob deftly wound spaghetti round his fork and speared a mussel.

'I'm picking them up from the printers the day after tomorrow. Don't worry; I'm making clear it's a surprise. How are you going to get them written without Mum seeing?'

'I'll manage. I can't wait to see her face when everyone turns up.'

They went home together talking over plans for the party. When would be the best time for the speeches? The playlist for the music was still to be done for Gabrielle was determined that the festivities should continue into the evening: there had to be something good to dance to. She longed to express herself in the usual abandoned way, the centre of attention with her uninhibited slinky moves. Running a few songs through her mind, she began to feel excited.

By late afternoon though, time was dragging as she sprawled on the bed in trying to dismiss from her mind the questions fired at her by the interviewing panel.

'Miss Unwin, Gabrielle, tell us your strategy…. Could you explain exactly how our objectives….'

Her throat was dry, her nose runny. Who would cheer her

up? Perhaps she would send Algie a bit of encouragement. They hadn't met up since the first evening together. She'd rather ignored his latest texts although they'd had a few humorous exchanges in the first place. He would be interested to hear about the interview. She would think of an upbeat comment. No way would she show her disappointment.

Had my interview today! Horrible!! Not my scene at all, luckily, she wrote, **didn't like the vibes. What u up to?**

She would have a date this evening if Algie hadn't arranged anything with his mates. She'd watch a film to pass the time and see if he replied. She typed Netflix into her laptop. Somehow she had forgotten all about her cold.

Chapter Twenty-Four

Nina, always sensitive to critical nuances, worried whether the earlier remarks about being 'far too young' were a warning shot over the bows. Carla was definitely over-protective of her son but all that 'you've both got your lives ahead of you' stuff was rubbish. The phrase had stuck in her head however. Had Pete said something? Or was Carla trying to get her out of the house? Surely not, Pete's mother had shown her nothing but kindness and his father certainly behaved as if he was fond of her. Those little jokes with her were nice. She'd loved feeling at home in Number 23. It was a long time since she'd had a proper home. She would never forgive her parents for splitting up without warning. Now, something had been spoiled; she did not feel quite as comfortable, in spite of the reassurance she gave herself. She sat in Melanie's studio on an unusually peaceful afternoon, brooding, instead of enjoying the intricate stitching she loved. She sewed a lace panel carefully into a silk bodice but her mind was elsewhere.

Something was up. Over the last few weeks Nina had become very watchful. Peter was far too easy to read to stop her from becoming suspicious. It was bad timing. She'd grown more and more in love with him over the winter and was convinced that he was right for her, long-term. To be brutally honest, she admitted, his apparent lack of funds and insecure employment had bothered her in the beginning but since getting to know the Unwins had ceased to worry her. His position as a cherished son provided her too with something that the split-up of her parents had wrenched away: the sense of belonging. She wanted Peter and had been reasonably sure he felt the same. Now something told her that he had changed. For a start, he'd never complained of being tired in his life yet some nights he crashed out before she'd even brushed her teeth. He seemed to be avoiding conversation with her. He was too careful with his phone and could not help looking up when she answered it for him, eager to get it back, a hand outstretched. Until now, it was always left lying around, often buried beneath Peter's untidy mess. These days the sound was switched off but the mobile tended to stay in his pocket to catch the brief vibration of an alert. Then he might leave the room on some pretext as he answered it. He was unreliable about coming home too. Regular as clockwork he'd never been but there was something about his expression on these occasions. He was just a little bit too Peterish. Trying hard to act normal was another way of putting it.

Nina had been cheated on in the past; she recognised the signs. Of course Peter had never sworn undying love, he'd always been like a large playful affectionate pet but she had believed that actions spoke louder than words. Had she read more into his expressive blue eyes as he gazed into hers than perhaps was really there? She had seen messages of love in those depths under his brown lashes, with the curly blond ends, that she often put her lips against as they shared the most romantic of moments. She was aware that his easy-going nature had been a foil to her, soothing the anxieties she was prone to. Her obsession with losing weight had morphed under his benign eye into just one of Nina's little foibles. The drama, even stigma of a 'disorder' had all but been extinguished. She had been getting stronger, not taking things so much to heart. Except for him of course. Times with Peter had been some of the most enjoyable, not the usual rollercoaster of her relationships. She could say anything, do anything and he would be there smiling, not the least bit perturbed.

Whatever it was, if he had his eye on someone else and his interest in Nina was fading, she was going to fight it. There was no way another girl was going to get him if she could help it. A panicky feeling had been creeping up on her recently, things getting out of control. She needed to think carefully before she lost him. Would it be counterproductive to try to beguile him again to stir up feelings that might have become drearily familiar? Should she make him jealous? It might be effective but could also backfire. No, that strategy was too risky. She chewed at a nail and wound a strand of hair round and round a finger. In the end she resolved to do the usual trick of letting her subconscious inform her actions. That was what always worked best for her. So, for the time being stay cool, enchant Pete with the little ways that tickled him. Keep him sweet and with luck, keep him keen.

Perhaps she would go to the club this evening, straight from the shop. It wasn't dark so early now; it seemed that the winter was packing away its most unpleasant tools, in retreat from the rising temperatures and the softening wind. It would be a change to meet him there. She would act unpredictably from now on. That should keep him on his toes. There was no doubt he took her for granted. She might treat him to a curry at that Indian place they'd been to once. Had she forgotten how to be fun? She would be light-hearted, absolutely certain not to provoke a heavy scene. She knew instinctively that Peter could not stand that.

It was time to go if she were to meet him at the club. She stitched the ivory thread over and over into an invisible knot and snipped off the end. She would get a bus up there and wait for him to come out.

At four thirty Peter was coaching a dozen youngsters who came straight from school every Thursday. They headed for the changing room in a shambles of outdoor clothing, weighed down by backpacks, brightly coloured trainers and racquets hanging off shoulders. In moments, they were transformed into his elite squad, bouncing across the court in warm-up exercises, cheeky comments and laughter after each routine. He enjoyed these sessions: really he was closer to them in age than many of the clients, those older men with dri-fit shirts stretched tight over the beginnings of a bulge, winter tans covering up the lack of muscle tone. Not all, of course, he corrected himself, some of the young middle-aged were active; they worked out religiously, did the weight training, put in time on the running machine and kept in trim, proud of their well-developed muscles.

His mind skated benignly over the women he taught, not dwelling on any over forty failings in the looks department; he tended to like them and according to Edwina, they all considered the new coach to be 'divine'. Peter smiled at that nonsense. He watched two of the beefy schoolgirls practising before him now, relishing their powerful ground strokes and sending down serves he'd measured at over ninety miles an hour.

'Okay you lot. Four to each court now. This is the routine I want you to follow.' And he ran through the series of shots they were to make. He moved around assessing and giving each one the encouragement that would enhance their game.

He enjoyed the repartee, able to keep it just on the right side of maintaining his authority. He was happy and so were they. This was what it was all about. He might discover a future champion, travel the world with his budding star, the next Andy Murray or some female equivalent and make his own father sit up and take notice. Rarely did he wonder what might become of him in his fifties or sixties but just occasionally his heart would fill with dread and he knew it was the future beckoning. This rare descent into a negative turn of mind would be shaken off like a dog out of the water. He even gave a little jerk of his head now to return to his usual ebullient mood.

'Come on,' he roared, 'you look as if you're hanging out the washing! Step in, hit out. Yes, that's better Giulio, good lad.'

The buzz in his pocket sent a thrill through him. He moved around until he was out of sight of the reception area and the manager who had a habit of popping up unexpectedly at the wide window in the viewing bay to survey the scene.

See u out front usual place 6pm?? Can't wait. xx

He had known it was Edwina. He shoved the mobile back in his pocket and continued the session. Guilt and excitement began their usual battle in him. Let her stew for a bit. The moment that thought surfaced, he had a vision of Edwina's small dark nipples under his fingers and knew he'd give in. Make hay while the sun shines, he told himself. What man could turn down such a juicy offering on a plate? He wasn't harming anyone after all. Far more danger to himself. He would not forget that the husband owned half the whole bloody Scimitar Club. Nerves added an extra frisson, no doubt about it. He did not know how he'd become such a risk taker. Any way he was hardly a threat to marital harmony: Eddy was perfectly happy with her alpha male. (Peter had seen a photograph of him and was under no illusions.) Besides, Nina should realize that he was still free as a bird. He'd never said a word to indicate theirs was permanent arrangement. No, to be honest, he'd taken pity on her when the flatmate chucked her out. Of course he was fond, more than fond—

'Hey, you two. Stop mucking about. Right. We will finish off with a game. Come over here. Come on, everybody over here!'

After he had dispatched the teenagers, he stood in the reception area as members greeted each other with upmarket voices and air-kisses while he filled in his mobile phone diary from the bookings on the club website, exchanging banter with

Lucia at reception. He stepped away and sent a brief response before deleting the messages. Just for half an hour, he promised himself.

Nina, on the crowded, jolting bus contemplated the other passengers, bundled in padded anoraks and sturdy woollen coats. She hated the cold, her chilblains and people sniffing. The year should have only eleven months and do away with the miseries of late winter in her opinion. She looked out of the murky window at the dispiriting sight of shops she could not afford to shop in and candlelit restaurants with clipped bay trees at the entrance, mostly out of reach as well. Between the smart doorways resigned figures sat with bowls, ready to climb into their sleeping bags after rush hour. Ah, she was not badly off, just tired and the anxiety gnawing a little.

Perhaps she should let Peter go. Struggling to hang on to him was undignified. In spite of her introspection, she became conscious of the stare from the man across the aisle. She'd been told once that she resembled a remote angel on a Christmas card. She cultivated her otherworldly look, her pale lips in a perfect bow, a serene expression masking the insecurities, the fair hair she could see mirrored in the glass, shining like a halo. She looked past her reflection, continuing to stare out, unseeing now, lost in a reverie of romantic renunciation. Snap out of it, she told herself. She felt for her phone. Perhaps she should send Peter a text; she didn't want to miss him. She saw that it was only ten to six; she would be there before he finished. Now she became absorbed by emails from her boss who was making the most of the quietest time of year to spend ten days in Antigua. Lucky Melanie. Nina frowned resentfully as she read. *Lazing on the beach, rum punch and coral reefs!* No need to rub it in thank you, Mel.

Here was the stop. She held on while the bus braked and swung in to the kerb and she hopped off, dodging the waiting queue. It would only take a minute to cut down the road and reach the club. Peter would be touched that she'd come to meet him and they could have a nice evening on their own for a change. She'd almost forgotten the reason for her journey.

There were a number of people about. Up ahead, a group of teenagers with swaggering postures and loud voices were loitering outside the building. Nina's head cocked to one side. Was that Peter just beyond them? A figure had come swiftly on to the street from the club entrance and continued straight across, dodging the traffic. That was surely Pete, in his navy fleece, the bright red and blue racquet bag over a shoulder. He disappeared down a small road opposite.

Damn, she swore, hurrying on, I'm going to miss him. She stared after him, waiting for a break in the traffic but a taxi roared past at speed then car followed car. She hovered impatiently, moving from side to side and peering down the road until she caught sight of him again walking on. Suddenly he ducked down to climb into a sports car that at once nosed out into the stream of cars heading the opposite way.

Nina stood feeling like a fool. Silly idiot, she ought to have rung him. He'd obviously been offered a lift this evening. Never mind, no point in ringing him now. She would walk home; she could do with the exercise.

She changed her mind a minute later biting her lip. Daft not to give him a bell. They could still meet up; have that meal. She pulled the mobile out of her pocket, tapped two or three times and waited for it to ring. It went straight to answer phone. He must have forgotten to turn it on after coaching. Bother, bother, bother. Perhaps she would catch a bus home after all.

She felt miserably guilty for not walking, a fat lump sitting there as the bus inched along, stop-start through the rush hour traffic. She watched cyclists overtaking the stalled traffic and wondered about getting a bike. She resolved to get off early, walk the last few blocks and work off some calories. Nina berated herself again for her stupidity: she should have let him know she was on her way. And who was the owner of that little silver car? Dejected, she sank into the jealous conjectures that were never far from the surface.

It was nearly half past six when she pushed open the door of Number 23. Her mouth watered at the smell of cooking. She went into the steamy kitchen where Carla was reading the evening paper, perched against the worktop.

'Any one seen Pete?' she asked Carla.

'No, I haven't been in long. Sorry. Cup of tea?'

'Oh, thanks. Any one seen Pete?' she asked the builders.

'No love, He's not back as far as we know.'

Nina wondered what he would say. If she asked where he'd been he might lie. If she told him she'd gone to meet him, he might think she was checking up on him. How complicated it was. She'd wait and see what he said. Did she feel like telling Carla that she'd caught a glimpse of him? No.

Half an hour later there was a commotion at the door and Rob and Pete came in with Terry.

'Come on through, Terry. I want to talk about the automatic blinds.'

The three of them entered before she had time to escape upstairs. She would slip out in a moment; it was difficult to smile, her mouth wouldn't obey.

'Shall I put the kettle on again?' she asked Carla.

'I was just about to. Thanks.'

Peter ruffled her hair in greeting as the men discussed details of the building programme. He plonked himself down in a chair, giving a sigh. He's waiting for me to ask what kept him, Nina decided. I jolly well won't. If he can't volunteer the information himself...

'What's been happening today?' Peter jumped up to check on the builders' progress, going out to the back door for a moment.

'Coming on well now, Terry,' his banal words were spoken

lightly while Nina's existence unravelled, putting tea bags in the pot, on the other side of the room.

'Yes, indeed, yes, indeed. Fortune favours the brave. We gambled on the weather holding up and have thus been able to complete phase two,' he gave a satisfied grin.

'So the boss is chuffed,' Peter looked at his father for confirmation.

Rob was helping to distribute mugs. 'Any one for a slice of toast?'

'No, Rob, it's suppertime soon. There's a lamb joint in the oven. I put it in hours ago. It's a Jamie Oliver recipe. I heard him on the radio this morning. Complete with veg, so there's hardly anything to do,' Carla sounded impatient. What was up with her, Nina wondered?

'Brilliant,' Rob conceded, putting the lid back on the bread bin. He stroked the smooth wood appreciatively. 'Where's Gabrielle?'

'I think she went to meet that fellow from Waterloo.'

'Wellington?'

'Very good Dad,' chuckled Peter, noticing that Nina didn't smile. Generally she was the greatest fan of his father's witticisms. Something was bugging her; he'd better be tread carefully.

'How was your day, my love?' Peter reached out to stroke her arm as he passed.

'As well as could be expected considering my boss is sunning herself in the Caribbean. Actually, I rather like being alone there. I pretend I'm in my own little atelier and that people are queuing up for my designs and that a celebrity is going to wear one down the aisle.'

'Yes, a famous film star or Russian billionaire's fiancée,' Peter joined in the fantasy as he often did. Nina smiled at him, disturbing thoughts forgotten for a while.

Chapter Twenty-Five

Carla arrived home from an afternoon spent in the local library. She had not taken much notice of its bulk on the street, its wide Victorian entrance. On an impulse she had stopped outside for a few moments; an empty crisp packet swirled around her feet in an eddy of cold wind as she decided to go in and register at the desk. There were a few people sitting at tables and two of the four computers were in use. She found the reference section and browsed the shelves, unsure what she was looking for. The self-help books she ignored. She knew what was wrong with her; there was no easy remedy. She began to realize that she wanted to study something. Hobbies and Crafts engaged her for a while and the variety on offer seemed well removed from the lop-sided pots she'd thumbed out decades ago. Was it just too predictable to say she wanted to get her brain working again? The wide books on Fine Art with their colourful fat spines drew her attention. She lugged one about Giacometti to a table and soon became engrossed in photographs of his drawings and sculptures. Although slightly repelled by the images at first she began to appreciate the unease and uncertainty that emanated from the pages. Aware that she was preparing herself for seeing some of his work in the flesh quite soon, she resolved to do her homework more often, pleased that she could add depth to her response to an artist. She took a cup of water from the fountain and lingered over some other books, elated at her discovery of a resource she'd overlooked and a place that she could use and enjoy. It was years since she'd studied but if she was a fairly blank sheet she must at very least have some potential. She smiled at the direction of her thoughts, reiterating her conclusion: she might never be a great authority on anything but that didn't mean she couldn't absorb a few facts and opinions.

At Number 23 the arc lights were bright in the dusk, reflecting her image around the recent glazing on the extension. Only one section left to complete, Carla noted, casting her eye over the day's progress. She squinted as one spotlight shone too brightly in her direction. That she did not need. Vanity, she reproved herself but still moved away, looking beyond the dazzle. There was Terry with his back to her, working alone on the far side. She filled the kettle and picked up a note from the table. An untidy scrawl told her that Peter, Nina and Gabrielle were meeting up to see a film. There was no sign of Rob yet. Terry began to turn off the lights as he finished and she waited for him to come to the door. He pulled off his boots before stepping inside in thick hand knitted socks.

'Come on in,' Carla said. 'I've got the kettle on.' She wondered who might have made those warm socks for him.

'Lovely,' he smiled his slow smile. On this particular evening he was quieter than usual. Everything was quieter than usual. Carla passed Terry the mug of tea. She pushed across the sugar basin, watching as he slowly stirred a spoonful. Round and round went the spoon for too long. She folded her arms in self-defence as a premonition struck her.

'You're looking pensive,' she said. He gave his hands a rub, cold from the outdoors. There was no preamble.

'Who's that girl, came yesterday? Looked just like Gabrielle. Cousin is she?'

Too late to cover her reaction, she was startled then prevaricated, getting out the biscuit tin and opening it. Swiss maids in dirndls danced round the sides. The tin was an unexpected reminder of afternoons leaning against the stove in the Old Manor on a cold winter's day, scones warming in the oven.

'Biscuit?' she offered. 'Oh yes, yes,' she improvised the vague answer to his question, covering up her shock, dipping the shortbread finger into her tea. 'Why? She was here?' she took care to smile a little.

'Yes. Yes, she was. Yesterday afternoon,' he shifted his weight, popped the remainder of the biscuit in his mouth.

'Was anyone in? What did she say?' It was an effort not to sound shrill.

'Nina let her in. No one else was about,' he paused. 'Funny thing.'

'Oh? Did you speak to her?'

'Not really, no. I'll tell you what happened. The three of us were about to pack in for the night. I'd just taken out some of the tools.' Terry was looking obliquely towards the dark square beyond the plastic. Carla waited.

'I saw this girl at the door, while I was locking the van. Nina let her in. I was back out there in a couple of minutes.' He jerked his head at the outside. "Well, bless my cotton socks," I told them, the lads. I couldn't help looking at her. "For Chrissakes, don't stare," I said. "Give it a minute. I'll be damned." He mimed how they'd cautiously raised their eyes to peer. 'I asked, "d'you see the face on that one? I thought it was Gabrielle, nearly said hello. Must be a cousin or something. Peas in a pod, aren't they? A looker, too. Don't stare," I had to say again, their eyes were on stalks. "Hurry up with that wiring," I told them. "It's getting dark out here." No, we didn't put on the light on for a minute. A bit nosy we must have been, I don't know why. That Nina.' Terry shook his head once more.

'Pretty girl herself, even if she's all skin and bone. I suppose it's the fashion. "Back to the job you flaming shirkers," I said; they were standing around still gawping. "Ok ok. It was my fault this time, I know, the engineer will be here Monday." He digressed, 'That snow was a bugger.' He looked at Carla. 'Then I heard something. What was that? Were they having an argument? I was sure I heard something kicking off in here. Quiet now we were, having a bit of a listen. Couldn't quite catch it but Nina is laying down the law. You could tell that much. Oh dear.' He shook his head. 'The other one is crying now. What to do? Ah, I hate to see a girl cry like that. I told 'em, "I'm going to nip inside. Just for a sec." Nosy bugger, you'll think.' Again he looked apologetically at Carla who raised her eyebrows, waiting.

'It'll be all kiss and make up in a minute, I was sure. That's girls for you isn't it? A spat and then friends again. She's a dead ringer for your Gabrielle, all right, that girl.'

'Did you say there was an argument?'

'I'd gone back out. "Time to knock off, lads," I told them. "What was all that about? The argy bargy?" they wanted to know.'

'That's what I'm wondering.'

Terry frowned, 'I don't know, Carla. I was trying to work it out. I could hear her being given her marching orders. The dark haired one. " You'd better clear off before they come back." That baby voice of Nina's, all bossy. I thought you might want to know. It didn't seem right. You can tell me it's none of my business but a girl crying like that. So I looked in to say I was putting the kettle on and did they want a brew? Very cool, she was, Nina. Doesn't say boo to a goose, usually. Just looks at you with those big eyes. Not last night. Cold as ice they were. And other the girl in a right two and eight. Well, she left then, didn't Nina say?'

'I haven't really seen her today. I expect she'll explain.' Why hadn't she said anything? 'Thanks for mentioning it, Terry. You know these girls. It will sort itself out no doubt. Well, I'd better get on.'

'Me too, Carla. Thanks for the cuppa. See you tomorrow.'

How dare she turn up here? Carla raged. She paced back and forth. She'd better talk to Rob. She knew she'd been too stubborn about the girl. It was time to give a little. Time to tell Gabrielle and Peter. Then it struck her and her heart sank. By now, of course, they would know all about Rose.

All day long, Rose had suffered agonies of remorse as she reviewed her actions. In the rush to work in the morning she had managed to put off considering what an idiot she'd been. Gradually however, the sinking feelings she'd had to endure in the past over other thoughtless and irrational acts came creeping back. Had her behaviour driven Adrian to leave her mother? Had she never learned to look before leaping? Rob would be livid. He would toss her aside. If only that awful girl hadn't been there. Why hadn't Rose turned tail and fled, the moment the door was opened by a stranger? How she rued the impetuosity that had sent her in a headlong dash after work to present herself to the Unwins. What had she hoped to achieve, a welcome with open arms? Rose no longer knew what she had expected. The conviction that had grown and grown over the afternoon before, had dwindled in a moment to total bemusement at finding herself being given a hard time by some jumped up kid, a friend or a lodger. Who the hell was she anyway and why had she shown no sympathy for Rose? Other people dropped in on friends without such dire consequences. She'd never felt so miserable, so convinced she'd fucked up. A tear escaped and trickled down her cheek. She brushed it away, taking in all the impassive faces in the office staring into space or at their monitors. They wouldn't give a monkey's anyway. The questions repeated themselves, taunting her.

Later, after a surprisingly productive morning at her computer, she gave up regretting her ill-considered visit and began to lay the blame on Rob and Carla for being utterly insensitive. She stood outside on the pavement, smoking a cigarette she'd cadged off the janitor as a cold wind cooled the take-away coffee and came at last to a conclusion that satisfied her. She'd forced their hand. Her brother and sister would know all about her by now. A meeting could not be far away. After all, she'd hardly committed a crime by hoping to catch them at home when she happened to be passing by. She exhaled a long plume of smoke. She felt a great deal more positive already.

Rob drove back up the motorway with an agreeable sense of satisfaction with his day. He had been gratified to be invited back to Gabrielle's old boarding school to address a group of sixth formers, part of the careers advice programme. He enjoyed the students hanging on his words, or so he believed, projecting the photographs and trying to inspire them. His enthusiasm had been infectious, he hoped, promoting a career in architecture as a marvellous way of life. It felt good to share his experience with the bright eager-beavers who asked serious questions and chuckled at his quips.

Afterwards, he dined in the canteen with some of the staff and youngsters amidst the rattling of school cutlery and the tables filling up with chattering pupils. They continued to quiz him, making a pleasant change. After all, who actually listened to him any more?

He had popped in to his old practice on his way to the school. That had been a bit of an effort, making out what a great time he was having since the move. Still it was early days, that over-used phrase. He thought he'd played the part okay, energetically embracing the new, while ruefully recounting the brushes with disaster.

'This will make you laugh. You know we wanted to be nearer the kids, see a bit more of them? Peter's found a new coaching post, in our part of town so it made sense, to him, to move in with us for a while. Not five minutes later, Gaby loses her job and you remember that ludicrously expensive flat she bought last year? Naturally, she can't pay the mortgage, so she's letting it out and has moved in with us too. Not quite what we'd expected.'

'Ah. The boomerang kids,' Hugh said, nodding, 'someone should have warned you.'

'We didn't sign up for that, did we, when we had kids?' Martha put in.

'Nor the bank of mum and dad,' chorused Steven and Catherine who had gathered round as well. Rob felt a powerful twinge of nostalgia for his old place there. What exactly had possessed him to leave? He should have hung on for a few more commissions.

'As I said, I'm giving a talk to the sixth form. Better get on. Great to see you. Give my regards to Phil. By the way, there will be an invitation to Carla's sixtieth in a week or two. We can have a good catch up then.'

The house had bloody well better look good he told himself, a few hours later, taking the slip road for home. He pictured the plan on his drawing board. They were nearly there. Glass extensions were not unusual, but the USP of his spectacular design would be the ground-breaking affordability, he was certain.

A sudden squall of snow hit the windscreen and he cut down the speed. The wipers made dark streaks in the white. He hoped desperately that bad weather would not hamper the work again. Once the vast amount of glazing was completed, they would be able to wrap things up quite quickly. There would need to be a lot of instant gardening to transform the site. He would get on to the suppliers next week. Get everything ordered. He also needed to put some good pictures on the web. After the party there should be some interest, with a bit of luck. Besides, it would be a great relief to get the builders out of the house. Good though they were, the sense of chaos that threatened to engulf all the family had been exacerbated by their presence.

A barrage of heavy raindrops was driving away the snow. He must remember to tell Gabrielle the bits of news about her old school. Oh Gabrielle, he thought with a pang.

He entered the house with a blast of wintry air and wet footprints. He retraced his path to the mat and removed his shoes.

'Carla, you there?'

'In here,' she called. She turned from the television to give him an odd look. A young actor he vaguely recognised was spouting sentimental twaddle and clutching an Oscar to his breast.

'This is for everyone,' he concluded tearfully, 'I shall be merely the keeper of it.'

'We ought to go and see that, when things settle down,' he looked back at her, 'someone told me it's a brilliant film.'

'It will be on the TV soon.'

What was wrong now? 'The talk went down well,' he said, aware he was sounding his own trumpet. She should have asked anyway.

'Oh good.' Did she sound sarcastic?

'All the old faces still in evidence?'

'I suppose so. The kids were great, though. Very interested. Gratifying really. Want a coffee?'

'No,' she frowned, 'Listen. I must tell you.' She turned off the television and looked up at him. 'I think Rose came round to the house.'

'Christ,' he was shocked. 'How the hell did she find out where we are?'

'I've no idea. According to Terry, a Gabrielle lookalike was here, yesterday, arguing with Nina. He assumed she was a niece of ours.'

'Have you spoken to Nina?'

'It's odd because she didn't say a word to me though I only saw her for a second this morning. I hadn't heard about it from Terry then. I'm sure she will have told Pete by now. I've been hoping you'd get back before they do. I can't think what got in to Rose. And why would they argue? I can't understand it.'

Rob was pacing up and down. He sat heavily on the arm of the sofa.

'Shit. Shit. Shit. We should have told them straight away.'

'I expect so. You can blame me. I probably got it all wrong.'

All through the film, Nina wondered how on earth to explain about the visit from Rose. In a panic to get rid of the girl before anyone came home, she had handled it badly and she was desperate now to break the news in a way that did not show her in too poor a light. Why had she acted as she had, trying to get her out before anyone came home? Did she think she was doing Rob a favour?

'Aren't you enjoying it?' Peter whispered as she fidgeted and sighed beside him. She nodded and stared at the screen unable to be distracted from the task ahead. If she waited to speak to Rob first, Peter would be puzzled as to her silence on the matter for over twenty-four hours. Now she bitterly regretted not telling him at once but the circumstances had not been right. It would have to be this evening straight after the film.

'I don't believe it. I refuse to believe it,' Gabrielle's usually animated face was slack-jawed in astonishment. She stared at her brother across the small pub table. 'Dad?'

'Tell us exactly what she said again.'

'First she said who she was. Then she said she's met your dad and mum once and she basically thought it was time to meet you. Oh, she was cocky enough, definitely pleased with herself. I was going to speak to Rob first, in case it wasn't true—'

'It isn't true. No way.'

'Gaby, we don't know that. Why would anyone make up a thing like that?'

'It seemed to be true,' Nina looked miserably at them. 'I'm sorry.'

The three sat frowning. Peter looked up from studying his pint.

'He's the last person I would expect to behave like that.'

'That's what I think,' Nina added.

Gabrielle took a vicious swig from her glass; her face was clouded with painful emotions. 'I can't believe it. Not Dad.'

The three of them linked arms as they marched along the wide pavements, Peter pressing the girls to his side as if to form a bulwark against the world and its bombshells. Gabrielle, in scuffed boots and a man's old overcoat fastened with a leather belt, clumped heavily, he almost had to drag her forward. Nina squeezed his arm, fearful of his parents' reaction and deciding to disappear upstairs as soon as they reached the house.

At the door, Peter said, 'Right, let's do it' and ushered them forward.

'Oh God, I can hear them coming in. Quick! Think what you're going to say. I'll get them into the kitchen.' Carla shot towards the door. 'Hi gang. What about a cup of something? How was the cinema?'

The three of them trailed after her pulling off their coats with unhappy faces.

'Dad wants to talk to you. Here he is.'

Gabrielle sat on the arm of a chair, her face closed as her father entered. Nina was about to slip out, having edged around Rob but he held her arm gently.

'You may as well stay too.'

Her instinct to bolt thwarted, she sat down and rested her head in her hands. Carla caught hold of Peter but he shook her off and she sat abruptly in the armchair looking upset. Rob stood where he could observe his children. The kettle rumbled to a crescendo before turning itself off with click.

'I'm not sure what you've heard,' he addressed them with a grave expression. He paused and Nina raised her head and spoke in a timid voice.

'I didn't know what to do. I'm sorry. I should have talked to you first.'

'Yes, you should,' Carla shot at her.

'Why didn't you tell us, Dad?' Peter's face was a mask of incomprehension.

'Obviously we were waiting for a good moment to talk to you. It just never seemed to be the right time. Look. I only knew myself, quite recently, that Rose was looking for me. She wrote me a letter, which was a complete shock. Before you start, let me give you the facts. I had never met the girl until now. I fully admit I made a dreadful mistake a long, long time ago and I was led to believe that there would be no consequences. She was to be a much loved child brought up in a happy family.'

'We would rather not hear any sordid details,' Gabrielle was curt, on the verge of tears.

'Don't interrupt, I'm trying to explain.' Rob perched his backside on the kitchen worktop.

'Spare us the explanations or excuses, Dad. What does she want, this bloody girl?'

'Let's all calm down,' Carla put in, 'we had no idea that Rose had the address or that she would turn up out of the blue.'

'Rose.' The name was spat contemptuously and Gabrielle stared into the distance.

'Can we just get back to the facts?' Rob folded his arms and waited. 'Mum and I have met her once and as far as we can gather, all she wants is to meet you and get to know us a little.'

'Why now? And how old is she? Frankly, I'm really hurt and

disappointed in you Dad. I can't believe you've behaved like this,' Gabrielle's voice wobbled. 'I wouldn't have believed you could be such a shit.'

'Look. I know. I apologise. Wholeheartedly. I couldn't be more sorry. I made an appalling mistake, a long time ago.' He met Gaby's eyes. 'She'd be, what, a little younger than you.' Peter was swinging a racquet round and round on a forefinger, not looking at his father. Carla's eyes were fastened on the floor.

'It's not something any of us ever envisaged but I think we should try to be sensible about it.' Rob was trying to remain composed. 'It's happened and as a family we can decide what to do about it.'

'Don't you mean *her*?'

'No need to be aggressive, Gaby.'

'If you want my opinion you can tell her to get lost. She's got her own family. We don't need her trying to wangle her way into ours. I'm sure you must agree with me, Mum,' Gabrielle looked pointedly at her mother.

'Why don't we give ourselves a little time to get used to the idea?' Carla's tone was neutral. Only the set of her mouth gave away the control she was maintaining. 'It's true we were about to tell you. It's just that things seemed to be a bit upset at the moment with job insecurities, flat worries and so on. We were only waiting for the right moment. Nina, perhaps you might like to enlighten us as to what happened the other evening. I do think you should have said something to us yesterday. Terry had to tell me that we'd had a visitor, for heaven's sake.'

Nina welled up; she couldn't bear being criticised.

'I'm really sorry. I wasn't sure what to do. She sort of barged in. When she told me who she was I just had the feeling I should get her out of the house before any of you came back... I had no idea who knew about her. I had no idea what to say to her. I suppose I panicked a bit, thinking of the upset she could cause. She said she wanted to meet you two.' Nina, eyes brimming, looked at her boyfriend and at Gaby. 'She said she had a right to meet them. I didn't like the sound of that: I told her to clear off. I didn't have a chance to tell you last night. I was going to, this evening,' she threw an anguished look at Rob. 'Then we rushed off to the cinema.'

'I don't like the sound of it either,' Gaby said. 'She's got no rights at all. It's a fucking nerve.'

Rob snapped, 'How many times do I have to tell you to mind your language?' He took a breath. 'I know it's not easy but she's a nice enough girl, as your mother will attest. She probably got over-emotional and behaved in a silly, thoughtless fashion. We can deal with this. She just wants to get to know us. It needn't be a problem if we are all very grown up about it. Can we agree to invite her to meet you?' he hoped his reasonable tones would defuse the moment.

'I am certainly not meeting her,' said Gaby. 'Barging into our home. Who does she think she is? I feel horrible, shell-shocked. How could you, Dad?'

'Don't be silly Gaby. We've just got to accept it whether we like it or not. I suppose we'll get used to the idea of her,' Pete said, 'and if she turns out to be a right cow, we can give her the cold shoulder later.'

'I can't believe I'm hearing this,' Gabrielle walked out.

'Let's meet her Gaby and get it over and done with,' Peter called after her. The door into the sitting room slammed. Nina shrank back hoping no one would attack her, still unable to comprehend the turn of events and that the Unwins, her ideal family, seemed to be combusting before her eyes. She looked anxiously around waiting for the next outburst.

'We'll talk about it tomorrow. I've got my early start; I must get to bed,' Rob too made his escape.

Carla held open her hands in a despairing gesture. 'I'm sorry it's all such a mess, Pete.'

Peter shrugged his shoulders and spoke with a catch in his

voice. 'He's let you down Mum, that's what's so hard to forgive. Come on Neen, let's go up.'

'Well, that went down like a lead balloon,' Rob aimed his clothes at the laundry basket, tossing them angrily across the room. 'I told you we should break it to them straight away. Everything would have settled down by now.'

'I know. I know. We should have told them sooner,' Carla replied in a low voice, slumped on the edge of the bed and undoing the strap on her shoe, 'but they'll simmer down. We knew Gaby would be upset but she'll probably come round. It's knocked you off your pedestal, I suppose.'

'Look. Lots of their friend's parents have gone through extremely messy divorces. That's far more damaging. It's a shock for Gaby and Pete but it's not the end of the world.' He stalked into the en-suite bathroom. The shower door shut with a bang and he stood unmoving under the powerful jet of water.

Carla gazed after him filled with a surge of resentment, thinking *he's washing away his sins. He'll assume we can all move on now.* Abruptly, she kicked off the second shoe and went out onto the landing to call up the stairs.

'Night, darling. Goodnight, Nina.'

A door opened above and Peter called down.

'Sleep well, Mum and no worrying, OK? We'll sort it.'

She stood on the landing, her shoulders sagging, listening for faint sounds from below. She steeled herself, went back down to face Gabrielle. Arms hugging her knees, Gabrielle with stony profile, was determined not to look round. Sitting down beside her, Carla could see the reddened eyes. She tried to hug the stiff figure. Their heads touched gently as Gabrielle responded for a second.

'Dad really hates to upset his girl. He's mortified about all this.'

'How can you forgive him Mum? He doesn't deserve it.'

'It all happened so long ago. He was a kid, I suppose. It just seems too late to be that angry,' she lied. 'I want everything to settle down and life to go forwards. Moving here was meant to be our big thing. I want to reclaim that.'

'He just seems so, so matter of fact about it, when actually, it's shattering. Did he know about her all along? It makes our childhood seem so false. It's horrible to think of someone else laying claim to my dad. I don't think I can bear it,' her shoulders convulsed as she broke down. Carla held her.

'You can talk to him about it, Gaby. He knew there was a child on the way but that was it. He was promised no repercussions. He genuinely believed that. Now, get off to bed. It won't seem so bad in the morning. Night, night, sweetheart.'

'Night, Mum, I'll go up soon. I won't be able to sleep a wink. I think I hate him.'

Carla took a glass of water with her. She was feeling so low, so emptied out it was an effort to drag herself to the bedroom, one stair at a time. Only the glow of her bedside light illuminated a corner of the room. A little patch of safety, it seemed. A few minutes later, she slid quietly under the duvet and turned off the switch. She lay on her back staring at the pale rectangle of the window. London was never pitch black. Rob was already asleep or pretending to be. She listened. Tonight he was turned away, his breathing calm while all at once she was agitated, seething with the anger she had kept hidden all evening. She forced herself to lie motionless, her fists clenched, concentrating on long slow inhalations, a lamentation of sighs, she would call it; the wry notion sidled in, diminishing the misery to the usual dull ache.

She awoke, cold and stiff. Drowsily, she pulled the duvet around her neck and snuggled down trying to go back to sleep. A chill seeped through the bedclothes. Had something happened to the heating?

They had told the children. The knowledge came as a great relief. She slipped an arm out to reach for the clock. It was just after seven. Rob was asleep still, turned away to the other side of the bed. She slid out, put on her dressing gown and opened the door without a sound, padded quietly downstairs and going to the thermostat found it turned right down. Of course, last night she'd got so worked up and overheated she had moved the dial. Now the boiler began its subtle throbbing. Going through to the kitchen, the words from the night before surfaced. It was anguish pure and simple that had overtaken her as they spoke about Rose. The disbelief on their faces nearly made her weep. But, at least, now they knew. What attitudes would they strike today? If only she could minimise the pain of it, kiss it better as if they were babies. Rob would no doubt slope off early; Nina was always out by nine. She'd try to have a word with her two before they all dispersed. They'd need to explore their reactions, express all the vitriol. They would accuse, show disgust, outrage, bafflement even. It would do them good to get it out of their systems if they could. She was tense with misgivings that a far greater storm was yet to break.

Chapter Twenty-Six

It was early evening the following day and Rob was rattling through the contents of a drawer in the kitchen when Carla appeared in a dark red sweater dress. A long gold chain and two bangles gleamed. Black suede ankle boots gave her a youthful look. After the sullen silence from Gabrielle this morning and the glowering brush off from Peter when she'd tried to raise the subject, she vowed to let them simmer down. She went across the kitchen to put some bread into the toaster. She'd better eat something before the theatre.

Rob had given up his search and leaned against the worktop. She could feel his eyes on her. As she moved past, he touched the small of her back lightly. So, he was taken in by her cool demeanour, happy to avoid another uncomfortable conversation.

'You're looking smart.'

'I'm going to that play tonight. I did tell you. Look it's on the board.'

'Who with?' his question was just on the petulant side of teasing. 'You didn't ask me to join you,' hands went into his pockets waiting for the justification.

'I knew you wouldn't want to. It's one of those progressive things. You'd hate it.'

'It might be nice to have been asked.'

'I'll read you the blurb and see if you want to insist on that.'

'Go on then.'

Did he think she was trying to cut him out of everything?

She put down the jar she was holding and began to dig about in her bag.

'Look, here it is,' she picked up her reading glasses from the table and after a quick glimpse towards the garden, began.

'Chock-full of meta-theatrical games for those who enjoy that sort of thing. The performers deconstruct their own characters.'

'Enough. I give in. Sounds worse than dreadful. I only hope you enjoy it. Are you going with anyone?' Rob started hunting through another drawer.

'What are you looking for? Only some of the Arts Club lot, you know, I told you about them. I got roped in at that meeting after New Year. You must remember. I'm going early because we're all having a drink first.'

'I should think you'll need one. Where's the garlic press? It should be here somewhere.'

'There's food in the fridge for you.'

'I know but having spotted the sausages, I fancy making some of those rosemary and garlic roast potatoes.'

'Oh, all right,' she took the garlic press from a magnetic strip on the wall. 'Look, it's up here.' She gazed out again, taking in the changes, aware of the lighter evening. 'They've got on well today. And tomorrow that comes down. It will be a bit awkward though. Let's try to keep out of their way during the daytime.'

Rob was staring out through the plastic too, a bag of potatoes balanced on one hand then tossed to the other.

'Yes. Nearly done now. For which we will all give thanks. God, I'm beginning to sound like Terry.'

'He tells me it should be finished in about three weeks.'

'Um. Not completely convinced but we'll see. Still, nearly done as I say. Do you know if the kids are going to be in tonight?' His voice was low and his eyes held hers. 'How were they this morning?'

'Looking pretty miserable, as you'd expect. Pete thinks you're an unmitigated bastard and Gabrielle is in a state of shock. Nina's not back yet. I can't see her eating those potatoes. Gabrielle might be back for supper. She didn't say. I suppose she didn't speak to you this morning?'

'Barely,' his shoulders slumped a little, 'she was always as stubborn as a mule. When she makes up her mind to be difficult...'

Carla's toast popped up. They both stared at it.

'What she needs is A, a job and B, a man. Then she wouldn't take everything to heart so.'

'She would no doubt take umbrage at your suggestion that a man would help. But not any man; she's got enough of those buzzing round. But a decent chap, someone who will stick around, that she doesn't get tired of in five minutes. Then I couldn't agree with you more.' Carla stopped and looked at him properly. 'As Nina would say, Gabrielle is not in a good place. I'm not sure it helps, her being at home. When we saw less of her she was ... busy, happy. You know,' she sat down with the toast and a jar of peanut butter. 'Oh never mind. We are all adjusting I suppose.'

'Are you? Are you sure?' Rob was looking intently at her. She started spreading the toast, sitting turned away from him. She ate greedily; she had forgotten how delicious peanut butter tasted. Rob shrugged, opening and closing cupboard doors. They did not speak as she ate but when she stood to put her plate away he insisted, 'Carla are you okay with it all now?'

Funny how we speak in such evasive terms, Carla mused. It's always *it* or *the situation* or *what's happened* never the bald terminology that might make people feel uncomfortable. *Illegitimate. Love child.* The words speared her. They were not even the right words.

'Yes. I'm perfectly fine. Got to go. We're meeting at a quarter to seven. I should be back about half ten.' She started for the door, went back and gave him a peck on the cheek. As his hand came up to her waist, she moved away.

'They've forgotten the lights out there; you'd better turn them off. I'll see you later.'

Why did it infuriate her so when he asked if she was all right? *Of course I'm not all right. I may never be all right.* Rose's mother could have been the start of a long line of other women. The past was a closed door until someone opened a crack and out came an infidelity, a girl, a life turned upside down. He wanted everything resolved so he could go back to his earlier, oh so pleasant existence, virtually the same but for an extra daughter. She could just imagine him thinking, is that so much to ask?

'Is that so much to ask?' Rob breathed out his frustration as the door closed behind her. All he wanted was a quiet life. If only women weren't so emotional. Look how calmly Pete had taken the news of Rose. Carla was wrong. Peter seemed almost ready to meet her. At least that was something. Rob refused to think about Gabrielle who would always be awkward if that was one of the options. He had spoiled her. Daddy's special girl, always. She would come round in the end. She just had to.

Silence ebbed and flowed in the deserted house. He could do some work on his website but it didn't appeal today. Perhaps Nina would be in soon. She was often the first and would slink upstairs if no one spotted her. Quiet little thing, he had a soft spot for her. She and Pete were far too young to be serious, even though people used to marry in their early twenties. It was different in those days. Peter needed to find his way in life; he could hardly take on any responsibilities at present. Rob crushed the garlic and began to put his potato dish together. He might have a glass of wine. He'd felt a great sense of relief all day; he would celebrate with a drink.

Smokers from the pub thronged the pavement. Carla made her way round several groups, trying not to breathe in the clouds of cigarette fumes and pushed open the door, feeling awkward as she searched for a familiar face. Again she needed to manoeuvre and slide through the crowd blocking access to the bar, mostly young people, fresh from their offices and noisily ebullient. Where was her party? She tried to shrug off her jacket; it was warm in the crush. She cursed her lack of height as usual, standing on tiptoe, craning this way and that before spotting them in a corner. She edged right up to the bar passing through a wall of suited young men, ties in their pockets and pints in their hands and tried to catch the barman's eye, holding her hand up as if she were in class. He was busy serving everyone but her. She squeezed her way along the counter, keeping her eyes on him. Another barman, mixing cocktails in desultory fashion watched customers in the mirror that ran the length of the room. Put a bit of effort in, Carla felt like saying. People were calling out their orders. Surely if she stared long enough, one of them had to notice her. She supposed it was the phenomenon she'd heard about: the invisibility of the old. Dammit, she wasn't old.

'Gin and tonic please.'

'Two white wines.'

Her voice was drowned by a giggling order from a rosy faced girl who had leaned towards the barman, waving the empty glasses rather too close to Carla. She held herself stiffly, determined not to give ground.

'I was first. A gin and tonic please.'

'Sorry, did I barge in?' A disarming smile and a lurch back was offered.

'G and T?' the barman asked Carla, winking at the tipsy girl.

'Thank you,' she gave the girl a prim smile.

Clutching her drink at last, Carla managed to make her way over to the group. She relaxed under their welcoming looks as they moved up for her in the circle.

'Lively spot,' commented one.

'I know. It took me ages to get a drink. Cheers,' Carla took a sip and began to enjoy herself.

'Did you see the review? Apparently the acting is outstanding.'

'I read out some of it to my husband. He was very relieved he hadn't got a ticket.' She was gratified that they laughed.

They walked together up the road to the theatre. Soon the small talk would soon be over and she could sit quietly and lose herself in the play, distracting herself from scenes of the evening before that ran on a loop in her head. She was delighted that Harry, the nice man, had arrived in the nick of time and had ended up in the seat next to hers. They exchanged a smile and she sat back as the curtain rose.

The production was certainly startling. She could barely watch, looking away or stopping the view with her hand as a series of traumatic events was enacted on stage. Abuse, a killing, a series of emotional torments made her shudder. Once or twice she shared a grimace with Harry. There was nothing left to the imagination, she concluded, wondering if there was any link between them all, the characters did not appear to know each other. Things became even less clear as an older actor delivered a monologue about examining the present from perspective of the past. Was that even possible? During the performance she ran a few lines of her own through her head, anticipating the end when the group would all shuffle up the aisle, no doubt making comments on the performance. It wouldn't do to have no opinion. She would try to think of something positive; the words 'exciting' and 'immediate' came to mind. 'Deadly' and 'unconvincing' on the other hand also surfaced. She came to the conclusion that she really did not have a lot to say. She struggled to remember what the review had made of it. Carla began to feel very sleepy.

Suddenly a round of applause announced the final curtain. Swiftly it drew back and the actors made their bows. Surely she hadn't nodded off? She clapped enthusiastically, giving sideways looks on either side. Harry winked at her. Had he seen her fast asleep?

With a colluding smile he leaned across, 'Better give them some encouragement,' his mouth twitched. The clapping slowly died down.

'Rather fascinating, didn't you think?' Carla turned to ask Heather, an earnest woman in her fifties, who had sat with clasped hands throughout the play.

'Splendid. Very moving,' came her verdict. 'They generated so much emotion,' she added, her own feelings bubbling just beneath the surface. She dashed away a tear.

'Are you okay?' Carla held her arm.

'Yes, yes. Silly of me. Must have been cathartic.'

At that moment the whole row stood and began to vacate the seats.

'Are you rushing off?' Harry asked.

'Why, do people go for a drink?'

'Nothing to stop us doing so,' he said quietly with a smile.

'Only my husband sitting at home.'

'Ah.'

His mouth twitched again with amusement and the faintest hint of regret.

'See you at the next one, I hope.'

Carla was caught up in the group for a few minutes saying their goodbyes.

'I'm so glad I came. That was really interesting. See you at the next one.'

'Don't forget we welcome suggestions for outings.'

Carla went home, wondering if she was a mug to sit through a production of such dubious merit. She was sure that's what Rob would say. She tried to think of something funny to make him laugh.

Over breakfast she managed to chuckle, reading the comments that members of the group were posting on their Facebook page. She was making the effort to keep things cheerful.

'Pseuds Corner or what?' she commented to Rob. 'Actually I'm sure some of them are tongue in cheek. This can't be serious can it?'

'The ill-fated isolated characters are doomed to be outsiders even while they seek to obliterate their true natures in order to meld with society.' She put down her mobile to butter a slice of toast. 'As far as I could tell, they gave full reign to their rather unpleasant true natures.'

'Are you sure you were watching the same play?'

Carla smiled, took a bite and looked at the emails again.

'Some fatuous observations on the human condition which left me cold. Harry.'

'Honesty at last,' Rob observed. He was looking drained; perhaps he needed some sun. His skin was sallow, almost tinged with grey instead of its usual olive.

'Are you all right? You look a bit tired. A rotten night? Did you drink all that wine?' she glanced at the empty bottle beside the bin.

'Pete might have had a glass,' he dismissed the accusation in her words.

'How did he seem?'

'He didn't broach the subject and neither did I. He was acting fine, normal, just a hint of uneasiness in his expression, avoiding a heart to heart. I think they've taken to watching films upstairs on the laptop.'

She looked thoughtful, gazing into the distance for a moment before flicking through the emails again.

'All very entertaining, anyway. You must come to the next one. It's got Kenneth Branagh in it. That's bound to be good.

I'm now a friend of The National, so I can get priority booking.'

'As long as you think I will like it,' said Rob, 'then I'm up for it.'

'You haven't exactly embraced the cultural scene yet.'

'Too much going on. But I will. Louise was only saying the other day, we should all go to the cinema.'

'We owe them. I suppose we'd better have them back soon. They were very welcoming.'

'All in good time. We might just wait for the party. Invite everyone. Not long now.'

'I'm not sure. The whole idea puts us under too much pressure. We aren't even absolutely certain when the merry men will be done,' she looked back at the screen.

'Let's not worry about it now.'

'Everyone knows we've got builders; it's not as if we're ignoring them.'

'I know. But they're all curious about the new house.'

'There's no rush.'

'Let's not stress over it. A party will do the job. Get them all here at once. Done and dusted.'

'Well. We'll see,' she did not rule it out but party or no party, she was determined it should be up to her.

Chapter Twenty-Seven

Was this what retirement was all about? The unusual sight a few days later, of Rob lounging about in the sitting room, disturbed her. Friends had joked about couples finding it hard to adjust to the constant presence of partners around the house. Carla stared at him, hoping it would rouse him to get up and do something. Why was some one else's inactivity so provoking? He was lying on the sofa, reading very, very slowly on the iPad.

'Where d'you get to this morning?'

'I spent a couple of hours at the Sudanese embassy with one of our people who's trying to get a new passport. Hopeless task. The poor woman is completely discouraged. Unlike many, she actually wants to go home.'

'What are you looking at? And you've got your shoes on,' she hadn't meant to speak in that tone of voice.

'I'm reading about life as an asylum seeker, the processes, hoops I suppose that they have to jump through.'

'You're getting awfully involved in that centre,' she fished the tea bag out of her mug, gave it a doubtful look and sipped cautiously, trying green tea for its supposed therapeutic benefits.

'I simply want to be better informed. What the rules are. Who gets to stay and who gets kicked out.' He had looked away from the screen for a moment then sat up, swinging his feet onto the coffee table. 'It's interesting.'

'It sounds rather like the dilemma we have here at home. I

jest.'

'True but that will sort itself out in its own time.'

'In the meantime the kids should pull their weight a bit more. Gabrielle is completely unhelpful,' Carla looked at the door.

'While Peter bends over backwards to do his bit?'

'Nina does offer at any rate. She's a sweet girl but he seems to take her for granted all the time.'

'Don't interfere. They'll work it out or not. I see she's here every night now.'

'She sort of materialised in his slipstream. There wasn't much we could do.'

Rob got up and turned off the tablet. His hair stuck up at the back giving him a boyish earnest look.

'We're the lucky ones. Even with the kids home we still have a spare room. The detention centres are horrendous.'

Carla said nothing. He was stating the obvious; it was the answers that were needed. It occurred to her that Rob was becoming just a little sanctimonious. Louise's influence, she supposed.

'The policies are in a mess,' he reverted to his earlier theme but least he was animated. She tidied up the magazines and mugs to take to the kitchen and looked back at Rob who stared into space for a moment before following her. Some of this concern for the refugees could be directed to his own family; with them he appeared disengaged.

They stood side by side for a moment to watch the workmen. A cement mixer turned kerthunk, kerthunk on the muddy grass. Sean and Jacko stretched measuring tape along lengths of wood.

'Haven't you anything to be getting on with?' she asked him. 'What about the apartment scheme?'

'Waiting for planning of course. As for home, it's just awkward! I can't do much in the garden while they are beavering away and I can't lock myself in the office all day either. If I so much as glance out of the window they seem to make a concerted effort to look busy. They probably aren't too keen on us having a bird's eye view of their every move, either. Still, they're hard workers; at least while we're about. He's a likeable chap, is Terry, don't you think? A rough diamond, in the best sense of the word. Clever too. Any idea what happened to the wife? I assume there must have been one at one time. He's mentioned a daughter in Australia.'

'I'm not sure but I get the impression he lives alone, don't you? There's a married son in London, definitely.' Carla stood beside him at the plastic sheet; drizzle ran down on the outside beginning to blur the view. She was very conscious of Rob beside her. Although they slept in the same bed, the distance between them was unbridgeable. He turned away from the awkward proximity.

'Mm. Right. Must try to get on. I'm going to work on a new idea I've had.'

Rob went through the hall to his office, a monastic space that had once been a family dining room. Scrupulously tidy, it was furnished with an ergonomically designed chair in brown leather, his solid walnut desk, an AppleMac computer and an extremely sleek and expensive cabinet for his files. He still took pleasure in its simplicity.

Carla winced as she took another sip from the mug. She peered into its yellow depths. Like pee. Was all this just because she was approaching sixty? She remembered the money she had spent on face creams and makeup, the daily reminder as they sat on her dressing table. She vowed to use them up, every last drop and then see if her wrinkles had diminished. She was aware she was becoming susceptible, not to the dream of eternal youth but more reasonably, the dream of eternal middle age. Every day she was assailed by exhortations to stay in shape and headlines about the latest superfood, a ubiquitous, inspired catchphrase from the advertising world. She and Rob, succumbing to the hype, had introduced goji berries to their muesli and Gabrielle was urging them to buy an expensive juicer.

She had better get started on writing up the minutes of the last meeting of the Arts Society. The secretary was away skiing; she was doing well for her age certainly, one of those breezy types whose parents had owned a chalet in Méribel, decades ahead of the glitterati and who'd learnt to ski before she could walk.

Carla was due out later at the sub-committee meeting on finance. Though why there needed to be a meeting to discuss the healthy balance sheet, she was not sure. She wondered if meetings were sometimes scheduled to feed the self-importance of the attendees. Turning the question on herself, she admitted to a desire to seem busy and needed.

Rob returned from the drop-in centre his face alight. He leaned against the kitchen units.

'We're doing a fund raising quiz at the hall. I thought we could make up a team. The whole family.'

His enthusiasm grated and she had to walk around his eager body, all enthusiastic gestures.

'Look, you're in the way. I assumed, having abandoned village life, we were escaping all the Harvest Festivals, the fetes every damn summer, the pantos. I was getting tired of the meals on wheels rota and those wretched coffee mornings.'

'You used to love all that. You hated to be left out. Anyway, it's hardly the same.'

'For heaven's sake. Of all things! I'm no good at—'

'That's not the point. It's supporting the centre and God knows we need all the funds we can get. I've got to go. There's no way I can get out of it. That's why I thought we could take the kids and make up a family team. With Nina of course.'

'You must be joking. They'll never agree.'

'I'll ask them about it. It will do us all good to be a gang again. It's ages since we all went out together. Besides, it will be over early and they can still go and do their own thing.'

'You can but try.'

'It should be fun. And we will meet some more people. I'll put it to them all tonight. Let's see if they have a social conscience.'

Carla was sceptical. The atmosphere in the house still prickled with resentment since the news about Rose; dismissive comments and sour asides accompanied any mention of her. Besides which, hearing him on the phone to Louise was unsettling: the tone of his voice suggested warm collusion while quiet laughter punctuated the call.

As Carla prepared the meal that evening, he announced that the young had agreed to the quiz. 'Gabrielle's to bring a friend to make up the team. I told you they would come. So that's decided. Now, what can I do to help?'

'Well, I'm amazed,' Carla said, passing over a peeler and a bag of carrots, 'I suppose it's a chance to do something together for once that isn't sitting round the kitchen table arguing while demolishing a ton of food.'

'Um. Speaking of tons of food, could we make a chilli con carne for twenty?'

'You didn't mention that—'

'I'll do it. You needn't worry. Louise says it's easy. Just tell me how much stuff to buy.'

At least it would increase his repertoire. She was a little weary of his 'signature dish,' a tagine that required its own special pot and the methodical measurement and grinding of spices in a pestle and mortar.

Carla's look softened as her two children came chattering through the door. She took in the striped purple and yellow bell-bottoms and the matted woollen jumper that barely grazed Gabrielle's waist. Her outfits were becoming increasingly colourful and mismatched. Gabrielle was harking back to her rebellious teenage years when conforming to school uniform was unthinkable.

'Is it okay if I invite Emil?' she asked, leaning against the cooker. 'He LOVES this sort of thing. He'll think it's very retro, a quiz evening. And, he'll increase the IQ rating of our team by about fifty per cent. Everyone knows his brain is the size of a warehouse.'

'We're not there to win necessarily,' Peter hoisted himself to sit on the worktop. 'Do you have to be so competitive all the time?'

'It's all for fun,' said Rob firmly, 'but Emil is welcome. He'll lend a multi-cultural aspect to our team.'

'Dad. Really.'

'Find out if he's free. We haven't seen him for ages. It will be nice to catch up.'

Nina glided in, looking astoundingly pretty tonight Carla thought, feeling sorry that the girl's mother seldom saw her. She put an arm round her shoulders.

'You look very nice.'

'Oh, not really, this is so old.' She looked at Rob. 'I hope I don't disgrace the team. I panic even if I know the answer.'

'Course not. Don't be silly. We all chuck answers in. No one gets put on the spot.'

The five of them squashed into the car on the Saturday night. Rob had nagged them to leave in good time, as they would hit the tail end of rush hour. It was stop-start all the way. Gabrielle moaned, convinced it was her fate to be forever impeded by lumbering vehicles; the nightmare of the journey to her last interview had scarcely faded over the past ten days. The brief letter of rejection had been tossed in the bin with a defiant shake of her head. Peter, in the front passenger seat was weighed down by a huge cast iron pot of food that Rob had managed to cook under scant instruction from Carla and a recipe on the Internet. Peter hoped the heavy lid would prevent spillages but had taken the precaution of spreading two tea towels over his lap. He gave a running commentary on the state of the contents swishing about as the car turned and braked, protesting at the uneven progress. Eventually, Rob squeezed into the hidden parking spot behind the hall and they clambered out and walked round to an effusive welcome from Charles and Louise on duty at the door.

'Wonderful to see you all,' Louise kissed Carla on each cheek. 'You must be Gabrielle and... so glad you've come to join in.'

'And this is Nina and Peter our son.'

After giving each of them a kiss, Louise excused herself to move on to the next arrivals. Charles shook hands and leaning forward with his good ear, had the young repeat their names. Carla had not seen the couple recently and touched by the warmth, was bolstered: they were making friends. Some others amongst the crowd waved and grinned. The noisy hubbub was cheerful. Places were claimed with bags and scarves. Their table was near the stage, only a short distance from the quizmaster himself and his two acolytes who presided from on high. Blue damask curtains framed the tableau of judges who stood ready with a laptop and three pints of beer laid out before them.

Rob unpacked glasses and dispensed wine to his party before he abandoned them to greet the other volunteers from his Monday and Wednesday mornings. He beckoned Carla over and other halves were duly introduced. The young people looked more at ease when Emil arrived. He had been part of the gang with Gabrielle at Reading University. They formed a distinct little group with plenty to talk about. The average age of the crowd was nudging fifty, Nina reckoned.

'Please sit down everyone. Please take your seats,' called out Louise a few minutes later. She seemed to be everywhere at once, getting tables organised, looking young and attractive in a loose white shirt and short black and white check skirt, her hair tawny with expensive streaks. Rob covertly studied the faces on her table with a calculating eye, asking Carla if she knew who they were.

'Of course not, how would I?' she said, looking away, aware that Rob would have liked to be among the chosen few. Soon the chairs filled up and at seven thirty, loud knocks rang out and the chatter subsided. The proceedings began with an explanation of the rules from Charles in his mildly authoritarian manner.

'First and foremost the judges decision is final.' He stared fiercely over their heads to emphasise the point, then grinned.

The door gave a loud squeak and a rattle as a couple bustled in with a large platter covered in silver foil.

'Take your seats quickly. I'm just going through the rules. I suppose I'd better begin again.' A collective chuckle encouraged Charles.

'Please appoint someone in your team to write down the answers. Team collaboration will choose one answer. A single answer only. No eavesdropping on nearby tables.'

'As if we would,' called out a man in a tweed jacket.

Gabrielle was poised, waiting in the wings for her star turn, while Nina giggled nervously. Peter rocked back on his chair until his mother shook her head at him.

'I'm glad you could join us,' Carla whispered to Emil.

'You'll find I'm clueless about sport,' he murmured with a self-deprecating smile. She tried to remember if Gabrielle had ever gone out with him. Her daughter could do a lot worse. He was clever, well paid…

'Question number one. There are ten questions in each section and we will go through the answers after every ten. So, question number one. I trust you are all ready with your pencils. You may find the early questions relatively easy. This is to help you get into the swing of it.'

'Oh, do get on with it,' a low voice complained.

'First question. Name the president of Russia before Putin.'

'Sorry. Didn't quite catch that. Say again old chap,' a well-spoken, elderly man requested.

'Who was the president of Russia before Putin?'

'Was that Gorbachev?' came a stage whisper from the same contestant who was roundly shushed by his team.

'Who was president? Who was it?' A tide of murmurs flowed around the hall. Rob had answered it just as Emil scribbled down the name and passed it round. He was not going to be overheard by anyone nearby.

'Ah,' said Nina, passing it on to Carla.

'Yeltsin, Boris Yeltsin.' Peter mouthed the words. Emil gave him a thumbs-up. They all nodded as if they were sure. Carla wrote it down on the form.

'Which is the largest bone in the human body?'

'Easy,' a sound of relief as every table got the answer and put it down.

'Which planet is nearest the sun?'

Grins were exchanged as they continued with all ten questions. The quizmaster called out the answers and they sat back feeling smug. Ten out of ten. A fresh bottle of wine was passed around. It was working; Rob caught Carla's eye with a pleased glint.

The team had relaxed into a coherent whole by the time the supper was announced. All were enjoying themselves. Nina contributed on a question about a famous showjumper; Peter remembered a scientific snippet that had them all raising eyebrows; no one felt ignored or ignorant. In a short lull after the chilli, Louise made sure to introduce the Unwins to her friends, bringing couples over for a moment. It was rather gratifying to be treated like minor celebrities by the queen bee and Carla was glad that she'd dressed up for the occasion.

'Do meet our lovely new neighbours, the Unwins. Carla and Rob—the absolute angel is helping at my Centre regularly,' she gave him a conspiratorial smile, 'and their charming family and friends of course. Please meet Donna and Francois,' and a moment later, 'William and Viv, such old friends of ours from Belvedere St.' It was quite difficult to collect the pudding when a stream of people were smiling and asking the usual questions.

'Where were you before?'

'How do you like it here?'

'Rob's an architect. You should see their new extension. Amazing.'

By round four, Peter had grown loud and ebullient, insisting on an answer considered ridiculous by the team.

'I think therefore I am. I'm certain it's the Dalai Lama.'

'Rubbish.'

'I'm sure that not right.'

'Wrong. Wrong.'

'It's on the tip of my tongue.'

'I know. I know! It's Descartes not The Dalai Lama,' the stage whisper came from Gabrielle.

'That's right.' Emil gave her another thumbs up, nodding eagerly.

'Could you kindly repeat the question?' the old deaf one repeated once more.

'Perhaps someone in your team could enlighten you?' Charles was getting a little tetchy. 'If everyone could be quiet and listen, you might hear better.'

Duly reprimanded, a hush fell over the participants as the remaining rounds were completed and marked. At a disagreement about one of the answers, dissension spread around the hall, heads nodding or shaking vehemently.

'The Quizmaster's opinion is final,' Charles reiterated

loudly, standing his ground. The contestant sat back with a mutter and crossed his arms in denial. His team shrugged their shoulders and began to count the score again. Carla watched as Louise circulated, collecting all the papers, making each table roar with laughter as she moved on, a lithe eye-catching figure. Was she witty as well?

The scores were announced to a roar from the winning team, 'Universally Challenged,' one of several names that made the Unwins feel they had failed in the humour stakes. Enthusiastic applause accompanied the winners to the stage to receive the prize of a case of Chilean red. The organisers were thanked to raucous cheers and Rob's team raised their hands, calling 'high five' for coming fourth, amid much self-congratulation and analysis. Driving home, regret struck Rob like a door slamming on the convivial evening. Crowds stood outside pubs and young people dawdled, chatting on corners. The thronged Friday night streets and the bright shop windows jarred with his sudden change of mood. Rose could have been with them. He glanced in his mirror to see Carla in the back. It was hard to read her expression. Perhaps her mind was elsewhere, though the others were talking loudly, in high spirits. Saying anything would only spoil the jollity. He resolved to contact Rose before another day went by. Conscience salved, he joined in the banter. 'Don't tell me which way to go. I do this all the time. I see I have a carful of know-alls...'

The following day, Rose tore downstairs and finding the door unlocked, went straight in to Luke's flat. Looking around, she called out to the closed bathroom door, 'Luke, Luke, guess what? Are you in there?'

The sound of flushing made her retreat to the other end of the room where she shoved aside a pile of clothes to sit on the sagging arm of a chair, smoothing her hair with a hand and composing herself.

'Don't tell me. Let me guess,' he said, doing up his flies and hitching up the waistband of his trousers. 'Our father who art not in heaven has answered your prayer.'

'Don't be mean. He has! He has. Let me read it to you. Oh, you don't want to hear.'

'Go on then,' he flipped the ring pull on a can of coke.

'I don't need to read it out. I just wanted to tell you I've been invited for dinner. Well, it says supper and it's on Friday week. Not long to wait,' she concluded almost bouncing up and down on the chair.

'Sorry, d'you want one?' Luke indicated his coke. 'That's cool, babe, really cool. You get your foot in door; get your name in the will next. Don't forget your mates when you're an heiress.'

Rose had not confessed the shameful weakness of her visit to the Unwins' home.

'Don't be daft. Hey. What about a bottle of wine and a take-away?' She jumped up to peer inside the fridge. 'You haven't got a thing in here.'

'Can't tonight,' Luke did not elaborate, he merely reached for his jacket from the back of a chair. 'So, you've got your invite. I hope it pans out for you, Rosie girl.'

From the landing she watched him skip down and out of the door. She went back up to her flat, refusing to be downcast. She might call in on her mother after work tomorrow, prove to her that the Unwins were keen to see her again. She knew she'd make it in the end; all they'd needed was a little nudge.

Chapter Twenty-Eight

You might be interested in some of these!

Oh really, do you think so? In her bedroom Gabrielle slumped against the headboard with her feet up, trying to quell her indignation with the agency. It was a few days since the quiz evening. The glow of affection among the family members had quickly evaporated when her father had informed them all that he had invited Rose to dinner the following week. He had gone straight out to avoid a row.

Gabrielle looked down the list of low-level vacancies the recruitment agency had sent that morning, scowling at the chirpy covering note. Her instinct was to grab her mobile to protest and had even found the number before reason prevailed. Her hand dropped submissively, knowing she could not afford to upset anyone who might be useful. She took a deep breath and tried to shut out the loud and insistent noise of drilling and the intermittent piercing blasts that rattled the windows. She got off the bed and went down to the kitchen to complain. A frown flitted across Carla's face as she looked up from emptying the dishwasher and Gabrielle almost refrained, suspecting that Carla was bracing herself.

'The racket is a bit much, today,' Carla offered, a glass bowl in her hand. 'I can't imagine what they're doing.'

'Whatever it is, it's bloody loud. I know you think I do nothing but moan,' Gabrielle began, moderating her exasperation, 'but I've been talking to that agency woman again. She needs such a kick up the arse. They all make these airy-fairy promises and then simply don't deliver. I've made it clear to them that I'm not going to apply for some piddling little job that I'm completely over-qualified for. Really, Mum, you should see the selection they sent me today. They're just a joke,' she leaned over the sink to drink from the tap.

'Sometimes it's worth getting in anywhere so that you can dazzle them with your brilliance and be promoted, fast-tracked or whatever,' Carla wrapped her cardigan closer as if for protection and waited, peering now into the fridge, contemplating the collection of yoghurts, packs of cheese and bags of vegetables.

'Yeah, yeah,' Gabrielle wiped her chin with a tea towel. 'What are you looking for?' she continued, the exasperation mounting. At once, the misery about her dad flooded in. Yes, it was still there under every aspect of life; she could not let go of the subject. In fact she had convinced herself of some extra grievances against him; she was ready to let fly with a barrage of them, if she could ever pin him down, he was so evasive. She was struggling to relate to her new image of him and as for Mum's restraint that was an added irritant that made the tears well up when she was least expecting it. Was her mother feeling nothing?

A sudden silence fell beyond the plastic sheet and she moved forward for a better view of the two men and an enormous sheet of glass.

'Oh my God, look at that. Anyway, I suppose I can do just as well job hunting online. Sorry to go on, Mum. Look, I'll take deep breaths. Some stress-busting yoga is what I need,' and she stuck out her chest and hollowed her stomach. She let her shoulders sag for the roll-down, exhaling all the daily provocations and the profounder woes that beset her as she let her head hang low and folded herself in two. Now she stretched to the ceiling before curling down again to touch her toes. Swinging arms up she abandoned the moment of calm.

'God. That agency woman gets on my nerves. I'm sure SHE enjoys her nice cushy number.' Her breath hissed then she swallowed, 'Life is so… first my job and then Dad. I still can't believe it about him.'

She lay down on the rug and began another exercise, waiting for the criticism that was sure to come. She gave it half a minute as she lifted her pelvis into a bridge and sent one black clad leg to soar in the air and drift down before repeating it with the other leg. Then she rested her back on the floor. Carla was looking out at the builders.

'Do you have to do that in here? You'll distract the men. Honestly, Gabrielle, you do behave in the most inappropriate way.'

Gabrielle continued with scissor movements. 'They can't see. They're far too busy to notice. Dad was cracking the whip earlier and now he's vanished. He's never in any more.' She began the fifty stomach crunches she'd vowed to complete each day. Carla turned away and ran a tap over some carrots, displeasure radiating from her stiff figure.

'Can you honestly tell me, Mum,' she just had to ask, 'that you're happy about this bloody girl coming?'

'Can you keep your voice down? You know, it will only hang over us if we don't give her the benefit of the doubt.'

The reasonable argument had already been aired several times but Gabrielle sat cross-legged, pursing her lips, biting back a retort.

'After all, it's not exactly her fault that we're in this situation.' Carla's voice was poisonous.

Immediately she could tell that her mother had let slip the mask and she dived in to encourage honesty.

'She could have let sleeping dogs lie.'

Carla however, restrained herself, obviously regretting the tone in which she had just spoken and began to backtrack.

'I met her the once and she seemed pretty harmless, quite

sweet, in fact. I think she just wants a bit of recognition.'

'What if she steals Dad away from his real family?'

'Don't be melodramatic, darling. She's probably been thinking about making contact for years and needs acknowledgement or something. Nobody is going to be stolen, as you put it.'

'Well, I don't want to acknowledge her and I don't see why I should. She might inveigle him into leaving her all his money, for example,' she sank back to the floor hugging one knee to her chest then the other, regretting in her turn that she had chosen such a mercenary argument.

'Just get it over with,' Carla retorted. 'No one wants to do this but we really haven't got a—'

'I do have a choice. You're forgetting that.'

'You could do it for Dad. You know he's very upset to have put us all in this situation.'

'Is he? You surprise me. I think to him it's all a fucking inconvenience.'

'Do you have to swear all the time? No, you're quite wrong,' Carla seemed determined to stick up for him now. 'Don't prejudge the situation. We may find that we all like her and that she's no problem.'

'I wish I thought you truly believed that. Have you any idea how awful it's going to be for me and Pete? I don't see why I'm expected to be pally with her. I might not even turn up to meet her, let alone sit round the dinner table, making polite chit-chat. I'll never forgive Dad for putting us through this.'

'If you take my advice, not to make a song and a dance about it, we'll work through it. She only wants to meet you, for God's sake. Let's wait and see what happens.' Carla sat down at the table and opened the registration form for the new cooker. 'It may not be such a big deal after all.'

'Not a big deal that I'll have to share my father from now on with some jumped up interloper whose been snooping around here?'

She stood up, pleased with the parting shot, unable to resist a glance at the audience for her histrionics: the men who looked away at once.

'Why don't you go and shout at your father instead of me?' Carla asked in reasonable tones. At that, Gabrielle departed, pulling down her skimpy top to close the gap over her bellybutton, a belated attempt at dignity. Was she the only one in the family who understood the enormity of what they were being asked to accept?

'That's a pity. I was enjoying the floorshow,' Sean remarked quietly to Buster, outside. 'Makes my day that girl does.'

'A bit of a show-off don't you think?' Buster secretly fancied Gabrielle.

'Legs like those, why shouldn't she? Did you see that? Another argument it looks like. Definitely looked like a row.'

'Let me tell you about life,' Terry lowered his behind onto a sawhorse, the better to reflect. 'Mothers and daughters engage in a power struggle. The young woman begins to flex her intellectual muscles; likes to argy-bargy, contradicts everything the parents hold sacred. But a father, now, he will be indulgent to his daughter. The mother will rise to the bait and take a stand. Then there's a clash as each tries to assert their personality. When a girl's beauty overtakes the older woman, it's a recipe for trouble,' he concluded.

'And sons?' prompted Jacko.

'Yeah. The mummy's boy,' chipped in Buster.

'Ah, they're always the apple of the mother's eye. Take Peter. Dads usually compensate for that. Try to toughen them up by being harsh; you've seen it I'm sure. But in my opinion, he's a good lad, Peter, still finding his way. They just take longer to grow up. He's got no airs and graces for one thing,' he stood up to indicate the chat was over.

On the other side of the plastic sheet Carla sniffed as she continued chopping onions. It's all me, me, me, she reflected. Gabrielle assumes that because I'm not making a fuss, I feel perfectly happy to go along with it. Little does she know.

She assembled a beef casserole, frying onions and meat before adding stock and a little red wine. She slid the pot onto the lowest shelf in the oven to cook slowly and set the timer. Tidying up took a few minutes; then she was finished and she looked over the builders' heads to the blue sky. Finally, the weather was offering a pseudo spring. There was a constant drip, drip from the leafless branches. In the extension they were finishing off the carpentry. The wine cellar was ready to be fitted out.

Carla checked the list on the blackboard. Mundane appointments she was grateful for. Read BOOK. Committee Meeting 6pm.

She'd better get on with the latest book club choice before too late. Not today, maybe tomorrow: her body was clamouring for its walk, the bright day beckoning. Then the Artfart meeting as Rob had christened it. So she'd be out again this evening. Let matters simmer down before the next Unwin family conference. Perhaps she should write it on the board for tomorrow.

Rose glanced quickly over her shoulder. Everyone in the office was occupied and she could continue browsing the net for examples of world famous architecture. She scribbled a few notes on a pad, key names that she recognised even though she had failed earlier to think of them. Gehry, Frank Lloyd Wright, Zaha Hahid of course: she marvelled at some of the iconic structures on the screen. Wow, the Crystal Cathedral in California, she couldn't get her head around it. What would Rob have to say? Mies van der Rohe… she heard her name and quickly closed down the page.

'Rose, the client meeting's in five. Have you got everything?'

'Of course. No worries. Be right with you.' When she saw Rob she'd be able to trot out some names; perhaps they could go together to Barcelona or New York. She'd develop an interest, he'd like that, she was sure. She dragged her thoughts away from images of futuristic buildings and concentrated on the brief.

Chapter Twenty-Nine

Carla's committee meeting broke up with a cheerful agreement to go to the pub for a drink to celebrate the group's tenth anniversary and the renewal of the lease. They were all glad that things could stay as they were for the time being.

'Convenience is an essential prerequisite of life here in London. Wherever it can be achieved,' someone pronounced.

'To get anywhere on time involves such lengthy and versatile planning,' another sighed, shaking her head.

'Fortunately most of the committee are retired or at any rate not working full-time, apart from you, Angelo,' Harry nodded at the flamboyant young set designer, all skinny jeans, velvet jacket and tousled long hair who had appeared unexpectedly and refreshingly at her second meeting and intermittently ever since.

'I'm working too,' protested Laura, a writer, as some of them exchanged a glance. Carla enjoyed their enthusiasm and commitment despite feeling they belonged to a cosy little clique who had known each other for years. She suspected that she, Harry and Laura were outsiders, expected to deem it an honour to be on the board. This view occurred to Carla during AOB while they still sat around the table, concluding matters. But perhaps she'd been unfair she mused as two of the women flanked her on the pavement outside the theatre.

'Have you settled in to the new house?'

'Yes, thanks. We're getting on quite well with all the alterations. Not long to go now. I'll be glad when it's over, though,' replied Carla.

'It was brave of you to come on the committee,' confided Anne. 'We were fairly desperate for some new blood. Truth is we're all getting a bit stale. Harry's great and of course there's Angelo,' she looked around in case he was near, 'but he flits about as he pleases. Not really a good team member,' she pursed her lips to her friend as they waited at the crossing.

Harry was holding the pub door for them; he was attractive, decided Carla as they gathered with the others at the bar. Drinks in hand, they stood talking for half an hour until a table became free. At this point four of them drifted off home. Carla decided that she would finish her wine and leave but found herself now sitting beside Harry while three others were deep in conversation at the far end of the table. 'Prize shortlist,' she heard, then, 'amazing, ten for only thirty pounds.'

'I still feel a bit like a new girl,' she confessed quietly to Harry. 'So many of them seem to have done this together for years. Ten years, I believe.'

'But you seem entirely in your element.'

'I must be a good actress then,' she smiled.

'You know, I think I'm rather enjoying it all,' Harry spoke as if he was wondering that for the first time. 'It's good to be involved with something that interests me and they aren't a bad bunch. I like the talks and visits. Never had much time for stately homes and museums before I retired,' he stared at his pint. 'Then when Maxine died I decided I had to get stuck in to lots of new things. Some good, some of which were a disaster. You would have laughed if you'd seen me.'

'Why, what did you take up?'

'I'd always fancied Archery. I said you'd laugh. Some boyhood dream of being Robin Hood. I don't know, I was hopeless at it. Could hardly manage to hit the target at all. Birds came next. Not to shoot them,' he chuckled. 'Bird watching, I mean. It's fascinating if rather solitary. Then I decided something more cerebral might be just the ticket and I started French lessons. Good for the brain so they say. I'm plodding on with it but last year I had a holiday in the Loire and discovered I could hardly understand a word. They just talk too damn fast.'

'Now you've discovered your métier, I see,' Carla smiled.

'Aha, mon métier. Peut-être. Well, I've been going to the talks for about a year and when someone suggested the committee I thought it would be good to have a role. What about you?'

'I accepted in a weak moment. Wanting to belong somewhere probably. You know, we've just moved to London and I seem to be floating about in a bit of a vacuum.' She pushed her hair back behind her ears, 'I'm not sure why I'm being so honest. I should have said my talents had been duly recognised and it would have been churlish to refuse.'

Her eyes crinkled then she looked at her glass. The other three began to make a move.

'Why don't we have one for the road?' Harry suggested to them all.

'Count me out.'

'Better get going I think.'

'No thanks, Harry, I'm off.'

'Another time,' Carla said. 'It's getting a bit late.'

'Just a quick one?' he gave a persuasive grin.

'Really, I mustn't.' Carla wondered whether he might be lonely and secondly if it was a good idea to be seen to be remaining alone with Harry. At the same time she asked herself, is this the twenty-first century? The others had reached the door as she stood up.

'Oh, let me get you one, Harry. A pint?'

'Sure you've got time? Okay, great.'

Half an hour later they walked along to the nearby tube station.

'I've really enjoyed talking to you. Thanks for the beer.'

She had a tingle of excitement as he left her at the barrier. Ridiculous but interest in one was always flattering. Harry had no idea how cold and miserable she was inside. How could he? She had been lively, amusing, a good companion. This was the old Carla, the one she needed to regain within the four walls of her home. Carla's journey, only one stop, brought her back to earth.

Chapter Thirty

In spite of her protests, a few days later, Gabrielle found herself part of the 'welcoming party' as Peter called it, tongue in cheek. She refused to change and ignored her mother's raised eyebrows when they gathered just before eight o'clock.

It was a Friday night and they had an air of being on parade. Rob had been quite clear, brooking no argument; he expected them to be polite and agreeable. A silence had greeted this announcement before a muted objection. Gabrielle had been distracted from her vehemently anti-Rose stance by a pleasing encounter with the engineer that afternoon. They exchanged only a few words but again she sensed a mutual attraction. This was not uncommon in Gabrielle's brushes with the opposite sex.

Peter hoped for an evening's relief from the shrewd contemplative gaze of Nina (who was confused by the step back in his affections while at times he was as robustly eager as before.) A break for him too, from the tumult of sensations stirred up by a breathless five-minute rendezvous he'd had with Edwina in one of the squash courts that had afforded the snatched moment of privacy.

'We may as well have a drink. Beer for me. Shall I open a bottle of wine, Ma?'

'Oh, do. What about you Nina, a glass?'

Nina, aware of a distinct apprehension that had taken hold of her, was girding herself for being very much a minor player in the evening's confrontation. At least they had taken it for granted that she would be with them: she'd feared exclusion. To Rose, Nina would look like part of the family.

'Please. And you, Carla?'

Carla was keeping her emotions under tight control. She wore a casual if impeccable outfit, pale grey trousers and a loose pink cowl neck jumper. The room with its gleaming floor and carefully placed lamps was an uncluttered set, ready for the denouement. She concentrated on providing as good a meal as she could within the limits of a simple family supper. Baked chicken and chorizo with jacket potatoes could sit as long as necessary in the oven and a humble apple and mincemeat crumble would not be overplaying her hand. She looked at her children, her darlings. Their lives would be different after tonight. Resolutely she blanked out the less than positive outcomes of this evening that she feared. In spite of her denials to Gabrielle, the implications regarding this girl were huge.

And Rob, where was he, she wondered as they stood awkwardly waiting? The doorbell rang and everyone froze.

Rob, in the summerhouse, unpacking the new shelving unit that had recently arrived had been keeping an eye on his watch, determined to spend as little time as he could with the rest of them in the oppressive atmosphere of their heightened emotions. They were all hanging about like spare parts. He was sure he would hear the bell from the garden. No need to hover near the front door, even if he could feel his heart thudding. That was only natural. He prayed that good manners would enable them to have a pleasant and civilised evening. Gracious behaviour. That's what he was counting on. Nevertheless he jumped as he heard the distant ring. Quick, she was here. He hurried into the house, wondering why no one had let her in.

He was struck again by the startling resemblance to Gabrielle and he had forgotten how pretty this girl was, as she stood back clutching a bunch of daffodils. A nervous smile and they exchanged pecks on the cheek. Then she was inside and he closed the door.

'Through here,' he murmured, 'let me take those.' Her fingers were icy as he touched them. He wished he could grasp them and let the warmth of his hand flow to her. He put his hand on her back instead to encourage her through the door.

Carla was about to step forward to kiss Rose just as Peter moved, putting out his arms and they almost bumped into each other. Carla waited and watched as half brother and sister embraced. Good for her son to do the decent thing, as she had known he would. Rose had tears in her eyes when they stood back and he introduced Gabrielle and Nina.

'My sister Gabrielle. My girlfriend Nina. Of course you two have met.'

An awkward moment was extended as Gabrielle merely nodded, saying a cool hello and Nina held up a limp hand as if to say 'Hi.' Unusually, Nina wore skin-tight jeans with a short crop top that revealed her midriff. ('You'll catch your death,' Carla had murmured.)

'Let's all have a drink. What will you have Rose, a glass of wine or a G and T?' Rob's voice sounded bluff in his ears and he felt foolish holding the flowers. 'For you,' he said to Carla, 'from Rose.'

Somehow the first half hour was endured. Rose looked nervous, her eyes shooting from one to the other and she overdid the friendliness, making conversation about the house and raving about the beautiful room. She was wearing a demure pale yellow shirt that hung outside a black skirt, work-wear she'd deemed more suitable than some of her outfits. Peter asked about the job and she made it sound more exciting than it was, moving on to talk about the music scene, her involvement with some bands and implying she was au fait with the latest waves in rock and blues. They all drank too fast.

Carla escaped to the kitchen, footsteps behind her.

'Okay?' she asked Gabrielle.

'God knows what I'm supposed to feel. I wasn't given a blueprint for this.'

'Let's just get through it. Food will help. Come on, get the chicken out of the oven would you?'

The evening was perfectly orchestrated by Carla. Small talk and impersonal matters were the order of the day. If it looked as if anyone might stray on to delicate subjects, Carla was there with a bland question, an offer of second helpings, diversionary tactics that were as natural as baby talk to a new mother. Only Gabrielle's sometimes sour expression gave the lie to the agreeable evening: unspoken thoughts stirring with volcanic intensity beneath the surface.

It was a relief when final drinks were refused and the cafetière was empty. Rob offered to drive Rose home at about half past ten. Everyone noticed her hand on his arm.

'Really, no. It's much too far and the tube couldn't be easier.'

Peter and Rob agreed to accompany Rose down to the underground station. As they set off, a sudden exhaustion showed in the fading smile and forced goodbyes, the bright, eager girl yielding to the strain of the evening. Carla did not feel sorry for her. As she closed the front door she wondered how much of the real Rose they had seen tonight. If the delightful amiable girl was a pose, no wonder the tension had suddenly shown. Well, they had all been on their best behaviour, she reflected and thank God for that.

'Ha ha ha,' Gabrielle had turned on the television as if she wanted no more to do with the earlier object of the evening and was laughing uproariously at a popular comedian. 'Have you SEEN this guy?' she called out.

Peter remembered his damp clothes in the washing machine and threw them into the drier before disappearing upstairs. Carla and Nina quietly loaded the dishwasher. They exchanged a meaningful look but said nothing. There was no post mortem that night as if they had all agreed to keep their own counsel.

Only Rob ventured a muffled comment in the safety of the bedroom as he pulled his shirt over his head. 'I think that went okay. Don't you agree?'

'Yes, fine,' came the reply in an equally non-committal voice. 'Did she say anything when you walked down with her?'

'Not really.' He turned out the light and got into bed.

He seemed to have fallen asleep at once. While she brushed her teeth, allowing the electric toothbrush to buzz away, Carla's mind began to zero in on a single conviction: for years to come, Rose would be part of the equation. Like it or not she had breached the walls and would be settling in for the long game.

Rose felt emptied out. The balloon had deflated as she waved goodbye and flashed her Oyster card at the barrier. She stood on the platform a weary figure gazing unseeing at the billboard across the track.

All her life, Rose had hungered for a stable, safe place. While her mother no doubt loved and mostly provided for her, there had always been an element of fragility about their lives. Her mother's marriage break-up when Rose was very young, had clouded all the later years with the possibility that things could fracture at any moment. Even though Adrian, her mother's long-term partner, had treated her with kindness, he was not a particularly demonstrative man. He had mostly stuck around, though there were periods when he had been absent, a marine engineer working abroad for months, quietly removing himself from the destructive atmosphere at home.

Even as she doled out the blame, she knew her mother had often had to cope alone, keeping a veneer of normality over the household when Rose was 'in a bad place.' Once as a teenager, during a bout of depression and aggressive behaviour, she was sent to her grandparents when her mother could not manage her. The rosy tinted reminiscences of times spent with them in

Bakewell in the Derbyshire Dales, were never wholly convincing to either of them. Under medication, the world had been dulled. Half-zombie, her visits were uneventful in the extreme: dreamy days passing in walks, blackberry picking and the telly; the rural idyll always compromised by the vivid recollection of fear, fear of the white hospital room and its locked door in her imagination. Over all that was spread the sadness of Granny's death at far too young an age. Grandpa had married again and moved even further north. Life was unfair, but there was nothing you could do. It was a defeatist philosophy: safer not to raise your hopes.

On the way home, after meeting her brother and sister, Rose could barely even think. The miseries of her upbringing were shaken off as the numbness gradually dissolved and a tarantella of emotions began with an elusive feeling of nervous jubilation. Misgivings chastened her while the longing to be back in her room, her own private space was dominant. The family, the scrutiny of all those curious faces had overwhelmed her. She needed to regain her sense of herself. Their ideas of what or who she was weighed her down.

The train rocked through the tunnels, the familiar platforms and signs and the lights of the stations beckoned; then they rattled into darkness. The seats were surprisingly full; extravagant praise for a team was yodelled down the carriage: it seemed the rugby had just ended. The rest picked at their mobiles. Passengers stepped out and in. She looked at her watch; somehow she had lost track of the hour.

She walked along a street, raucous shouts and laughter spilled from bars and pub doorways and groups loitered on the pavement with their cigarettes. Taxis coasted by, the drivers in turbans, arms hanging from the windows. A whiff of pungent food mingled with exhaust and marijuana smoke clinging to the night air.

Her mobile beeped with a message. She stopped and fished

it out of her bag.

It was good to see you tonight. Rob

At once, jubilation got the upper hand. Delightedly she tapped back a reply.

And you. Thanks for a lovely evening x She hadn't expected that.

She'd done it. She broke into a triumphant grin that encompassed the whole street. It would be all right. In time she would get what she craved. He was on her side; she was sure of that now. She passed Ahmed running down the stairs. Noticing the radiant smile he called out, 'On cloud nine are you, doll?'

'Too right! You off out?'

'Yeah, meeting the lads. Laters.'

'See you later, have a good time.' The pointed shoes and flashy jacket looked terrible, Rose decided, not cool at all yet tonight she sensed his vulnerability. He just tried too hard.

Now, she lingered at the landing, undecided. She stared at Luke's door, listening. Sometimes she could hear his music but often he wore headphones. He was the only proper friend in the house; the others were ships in the night. He was hard to pin down, his emotions locked fast, she reckoned. Occasionally, she tried to rekindle something between them but she suspected it was a lost cause. He was a mate though and that was probably better. She'd relied on him during a couple of 'down' patches the year before. At least he was a consistent if unimaginative support. She might bang on his door and tell him the good news. Perhaps not, he had been up most of the night before and would have 'crashed' early tonight. Anyway, she knew what he'd say: keep it real, Rose. Familiar words: a damper on her good mood. Open the door instead, Rose, she told herself. Go to bed. She was far too excited to sleep.

In the morning after the elation and the alcohol had worn off, she sank into a more contemplative state of mind, assessing their reactions. How had they seen her, judged her? She knew she had talked too much in her nervousness. That fatal habit of jabbering on in case there was a moment's silence. Idiot. Never mind, Rob was a pushover. He'd been so sweet and charming. She could have done this, years ago. She had a savage insight that the miserable decades should have been completely different.

It had been easy to make Peter like her. He was uncomplicated, a soft touch, probably spoiled by his mother; you could see that. She could tell life had dealt him no blows. The girlfriend, the one she'd met before, hardly giving her the time of day; that was to be expected: an out-and-out bitch. Possessive of her boyfriend, that's for sure. Thankfully no one had mentioned her earlier visit. Rose squirmed. In time that mistake would be forgotten.

She sat up in bed and reached for her glass of water. She was parched, her mouth dry as sand after the wine. The clock said eight. No hurry today. In a minute she would make a cup of tea. Gabrielle was a tricky one. Rose had nearly quailed under the cool gaze. It had been a shock to see herself reflected in the dark eyes and precise features but she'd never be that pretty. Or striking. Gabrielle seemed very sure of herself, giving away little.

Carla had been less hostile than before. Trying hard to be decent. She had nothing to lose, Rose supposed. Still, better than Rose had expected. The mother vixen was allowing someone to play with her cubs. But remain on your guard, she told herself, Carla's the one who could put the kibosh on all your plans.

All in all, Rose calculated that the evening had passed off all right. So what, if she'd been a little OTT? A certain excitement was only natural. She would win them over no matter what. She'd had enough of struggling along on her own.

All her life her mother had been the unreliable narrator, peddling a story that had been inconsistent from the start: a story that had kept her away from her father all these years. Pure hatred shot through her for a second. Her mother was PATHETIC. All right then, she acquiesced, she might have done her best; she couldn't help the way she was.

For the moment, more patience would be required, *softly, softly catchee monkee*, she reflected but she could plan her campaign nevertheless. She sprang out of bed. On a high now, her thoughts ranged over the whole 'package' of the family. There was so much about it she yearned for. Restitution she called it. They could all move up and make space for her. What a good sister she would be to Peter and Gabrielle. She saw herself listening to their problems, full of empathy and wisdom. She'd attended the school of hard knocks. It wasn't all about taking. If only she could make them see that. She just wanted the place she deserved.

Chapter Thirty-One

After work one evening, Nina made a detour to the new health food shop she'd heard about. She hopped over the puddles on the pavement in her cosy sheepskin boots trying not to study her reflection in the windows, stealing a joyful glance one moment, the next cast down in the usual rollercoaster of perception about her figure. The family were liars, telling her she was fading away. She should get rid of this jacket. It didn't do her any favours.

She passed a row of ethnic food outlets; on the pavement were stands full of luscious imported fruit in neat pyramids, then a down-at-heel launderette, a shop selling beds and mattresses and a printer's boasting cheap photocopies. Along here, surely. Ah, there it was.

The display of immune boosting, vitality enhancing supplements was extensive. She nodded to the man on a stool at the cash desk who nodded in return before he resumed staring listlessly out of the window. She wandered up and down the two aisles. Packets filled the first shelf, grains, nuts, gluten free flours, spelt then phials of elixirs, cartons of muscle building protein and giant bottles of vitamins and minerals, oils and probiotics. Where was the spirulina? Something new to try and this other one that boosted the metabolism was what she'd come for. It wasn't just about losing weight; she wanted more energy, to get fitter. She thought of Gabrielle wolfing down her food; it was not fair. That girl Rose was skinny too. There was something about her that made Nina uncomfortable; she had to admire Peter's sister, she was strong and direct while Rose was— two-faced, was that it?

A few minutes later her backpack was laden with packets of flax and sunflower and pumpkin seeds and the powdered seaweed she'd come for. She fingered a stick of liquorice in her pocket, keeping it for later: a treat. She hadn't craved anything sweet for ages. She remembered her mother's excitement at finding old-fashioned Pontefract Cakes, the oily black coins from the sixties, in a little shop in the Pennines.

About a mile from home she wondered if she'd taken a wrong turning. It was only the second time she'd been this way. Suddenly a church loomed ahead. This wasn't right. She took down the bag from her shoulders and dug about for her mobile to check the route. Nina stood with the bag between her feet, searching for her location. If she continued and made a right turn then a left she would soon be back on her way. The cars passing by sent a spray of mist from the wet tarmac and then slowed for the turning by the church with a flash of red from their brake lights. A cross mother, holding a child by each hand, hurried by, grumbling. She pictured all the mothers in England standing by cookers or chopping vegetables, buttering bread and frying chops. Her mouth began to water. She peeled the wrapper off the liquorice and took a bite of its unimaginable sweetness, trying to chew slowly. It was sublime. Soon she was running her tongue all over her teeth to finish the sticky remains. She screwed up the wrapper thrusting it into her pocket in disgust at giving in to temptation.

Several cars went by and made a short queue waiting to turn at the junction. She caught up with a low whitish-grey sports car, the last in the row. It was the racquet bag she recognised first, squashed against the rear window. In a split second she was going past. Glancing into the interior, she saw only a large pair of blue-clad thighs and a woman's hand resting on the passenger's lap. Nina's mouth went dry as the car moved forward overtaking her again as she stared after it. A moment later it swept from view around the corner.

She was certain it was Pete. Yet it was hard to be certain in this light. The shape of the head and tall bulk of the figure was evident but the bag with its familiar red and blue stripes and bright yellow logo was common enough, probably made in its thousands. Her heart was hammering. She concentrated on finding her way, crossing carefully. In her mind's eye a tape was running. Pete, some weeks ago, climbing into a silver two-seater while she stood on the corner like a fool, watching him ride away with somebody else.

Ten minutes later she entered the kitchen telling herself she was mistaken, a jealous cow who'd lost the plot. Peter's hands were warm as he hugged her even though he'd only just come in.

Along the edges of the paths and under the trees the green shoots of crocuses and daffodils were pushing through the soggy grass. These were an affront to Gabrielle as she ran through the park. Yet another sign that time was passing and she still had not found a job. She was nearly at the point of settling for something way beneath her capabilities just to get out of the house and start earning again. On the positive side, it was surprisingly cheap to live at home. The monthly rent on her flat not only paid the mortgage but gave her quite a lot of extra money too. Prudently she had begun to save it in the building society along with the redundancy payment. It was gratifying to think of the account growing in spite of her lack of a job.

She hoped the tenants were looking after the place; it was her pride and joy after all. She'd been too proud, though. What a glow she had felt, when friends first came round. She'd been one of the first to raise a mortgage. They were impressed that she'd picked such an up and coming area (really sheer luck) and could afford a place like that: two bedrooms and a decent sized living room with a tiny balcony. Of course, she let them know she'd achieved it mostly off her own bat. A few quid from Granny on her twenty-first had been a godsend and the significant bonuses from her old job in the city to put down as a deposit had enabled her to go for it before the latest boom. She prayed she wouldn't have to sell. She could carry on at her parents; it was a good thing she was there, what with everything kicking off. She had nearly offered to pay something towards her keep at Number 23 but it was better not to commit to that yet. Anyway, Dad would refuse, she was sure. Dad. She swallowed then clenched her jaw. What a bastard. So much destroyed by a few mindless screws. His carelessness was almost as great an affront. Spilling his seed. The biblical phrase repeated itself, disgusting her. Meeting Rose had stirred up even more unpleasant emotions. She'd looked like a receptionist at a two star hotel and that big mouth talking non-stop.

She ran past the small bandstand. Her fitness was at a new level and she felt lithe and muscular. The running had become a pleasure, nearly a pleasure, something she depended on. It gave some structure to her day. Besides she felt good in the gear and while outwardly disdaining them, enjoyed the appreciative looks she got. And while she was on an ego trip, which she fully realised, Algie had seemed extremely interested in seeing her again and dishy Aidan, how funny they both began with an A, now stopped to talk whenever she encountered him. She daydreamed over possibilities. When the extension was finished she was certain that Aidan might invite her for a drink. For the present it tantalised them both to have this constraint putting paid to anything but mild flirtation.

She slowed as a small rough haired dog ran towards her. It was a popular spot for dog walking and some could be aggressive. Not this one. She recognised it as it ran round her and then sat and looked at her, exactly as it had the day before.

She scanned the park in each direction but for once there was nobody about. The dog appeared to be quite alone again. No collar either. She bent to check in the pelt of its neck.

'Good dog, stay.' Gabrielle started to jog on, her trainers squelching. She liked the way they ate up the distance, could bounce lightly over the uneven surface. She could sense a padding of paws behind her and glancing back could see the terrier's hopeful progress a couple of yards away, keeping pace. She stopped again, panting. The dog stopped too.

'Shoo!' she tried but the walnut coloured eyes were fixed on her. Perhaps she could outrun it. No, that was daft; she would just ignore it and hope its sudden infatuation with her would abate. The next ten minutes would have been amusing to a spectator. Gabrielle set off again, a little faster than before. Each time she tried to veer away, the tufty brown dog veered too; she retraced a complete circuit of the park in case the owner might appear. The animal had latched on to her and wouldn't be dissuaded. She approached the few people she encountered but none were interested in helping. Tired of negative answers and vague gazes into the distance, she relented and she and the dog trailed back along the streets to the house, the dog obediently trotting along the pavement. Gabrielle opened the door and it shot inside, its claws scratching noisily along the hall floor. She picked it up and carried it out to the back.

The men stopped work to look as she appeared in her running gear, a faint sheen of sweat on her face and arms, a hairy bundle in her arms.

'This bloody dog's adopted me. It's been following me everywhere, all over the place and now we're here.' A broad grin belied the words. 'You haven't got a bit of rope I can use as a lead, have you? I guess I'll have to take it back when I've showered. Maybe I need to put up a notice or something.'

It was nice that Sean squatted down at once.

'Hello Scruff,' he fondled the dog's ears, 'noice little fellow. Oops no, she's a bitch.'

'Can I leave her out here for a minute?' Gabrielle was rapidly cooling from her run. 'I'll just get her some water.'

'She may have been dumped,' said Terry, 'unwanted Christmas present, I dare say, though she's no puppy. What do you reckon?'

The dog began to explore the garden, sniffing here and there while the men stood enjoying the distraction.

That evening, Gabrielle tied up a notice on the railings at the entrance to the park and telephoned the police who advised her to take the stray to the nearest animal shelter.

'I shall put another notice in the corner shop by the park. We'll just have to hang on to her for a day or so I expect,' she told her mother.

'Don't get any ideas about adopting her, that's all. And keep her off the furniture.'

'She's sweet though. Aren't you, little Fudge?' Gabrielle nuzzled the dog's warm neck and put her nose to brown button nose.

'Really, Gabrielle. You don't know where it's been. You should never put your face near a strange dog.'

'Who's this?' asked Peter, coming in. 'Hello, beautiful,' he took the wriggling creature from his sister and held it up, 'yes, you're very cute, aren't you?'

'I'm calling her Fudge. I went all over the park looking for her owner but she just followed me home. We have to keep trying, somehow.'

'You could do with a dog, Mum,' Peter told Carla.

'A dog is the very last thing I need, thank you very much. Have you fed her? There's a bit of left-over stew in the fridge.'

In front of the television after dinner, Carla looked across at Nina and Peter squashed together at the end of the sofa, the dog on Peter's lap in a posture of complete abandonment. Nina's arm burrowed under his and stroked its warm pink stomach as she rested her head on his shoulder. Rob caught Carla's eye and raised an eyebrow. Her expression mirrored his exactly. Perhaps, for once, their thoughts were in tune.

Gabrielle had gone straight out after dinner. A girlfriend had telephoned with news of a job in a well-known internet retail company. Carla looked at her watch, back to the old habit of worrying when her children were out at night: muggings, drunks, stabbings, speeding cars, lorries out of control or worse. Gaby had said she wouldn't be long but perhaps the girls had gone to the pub. She wouldn't ring yet. Her eyes drifted to the screen and across to Nina again, nestling as comfortably as the dog. Peter was asking for trouble there: he was too laid back by half. Day by day, Nina's expectations were probably growing just as Gabrielle had predicted. It would be a messy break-up, something Peter would be ill equipped to deal with. In the past he'd blithely moved on after a few weeks with a girl. He was undoubtedly fond of Nina but 'in love?' She gave a tiny shake of the head. Carla turned her gaze to Rob as he lounged back with eyes narrowed as if focused on the screen. She knew better. The hint of a preoccupied expression flitted across his face every so often. Was he too, worried about Gabrielle? She doubted it; he had faith that his daughter would overcome all obstacles, blazing her way through the next company as she'd done before. Rob had given up confiding his preoccupations; anyway, she wasn't really interested. In spite of that denial she scrutinized his expression frequently when he was unaware of it. Carla's unrelenting internal commentary began. Soon it was in full flow. Not only did her mind provide an unspoken script from each member of the family, she could routinely predict the scenes that were to be enacted on the television. It was doubly sapping to have everyone's reflections going round in her head as well as the programme unravelling exactly as she'd anticipated. Perhaps she was going mad. And now a phrase from Rose slunk in. *Persona non grata*. Was that how Rose thought of herself? It had a depressing if truthful ring. Was she beginning to feel sorry for the girl? A shiver of distaste contradicted the notion. She half-closed her eyes weary from a long day, the early start with Rob's alarm and an expedition on foot with her copy of Secret London leading her on and on.

A scream and another body was unearthed on the television. Even Peter exclaimed, 'yuk.' Nina had her hands over her eyes. The camera lingered on the grisly torso. How Carla longed for a really good drama without a single murder. There was still half an hour to go before the news if only she could keep awake. She would much rather go up to bed and settle down with her book but that was anti-social, three nights running. She sat up to shake off the drowsiness, stifling a yawn.

'Haven't we got anything better to watch? Rob, where are those box sets you had for Christmas?'

'We're enjoying this,' Peter protested mildly. 'Anyway it's nearly over. You can choose after that.'

'How kind,' Rob inclined his head in appreciation, 'very good of you.'

'Right. Our choice next.' Another yawn. The temptation to go to bed was becoming more and more overwhelming. By ten o'clock every evening a stupefying inertia overcame her.

The front door could be heard opening and closing and the small brown dog leapt down. Gabrielle came straight in, taking off her coat and flinging it over the back of a chair before dropping on to the seat.

'Up you come,' she patted her knees and Fudge leapt up, gave a warm lick to Gabrielle's cold cheeks, curled up and went to sleep. 'She is the sweetest thing.' She noticed the eyes on her. 'The job sounds really exciting,' her face lit up. 'A definite possibility.' Her mouth turned down, 'At least it's worth a try. If it does actually come up.' She stroked the rough fur, smoothing the ears. 'She been good?'

'Shush—' Peter reached for the remote control and turned up the volume.

'Too loud.'

'Where's the job?'

'Shush please. We're trying to watch.'

'Thanks for the interest.'

'It's nearly over. Then I will be interested. What did he say, Nina? Oh fuck it.'

'Just watch it then.'

'I'm trying to—'

'Oh, eff off,' retorted Gabrielle.

'For God's sake,' Carla and Rob spoke as one.

Even the builders sensed that something was amiss and wondered what they had done to displease the Unwins. Terry was in a philosophical mood.

'Clients nearly always fall out of love with us at the point when their dreams are about to be realised. A sudden panic that reality will not live up to the vision they've cherished through long weeks of disruption.' He drove a fist into his other palm. 'Bam. What were they thinking of, why oh why didn't they, why shouldn't they, why hadn't someone said? Just the usual attack of nerves, before the final financial reckoning. Then joy of joys, we complete the project and they become sweetness and light again, overflowing with gratitude. Wait and see.'

The men acknowledged the likelihood of this with sniffs and shrugs. Conversations with the Unwins were brief, smiles appeared wooden and the relaxed atmosphere over cuppas had all but disappeared. Averted eyes, glum looks and an air of disagreement had been simmering within the family for the past few days.

Peter nodded to the men as he passed them on his way out.

He was embarrassed that a conversational opening had not sprung to his lips. He busied himself with the bike to cover up. At home, his mind was forever concerned about averting a blunder that would give away his meetings with Edwina. Deleting texts had become a routine activity. It was so easy to get tripped up by arrangements: the when and where and how. Her admission, in a rare moment of tenderness, that he made her feel young and desirable, had touched him. Yet Nina was wonderful, he told himself as he rode off on the bike but the fact was they'd been together nearly two years now. He took the bend too fast, nearly mowing down a teenager foolishly dashing over when there was a perfectly good zebra crossing just up the road. *Brainless idiot.*

No. He'd be getting himself tied down if he wasn't careful. He should be out playing the field as his mother put it. He shook his head over the idea of *settling down.* Impossible. He braked at the lights and noticed a girl in a blue anorak going across, a girl who reminded him of Rose. He still could not make up his mind what he should feel about the half sister who had appeared out of nowhere. Surely she had her own life to lead and need not bother them unduly? He had quite enough on his plate, right now. The lights turned to amber and he pedalled on.

Not only had Carla gone all negative about the sixtieth birthday party, as Rob put it to himself, his suggestion that Rose should be invited and formally introduced to everyone had caused a furious debate which was not resolved.

'It's the perfect opportunity,' he insisted again when they were gathered round the kitchen table over kedgeree, having exhausted alternative arguments. It was blindingly clear to him. Get her to meet everyone and then it would be a done deal, no need for tittle-tattle from old friends and acquaintances: Rose would be out in the open in the bosom of the family. He ignored the mixed metaphors.

'We could take a vote on it,' Peter put in.

'No way,' Gabrielle was adamant, 'Mum's birthday is bugger all to do with Rose.'

Carla's face was closed. Let all their friends know she hadn't been able to keep Rob in her bed? No thank you.

'Let's think about it. Decide later,' Rob made a concession to keep the peace. 'I just feel it would be the magnanimous thing to do,' he could not resist a parting shot, before forking the yellow rice into his mouth.

'Atoning for the past, is that it?' countered Gabrielle capturing the last word as usual.

'Shut up, Gabrielle,' snapped Carla. 'That's enough everybody. I'm sick of the whole subject. Can I make it quite clear to you all? I've said it before and I'll say it again. I have no desire for a party in my honour.'

'But Mum, you agreed ages ago.'

'Be quiet. I mean it. Not another word,' she collected up the plates as the family simmered with unspoken remarks, exchanging glances, 'and don't have that dog on your lap at table. Really.'

Gabrielle stood up, 'I've finished anyway.' She began to coo in a baby voice to the shaggy terrier in her arms. 'Who's looking so very lugubrious now? Big soppy brown-eyed girl. Doesn't mummy love you? Yes, she does my petal. Ooh yes, you're a good girl.' She looked up at Rob. 'If no one comes forward to claim her, I'd really like to keep her. You know, I think I could manage it if I was in my own place. Which I will be soon.'

'That would be completely ridiculous. Do see sense Gabrielle. You'll be back at work any day. If you don't take it to the dog's home you will get more and more attached to it. You should take it tomorrow.'

'Dad. She's a girl.'

'She's not staying here,' Carla wondered for the hundredth

time why nobody ever listened.

'I'm taking her out for a last pee.'

'Gabrielle wants her head read.' Rob observed. Nobody disagreed.

'I don't understand why it's taking her so long to find a job,' Peter offered. 'She could easily go back into some investment house. She did so brilliantly before she got into this marketing stuff. She certainly earned a packet.'

'I think she's broadening the search. Something might come of that chat with Anna. She's completely wasted, hanging about here,' Rob leaned back in his chair, 'though I dare say it's character building.'

'If at first you don't succeed...' Nina added. 'I try to remember that myself when I'm ground down by my boss.'

Peter stared at her. Sometimes she could be quite self-centred. 'At least you've got a job.'

'And one where you are getting invaluable experience,' Carla pointed out in a nice way, encouraging rather than correcting.

Nina tried not to look upset, her lips in the slightest of pale pink pouts. Sensitive to criticism, she retreated inside herself. Most of the time she relished any small signs of affection from the family, lapping up the crumbs. Like that poor dog, she thought. She could take a hint, though. Tonight it was going to be all about Gabrielle. Again. She stood up to clear the last few things. As she reached past Peter for the salt and pepper, he slipped his hand around her hips squeezing her gently towards him until she straightened up, sliding from his grasp. Maybe later tonight she could broach the subject of moving out. It would be wonderful if they could look for somewhere together. As she walked by him a moment later she stroked the back of his neck with her fingertips and gave his earlobe a little pinch. She'd read in a magazine that the neck was an overlooked erogenous zone. Since her suspicions had solidified, she'd done her best to figure out a plan. Confrontation was not part of it.

News at Ten showed a crowd of despairing refugees. Everyone in the comfortable sitting room frowned and looked grim. *Something should be done*. The front door slammed. Gabrielle came in, texting cheerfully on her phone. She unwound a long scarf from her neck. Carla turned away from the misery on the screen to look at her daughter. How lucky to have a home and two children safe from harm.

'Brr. Bloody cold still. I thought I might watch that film I told you about. Unless of course you'd rather see something else, my dear mater and pater?' she looked at them with ironic politeness and a lifted eyebrow.

'I sometimes feel you children never grew up, never left home, never went to uni. Because when I look round, it's life just as it was ten years ago,' Carla protested.

'Come on, Ma, don't be an old ratbag. You know you love having us here,' said Peter, 'go on admit it.'

Carla put her head in her hands in mock despair.

'It's time I went,' said Nina bravely, stressing the personal pronoun, darting a glance at Rob.

There was a fraction of a second's pause before Carla spoke.

'You must stay as long as you need to, Nina sweetheart. My concern at present is getting rid of that moth-eaten pooch,' cleverly she brought the subject around, hoping she had got away with it.

Chapter Thirty-Two

The next morning, Carla stood waiting at the dry cleaners with a jacket bundled under her arm. She sensed something familiar about the man ahead of her. He was leaning forward in a khaki parka she'd noticed before, tapping his pin number into the card machine.

He turned and she said, 'Harry.'

'Carla.'

'Hi, how are you? Have you recovered from that dreadful play?'

'Now the truth will out. I thought you rather enjoyed it,' he looked stern.

'Not really. I loved everyone's comments afterwards.'

'I suspect you have a subversive streak that will shock the committee at some point.'

'Oh no, I'm awfully conventional. Not likely to rock the boat at all.'

'I'm not convinced. We will see.'

Carla put the jacket on the counter, aware of the assistant's eyes.

'Sorry. Just this.'

'Name, please?'

'Unwin, Mrs Unwin.'

'Thank you,' she took the blue ticket and tucked it quickly in her wallet aware that Harry was holding the door for her.

'I don't suppose you've got time for a coffee?'

'I shouldn't really. I've got masses to do.'

'Ah, you might be persuaded. How about coffee and a doughnut? They have delicious ones, just over there.'

'No, really, I mustn't. But which way are you going?'

'No particular direction. I was just collecting these,' he indicated the parcel. 'Clean shirts. Ironing's not my strong suit.'

'I rather like taking a detour through the park on my way home. Bishop's Park. Do you know it?"

'Of course. Shall I walk along for a bit?'

'Yes, do. I had no idea you lived round here.'

'Mortimer Rd. in that direction,' he waved vaguely.

Carla felt a creeping embarrassment as they moved between the shoppers and she walked a little faster until they went through the park entrance, past a young man sitting on a frayed rectangle of old carpet atop a sheet of plastic, leaning back against the parapet. He began to sound a few hopeful notes on a saxophone but they did not look round.

'Has your daughter managed to find a job?'

'Not yet, the job market seems to be rather difficult at the moment. She moved from fund managing to marketing, which we thought was mad at the time but then she did pretty well. She's frustrated but won't lower her sights. I think she should. She'd get promoted soon enough. She's a capable girl.'

'She probably knows her value.'

'I hope so.'

Harry was easy to talk to; she would give him that. For a few minutes the conventional small talk entertained them both. A pair of runners dashed past with ragged breaths. She gave a burst of laughter when he asked if she ever went jogging.

'You're joking of course.'

He took her by surprise then, looking quickly towards her.

'I like your laugh. You're awfully attractive you know.'

'Don't say that,' she said at once, 'you'll spoil it. I'd much prefer you as a friend than a flirtation.'

'I'm an idiot. Okay. You make the rules. No flirting, that's fine. Besides, I was only telling the truth. I shan't say another word, I promise. Tell me about your husband. You see I shall make polite enquiries about him and show you that I have absolutely no intention of chatting you up.'

'Hm. Very droll,' she'd laugh it off. 'Anyway, what would you like to know about Rob?'

'Was it his idea to abandon the countryside?'

She squinted at a figure walking along towards them, making her uncomfortable. It was a stranger; she hardly knew a soul anyway, just a few of the other residents in their road exchanged smiles and greetings. What had Harry asked? His pleasant face was half turned, quizzical.

'Oh, not really, it was probably mine in the first place. Then it sort of brewed quietly between the two of us. A joint initiative you might call it, in the end. It had to be. Rob always had it in mind to retire at sixty and maybe do a few freelance projects, take up new hobbies, you know, the usual sort of thing.' Why wouldn't Harry go? Couldn't he take a hint? He chatted on; he was far too agreeable.

'Has he tried archery?' They laughed.

'Of course we've only been here a matter of weeks,' now she was babbling away as if she hadn't a care in the world. 'He's designed a fantastic extension for the new house, state of the art kitchen et cetera and he's got very involved in some charity work,' Carla's tributes tailed off and she eyed a man on a bicycle freewheeling towards them.

'Oh, what sort of thing?'

'He helps out at a centre for the homeless.'

'Good for him.'

The topic of Rob seemed to have been exhausted. Harry looked as if he would stroll along all day. Then he stopped unexpectedly and pulled a small pair of binoculars from his pocket saying, 'See that owl? There, in that tree, on the second branch to the right. Have you got it? Here, have a look at it through these. Unusual at this time of day.'

She peered through the glasses. 'I can't see it. Is that it? Yes, there it is. I do love owls: they have such funny faces. I'd forgotten you're quite the twitcher.'

'Guilty as charged. I suppose I'm interested in what's around; I certainly don't claim to be a huge expert but I join in the RSPB surveys, that sort of thing,' he took back the binoculars and they walked on while she digested this latest clue about him.

'It's quite amazing what you can see in the city. Hyde Park is marvellous and I tramped round the Walthamstow marshes recently. Ever been there? It's a great place for migratory birds.'

'I'm not sure exactly where that is. When we've settled in I'm sure we will do a bit more exploring.' She stared at the sky but could see only rooks and pigeons. She needed to get on but it seemed impossible to walk off when they were proceeding side by side along a path. Wasn't there a gate along here?

'How's your cooking?' she cast about. 'Do you manage okay?'

'I can see you think I live on coffee and buns. Oh, I'm not bad. I can knock up quite a few dishes. I even give the occasional dinner party; no one has died yet.'

'I used to love cooking,' Carla mused, 'but I've rather lost interest, what with the move and everything. Once the building work's done, I think I'll flit about my wonderful new kitchen knocking up cordon bleu meals in style. And now I really must dash on. See you at the next meeting? Lovely to bump into you.' They both halted and smiled brightly.

'And you.'

'See you,' she ended gaily before turning away.

Carla remembered at last the other errands she had meant to get done. A flustered feeling sent her hurrying down the path in the wrong direction.

The pigeons, pecking half-heartedly amongst the rubbish that collected along the edge of the pavement, were looking as disenchanted as Gabrielle. They ignored the terrier whose ears were cocked, anticipating the destination. Today, Gabrielle was particularly annoyed with her parents as she racked her brains for a solution to finding a home for poor Fudge. A temporary home. Once back in her own flat back she would see if she could manage. You could pay dog-walkers, couldn't you? At once, she faced up to the fact that it would be well-nigh impossible. Very often she would be out for hours. Of course they were right. A dog was a tie but her mother would grow to love Fudge, surely and they'd always had a dog before. Imagine giving her an ultimatum.

She waited reflecting, while Fudge squatted beside a wall. So much of what she had relied on had evaporated into thin air. *Don't let me even start on Dad.* Her mother's reticence was typical. Peter was completely wrapped up in his own affairs, no longer sharing or asking for her advice. Her older-and-wiser sister role was out of kilter with the more independent even aloof new Peter. They'd been close, in spite of her put-downs to the pain-in-the-arse teenager, her childish jealousy from vying for the attention he stole with his illness. Yet he was out of reach somehow; perhaps she'd been swapped for Nina.

Her reflections now changed focus. That girl was an attention seeker if ever she knew one: all that posturing, expecting everyone to cajole her with kid gloves at every meal.

'Come on sweetheart, another bite.'

'Nina, have the last spoonful of custard. I know you like custard.'

'This one's a small helping. Pass it up to Nina, please Gabrielle.'

The exhortations were a frequent feature at the dinner table while Gabrielle raised her eyes. Was she the only one to see through her? In contrast to Nina's dainty appearance, Gabrielle had abandoned her fashionable, well-groomed image in order to cultivate the look of an unconventional toughie with a few vintage finds in down-at-heel second hand shops and market stalls, a sort of two fingers to her middle-class upbringing. She passed the corner mini-mart and glanced at her card behind the glass. In a mass of small advertisements she could just read FOUND in large red letters. She was coming to the conclusion that someone must have dumped poor old Fudge; no one seemed to be searching for her.

'Come on, Fudgie,' she flicked the lead lightly, taking pleasure in the small head nodding along beside her.

As for her father, resentment flared as she returned to her complaints, his pathetic attempts to reassure her that she still held the number one place in his heart, hardly rang true any more. The old Gaby who'd doted on him even during the rebellious years now seemed such a sucker. Frankly, as the 'apple of his eye' her childhood had been a lie: all along he must have been thinking of Rose too. Her gentle father would not have turned his back without any lingering regrets.

Perhaps Mum had stayed true after all. They hadn't seen eye to eye, but maybe she hadn't really changed. Still trying to keep everyone in order, in spite of her own feelings. Whatever they were. Only a recent impatience in her manner, being somewhat abrupt on occasion, was a clue that for once things had not gone according to plan. For the first time in her life was she actually feeling a bit sorry for her? She'd never had reason to before. She pictured her mother's appearance, a source both of pride and irritation. Was there just a hint of the elegance slipping, the look slightly more bohemian with unpolished nails, hair almost curly at its new length and the slightest flash of grey when she tucked it behind her ears? She smiled at the idea of Carla embracing the alternative look in her old age. Like mother like daughter? No chance, her mother would take umbrage at such a suggestion.

Gabrielle bent to unclip the lead, looping it around her neck so as not to lose it and fastening it again. She marched past the tennis courts and into the park, missing her mother by five minutes and going across through the wooded area. She would take a less familiar route for a change.

'Come on, hurry up,' she called, stopping to look back. How adorable was the dog, trotting along with that purposeful air. Dogs were always there for you weren't they? She would talk to Pete again. Maybe they could come up with a plan. Then it came to her. Granny. It could be the perfect solution. Fired up with the idea, Gabrielle performed a few sideways skips in each direction to warm up.

'Come on Fudge,' she called again, 'I'm not waiting.' She jogged on the spot, before setting off at a medium pace. She sucked in the air, feeling liberated, slowing only to check on the dog and pausing now and then to do some lunges while Fudge caught up. She had reached the far side of the wide lawns and could see the river when the dog tore past her making a beeline for a gaunt figure carrying a rolled up mat and some plastic bags. The man dropped to his knees and picked her up, hugging and kissing the ecstatic animal.

Gabrielle walked up slowly and waited until he looked up with a rapturous smile. To her surprise he was young with a short wispy beard.

'I never thought I'd see Cassie again. My little beauty,' he finished in a northern accent, with his face in the dog's neck.

'She's yours?'

'Aye, she is.'

'Didn't you look for her? I put notices all around the place. I suppose you thought you could just abandon her?'

'Hold yer horses. It weren't like that at all.'

Gabrielle took in his appearance, the pallid skin, eyes ringed with smudges, lank brown hair to his shoulders, anorak, jeans and worn trainers: a uniform common enough. It was the tattered piece of carpet and the bulging plastic bags that told another story.

'Did you lose her then?' she demanded, upset that Fudge/Cassie was ignoring her.

'I were in hospital. Pneumonia. Someone called an ambulance, thought it were an overdose. Kept me in for ten days they did.'

'Oh.' Gabrielle was taken aback. 'Well, couldn't a friend have looked after her? The poor animal was running all over the park looking for you.'

'I never thought I'd see 'er again,' he repeated, burying his face in the dog's neck. A realization hit him, ''ave you taken care of her?'

'She kept following me, so after hunting in vain for her owner I took her home and put notices on all the gates and the shops. Didn't you see them?'

He shook his head, 'I only got out yesterday; had to find a new pitch. Never saw nothing,' he paused. 'You can't keep 'er. She's mine. You're my only friend in the world,' he told the dog.

'I didn't want to keep her. Just wanted to make sure she wasn't rounded up and put down or something.'

'God forbid. Well, I should thank you. Ta for looking after 'er. She's put on a fair bit of weight. That's good. Skinny little runt you was, eh?'

'Listen. You're better are you? You can take care of her?'

'We'll get by. I do a bit of busking with me sax. I need to get me puff back first.'

'Where are you staying?'

'Here and there. I expect I'll see you around. Say ta ra then, Cass.'

'Bye bye, sweetheart,' Gabrielle gave the dog's ears a rub and turned away. Tears pricked the back of her eyelids. She looked back once to see him knotting a length of string to the collar and hefting the piece of carpet under his arm. She touched the leather lead she'd bought, still hanging round her neck.

'Hi,' she called out, waving it, 'look, you may as well have this. A present for Cassie. She's been sweet.'

He took it and wound it round and round, thanking her.

'By the way, what's your name?' she asked.

'Tim,' he said, 'ta again.' He walked away, holding Cassie by the string, the lead safely in his pocket.

'I'm Gabrielle, nice to meet you, Tim,' she called. There was a glimpse of a smile as he half turned his head, trudging on to who knew where.

Chapter Thirty-Three

The alarm beeped at seven and an exhausted Nina reached out an arm to switch it off. She hadn't slept well, clinging to her side of the bed in a mute rebellion as pictures of life without Peter besieged her. He had come home early the evening before but a row with his sister had escalated from familiar grumbles to an argument, spoiling the atmosphere. Peter's freewheeling lifestyle as she considered it, riled Gaby who needled away at him. Leave him alone, Nina wanted to shout, he's got a job for God's sake, which is more than you have. Standing in the kitchen with an armful of dirty washing, Gabrielle's frustration with life had exploded. All the old criticisms came pouring out. She was suddenly furious.

'You haven't even sorted out that business with the deposit. No doubt Dad paid it in the first place, so you're not bothered.'

'I'm on the case, if you must know. You're the one who needs to get off her fat arse—'

'It strikes me that you're perfectly happy to enjoy the fruits of Dad's labour, living in this comfortable house, without demonstrating any ambition whatsoever to achieve the same for yourself. Surely there's more to life than earning a few quid an hour teaching people to play tennis? Can you see yourself doing the same old thing when you're fifty?'

'If anyone's sponging off the parents, it's you. After all, your flat must be a nice little earner,' he struck back. 'At least I've got a permanent job.'

'And I'm trying to find one that will reward me with a

decent income so that I can stand on my own two feet.'

'We are looking for somewhere to live,' Nina pulled a sheaf of estate agent's brochures from her bag. 'Some of these are quite promising, Pete,' if only he hadn't looked so surprised, 'better than those other places,' she improvised.

'Well, I'll believe it when I see it,' Gabrielle recovered and stalked out with her washing to the machine in the utility room.

Peter threw himself into a chair. He had never liked facing up to uncomfortable criticism.

'What's got into her? Fucking nerve. God it irritates me when she looks down her nose at me. Something's got under her skin. I'm having a beer. Come on Neen, you'll have a drink won't you? Fucking sisters,' he glowered. Rows always distressed him until he dismissed them firmly from his mind. Today the unfair accusation niggled. 'I do stand on my own two feet,' he grumbled. 'Anyway, where did these come from?' he poked at the papers on the table.

'I think it's time I moved out. Your parents have been amazing but I don't want to overstay my welcome. You know. Everyone must be fed up with the sight of me by now.' She laughed, ha-ha, anxious for his denial. The infinitesimal pause dealt a stab.

'Don't be daft. The trouble is it's bloody convenient here. I can walk or cycle to the club. Renting is so flaming expensive and its been nice to have a bit of dosh in my pocket for a change,' he reached for the agent's details, scowling as he read.

'Some of them aren't bad. The one in Lamartine Road has got a decent sized living room.' Nina could not bring herself to say that a share of the rent would be manageable between the two of them. Never had Peter suggested moving somewhere together. His face was troubled and for once life seemed to be impinging on him. He had gone to listen to music in his father's office. She had glimpsed in; he sat with eyes closed, wearing headphones, withdrawn from her.

Nina went upstairs early, demoralized. His complete lack of enthusiasm for looking at flats to rent had intensified her conviction that Peter was no longer in love with her. She knew she was overweight and downright plain with her washed out colouring that made her disappear into the background … what had he ever seen in her? Now, at seven in the morning in the aftershock of the alarm going off, the negative thoughts of the early hours surged back. She searched in vain for anything that might bind him to her. She inched closer to his warm sleepy body, breathing in the familiar scent of him, something between coffee and cocoa, for a few painful seconds before climbing out of bed to get ready to go to work.

All morning the suspicion of Peter's indifference kept her on the verge of tears. She drew a sketch of a wedding dress that she would never wear, sewed silk embroidery onto another that she would never wear and helped over-excited girls try on the beautiful confections of lace and tulle that would never be hers either. The refrain of never, never, never had dogged her right through until her lunch hour. Nina supposed that it would come down to an out and out accusation in the end. She was almost sure that Peter was having an affair with someone else or he'd merely fallen out of love with her and was prepared to drift along, offhand and cheerful. She gulped back a tear. All her pathetic little plans to keep him keen had come to nothing. He had not even been sensitive enough to realize just how miserable she felt when she grew tense under his touch, refusing to go with the flow when he was amorous. He didn't much care. Abstracted was probably the word. Could he even be bothered to dump her? She wasn't sure he had the energy. The apathy was almost worse than a bust-up would be. He had always been so transparent but now his attitude was 'don't rock the boat.' Avoiding a scene: that was what he was doing.

I'm behaving like a doormat, she told herself. Once again she made up her mind to confront him.

'I've got to go early today,' Melanie interrupted Nina's despairing thoughts. 'Will you close up after the four o'clock appointment? It's just a first fitting: the Alvares girl, shouldn't be any problem.'

'Everything okay?'

'Fingers crossed. Just something that's been worrying me a bit.'

Peter had started meeting Edwina in his lunch break. Safer than after work. He could cycle to her house from the club in eleven minutes or take the car and be there in eight. After a few polite sips of icy white wine they would move towards each other in an irresistible draw that wasted no time. Rarely did they make it upstairs. Once or twice they had gone up to a spare room with a wide inviting mattress. They never turned right at the top of the stairs to the other rooms; he assumed that the marital bed was out of bounds. His mouth twitched at that.

The exquisite thrill of the forbidden had begun to wear thin. He had never been sure who was the puppet on a string as the song went, but he was beginning to suspect that it wasn't Eddy. Peter had nearly made up his mind to pack it in. Yes, he would tell her today. He felt a shaft of jealousy as he realised that she would soon find someone else. He closed his eyes with a longing to be there in her arms and a wobble brought him back to the street. Chastened, he freewheeled down to the corner of her road, braked to balance a toe on the edge of the pavement and sent an innocuous word by text, warning of his arrival. They always kept in communication so that she could open the door quickly. Neither wanted Peter to hang about outside. He slipped through and was in her eager arms at once.

'Would you like a drink?' she pulled back to ask. That was what he needed and he took a hefty slug of the chilled

Sauvignan.

'Shall we talk for a minute?'

'Don't be silly. I want you too much for that. Come here,' she pulled him closer and still kissing him began the sly drag towards the living room.

'We should talk.'

'Later,' she was sliding down onto the creamy white carpet, holding on to him. Going on to his knees so as not to overbalance he realized that she had never been very interested in his conversation. Peter gave up and began to undress her, sliding his hand under the sweater and undoing the buttons on her shirt.

The noise of the front door being unlocked was terrifying. They rolled away from each other and Peter shot to the other end of the room and ducked behind a sofa. Edwina was into the hall in a flash, smoothing down her clothes.

'What's up, Ian?'

Christ, thought Peter flinching, it's the husband.

'Got to go over to Paris for the night. Just popped home for my toothbrush.'

'Have you had lunch?' she asked, cool as anything. Peter hoped she'd had time to do up her shirt.

'I'll grab something at the airport. Can't stop.'

'No time for a cuppa?'

Was she mad, he wondered? He could hear only quick footsteps up the stairs then silence. He wondered if he should make a run for it. He remembered with a shudder that Edwina's husband was a hefty bloke who'd played outside half. The co-owner of the Scimitar. How had he got himself into this mess? He curled up even tighter, the premonition of a tickle in his throat, dreading the sound of heavy footsteps entering the room. Hardly daring to breathe, he stared over his shoulder at the cold expanse of grey terracing outside. He'd lose his job; never get a reference. Visions of doom shot through his mind.

He'd never live it down.

Where was Eddy? He strained to hear voices but there was nothing, only his heart going at a rapid clip. The best he could probably hope for was a beating. A memory of a boxing match at school flashed through his mind. Keep your hands up to protect yourself.

To his immense relief there was chatter outside the room. He had never heard the word 'goodbye' with such relief and joy. Never again would he risk this, he vowed. He heard the front door opening and closing but remained in his agonising crouch waiting for Edwina.

With a burst of nervous giggles she peered over the back of the sofa at him.

'What a scream! Oh my poor Petey.'

'Not my most edifying moment,' he got to one knee and watched the far window. 'For Christ's sake, Eddy, enough is enough. I can't take any more shocks like that. I'm off. Going to be late as it is.'

'Come here. Calm down. How do you think I felt? My heart was hammering like a drum! But nothing happened. You could come back later, stay the night.'

'What? No, I can't. Today must have been a warning.'

She curled her arms around his neck. 'I'm sorry. It was a close thing. But he never comes home unexpectedly.'

'Well, he did today. We should cool it for a bit.'

'Don't you dare,' she wagged a mischievous finger at him. 'I'll see you in a couple of days.'

'I'm not sure,' Peter shook his head. 'I'd better go.' He unwound her arms and stepped back. He wanted Edwina to protest, to look upset, put out that her husband had nearly caught them in flagrante but her amused demeanour was disconcerting to say the least. He went straight out without a backward glance, refusing to look about in a guilty fashion. He made a beeline for his bicycle, padlocked to the railings further up the road. It was obvious that Edwina considered the whole affair to be a bit of a joke. His hands shook as he reset the combination. He sped away, full of adrenalin, his mind grappling with images from the worst-case scenario that by the skin of his teeth, he had just avoided.

Chapter Thirty-Four

Carla went back to collect the jacket from the cleaners. She stood there nervously, convinced that Harry would materialise at the door and knowing she'd go bright red if he did. He was at fault, she decided; he should not have flirted with her. Yet she berated herself for playing the coquette. She had allowed him to see that she warmed to him. It was the age-old question. Is it possible for a woman and a man to be friends? She left the shop holding a cumbersome plastic bag over her arm, escaping to the cold damp air with relief, hoping she would not be bumping too often into Harry by the local shops but at the same time she fantasised about inviting him to dinner, along with others, of course. That would be a grown-up thing to do, picturing an easy guest, interesting and light hearted. He would be able to appreciate the evident solidity of her marriage. She turned back towards the supermarket and her car and as she walked along carrying the awkward bag in one hand, then the other, images of her old life sneaked in, tinged with regret. That way madness lies, she told herself. The occasional congenial lunches with old girlfriends in the weeks leading up to Christmas had petered out with the bad weather and the planning application. Since her annoyance at the New Year's Eve dinner, she had not been in touch with the people she had once considered her closest friends. She had sent a thank you note; yet she who had never been quick to take offence remained bruised by the cynical remarks and insinuations. At the bottom of it, of her isolation, was the dread of scorn or pity when the knowledge of Rob's affair and the existence of Rose became public knowledge. How people would relish the blow to her self-satisfied personality. Schadenfreude: it was an ugly national trait. She winced, as she remembered her pleasure and pride in their close family unit, (a sham when Gabrielle was at her worst) and how mortifying now, the way she had assumed she was indispensible to so many village projects. Oh yes, she feared the contempt of her old community.

She found herself by the car, neatly parked in its bay at the supermarket. She put the bag on the back seat and took a deep breath. Where was her focus? She hadn't even done the food shopping.

Entering the house, a swell of excitement pushed aside all Carla's concerns. Tomorrow the plastic sheet was coming down; all the carpentry, decorating and flooring would have to be done right in their midst. And then they would see the back of the Merry Men. That gave her mixed feelings. For a moment she watched the builders from a distance, planning to bake a cake for them. They had been her excuse to distance herself from Rob; now there would be a second chance at beginning their new lives.

'There's something funny going on,' Buster announced the following morning, giving just the slightest nod, accompanied by a swivel of the eyeballs, in the direction of Nina and Gabrielle who were having breakfast.

Unless Terry's remarks had inspired a discussion in the kitchen, the conversation tended to be laconic after muted morning greetings and a wave to the men outside.

'Have you noticed there's still a bit of an atmosphere?' Buster swivelled his eyes back in their direction, 'There's not many laughs going on these days.'

'They're not happy. That's for sure. Long faces. Look at

them. D'you think there's gonna be a big bust-up or something?'

'You've got a very vivid imagination, Jacko,' Terry said. 'How do you know they're not just discussing who won the snooker last night?'

'I overheard something about keeping it quiet,' Buster insisted.

'It's a surprise party, you idiots,' Terry shook his head. 'Don't say a word, though. Carla doesn't know. Get on with that plastering. It's worse than the Mother's Union, you lot gossiping. Idiots.'

'As you said yourself, we're taking a polite interest in our employers,' Sean was quick with a defence.

'There's a difference in my book between a polite interest and being downright nosy,' Terry slapped down a box file on a pile of paving slabs. The four of them concentrated for a few minutes.

'Look. Now it's Nina and Rob having the chinwag,' Buster nodded gleefully. 'So it's a party they're plotting. Ah, that accounts for it.' They scanned the scene from the corner of their eyes.

'Watch it, he's coming in this direction.'

Rob came through and sat on one of the new windowsills after testing it with a finger. The weak sun through the glass warmed the room.

'Nearly there, aren't we?'

'We were just saying, we hope it won't be too intrusive when the plastic comes down later today. We'll do our best not to get in your way.'

'No no, on the contrary we'll do our best to let you get on,' said Rob. 'By the way, if my wife makes any last minute suggestions I do hope you'll run them past me. Hopefully we've covered the lot but she often gets a bee in her bonnet about something,' he laughed to soften his words. 'I trust you're on my side on this one.'

'You've got to ask yourself who's been giving us tea and cake,' came the response.

'OK Terry, so you're siding with her. The tea and cakes are merely bribery you know.'

'But none the less effective for that,' Terry gave a smile.

'You win,' Rob got up. 'Let's have a beer to celebrate before you leave tonight. Enjoy the new dimensions. I'll see you later.'

'Cheers, Guv,' chorused the men.

'Right, you three. Everything superfluous removed. Let's give them a tidy spot for the celebration.'

At four o'clock Terry gave instructions to remove the wall of polythene that had separated the family from the workers.

'No one's about right now; let's get it down.'

Sean climbed the scaffolding tower to remove the wooden frame. The heavy sheets creaked and rustled as they were folded and carried out. The men stood back whistling in appreciation of what they had achieved.

'Bloody hell, what a difference it makes.'

Various expletives echoed round the space.

The high ceiling of the old kitchen had become one with the soaring glass and steel extension, almost as wide as the rear of the house, the huge sheets of glass allowing an unbroken view of the garden.

They turned slowly to absorb the transformation, giving appreciative whistles.

'Go on, now. Get on with the tidy up. Buster, you can finish steaming the labels off the glass.'

'Sean, Jacko, get the tower down then deal with that mess out there,' he pointed to the garden. 'Bit of a clear up needed.'

They set to eagerly. Most stages in building work were a matter of regular incremental advances. There wasn't often this curtain up moment to be appreciated.

Carla was first home. At the door of the kitchen she dropped the two bags she'd been carrying and stood there wide-eyed.

'Oh my goodness. I've imagined what it would be like, having been out there often enough but I never guessed it would look this good. It's brilliant.' She moved through, a hand to her mouth. 'Oh, well done. You are all so clever. Amazing. Even better than we dreamed it would be.'

'It would be a bit late now, if you didn't like it,' said Terry, smoothing his non-existent hair, 'though I suppose we could knock it down and start again.'

'I love it. You've done a grand job,' she walked around, looking from every angle. 'What a marvellous space. Really, it's spectacular, isn't it?'

The men sat in a row on the sill, exchanging looks. They heard the front door open and Carla called out, 'Come and see. Come and see.'

Peter and Nina came in.

'Wow,' Peter flopped into a chair, gaping. 'Pretty amazing.'

Nina walked about with her dainty steps, her head tilted, taking it all in.

'It's beautiful,' was the verdict. 'You must be so happy.'

There was something self-satisfied about Rob's expression all evening. Of course, he was gratified and thrilled with the room and yet something grated on her. It was as if she'd never seen him clearly before. The champagne and beer flowed as everyone celebrated amid much congratulation all round. A probable date for the builders to pack up had been suggested. The young were full of high spirits over dinner, continuing drinking in the rather determined way that Carla abhorred, empty bottles despatched and replaced on the table by new ones without a by your leave. A short argument had erupted over an ancient dispute that had a habit of rearing its head just when family harmony was reigning.

'You still owe me—'

'Rubbish. I did not lose your camera. I've got one on my phone. Why would I want yours?'

'Well you borrowed it and I haven't seen it since.' Gabrielle was adamant.

'I used it once then I definitely put it back in your flat, way before last summer.'

'Agree to disagree,' Carla begged, 'you're spoiling the evening.'

Gaby continued eating her salmon in silence while Peter shook his head slowly, slowly with a mocking curl to his lip. She watched Rob downing his own fair share of the wine while she remained coldly sober. Would she ever regain that *liking* for her husband that she'd had? There was a look of triumph in his eyes. She could read his mind, his complacent conclusions: *Carla will be satisfied now; Carla will forgive and forget*, and following on from that she supposed, *welcome Rose!*

After a morning at the Centre, Rob invited Louise back to Number 23. The building works had been a frequent topic of his conversation for quite some time and he'd been waiting impatiently to show it off. He was proud of it, why shouldn't he be? He had been revelling in a sense of achievement, something one lacked in retirement. For once, Louise had not been hurrying off and he posed the invitation in a nonchalant way.

'I've been dying to see it. I'm sure we will all be frightfully jealous,' she spoke with genuine enthusiasm, wiping down the final table with a dishcloth, her hair a shining curtain swinging back to hide her face. The other helpers had left promptly as usual, giving Rob the chance to raise the subject.

'It's not absolutely finished of course,' he pointed out. 'It's still not properly painted or furnished but you can see the general effect.' He continued to downplay it as they stood still for a second, surveying the hall. Regulations and etiquette demanded it be left spotless for the imminent invasion of the toddler group. Satisfied, they walked round to the small parking area at the back, pine needles from a neighbouring tree crunching under their feet.

'I bet it won't be long before this whole place gets flattened for building,' Louise spoke despairingly.

'That's not going to happen, surely?'

'Oh give it time. It's inevitable but such a shame. There's not much going on for the community round here. You probably never saw the old swimming baths that were up the road. A Victorian triumph. They should have been listed. A hideous block of flats now. It's all about how to make a quick buck; you should hear what Charles has to say about the Council,' she rubbed thumb over index finger and gave him a disgusted look. 'You know, it really gets me down. Ridiculous property prices have had such a detrimental effect on the poor. People see gentrification and think it's great. Well it is, if you're on the right side of society. Oh, don't let me start. I could go on and on.'

Rob murmured agreement and as he pulled on his seatbelt, she turned the car around in two easy moves, crept up the side of the hall towards the road and waited to pull out. A group of mothers with buggies were gathering. In a moment a car slowed to give way and she set off. Rob sat quietly, enjoying the languid way she drove. Unlike Carla who sat up straight, her forehead creased in concentration as she gripped the wheel with both hands, Louise made minimal effort. She merely raked back her long hair as she glanced left or right at the junctions, staring down the oncoming traffic.

'Carla must be thrilled about the house.'

'It's sometimes hard to tell. It's been a bit full-on recently,' he regretted the frankness at once and stopped. It wouldn't do to moan after all the destitute clients of the morning. 'Builders can be quite trying,' he turned it into a joke, 'Terry and his merry men we call them.'

'They're robbing the rich to pay the poor?'

'Got it in one,' he caught her eye and chuckled.

'By the way, you won't forget will you? No mention of the party.'

'I won't. Are you sure she hasn't got a clue?'

'I'm pretty sure she hasn't. Gabrielle is going to take her off for a few hours while the preparations go on.'

For heaven's sake! Carla gave a welcoming smile that she feared might have been a grimace, wishing she'd been given a little warning that Rob was bringing Louise over this morning. She hadn't even had time to put on any makeup or to shove the mess out of sight. It was a tip. What would Louise think? At least the men were outside finishing the landscaping, doing their best to restore the garden to its former neatness. (The 'purity' of form mentioned in the sale brochure remained an aspirational ideal.) Unfortunately, today, Rob's antique urns were sporting on the left hand a tray full of mugs, while on the right an untidy pile of newspapers flapped in the wind. The final urn was draped with discarded jackets. *What a mess*, Carla grumbled, seeing everything through the critical eyes of Louise.

'Wow. This is fantastic,' the visitor looked slowly around to take it all in, 'you've done wonders. I love the height. Fantastic.'

'All Rob's idea. Sorry, I haven't had a chance to tidy up yet. Everyone was rushing about this morning getting in each other's way,' she smiled the excuse, removing some used plates from the table to put them in the sink. 'A shame you've missed them. They've only just left, actually.'

'Heavens. Don't worry; it's fine. You should see our house. This is really brilliant, wonderful light and seeing the whole garden.' Louise smiled at Rob and Carla with her lovely white teeth. How could she look this good after working since dawn cooking breakfasts and dealing with dozens of hungry refugees? Carla was impressed and smiled back.

'Do grab a chair. You must have been on your feet all morning. Makes me feel very lazy.' She filled the kettle and wondered about biscuits. Louise did not look as if she indulged in biscuits. Her ears pricked up when she saw the visitor pointing across the garden at the summerhouse.

'Is that where you meant?'

'As a very temporary solution, it might have worked.'

'Oh, what's that? What could have worked?' asked Carla.

'Rob had this amazing idea of rescuing one of our lot off the streets.'

'Tell me I'm imagining this,' she looked from one to the other.

'Don't worry, it's not going to happen,' Rob said. 'Anyway, it was merely an impulsive suggestion. Don't get your dander up. It would only have been till we could get him into a hostel. A few nights. You wouldn't have known he was here. A decent bloke, Dirik. Educated,' he nodded and looked across the table to Louise.

'We are all so privileged aren't we,' she sighed as Carla decided it must be her favourite saying. 'What's amazing is that a garden shed could be a real lifeline for someone like Dirik. He's one of our Eritreans. A breathing space, that's what they need. They're fleeing war, persecution, every single kind of ghastliness. But sadly it can't be done; too many rules and regulations. Mind you, I'm impressed. To offer part of your home like that, even for a few days, would have been a generous and unlooked for gesture,' she smiled at Carla, 'devotion beyond the call of duty, absolutely,' and she swept the long blonde hair back, turning to Rob. 'An extremely kind thought.' She was buttering him up, it was plain to see. St. Rob, of course.

'I'd better be off,' Louise drained her mug. 'That was lovely. Thank you. I'll be chasing every avenue to find a hostel somewhere, for this chap. The trouble is there are so many of them. The ones with genuine cases of persecution are utterly tragic. Especially when there are children. But even the economic migrants suffer the same in hope of a better life. This sort of work can be really distressing. Your instincts are right though, Rob, you're a Good Samaritan. If the rules change, they are talking about it, we might all be able to offer a temporary home to any bona fide refugees,' she slid back her chair. 'Completely settled in now?' she asked Carla, picking up the car keys. 'You must come over for dinner. I'll have a look in my diary and give you a ring. Thanks again for the coffee. It's lovely to see the house now it's finished. It's absolutely stunning.'

The argument had blown up almost as soon as Louise had gone.

Carla rested her head in her hands and massaged her temples. Her head was pounding like surf crashing on shingle. Perhaps this was what a stroke felt like.

Rob must be losing his marbles, the insanity of the idea. How dare he even think of offering their home to some hapless asylum seeker without consulting her? Not a word. It was all down to that woman; the way he tried to impress Louise was pathetic. Thank God, it was against the law. No way would she have put up with some unfortunate African, not that she was prejudiced, no one could accuse her of that, no matter how difficult his circumstances, living in the summerhouse at the bottom of the garden, for God's sake. Calling it a garden shed, indeed. She didn't care how heartless she seemed. Naturally she felt sorry for the unfortunate souls from the Centre, she really did, she'd heard some heartrending stories but honestly, when she and Rob had hardly been in the place for any length of time, it was unbelievable. Rob's complete lack of empathy for her feelings once again demoralized her. It was obvious they were no longer on the same wavelength.

Chapter Thirty-Five

Peter's cold feet with regard to Edwina persisted. There was no way he was going to risk seeing her alone again. He must have been mad, off his trolley. The husband owned half the club for Christ's sake: what had he been thinking of? It was very difficult to avoid her altogether and he resorted to subtle prevarication, not much liking the look on her face when at the third or fourth rebuff, she shrugged, then softened it with a come-hither sulky pout that turned into a genuine regretful smile.

'I'm missing you.'

'Shit, Edwina, I've got to watch it. It's my job and everything.' He opened his hands in appeal as she walked away across the wide foyer, car keys twirling on a finger.

A few days later she gave him a flash from her eyes. What the hell did that mean? In desperation he tried some flattery the next time she cornered him. It was not too hard. Edwina wore as usual a figure hugging tennis dress, her legs lustrous and golden, in mid winter and her face as pretty as ever.

'You know you're too gorgeous for words. Can't you see I'm doing my best to resist you? It's not easy.' This was the line he clung to. He resorted to whispering excuses in her ear as he passed close to her.

'You're too much for me, you'll end up breaking my heart.'

Her narrowed eyes at these moments were not comforting. He became aware quite suddenly of a vindictive streak at odds with her essential good nature. 'No one dumps Eddy' was the implication when she ignored his attempt to remain aloof.

'Do you know what you're doing to me?' he pleaded. 'You're tearing me apart.' This much was true; he was beginning to find her presence excruciating. Trying to placate her made him loathe himself. With guile, he persuaded her to join a group session for her tennis lessons, a lively bunch of 'young marrieds' who'd joined the club after Christmas. In the reduced time alone with her she occasionally let her eyes linger on him or an innocent text message would ping on to his phone making him wince. Fear had driven away his desire: the words *a woman scorned* repeated themselves, a tardy epithet that was no use to him now.

He left the club at five one afternoon, in a heavy drizzle and taking his usual route marched nimbly between the pedestrians, carrying a take-away cup of tea from a kiosk. He slowed to sip now and then, loping on until he could fling the cup into a bin. Unimpeded he hurried along. A few minutes later the familiar sports car pulled in rapidly at the curb and Edwina called from the lowered window. 'Peter, get in.'

'I shouldn't,' he muttered, weak and undecided, bending to see her face.

'Do get out of the rain,' she commanded, opening the door.

Once in, he looked across at her. His mouth turned down as she revved the engine and shot into the traffic.

'You can't escape me now,' she taunted him with a tight smile.

'Look Eddy, you're not being fair to me,' he smiled back to win her over, taking a moment to think. Go for the flattery, he told himself, 'you're completely irresistible. You know you are. I'm all at sixes and sevens over you. You do realise that?' he repeated. 'Admit you're just playing games with me. You've always had the upper hand.'

Suddenly she grinned.

'You didn't need much encouragement,' she darted a glance

as the car speeded up. 'You have dirty thoughts, my darling. I can read your mind perfectly,' her hand strayed to his lap. Her boldness only sickened him but he pressed her fingers against himself then pushed them away.

'Admit it, you're only toying with me. I doubt you've got a single genuine feeling for me.'

Edwina swung round a corner and slowly crept along the road until there was a space.

'My darling, you are such an idiot. I've never fancied anyone so much. You're utterly delicious,' her gurgling laugh teased him. She undid her seat belt and moved towards him. 'Are you really falling for me? That would be so sweet.'

'Now you're patronising me.'

'Kiss me,' she tried to pull him as close as possible in the cramped space. His knee banged on the CD player as he turned towards her. Her mouth met his and he felt desire jolt through him then dissipate at once, 'I can't go on any more, Eddy. I told you.' He held her head away, hands gentle in her hair, wanting her to get the message. He looked into her eyes. 'I want you so much it's unbearable but our lives are miles apart. I'm no use to you really.'

'Don't be feeble, Peter. We've both enjoyed it. Why don't we let it run its course? You wouldn't want me to get cross with you, would you?' her voice held a hint of venom and she slid away from him, staring through the windscreen.

'I'm sorry, I've got to go. Actually, I really am busy tonight. I'm sorry. I'll see you at the club,' he fumbled for the door handle as she stared straight ahead. 'I'll see you.'

'Maybe.' She drove off before he'd closed the door properly, leaving him standing like an imbecile, disgusted by his pathetic excuses.

A few days later during a lunch break the manager of the centre appeared and jerked his head once unsmiling.

'Peter, could I have a word please?'

His insides curdled with foreknowledge.

'Sure. Here?'

'In my office.'

As he followed, Peter looked about with a sense of desolation. He'd begun to take for granted the opulent lounge and bar, the sporty, affable clientele and well-equipped gym and courts. One or two people looked up to wave at him in the friendliest manner. He'd been in clover here. Had he really risked all this for a randy married tart? They went through the building while his dread mounted and he flinched from a rush of acid reflux.

'Look, it won't happen again. If there's been a complaint I can sort it out.'

'A complaint? On the contrary we've had some excellent feedback from the members. Come in, come in.'

Peter was reeling, certain that relief must be spread all over his features. He held the back of the swivel chair for support.

'Yes, Peter. The management are very pleased indeed. We'd like you to have a look at a new contract, a change in the remuneration level, expand the job description, that sort of thing. Good man. Sit down and we'll have a chat.'

That night while Nina's warm even breathing told him she was asleep, Peter resolved to put his life in order. First he prayed that Eddy would not accuse him of improper behaviour, rebuking himself for his stupidity. Never again. As for Nina— she deserved better than a half-hearted streak of piss without the guts to tell her it was over. He would sort that out and then he would work harder than ever to show his father just how much he could achieve. They had faith in him at the club. It was about time he grew up.

Gradually order was being restored to house and grounds. Each day the paint pots, boxes of screws and lengths of wood strewn on the new sleek floor of polished concrete were reduced. Appearances were deceptive however. Outwardly things were tidied up but the Lord of Misrule was still at play. Mercifully out of the house most days with a temporary job at an estate agency, Gabrielle could still be capricious in mood. Lacerating wit about the new workplace had them in stitches but sometimes the chip on her shoulder was plain to see, her disgust that she was merely an administrative assistant was all too evident. On her way home, she stopped regularly to chat with the dog's owner; there was a wounded depth to his eyes that got to her. She was sure he needed rescuing, she told the family. Nina and Peter's relationship was running a rocky course. Bite the bullet, Carla wanted to say; it's going to be bitter and nasty, get it over. There was something uneasy about her boy's face; she did not like to see it. One minute he would be open and enthusiastic then his expression would shift, his eyes resting on Nina and his brows knitting while he gnawed a thumbnail in an anxious way, before his eyes drifted uncomfortably round the room. He was defensive, off-hand when she probed. After work Nina went flat hunting and once back, spent more and more time in the room at the top of the house.

Carla was excited by the sensational extension and yet in a heightened mood of vulnerability she panicked that the children would never leave or that they would leave too soon and she would lose control over them, her role diminished for all time. Rob was miles away beyond an invisible barrier. She recognized it was a sad cliché. She could see him speak but the words hardly impinged on her. They were going through the motions. Why did every thought have to turn into a hackneyed phrase? He appeared puzzled by her, his usual nonchalance absent; they were at an impasse regarding Rose, saying nothing. Carla had backed off but he had taken no action as yet. She was sure the girl was pestering him: oh let him do as he wished.

He was walking a tightrope between his children. She would watch him fall if she had to. The bitterness of her response sickened her, but there it was.

A visit to Tate Modern with Harry and the others (safety in numbers she decided) was planned. Rob meant to go, he had every intention, he told Carla but at the last minute something had come up. A Planning officer was to meet one of his new clients on site and it was vital to be present.

The Arts Club members always communicated by email; that was good; it gave one time to decide. The informality offered a chance of backing out if necessary but Carla was finding it more enjoyable to go out in a group than alone. She didn't dwell on the hurt that her old friends inflicted by their silence. She would make the effort later on; it would be easier once the application for sixty, sixty! houses opposite The Old Manor had been decided. Rob had mentioned public meetings and consultations with the Highways Department, something about the Local Plan. She willed the development to go away.

Today, the gallery visit would begin with a light lunch at twelve thirty and then they would wander and see the pictures. She had no chance to sit near Harry; she gazed at the view over the river trying not to look at him at the other end of the table though absurdly, her heart beat a little faster when she felt his eyes on her. She was at ease with the group now, enjoying getting to know the different faces.

She lost sight of Harry quite quickly in the afternoon and walked around with one of the women. Peggy made erudite comments with a serious expression that seemed to disapprove of the occasional irreverent remark that Carla could not suppress. It appeared she had donned a cloak of blasé sophistication unlike her normal self. The vast Turbine Hall was always impressive although the installation of sculptures left her cold. Later, tired of looking at the paintings in the upper galleries she sloped off, declining a cup of tea in the café. She felt a little pang on leaving; she had not exchanged two words with Harry all afternoon.

The resentment in Rose had built up over the weeks into a very black mood. She knew she had every right to feel bitter. Hadn't Rob promised he would be in touch? Three short-lived telephone calls had only exacerbated the situation. She gave up replying to her mother's calls in indignation that it was not her father. Her mother had called her work number wanting an assurance that Rose was all right and taking her pills.

'I can't talk. Yes, of course I'm fine,' she protested, cutting her off. She gave no credence to her mother's fears and ignored the warning signs she'd learnt to recognise in the past.

Carla was an obstacle looming grotesquely in her imagination, denying her a future. In the depths of night, Rose vowed, 'I'll show her.' Yet the way ahead was unclear. Luke had gone to Berlin for a short tour with a band and Rose missed her sounding board. One conviction dominated her mind: Carla had poisoned the family against her; it made her throb with anger. At work she struggled to keep the ideas flowing. Let the others give her a free ride for a change. They had coasted often enough on her creative output.

This evening, Rose had lain in wait for Rob for over an hour. She craved a few words to comfort her. Catching sight of Peter or Gabrielle gave her a quick fix that dulled the pain for an evening. She had taken to hanging about near the Unwins' road, with her parka hood pulled up or wearing a woolly hat and scarf so that little of her face was visible. Anyway it was a free country wasn't it? It was difficult to get much of an inkling of the times they might appear. Peter was the most regular; she was building up courage to say something soon. He had seemed friendly enough at the dinner. Gabrielle had been cooler, not glacial but impervious to her overtures. Gabrielle was often hurrying away from home, heading who knew where. If she spotted Rob today and he looked approachable, she was determined to talk to him. He owed her that at least. She'd crossed London to see him. Carla was malignly elusive: she never caught sight of her. There was a route Rose could take on the underground that enabled her to emerge from the tube station nearest the house, walk along for ten minutes and then dawdle, a bus shelter for cover halfway along, keeping the end of the road in view. It was busy enough at that time of day for her feel safe, reassuring herself that she was a loving daughter wanting only to catch a glimpse of her father.

Standing back against the corner shop window, she began to feel conspicuous. What if the witch came by? There were usually enough pedestrians about to act as camouflage but the street was strangely quiet for once. Chewing her nails, she stared along the road at every figure that came into view. She had no idea whether Rob might appear or not. His movements were mostly unpredictable.

Be lovely to meet, she had sent a text to him first thing but no response had come to soothe the tautness of her nerves. She pulled up her hood, paced up and down to keep warm, shrank back against the shop, checked her phone again and again. Then all at once, he was just yards away, behind a woman bending to push a buggy while her child sucked on a lollipop. There was a shock of recognition as he caught sight of her, followed by a broad smile. Too broad, she thought at once and then he was right in front of her.

'Rose? Good Lord. Hi, what are you up to? Oh God, I never answered your text. Forgive me. So much on today.'

She could tell he was put out but he kissed her cheek, looked each way and said, 'Come on, lets walk. What are you doing in this neck of the woods?' He eyed her brightly, a red woollen scarf cheerful at his collar.

'Just an errand for work,' she nodded vaguely up the road,

feeling dowdy and insignificant. Pulling back the hood of her jacket with a frown and avoiding his eyes she muttered, 'I'm an embarrassment to you.'

'Don't be ridiculous,' he patted her. The brief touch on her back was astonishing; at once she felt his affection envelop her, bringing a sudden glow to her face and she felt pretty, loving, not needy that foul word that Luke had tarred her with.

'How are you? Come on tell me what you've been up to. You're looking well.'

She found herself strolling with him, warmth lingering between the shoulder blades, chattering too much as ever.

'Well, work's been a pain. I seem to have lost my inspiration somehow. I'm hoping it will come back. Though my boss is being quite the taskmaster, very demanding. A bit of a bully at times. You know. Things will improve, I expect. I'm starting a course next month, design based. Everything else is quite quiet. The time of year, I suppose. A bit depressing.' They split up to walk either side of an elderly woman in bedroom slippers pulling a shopping trolley, then joined up again. 'But how are you and the others? Have they got used to the idea of me?' she gave a beseeching look at him. 'I loved meeting them. I hope I didn't give the wrong impression.'

'Nonsense. You must come round again. The house is very nearly finished now. There will be lots more time soon. I'm getting some projects set up. The planning stage is quite tricky. Getting all the ducks in a row; you know how it is.'

Something was making him stumble in his sentences. He appeared uncomfortable, unsure what to say; he did not seem so charmed by her, the thought struck her like a blow. She made a last desperate stab.

'Could we have lunch again, perhaps the two of us? Oh no, that's just silly. You're far too busy.'

'Of course we can, we must. Let me get Carla's 60th party out of the way next weekend then we shall make a plan. Where on earth does time go?' he shook his head, looked enquiringly. 'Are you okay for money, Rose? I could help if you need anything,' his hand went to his pocket. 'I expect that course is costing you…'

'No, thanks, I don't need anything,' she spoke dully, shaking her head. Did he really think she was after money? What a fucking idiot. She could have wept with disappointment.

He had stopped walking. 'I need to head up there. Look, I'll be in touch, Rose. Be a good girl and be patient. And look after yourself,' he gave her a brief hug before crossing the road.

He couldn't wait to get away. Rose stared miserably after him.

Nina's resolve was building and she began to face up to difficult decisions. At work, Melanie's moods were even more volatile than usual. What was wrong with the woman? Once Nina had found her in tears, tears that were dashed away, the unhappiness covered up by ordering her assistant about. The studio behind the showroom had a less comfortable atmosphere; the racks of dresses in their dust-proof bags were a reproof she tried to ignore. She would flower in the months ahead, she insisted to herself, her single status nothing to be feared. She might even leave the protection of Melanie's faltering guardianship and look elsewhere.

It was no longer a relief to be at home with Peter, either. She could sense his feelings for her ebbing away, week by week. There was an inevitability about it that crushed her. Tonight, they'd watched the television after supper with the others. Looking around the room at them, lolling in chairs, Rob with the paper, Carla fussing over hot drinks or fiddling with the pages of a large art catalogue, Gabrielle flicking at the screen of her mobile, Pete a sprawled lump beside her. Nina was overwhelmed with a strong sense of being an outsider.

Now, she sat up in bed pretending to read while he

pottered, taking his time. Her shoulders grew cold in the thin slip as she waited. Eventually he had no alternative but to climb into bed with her. He settled beside her and after a moment she turned her head to look evenly at him saying nothing. There was an uncomfortable moment.

'You're not too happy right now, are you Neen?'

This was her opportunity, if she dared.

'Not very.'

'Is it work?'

'No. It's not.'

'You'll feel more cheerful tomorrow.' What a coward he was.

'Mm. Not if things carry on like this.'

They were half sitting up. He dragged the duvet closer and gazed down at the pale blue and white stripes, looking fearful of what was to come.

'You're seeing someone else.'

His shoulders relaxed and his head came up to look into her eyes.

'Of course not. For God's sake, what do you take me for? I can put my hand on my heart and swear. Look, I'm sorry things are a bit strained, living with my parents; it's not easy for you. I could tell you weren't exactly on top of the world but you're being ridiculous. You're right to hunt for a flat; things will look up when you get your independence back. You need your own space, then you can see the wood for the trees.'

She could tell he was wildly improvising, but was he being honest?

'I've seen you in someone's car. Don't deny it.'

'Fuck's sake, Nina, people give me lifts. All perfectly innocent. I promise I am not seeing anyone.'

'Okay then but you've changed.'

'People change all the time. It's part of life's rich pattern. We don't want to tie each other down yet, do we? Perhaps we just need to live apart for a bit. Have a breathing space,' he laid his head on her shoulder. 'Don't let's be cross now. Here give me a hug. We'll see how it all pans out. We don't have to do anything drastic. You're still the most beautiful girl I've ever met.'

Now he was sugaring the pill: Nina closed her eyes. A slim white hand on his thigh flashed into her mind. Perhaps it had never gone further. He sounded indignant enough but the words 'I love you' never came. She would get out as soon as she could. See how he liked that. She bit back a sob. She would not howl with misery; she would not.

Chapter Thirty-Six

The brakes screeched on the wet road as Gabrielle waited on the edge of her seat for the stop, ignoring the bold stare of a short, muscular individual standing in the aisle. She wasn't in the mood. The door of the bus whooshed open and she dodged past, leaping down, just avoiding a large puddle. She pulled a loose woollen hat out of her pocket and tucked her hair under as she walked on towards home. Her striking face with its chiselled nose, lips and chin wore a perplexed expression. Gaby's mind had not often been quite so scattered as it was these days.

Across town at a friend's flat, they'd spent the evening half-watching a film (while discussing the pros and cons of various men) and polishing off a bottle of wine. Kat had offered her a tiny bedroom from the end of the month, at mate's rates and Gabrielle was inclined to accept. She asked if she could think it over for a day or two. It would eat into her savings but would relieve the hassle of home.

Gaby pulled at strands of her hair that had escaped the hat, checking the new length. The two girls had trimmed each other's hair, a favour they'd exchanged many times over the years. Katherine's fine long hair was easy, a few snips with the dressmaking scissors and it was done. Pale wisps were hardly noticeable on the beige carpet.

'Your turn.' They swapped over and when the tea towel was draped on Gabrielle's shoulders, Katherine lifted heavy hanks of the damp mop and hacked, there was no other word for it.

'I'm keeping a few layers in, okay?'

'Do what you did last time. That was fine.' Gaby held still, not the least concerned about the shower of hair descending to the floor. In spite of the heavy-handed approach, Kat achieved a tousled, face framing style, falling down to the shoulders at the back.

'Just let me even it up along the bottom,' Katherine combed and snipped, her tongue poking out of her mouth in concentration. 'You're so lucky to have such a mass of hair.'

'Well, I envy you your dead straight locks.' In fact this was a fib. Gaby was fond of her hair and unlike most women never despaired of it. The usual paraphernalia of hair care: serums, tongs, straighteners, hot curlers and blow dries were not needed to achieve bouncing glossy locks. She ran her fingers through the still-damp strands and suddenly as it often did, the thought of Rose sent an angry dart through her. Fuck it. She'd been happy all evening, planning a possible move to this slightly cramped environment with Kat and Emma who were full of feminist strategies and an engrossing interest in each other's lives. It would make a change to be enveloped in their solicitude. At home she was aware of an indifference or disinclination to share her concerns. She could see a clear-cut divide: before and after. Faith in the decency of her family had been a given, even if she had always needed to impress them. What else could be lurking in muddy waters, poisonous things she had no control over? She could not talk to Pete any more; he hardly seemed to care, wrapped up in his own affairs. Neither had she confided in Kat; the subject was still raw and she had no desire to add any more criticism of her father to her own chorus.

She scuffed along towards home, heedless of the shower that had pedestrians ducking into doorways, pulling up hoods or hurrying by, jostling her with their shopping. She frowned as she imagined Tim and his dog, dear little Cassie; where were they sheltering from the pelting rain this evening? She had very nearly latched on to him as a cause to embrace; ideas of finding him accommodation through her father, or a job — he was bright enough, of steering him into a rewarding and more comfortable place in the mainstream, had dwindled away. Tim was too elusive, his past was not for delving into; he wouldn't disclose the reasons for his homelessness. He was unreceptive to her subtleties and she was in danger of making a fool of herself.

A fool in more ways than one, Gabrielle reflected. Some of the recent barbs from her mother had got under her skin. Was there perhaps a grain of truth in them? If she was arrogant, her upbringing had cultivated that, reinforcing her superiority with prizes and rewards. Was she unrealistic about her job prospects since the redundancy? She'd had rapid promotions before; the recent knock-backs would surely be forgotten soon. Besides she was doing fine at the estate agency, a temporary job she could do standing on her head. Her mother could hardly complain about that. One criticism from Carla niggled more than the others. *Man-mad. Promiscuous. Can't stick with anyone.* Various withering ripostes had sprung to her lips but she had walked out in a contemptuous silence. Staying power was irrelevant unless you wanted to settle down with a man; her mother's ideas were fixed firmly in the twentieth century, decades out of date. There was no point in tolerating a bloke if he failed to measure up to one's standards. *Set your standards higher!* was the unspoken reproach Oh rubbish, Gabrielle reasoned, it was more fun to play the field and sitting waiting for a prince to ride up on his charger was simply laughable. Any little ache of yearning could be obliterated by a damn good night out.

She sidestepped a couple with arms wrapped around each other, oblivious of the rain and blind to other pedestrians. *Look where you're going.* Her mobile rang and she delved under her coat to reach it.

'Hi, Algie.'

'How you doing? What say we go out for a meal one night next week?'

'Could do.'

'Don't be so enthusiastic. Are you okay? You sound a bit down?'

'I'm absolutely fine, thanks,' she could do without Algie feeling sorry for her. 'Life's a breeze. Well, what about Tuesday?'

'Good. Tuesday it is. Let me text you when I get out of work. It will be about eight.'

'Thanks,' she relented. 'Great.'

'That's more like it.'

She was glad she had something to look forward to.

Chapter Thirty-Seven

The bus roared to a stop and Carla nipped into the last free seat beside an elderly man holding tight to a walking stick between his knees as he sat upright, looking ahead with a stern expression. Did she still expect Londoners to acknowledge her presence? Carla placed her bag on her knees and keeping her elbows in, reread the notes she'd made on her phone while browsing in the kitchen shop. The basics had been fitted weeks before but ideas for up to date accessories were needed. She was shocked by the prices she'd seen in the smart shops on Marylebone High St. Yet the small appliances were rather beautiful. Still, perhaps she should stick to John Lewis. She stood to allow her neighbour to move out and inch slowly along the aisle, his stick wobbling as she slid across to the vacated seat.

She looked to see if Uldis had replied to the email about her return. It was quite possible she'd found work somewhere else. Had she looked a little surly recently when Carla smiled and flapped her hands to communicate? Carla sighed. The other passengers dreamed, breathed, coughed, spoke in staccato bursts into their mobiles. Soon, worries about her children took over; in some ways Gaby had misplaced her life as much as her mother seemed to have done. Soon, unbelievably, she Carla would be in possession of a Freedom card; she could apply for one as soon as her birthday had passed. Sixty. Old Age Pensioner. Senior Citizen. She didn't feel ready for old age however it was labelled; her instinct was to keep quiet, not let anyone find out. Who would care anyway, she reflected dully? A sharp jolt as a girl bumped down beside her and they exchanged a quick smile. She made a To Do list, vigorously planning her week with its tasks and errands, tap-tapping intently on the little keypad.

Ten minutes later a message alert pinged. Harry. A photograph of a small bright bird on a twig accompanied the brief exclamation.

Waxwings have arrived en masse! Stunning. A rare sight this far south. Hurry if you'd like to see them, they may move on.

Carla, bemused, tapped back **where?**

In the park just where we walked the other day.... am there now

She looked at her watch. She could be there in about twenty minutes. It seemed mean to quash his enthusiasm. She studied the picture again, unsure if she'd ever heard of the birds.

They'd better be good. See you in about half an hour.

She reassessed her journey. She could stay on the bus for an extra stop and then it would take no time to reach him. You could almost say it was educational.

Engrossed on his computer, Rob had scarcely been aware of the afternoon going by. The builders had completed the finishing touches and the house was ready to be christened; the bottles of bubbly safely stowed in the summerhouse, well out of Carla's way. She would appreciate all the arrangements, be grateful for the trouble he'd gone to. If no one made a fuss about the birthday, she would be upset. Rob quelled any niggles of doubt.

The photographs on his website were good, bloody good. So they should be; he had a more than decent camera. The pictures followed the stages of the build, culminating in the end result that looked fantastic. Rob leaned back on his office chair and rubbed his chin as he glanced over some of his earlier designs on the screen. Where to go from here? He could not utilize the Angus and Latimer client list but word of mouth would spread if he put in the time to network. Planning for the apartment was in the pipeline; a separate small project looked as if it would be commissioned too. He had recently become a trustee of Louise's charity; he half despised himself for succumbing quite so readily whenever the spotlight of her attention fell on him. It was very hard to say no to her. Besides which, they got on so well it seemed like a waste of a good rapport not to go with the flow. The flow in this case being trustee meetings and responsibilities which he simply did not need. Still, it was nice to be valued. Through the window, he watched a Range Rover draw in to the kerb and the couple carry loaded carrier bags into the house. The hum of traffic in the distance grew louder as the afternoon passed; these calm days allowed the persistent drone to creep into the house. It was only three o'clock.

He must consider Rose. Rose, Rose, Rose. He looked up at the ceiling, rolled his shoulders and stretched his arms to remove the tension. He must talk to Gabrielle or maybe just to Peter and arrange for the poor girl to come over. Again he berated himself for his cowardice on the night of the quiz. It would have been the perfect introduction to the whole family. Emil would have diluted the intensity with that charming air of the friendly boffin. Rob had not dared suggest it. He had begun to wonder why he had no great desire to spend time with Rose on his own. She was too emotionally draining perhaps, though he could help to remedy that; even in small doses her company was somehow exhausting, he could feel the energy seeping from him. He did not have much oomph these days. He supposed the strain of getting the extension right and the cool atmosphere between him and Carla, their absurd tiff yesterday over arrangements for a weekend in Somerset, Gabrielle's tiresome histrionics, not to mention Nina's soulful gazes, were all a bit much. Throw in the clamour of Rose's unspoken entreaties and it was an effort not to snap at the lot of them. Hurrah for Peter though, he was doing well at last. Don't go and blow it, he thought. He considered the arguments that seemed to flare up all the time: kids sniping at each other, incapable of a quiet discussion. They got on his nerves. He would kick them all out one of these days. No excuses, just bugger off, he would tell them.

Rob went into the kitchen. God, what a mess it still was. No one had cleared up since the night before. If he hadn't had to go out he would have got on with it himself. How could his beautiful new room get so trashed? He stood looking around, stiff with disapproval. He'd crack the whip when he got back and get those idle youngsters to tidy up. Of course, they'd had friends round last night, played poker noisily until late. He'd had to go down and read the riot act. He shook his head over the spread of bottles and cans on the floor near the bin. They took everything for granted. He simply could not believe they'd gone off to work without lifting a finger. Where had Carla gone today? She would not have been impressed. He gave the room a disgusted look, turned his back on it and went through to the front door. Plenty of time to sort it out, before dinner. Why hadn't the cleaner been? She couldn't still be ill, could she? Perhaps she'd buggered off back to Budapest, leaving them in the lurch. He looked at his watch again. He would be back in an hour or so and Gabrielle would be in by then; the pair of them would knuckle down and have it all shipshape in no time. He almost left a note for Carla to tell her not to worry, he'd be back soon to tidy up and lend a hand with the meal.

It had become an obsession. Rose had set Rob aside, the better to focus her resentment against Carla. A party for her, Rob had mentioned. So Carla was to have a massive celebration when Rose had missed out on twenty-seven birthdays and Christmases with her father. Carla had prevented it, playing happy families with her darling Gaby and Peter, never allowing him enough slack to see his middle child. Had Carla not been such a bitch, Rob would surely have felt able to include Rose in his life. Even her mother had implied as much. How she'd dreamed of him meeting her at the school gates, picking her up from some teenage gathering where she would pretend to be embarrassed. Something about the short brunette woman stirred Rose to a fury. She'd watched her leave the house more than once recently, bustling like a guinea fowl full of self-importance, heading off to spend his money, Rose was sure.

The usual compulsion had drawn her back to the streets near the Unwins' home. Getting out of work early was simple enough. Some days she used a different route and would emerge into the stream of people by the shops. She hung about for half an hour before deciding that she would look for her half-sister. She nursed a fantasy of Gabrielle taking little sis under her wing. Perhaps she was the one to win over. She'd seen Gabrielle in her running gear several times and once had hurried after her into a nearby park before being chicken and turning back, letting the vigorous figure jog away out of sight. Perhaps today she might be brave enough to say hello.

The afternoon light was going fast, an evening mist blurring the outlines of distant trees and buildings. Glum apathy alternated with adrenaline pumping, as Rose waited on a wooden bench near the Pavilion. She sat up suddenly, recognising Carla's back view. The compact walk was unmistakeable; it had an urgent quality to it. Carla was in a hurry. She must have sprung into view from the adjacent path.

Rose got slowly to her feet and followed the hurrying figure, fighting the instinct to turn away. Then she stood still, staring. As Carla came to a sudden halt some little distance away, a man emerged from the trees to meet her, touching her arm for a second. They walked on together, leaving Rose open mouthed. There was something intimate about the way they looked at each other, Rose could tell. Was it a tryst? She was only about fifty yards behind when they turned down a narrow side path between thickets of bushes, disappearing from sight among the trees. Rose walked straight on, disturbed and triumphant. That holier than thou bitch was up to something. Her mind reeled as she hurried on, making for her usual vantage point near the corner shop. If Carla did not appear within a few minutes she had to be guilty. Rose held her breath. She faced the window and did not register the tins of soup in a precarious pyramid or the colourful arrangement of linen tea towels for sale. The sight of Carla inexplicably meeting a man had released a burst of consternation quickly turning to anger. A wife like that did not deserve Rob. And still she had not appeared in the street. Rose walked on to another of her 'spots' where she often attempted to keep a discreet vigil on the comings and goings of the family. The bus shelter was smelly and dank with cigarette ends littering the floor and a used nappy discarded in a corner. After ten accusatory minutes she moved further along, drawn by a thread to Elmwood Rd where she waited again. She looked at her watch, panicking that she should flee: she was too exposed, too vulnerable just here in the grey late afternoon. She darted from the protection of a large stone gateway to make for the tube, putting up her umbrella to hide her face, hurrying along the road while carefully watching figures in the distance coming towards her. Near the Tube station, Rose rested the umbrella on her shoulder, ready to duck out of sight out as she waited to go across. Mercifully a few heavy drops of rain had begun to fall. The umbrella did not look so silly now.

Nina was often amused by the goings on at the end of the week in the studio. You just had to hold on to your sense of humour, she reasoned. In theory, every bride would be in possession of her wedding dress a fortnight before the big day but in practice, panicky phone calls would routinely interrupt the studio as the bride scrutinized her dress for the umpteenth time and decided to panic about the fit, the veil, the silk roses around the neckline, matters which had been finalised long before. The clients would need to be squeezed into the few slots kept free for just these changes of mind and the calming strategies worthy of any psychologist, would be fully deployed. Serenity was also encouraged by the aromatherapy candles wafting perfumes especially recommended for the purpose: ylang ylang and the like. Melanie was an expert. Her voice too took on a more soothing tone and with a few tiny alterations the last minute anxieties would be smoothed away and normal work resumed as the bride and her maid of honour went happily out of the door, holding at each end what looked like a vast white body bag containing The Dress. Nina and Mel would give each other a despairing look and then burst into giggles.

After another pair of squawking young women had been pacified and the morning was edging into Friday afternoon, Melanie's face looked haggard, pale beneath the remnants of the Caribbean tan. Something was wrong. Her exchanges with the next pair of girls as they tried on at least a dozen dresses, with rows of miniscule buttons to be hooked up, were almost curt, very unlike her usual self.

'Shall I take over?' Nina had whispered twice but the barest shake of the head was all the response she got.

Finally there was the chance of a break.

'I'm popping across the road to Costa,' Nina grabbed her purse, 'Cappuccino as usual, Mel?'

'Thanks. I need a bit of perking up.'

'Are you okay, Mel?' Nina placed the cardboard cups on the table, 'you're looking a bit down.'

Melanie's thumbs circled and she glanced at the clock. 'I was going to talk to you later but we've got a few minutes. I've had a bit of bad news.'

Nina stared at her; Mel looked away for a second then held Nina's gaze.

'You know those appointments I've had? Well, I've got breast cancer. It's a sod but there it is.'

'Oh my God. I'm so sorry,' Nina bent down to give her a long appalled hug. 'That's awful news. How horrible for you. But you'll start treatment right away, won't you? The docs are fantastic now with what they can do.'

'Oh, yup. It looks like I'll have to have the works,' she blinked hard and blew on her coffee, then looked across at Nina who had sunk down to perch on the nearby chair. Melanie rallied herself.

'What I wanted to say was that I'd like you to carry on the business, run it for me. You know every aspect of it anyway. I expect you were thinking of going it alone soon weren't you?'

Nina was sure she looked astounded. 'Run it for you?'

'Yes, take over everything; use the flat upstairs. I'm happy to give advice but I want no responsibility until I've kicked this bloody disease. You can use my name till you've built up your own clientele. Maybe, buy me out. Think about it. You'd be doing me a huge favour,' Melanie gave a reluctant grin. 'You can do it you know.'

'I don't know what to say,' Nina blurted out, 'I'm so sorry about your news.'

'Don't worry. I'm going to beat it,' she sat up and straightened her shoulders. 'You will take over, won't you?'

'All right. If you really think I can,' she nodded, 'thank you. Thanks for believing in me.'

Walking the short distance home after the delight of watching the flock of waxwings, the irruption, to use the correct term, all fluttering deliriously with their red-tipped wings as they feasted on the rowan and hawthorn berries, Carla's mood faltered and dipped. Only minutes earlier she had been utterly engrossed in the spectacle, amazed in fact, that she'd never been aware of the waxwing in spite of years of David Attenborough and Nature Watch. The mass of colourful birds greedily crowding the branches was spectacular. She felt at ease in Harry's company but any romantic inclinations had fled, thank goodness, she told herself. She put the nonsense down to her loneliness in the midst of the whirlwind that seemed to swirl around Number 23. She was tired of her family's constant bickering and as for Gabrielle's odd friendship with that homeless busker, parroting his ludicrous anarchical view of the world (throwing in some articulate anti-globalisation opinions and environmentalism which heaven knew most people supported in a reasonable, moderate sort of way) and demanding now to bring him home for a meal, to find him a job, give him a room, that was surely daft. The missionary zeal to rehabilitate the poor boy would only bring complications. At least Gaby had been out of the house for a few days and earning a bit of money at the estate agency. Carla pictured her bleary-eyed daughter who'd stayed up half the night with those noisy friends, blithely ignoring the fact that she had another interview today. How had their prize-winning golden girl turned into a weird amalgam of fitness freak and third-rate hippy in her tatty clothes from the charity shops, chasing after every man who looked at her? The trouble was, they all did. Why couldn't she find a steady boyfriend? Going upstairs two weeks ago with an armful of washing and hearing a male voice from Gaby's bedroom had felt like the last straw. Carla had rapidly retreated, had had it out with her later in a furious exchange.

'Appalling behaviour under our roof! Makes me feel really uncomfortable. Dad won't like it at all,' Carla accused.

'I find that pretty hypocritical coming from him!' Gabrielle had retorted, her lip curling and eyes flashing. 'I can have a nice chat with him about double standards. Anyway, I shall be out of here soon.'

Oh, she was sick of them. Even darling Peter: he was right under the thumb of Nina now, it seemed. The girl's slender appearance came into in her mind. Unworldly or not, Nina worried her; she was becoming rather withdrawn. The whole family should pull together to give her some support, Carla had suggested. She'd seized on a book in a charity shop, kept it hidden under her pillow and had pored over some of the pages for advice when she had a moment. Eating disorders did not make cheerful reading.

The Rose problem still simmered, of course, the source of so many uncomfortable musings. In addition, she was missing, actually missing Terry's friendly features. Carla counted up all the elements that made her life ridiculous. She herself was utterly ridiculous. Her pace slowed. She was nearly home. She gave the monkey-puzzle tree on the corner a scathing look for its ugliness. Dismiss those negative reflections, she snapped. On the contrary, life was marvellous, get a grip, keep everyone calm and happy; all the little provocations would come out in the wash. She'd lost utterly all sense of proportion. She almost managed a smile as she reached the front door. It never entered her head that last night's mess would still be arrayed in all its tawdry glory.

As soon as she walked through the house the resolutions vanished. Really, she'd had enough.

Carla contemplated the room. The detritus of family life: Tracey Emin should use it for inspiration. Dirty glasses, bottles and beer cans, plates, take-away cartons and poker dice still littered the table along with papers and post, a racquet with a broken string, sticky bottles of medicine, a makeup bag, chargers for phones and laptops abandoned on every surface.

A pair of shoes under a chair, a hat with earmuffs, if she cared to do the full inventory of superfluous items it would probably fill a page. Her dream kitchen. How quickly it had turned into the family dumping ground. She could cry. Well, she for one was not going to clear up again. Going without breakfast, walking straight out after putting her nose round the door, she hadn't expected to come back to it. Well, she vowed, it was not going to be her problem any more. And where the hell was Uldis? She should have got over whatever it was by now.

So readily had they planned tonight's supper! All of them getting together, assuming that she would do the shopping and cooking. Not one of them had expressed the slightest interest in her for months. Only the wretched party they wanted to give. Thankfully they'd finally abandoned that idea. She'd had to put her foot down, all right.

Fretting about one's children: she hadn't realised it would never end. As for Rob—just don't go there, Carla ordered herself. How could she live with so many areas of her life off limits to rational thinking? She was tired of holding it all in, tired of keeping up the façade of their new lives being all hunky dory when the reality was a shitty muddle.

Was that a sound overhead? Carla started like a teenager caught smoking. No chance. No doubt they'd all keep clear until someone else had done the tidying and the supper. Her shoulders drooped. Why should she feel guilty over a bit of self-indulgent ranting? She should probably be doing more of it. Rant, rant and tell them what she felt. It would be hopeless though, too many voices drowning her out rather than listening. Angry complaints seemed to be crammed into her head like feathers forced into an over stuffed cushion. Serve them right if she left them all to their own devices. That's what she should do. Why not? Clear off and shed all the conflicting pronouncements that her over-verbalising family was prone to. It had become like the Tower of Babel. Their words still reverberated in her mind, sniping, insinuating, arguing, opinionated.

Carla tiptoed up for her toothbrush, crept down for her bag, checked it for her wallet and grabbing a coat, went silently out of the front door, resisting the temptation to slam it.

The street looked just the same; she had expected a more dismal hue than the bright winter sun bathing the west facing houses, their colourful front doors picked out like a child's drawing.

No one about. A qualm was quickly stifled. That was what she wanted didn't she, silence and a breathing space? She gave her indignation full rein as she marched along. Then she slowed the fierce exhalations and counted each breath steadily, recollecting a short-lived interest in meditation and relaxation that Gabrielle had inflicted on them. Breathing was key. One two three four in, five six seven eight out. One two three four, five six seven eight. By the end of the next road she grew calm knowing she would have to decide what to do. She could blow a couple of hundred pounds on a decent hotel room, indulge herself with room service, and let the family do the worrying for a change.

She remembered the small hotel where once they'd celebrated a birthday, an award or whatever it was. They'd had a wonderful lunch in a shady courtyard beside a conservatory, lush with trailing plants. That was the place. Someone famous had lived there in the nineteenth century. Gracious and peaceful. You would hardly know you were in London.

Carla straightened her back and picked up the pace again. She mustn't bump into any of the family. They'd be on their way home at this hour. She went quickly down the busy steps to the underground, heading with determination for Holland Park.

At that very moment, Rose swiped her Oyster card at the barrier and looked up to see Carla hurrying through the station, her eyes fixed on the signs above the District Line escalator. Not heading home then, Rose decided, I wonder where she's off to? She turned to follow, a strange instinct leading her on as she ignored the exit and passed through the barrier in pursuit. A reckless exuberance filled her, drowning out the foolishness she refused to acknowledge.

Keeping her quarry in view was not difficult although the carriage was packed. Rose craned her neck and spotted her sitting at the far end. Carla did not look about her but picked up a newspaper lying on a seat and seemed absorbed in the pages. As she followed her off the train, a few minutes later, Rose was sweating, feeling a fool, almost dragging her heels now. At any moment she expected Carla to wave at someone and embrace the friend she'd come to meet. But Carla walked on, never looking behind, her back straight, an arrogant sort of pose, Rose considered. Then her footsteps slowed and she looked up into the entrance of a small hotel.

Rose was on the other side of the road, watching in surprise and then comprehension. There was a glimpse of a doorman and the neat figure in a navy coat disappeared. 'I've caught her in the fucking act,' Rose crowed before she panicked and scuttled away back to the tube station. 'So that's what you're up to,' Rose accused, instantly linking the disappearance in the park with the discreet hotel, feeling real pain as she thought of Rob, unaware, decent Rob, in need of her. For the first time she could see that he needed her. She headed for home, her mind whirling with the impulse to save him.

Chapter Thirty-Eight

Gabrielle fairly bounced along the pavement, conventional today in a neat suit with a short skirt, thrilled to have the successful interview behind her. The job would be a challenge but that was what she relished. The offices were just off Oxford Street. *So, all in all, brilliant. Pack in the temping. Hooray.* She pictured her parents opening her joyful email. WOO HOO nailed it, she had crowed. She skipped past a crowd of school children, hoping she would not scuff her good shoes and ten minutes later was to be found sitting carefully on a corner of a grubby piece of tarpaulin stroking a silky fawn head and discussing the iniquities of capitalism with the dog's owner.

'I call it market manipulation,' she sighed.

'Everything should have gone tits up with the financial crash and a better system evolved. Okay, not Communism, that doesn't work…'

'Except in Cuba,' Gabrielle interrupted.

'They're poor as anything. The trouble is finding a fair and honest system under a benevolent democratic set-up. Shush, Cass.' The dog whirled round to bark at two teenagers kicking a ball to each other as they ran past. Tim laughed and held up Cassie with both hands, pretending to be cross with her, 'Bad dog, noisy dog. No barking.'

'I'd better go. We've got loads to do at home. See you next week.'

Gaby hurried off, pleased that she had not boasted about the interview (Tim did not appear to be interested in job hunting at all) and glad that there was someone who did not feel the need to chat her up. Tim was authentic in his gentle rebuke to a society that driven him to sleep rough. She wanted to help him but she would make do with the scraps of friendship instead.

She passed the corner shop and took in an enticing waft of spices from the open door. She frowned, thinking now of Algie. Was she going to call him? No, she wasn't. He'd been sweet but it was a mistake to sleep with him. She'd not spared his feelings, making it clear she didn't want a boyfriend. He'd accused her of using him and discarding him without a qualm. The uncomfortable truth made her squirm. If only Aidan would make a move.

'Where is everyone? Mum?' called Gabrielle, running downstairs a little later. She heard a key in the lock and paused as it opened. 'Oh, it's you, Dad. Where's Mum? Pete hasn't seen her.'

Rob shrugged off his jacket and gave her a hug.

'Hey, clever girl, well done. When do you start?'

'As soon as I can. I'll have to agree the package and do a last week or two at the agency. Where's Mum?'

'I'm not sure. I've been out for a couple of hours.'

'I wonder what she had planned for dinner? We all agreed to be in tonight,' her voice dropped, 'she was keen to tempt Nina. She's worried that she really has got a problem. Says her eating habits are getting very minimal. Ma has a plan to entice her with special offerings. Do you think Pete, for once in his life, is quite worried?'

Rob sighed. 'I think he is but it's a tricky situation. If only her parents hadn't pushed off with their new partners they might take a bit of interest in the poor girl. I do feel sorry for her.'

'She's good at getting the sympathy vote, anyway,' Gabrielle turned from looking in the fridge. 'There doesn't seem to be much in here. I'll check the oven just in case. There may be something ready for us. No luck. I can't understand it when we definitely said we would all eat together.'

'It's not that late. We can always have a take-away but I'm sure she'll be back soon. Probably one of the committee meetings at what d'you call it, that stuff she's into?'

'No idea. Let's have a drink, shall we? I can tell you all about my interview.'

'Hey, you've got a job.' Rob waltzed Gabrielle round the kitchen. ' She's got a job,' he told Peter as they stumbled to a halt.

'Told you you'd get it.'

'All right, know-all.'

'I'm chuffed for you. What were they like?'

'Nice. It was all good. Pete, open some wine. Let's have a few bevvies. Is Nina deigning to join us?'

'Don't be a bitch, Gaby, though I suppose you can't help it.'

'Only kidding.'

They sat down at the table. Peter poured three glasses and plonked the bottle down in front of his father. Rob swept some of the clutter to the far end. 'This room is an absolute disgrace. We'll have to have a major clear up in a minute. By the way, I'm not happy about the way you kept us awake last night. For God's sake you're not sixteen any more. Behave like adults if you want to be treated like adults. I bet Mum had a terrible night. And not to tidy up after yourselves...'

'We thought Uldis was coming today.'

'No excuses. You left a dreadful mess. Congrats, Gaby. Well done,' her father held up his glass. 'Now, where is your mother? I must confess we had a teeny bit of a disagreement last night. Then I was out early this morning and she wasn't awake when I left. I'll give her a bell.' Rob stood by the glass doors, looking with satisfaction at the garden while he held the phone to his ear. The new paving slabs were pristine under the moonlight, the square of gravel had been swept, dust hosed off the specimen shrubs and the stone urns overflowed with pansies and hyacinths.

'Where are you Carla? Just wondering about supper. We could get it going. Give us a call.'

'You could try to sound contrite Dad. If she's pissed off with you, demanding your dinner is not the most winning formula.'

'Hi, everyone.' It was Nina in a dress that floated above the knee and pink ballet slippers. 'Are you in trouble, Daddio?' her soft voice was babyish, teasing…

Rob frowned at Nina's pet name for him.

'Nina,' he said reprovingly but his gaze softened as she looked at him. 'We had um, a few cross words last night and now Carla's rather late. Did she say anything to you about supper?'

'Not since we all decided it would be nice to eat together tonight. Have you tried her mobile? How did the interview go, Gaby?'

'Yeah! I got it. Woo hoo,' Gabrielle sang.

'Brilliant. I—'

'Where's that leaflet from the Indian take-away?' Peter began to rummage under a pile of newspaper. The others looked vaguely about.

'We must have a massive clear up after we've eaten,' Rob insisted. 'I'm hoping Uldis will have got over her flu and be back in the morning. We've certainly missed her the last couple of weeks. She must know we're relying on her.'

'Mum has probably remembered some meeting at the last minute and had to fly off. I wonder if she even bothered to read my email?' Gabrielle said.

'And no doubt had to turn her phone off. She'll see there's a message when she gets out. Nina, tell them your news. It's very exciting. Ah, here it is,' Pete brandished a menu. 'I'll write down the orders. Dad, your usual?'

Rob's kindly look moved from Nina to the choices before him.

'Um…' he ran a finger down the list.

'You like the fiery ones, Dad. Chicken vindaloo? I'll have a rogan josh I think.'

'Lamb dhansak, for me.'

Was anyone going to be interested, Nina wondered?

Carla could picture the scene as she listened to Rob's message on her voicemail. She shook her head. *Typical. He just doesn't get it.* Her uncertain intentions gained some backbone. She would put off ringing them for a while longer. They were hardly likely to call the police just yet. She looked about the hotel room with its sophisticated décor in cream and grey. Yellow highlights brightened a lampshade, the piping on a chair and the picture on the wall of a woman in a gauzy summer dress and a large brimmed hat.

She would have dinner and then watch the television. Should she text them first? The impulse was nagging at her. She'd rehearsed what to say, had considered the tone carefully: something precise, not whiney. She took up her phone from the table, weighed it in her hand for a few moments then turned it on and read Gabrielle's ecstatic email. Relief swept through her. That was something, something to cheer about. Gabrielle would be out, painting the town red, no doubt. Carla could not help but see that she had another voicemail. She had no intention of listening to Rob's voice again. She opened the messages and sent the briefest of texts.

Felt like a break. Back in a day or two. She resisted the habit of adding the ubiquitous x. She tapped SEND, turned off her phone again before a deluge of reproaches could ping back at her and after combing her hair, took the lift down to the restaurant. Her steps were really quite jaunty now the deed was done. She would not allow doubts to creep in. She'd have a nice glass of wine. Now you're talking, she told herself.

Rob knocked his mobile on the floor so clumsy was he in his haste, his fingers misbehaving. Pete knelt down, stretching to retrieve it from under a chair.

'Is it Mum?'

'Let me see.'

Rob snorted. 'Bloody hell—'

'What's up, Dad?'

'What is it? Is it from Mum?'

Rob handed his mobile over. His fingers tapped nervously on the table and he leaned back considering his options. 'Hey. Give it back,' he gestured towards Peter who had begun to tap out a few words.

'I was just going to put 'Don't be a berk, come home.''

'Hold on. Let's have a think first. What exactly is bugging her?' Gabrielle was perplexed.

'She was longing to get rid of the builders so she ought be ecstatic.' Rob complained. 'Felt like a break? Terrific. We'd all like a break, wouldn't we? Where the hell is she?'

'She's completely ruined my celebration about the job. It was meant to be a bit of a family beano tonight. You'd have thought she'd be pleased for me. I was really looking forward to it. I wonder.' She pursed her lips and sat back, arms folded. 'You don't think she's found out about the party? I warned you a surprise might backfire. Any one let slip anything? Nina, have some wine.'

'No one's said a word. You haven't, have you? Good God. The tent people will be here tomorrow. This could be an absolute disaster,' Rob fumed. 'It's just not like her. Buggering off in this fashion.'

'I'm going to try to ring her again. Something must have got her goat,' Peter frowned.

'No. Dad should do it. And this time say you're sorry she's upset, before anything else,' Gabrielle pushed the mobile across the table. 'Make sure she comes back in time for the party. You'll have to tell her about it. Yes, tell her there are loads of people all coming to see her on Sunday.'

'Right,' said Rob biting his lip, thinking *bloody woman* while he tried to get her.

'She's turned it off. I'll have to leave a message. Let me think. I'm going into my study. Get rid of those bottles. And take those cartons to the bin.'

Carla's behaviour was inexplicable. Rob sat at his desk, seething. *Sixty people coming to lunch in her honour and she does a runner. What's got into the woman?* For years he'd relied on her for that marvellous down to earth grip on things and now you could almost call her unbalanced in her temperamental departure. He could not imagine Louise stomping off in a hissy fit; she was the epitome of cool, yes, cool, calm and collected and decorous besides. A model wife, as far as he could tell, devoted to Charles. He marched back to the kitchen to check on the tidying and frowned as he looked at the faces of the children who still sat there looking equally baffled. He clasped his hands together to prevent himself hitting something.

'It's no good sitting there looking stumped for ideas. You lot clear up. I'm going to send her another text.'

'The last one didn't work,' Peter said.

'Dad. Be tactful.'

'Be nice.'

'For God's sake. What do you take me for?' he stood glaring with poisonous suspicion at the phone before grabbing it. He walked out again and ran his finger around the collar of his shirt. Everything felt tight, uncomfortable. He needed to vent his frustration with the woman. He tapped the keys of his mobile in a resentful tattoo.

I wish I knew what you're playing at. Have you any idea of the havoc you're causing? I know you were feeling aggrieved about the past but I assumed we'd all come to terms with that. Just when everyone is trying to do things for you for your birthday, it is SELFISH to bugger off and let us all down. We want you to enjoy your day on Sunday and are doing EVERYTHING to ensure that you do, but you need to be here with us! Please calm down and be reasonable. Come home. Besides which, you are upsetting Peter and Gabrielle. We'll all stay cool if you give up this nonsense and come back. Tonight, preferably. If I've done any thing wrong, naturally I'm sorry. Rob x

He read it through, corrected the predictive text that had exchanged cordial for causing and pressed Send. *Well, if that wasn't clear enough, nothing would be.* He stared into the dark, expecting an immediate response.

'What did you say to her?' Gabrielle had come in.

'I've just asked her to come back.'

'Are you sure? You didn't send anything too hasty did you? Let me see.' She snatched his phone as he tried to pull it away.

'Give it—'

'Let me see it. "I wish I knew what you're playing at." For Christ's sake, Dad, did you want to make matters worse? You have no effing clue. Get off, I want to read the rest of it.'

'Who has given you the right to read my message? It's purely between your mother and me. Now, give it—'

'No, Dad. You're unbelievable. Couldn't you have backed off for once in your life? "If I've done anything wrong I'm sorry." A fine apology, I don't think. We'd better repair the damage or she'll never come back. You've got to send another one. Think sensitive if you possibly can.' She gave a deep sigh. 'You'd better be a bit abject this time. I'll help you write it. Come back into the kitchen and we'll make it a joint effort. She'll be climbing the walls after the last one.'

Peter and Nina had had enough of the simmering atmosphere, leaning back in the new leather chairs, oblivious of the surroundings.

'It's not like your mum at all,' Nina repeated, 'it's just not like her.'

Pete was confident that she wouldn't let them down. The small matter of her ignorance of the party had yet to be faced.

'She'll get over it. I expect it's just the mess. She never did like mess. I expect she just flipped at the sight of it. We may as well go and get the curry. They said fifteen minutes. Come on.'

'Hasn't Mum replied?' he called out as they passed the sitting room.

Gabrielle raised her eyebrows, shrugged and rolled her eyes.

'Not yet. We're still on the case. I'm starving, so hurry up. Don't forget the naan bread.'

Rob and Gabrielle went back to the kitchen as the others went out into the night. He went straight to the wine bottle and filled up his glass.

She took her father's mobile while he sat nursing the drink, swirling it round and round. Gabrielle sat beside him rapping her fingernails on the wood then took a swig of wine. She stared at her father, thinking for a moment.

'What about this? Forget the last message. A bit stressed. I'm sorry you're fed up. What else should you say? Um. What say we tell her about the party? She'll come home for all your friends, I reckon.'

'Yes. That's probably a good idea. It should bring her back if it doesn't freak her out altogether. Say there's a little lunch planned for her old pals on Sunday.'

'Shall I put, Gabrielle and Peter have planned a surprise for you?'

'Better just say it's lunch, I think, and hope for the best.'

'There. I'll put 'all my love' too. How many kisses do you think?'

'Just send it for God's sake.'

They listened for the faint noise, the brief whirring of tiny wings carrying their plea.

Chapter Thirty-Nine

She had dinner before the restaurant filled up, quickly squashing a little self-consciousness at ordering a fancy meal all alone. The maître d' was charming, if verging on the obsequious. Carla had grown up long before power dressing business women owned the restaurant tables as much as any male. She made sure to savour every mouthful of the sea bass and each sip of the two glasses of house wine. All the same, it didn't take long. She paused at the door of the bar but that didn't feel right and she retreated to the room. Now she slid off the silky bedcover where she'd been propped up against the dimpled velvet headboard, watching but hardly taking in the television and made herself a coffee with a little pack of rare Guatemala blend from a bowl by the kettle. She supposed she would let the family off the hook in the end. She was beginning to feel unsure of herself. Had she simply overreacted? She paced the room feeling foolish and full of misgivings. She dismissed the childish notion that no one cared about her. It was nearly ten. She would send a message in a little while. Let them wait a bit first. She sat at the desk and doodled around the address on the hotel notepaper wondering what she would say. The ping of a text made her jump.

Now what? Ah, so that explained what they were panicking about. A lunch party: she should have predicted it. As usual, not one of them had been listening when she opted out, their minds made up, no rebellion expected. She shook her head in disbelief. It was so like them all: not concerned that she would vanish from their lives but that she might spoil their damn party. A party she'd like to remind them that she had declined in no uncertain terms. How dare he say that she was upsetting Gabrielle and Peter? Her eyes filled with indignant tears. All through the early years, arguments between them had been avoided for fear of distressing the children. Perhaps it had given them all unrealistic expectations. They were grown-up now! She could picture her family so clearly. Gabrielle in command, issuing instructions, full of herself and the job offer; Peter not sure what to think, trying to posit a positive spin on her going away, that dear puzzled look he'd never grown out of and Rob's expression, put out, even furious. Concern for her didn't seem to come into it.

They were a sorry bunch sitting despondently as they finished off the last scrapings of curry. Nina wiped a piece of naan bread around one of the foil containers.

'I really shouldn't. I'm stuffed.'

'That's the lot. Nothing wasted anyway,' Gabrielle held open a black bag as they dropped in the containers. 'It's not bad, that take-away. What did you think, Dad?'

'Oh, fine,' Rob had hardly spoken during the meal; his annoyance was still bubbling. He could not for the life of him understand the on-going resentment from Carla. Since they had arrived in London there had been moments of closeness but the norm had been unmitigated indifference enlivened by occasional outright hostility. Perhaps she needed therapy. She appeared to be stuck in an emotional response that bore no relevance to the here and now. Would it never end? He glowered at his children who stared back defiantly. No doubt where their allegiance lay.

'Time to tackle the mess,' he eyed the yellow stains on the table. 'Get everything cleaned up. God alone knows when Uldis will honour us with her presence. It's going to be hectic here tomorrow with the preparations. I suppose we must hope that Mum will be home, protest over,' he shoved back the chair and walked out of the room. The three young people exchanged wary looks.

She brushed her teeth and wiped off her makeup. How she was going to love the vast spread of this comfortable hotel bed; she was determined to sleep like a top. Tomorrow would be plenty early enough to give in and go home with her tail between her legs. Mum's little wobble it would probably be called, an amusing paragraph in the Unwin family saga. Still, what had she hoped for? A major drama, the police called in, wailing and hand wringing? Hardly.

She turned on the television to watch the news with its reports of arrested terror suspects and the latest on the political posturing of the Middle East nations, the refugees crowding the boats and shockingly the bodies of the drowned. Unable to watch the misery, the stories depressing her and filling her with fear for the future of her children, she extinguished the scenes, uninterested in channel hopping.

She sat uncertainly on the edge of the bed, staring blindly at her feet. All through the meal, beneath her determined delight in superbly prepared dishes, she'd been hardening her resolve, justifying her getaway. In the midst of the well-dressed clientele, the attentive waiters bending towards the guests, the pop of corks and the clink of silver on porcelain she had reprised the list of grievances. Was she indulging in mere posturing? Now, she sagged, giving in to a wave of regret. There was too much anger in the world and too many people running from war and oppression. The bitterness she felt seemed so petty in comparison. She gazed around the luxurious room, imagining a hungry family huddling beside an icy roadblock, in thin rags, forbidden from moving on.

She'd resented being taken for granted but wasn't that

exactly what being 'family' meant? Making assumptions, treading wilfully on each other's toes, being selfish because you could be, treating love carelessly. A family was the only place you could get away with all these things; it was pointless to rail against them. Make your stand, by all means, complain a little, throw up objections to this and that, let them hear your views loud and clear while hoping for the best. A little notice taken, some small consideration or concession given, a word of appreciation now and then was all you should probably hope for.

No wonder Rose was longing to be part of the Unwin family. Carla realised for the first time what it must be like for Rose to dread being forever the outsider; the lonely desperation of being disregarded, to be Rose and her mum, just her mum and Rose: a team of two. It really wasn't enough.

Carla stood up and walked about the pretty room, confronted by a ghastly shift of perception, guilty thoughts swarming suddenly in her mind. She had a cold stomach-churning view of her conduct, behaviour so uncharitable that at once she felt her self-righteousness lurching towards remorse. No wonder Rob had been dismissive of her objections to the girl. Yet he had listened, taken notice, not acted unheedingly. Thanks to her, Rose had been ostracized and Rob had nearly drifted away. Carla pulled back the curtain and stared down at the street and its reflections shining from the windows opposite. A taxi raced up to the entrance while the doorman in frock coat and top hat hurried out. Carla stood thinking, her cheek pressed against the cold glass, allowing her resentment and hurt to surface. She'd been badly treated, hadn't she? Just accepting everything made her a doormat, surely? Now, for the first time, the utter pointlessness of her role as slighted wife became apparent to her. What was she likely to gain from this pathetic little protest, wasting money on a hotel? Again she seesawed from blame to contrition.

She had been too hurt, too inflexible to accommodate the new situation. Once, she'd been proud of her fearlessness, always sticking up for what was right and true. It was one of the qualities Rob admired in her; he'd told her so, at times when they were up against it. How petty she had become; after over thirty years she had not found an ounce of forgiveness for the early error of judgement, an everyday transgression (when you thought about it in today's terms) that Rob had stumbled into in his twenties. A brief liaison. What on earth did it matter in the great scheme of things?

For months she had wallowed, there was no other word for it, in her presumed misfortune, poor wronged Carla, to exact payment from him. She had chosen months of hostile attitudes and non-engagement to deal out the retribution. She let the heavy damask curtain fall and walked over to the bed. Head in her hands, she submitted to the avalanche of regrets, recognising the miserliness of her instincts in shutting out Rose. She picked up the phone to ring home.

In the morning, after a long soak in the bath, making sure to use all the bottles arrayed by the basin, she wiped away the steam and stared at herself in the mirror. Her change of heart had made an unmistakeable difference: her face had lost its moue of reproach and the deeper frown lines between her eyes. Wet hair slicked back, rosy cheeks and pink lips recaptured a girlish look; she should be so lucky. She pulled a funny face at her reflection before dressing and going down for breakfast with a lighter step. She settled her bill at the hotel before strolling round to a nearby row of shops, expensive shops but what she needed as the birthday girl. It had not taken very long. The blue dress fitted like a glove.

They had told her not to hurry home, to let the house be prepared for the party.

'You're not to worry about a thing; we've got it all under

control.'

After finding the dress, she bought a paper and sat outside a café to read it. Out of the wind, it was almost like a summer's day. Fingers crossed it would hold for tomorrow. Now and then a pensive look crept over her face. Would her resolution of last night hold up? Rob had been a little curt but the sense of relief at home was palpable even over the phone. She would get back just in time for lunch.

Chapter Forty

For days Rose had seethed on Rob's behalf. She could have wept for him, having a wife like that. How would he cope with Carla's infidelity? No doubt in her mind about it; the familiar grasp on the arm, the scuttling to a secluded spot were dead giveaways, not to mention the blatant visit to a hotel. It would serve the woman right to suffer. How sordid it was. No wonder her poor father had been looking stressed and out of sorts.

Rose was buzzing. She had given up her pills, putting the packet out of sight and out of reach in a high cupboard. She just couldn't think straight when they when they left her feeling so hung over and drained of energy. This was more like it. Her mind could focus at last. An avenging angel she would be.

On the Friday she went to work as usual. She'd thrown too many 'sickies' to take another day off; anyway, Sunday was the day of the party. It would be divine justice to take Carla down when she thought she would be celebrating. Rose smiled, tickled by the idea. She'd be around to help Rob pick up the pieces. He would thank her in the end for opening his eyes. She walked tall, feeling purposeful, totally alive, not noticing the glances exchanged by her colleagues as she drove through her proposals, sparkling with an overflow of creativity. She dragged Simone out to lunch, explaining over the falafel that her real father had managed to track her down and was making her a part of his family: her new brother and sister welcoming her with the most amazing warmth and affection. She talked quickly and her eyes shone with restless anticipation.

'Everything will be different now. I never really had anyone rooting for me before. All my life I've dreamed of him turning up out of the blue, searching for me. It's unbelievable.'

'I'm so happy for you,' Simone said, 'I could tell you were on a high.'

On Saturday evening, Rose was agitated, jumping up to pace the room every few minutes, poring over Facebook with its photographs and trite remarks. It had been clever of Steve, the IT wizard in the flat above, to hack into Gabrielle Unwin's pages. Fuel for the fire, considered Rose, her indignation burning brighter. After two glasses of wine she rationed her drinking, some sense of 'saving herself for tomorrow' prevailing. Yet not for a second did she look properly into the future; she was consumed only by the knowledge that she needed to share with Rob, to lift the scales from his eyes.

As promised by the long range forecast the unseasonal weather continued over the weekend. On Sunday morning, Carla leaned out of the window to hear the strains of music. She looked over to the striped gazebo, breathing in the luscious air with relish. The sky was a limpid blue; you could imagine lambs frolicking in fields of daisies. There was Nina carrying a vase, ravishing in what looked like a cloud of spring flowers, a full skirted billowing froth of a dress. How marvellous that she had taken on the challenge of running the studio. She'd always suspected there was latent toughness in the girl. She would miss her quiet presence, in a way. There was Peter, moving a table under the direction of a waitress who laughed up at him, all red lipstick and restrained ballet dancer hair.

She had come upstairs to change; people would be arriving shortly. She touched up her make-up and slipped into the new dress and her smartest shoes. She would put up with the discomfort of high heels today; she had to look her best. The house had been transformed in the last twenty-four hours with nothing out of place, all the glass gleaming and every cushion plumped and ready. Even the kitchen, under the direction of the caterers was orderly, with food prepared and refrigerated, the staff outside checking the distribution of tables and chairs. Again she blessed the weather.

A dab of perfume behind each ear and she was done. She checked herself in the mirror, smoothing the fabric over her breasts and hips. At that moment Rob burst into the room.

'We're nearly out of time,' he stopped to stare at her. 'That's beautiful.'

'New dress,' she shrugged, 'if I'm to be the belle of the ball.'

He put his arms gently round and spoke into the warm sweep of hair at the side of her face. 'You look nothing like sixty. No one will believe it. I'm sorry if I drove you away. I've been,' he paused, 'thoughtless. Always felt that least said, soonest mended. Not the best approach, perhaps, for us.' He searched for the right words but Rob was not well practiced at apology. Had Gabrielle instructed him to grovel? 'You were quite right to make a stand. The kids have been appalling. And me, of course, at times, I'm sure. But thank God you're home. That's all that matters, anyway.'

Carla found that her arms had crept up round Rob's neck. She was touched by his almost humility; really he'd acted in character for the last few months while she had been trying out a whole new role of tragic heroine. Their lips brushed and she moved away.

'Did you text her?'

'Just going to.'

She made sure to smile as she watched him tap out the message.

Rose, come over to the house, join the party.

She turned away and went out onto the landing.

Rose waited until mid morning, watching the sun slide round the corner of the terrace of houses opposite, feeling nail-bitingly on edge as she checked the time again and again. It was impossible to settle to anything. She chose her smartest dress to wear under the usual anorak. She'd bought it for a cousin's wedding. Now, it lay on the bed waiting for her. When it was time, she stepped into it and pulled up the zip at the back using one hand then the other. She thought purple had some kind of mystical significance. Her bag had been prepared in good time. She put the strap over her head and adjusted the weight to hang against her side. Once out in the street her mind cleared; she moved full of determination, ignoring the humdrum surroundings, the passers-by and the fumes of traffic idling in a queue.

Going down the steps to the tube she did not hear the beep of a text message from Rob.

For half an hour she sat unmoving, her eyes fixed on the trembling floor of the train. Only the passing stations elicited a stare for a few moments. The train slowed again, the sign with her destination sent a shockwave that had her stumbling towards the doors. Then she was stepping down and walking along the platform as the train rumbled on. At the exit, the harsh daylight made her screw up her eyes as she followed the familiar route. It took her barely ten minutes.

At the top of the road she hesitated for the first time, clutching her bag to her, a lost look in her eyes. In front of her, a car manoeuvred into a tight space and every door opened as four people clambered out.

'I never thought we'd get here on time.'

'That was lucky,' a man said.

'Have you got the present?' another voice called out.

Rose lagged behind the couples as they tripped along the road that she'd peered down so often. Tripped was the only word for their pattering, excited feet, hurrying a little as they checked their watches, the very opposite of Rose whose slow heavy tread began to douse the flame of purpose that had brought her here. Reluctance undermined her. The possibility of Rob's disbelief occurred to her for the first time. The four guests turned in at Number 23 and a red haired woman in a cerise silk dress darted forward to ring the bell.

She couldn't see who had opened the door and the two couples disappeared inside. She almost stayed back, yet somehow her feet climbed the steps, her arm rose to the knocker and rapped twice, not too loudly.

'Hey. I'm so glad you've come. Carla said you should be here. Come in, come in. Let me hang your coat on that rail.' Rob's face was open, happy, the reserve and the usual expression of wary misgiving completely absent. It struck her forcibly in that split second that he was delighted to see her.

'Lastminute.com and all that,' he grinned the apology. 'You'll meet lots of our friends; we're expecting over sixty. You mustn't be shy. No one's going to bite. Anyway, you already know Gabrielle and Peter. Here, a glass of bubbly will help.'

He kissed her cheek and as she stood open-mouthed, took a foaming glass from the tray on the hall table and held it out.

'Really, it's just a few friends from our old village mainly…'

A ring at the door cut him off and he turned back to her as he took the handle, 'Go on through, everyone's outside. Thank God for a decent day.'

She moved obediently towards the back of the house. Now was definitely not the time.

In the kitchen the smell of toasted cheese and basil wafted towards her as two women, dressed in black with white aprons, lifted canapés from the oven. A few guests stood inside the sliding doors, craning their necks to soak up the height and space, while outside a small crowd gathered under a striped awning. She could see the builder bloke on one side with his young men holding pints of beer. Rose downed half the champagne in her glass as the latest arrivals came through behind her, looking around, holding their drinks carefully, taking a canapé, making small talk and giving her a half-interested appraisal. She moved towards the open doors across the enormous room feeling over-exposed in the aggressive daylight.

Outside, the light softened with shadows and she hesitated, downing the dregs of her glass. She noted the immaculate paving slabs beneath her feet, looked up, right into the gaze of Carla. For a split second, shock registered before a slow motion softening of Carla's features while Rose gave an involuntary jerk backwards, disguising it as a trip on the flags. 'Oops.'

'You made it. Great.' Carla's hands flapped, slightly lost for direction. 'But look, your glass is empty. That won't do.' She turned her head this way and that in search of a waitress as Rose offered birthday greetings, feeling they were both nonplussed. Close up, Carla seemed a slighter being, both in size and luminosity, her makeup perfectly unobstrusive, brown eyes more golden than dark.

A head interposed between the two of them.

'Carla, darling. Happy birthday,' two air kisses were delivered and eyes now rested on Rose. 'Hello.'

'Meet Rose, Rob's daughter from an earlier relationship. This is Cameron. You're looking so well. We're doing the doing rounds. Catch you later.' Carla put an arm out and pulled Rose gently to the next subset of friends. In a daze, Rose submitted to the progress with an uncertain smile and continued around the party. This was undermining her plan, a crafty move by the rook woman in a metamorphosis of motherliness that Rose distrusted with all her being. Yet she was powerless for the moment, succumbing to the animated introduction that Carla trotted out, which left no room for any expression of surprise until the two of them, joined almost at the hip, moved on, only vaguely sensing a few puzzled glances in their wake.

Round one to you, Rose thought as Carla swept away at last leaving her to Peter who was shouldering through the crowd at his mother's beckoning.

'God, you must need a drink,' he told her, 'come on.' She moved just ahead of him, a forced smile stretched across her face.

'Over there,' Peter said nodding towards a trestle table laden with bottles. 'Shall we sit down for a bit? I'll grab us a fill-up.'

He poured her a glass and then his own. 'Cheers.'

'Cheers.'

'Must be a bit boring for you, all this lot.'

'More like daunting,' Rose admitted.

'They're all pussycats. It doesn't matter what anyone thinks, anyway. You're part of the family now. Let's drink to that.' He clinked glasses with her and settled back, stretching out his legs. Almost immediately a beaming middle-aged woman came towards them, winding her way around the tables, her eyes fixed on Peter. As he stood to be kissed, Rose melted away through the throng.

Ill at ease, she looked about for Rob, edging her way past loudly chattering guests, despairingly clinging to the last vestiges of her plan. When, when to do it? Would she ever get Rob alone? A realization suddenly dawned that she could ditch it, chuck it, simply forget it. What had she been thinking of? Wasn't everything going to work out after all? Suddenly there he was, climbing on a chair, laughing and announcing lunch.

'Help yourselves from the buffet and find a seat.' He spotted her and jumped down, coming across to lead her over to the spread of cold meats and salads.

Gabrielle was back to her effervescent air of knowing she was loved by the world: the presence of the engineer with his obvious eye for her, the old family friends who still took a genuine interest in her life, contributed to her high spirits. Drunk on Dom Perignon and optimism, squashing barbs of resentment and ideas of future rivalry, Gabrielle decided that generosity to Rose, no need to go overboard, would cost her little; she'd see how things panned out. She'd take a bottle round the party again; head over towards Terry and Aidan, offer them a top-up.

Rob was riding high, applauding himself on the signing of the non-aggression pact as he called it privately. It was a while since every member of the family had looked so much at ease. Perseverance, not forcing the issue, had succeeded eventually. It was a relief that his passivity could be thought of in these fresh terms.

Late on, Rose had spotted Gabrielle and Aidan kissing in the utility room, oblivious of the catering team bustling past. Anxiety that waves of resentment from Gabrielle would drive her away was unfounded. Gaby had been friendly enough over lunch, passing along food and bottles with a grin; at least her mind was otherwise engaged for now. Peter and Rose had talked for ages. They'd found another quiet spot on a window seat in the kitchen while the party went on outdoors and had polished off nearly a bottle of wine during the heart to heart. He was easy to talk to; they both traded personal details that no one had been much interested in before.

'Do you think Gabrielle's okay with me now?' Rose asked eventually.

'Don't worry about Gaby. Her bark's worse than her bite,' he took a mouthful of his drink. 'We fought like cat and dog when we were kids. Still do at times but let me tell you a secret about Gaby. She may be spiky but she'll never bullshit you.'

'I longed for a sister or brother.'

'It's not always a bed of roses. I was rather ill, actually, in and out of hospital when I was a kid; she thought she got short-changed or something and had to toughen up. Resented me for a while.'

'Really? You know, I wasn't too well either,' Rose confessed, 'sort of bi-polar. Bi-polarish. It was pretty horrible. Mum still says I live in cloud cuckoo land half the time. It's funny though, since I've met you all, I feel, like, more complete. I know that sounds a bit soft but it means the world to me, being here.'

Peter was seldom introspective; this chat where they had both 'opened up' had accelerated an intimacy between them that surprised him. His sunny nature had returned recently with Edwina's slightly mocking acceptance of her dismissal; she had relinquished flirtation for the occasional deliciously complicit eye contact and teasing respect for his new status at the club. And thank God he'd been able to tell Nina the truth when she accused him. Now, pleasantly well-oiled, he gave Rose a sympathetic look and held up the bottle to see the inch or two of wine at the bottom.

'There you go,' he filled her glass and poured the dregs into his own.

'Here's to health, wealth and happiness,' he clinked her glass and drained his own. 'I must go and find Gaby; we're doing a speech for Ma. It's a bit cheesy but appropriate for the occasion. Come on, Rose, you can give me moral support.'

As she waited at the side of a large circle of guests, the urgent imperative that had faded over the last few hours overtook her again. Digging her nails into her palms, Rose assessed her chances. Rob stood beside Carla as Gabrielle and Peter called for quiet.

'Hallo everyone! We're just going to say a few words about Mum. Embarrass her no doubt,' Peter pulled a sheet of paper from his pocket and nodded at his sister.

Hardly embarrassed, Rose decided, staring at Carla, seeing her take her dues with mock modesty, the fulsome praises and gentle teasing wrapping her round. Now, her eyes fastened on Rob, would he join in the cheers and clapping?

Terry, standing on the grass just outside the marquee to hear the speech, was feeling gratified that Rob had introduced him to several residents of the street, insisting on handing over cards with the smart new logo and contact details designed by Gabrielle. A pristine pile of them had been waiting for Terry. It had given him a great deal of satisfaction to hear his praises being sung by Carla and Rob; they'd been a decent pair to work with and Rob had mooted a potential partnership on some projects under consideration. So it might not be goodbye to the family: he'd like to know what would happen to that minx, Gabrielle and whether Peter and Nina would hang in there. He looked across at Carla. She had handled herself well, that time after the girl had barged in. A bit of a turn up for the books, he concluded when the 'cousin' had been introduced today. Well, well, well, he'd thought, life was full of surprises. He wouldn't stay long at the party, the lads had escaped earlier; it wasn't exactly their scene or his for that matter.

'…keeping the show on the road…putting up with us all. Thanks Ma.'

Someone started singing Happy Birthday and Terry joined in with vigour.

After the toast, Carla had taken Rose under her wing, making sure she was introduced to anyone they'd missed earlier, stumbling occasionally over the awkward words, until 'Rob's girl, Rose, you know, from way back,' became a fluent opening to the animated greetings which followed, swallowing up any flicker of surprise from the Unwins' old friends in a charming fait accompli.

'Thank you,' Rose had felt compelled to whisper several times as Carla squeezed her arm in encouragement. Perhaps she was no longer pretending. Was this the real Carla not the monstrous figure of her imagination? How could she tell? Mortification accompanied Rose around the party; never again would she allow that vindictive tide to overwhelm her as it had over the last few days. She felt sick at the thought of what might have been. Minutes later she was swamped by scepticism; was it all an act on Carla's part? A clever ruse to win her over?

Gaby had got her wish with the music. The old favourites had people on their feet, knots of friends, young and old dancing all through the early evening. A benign audience sat around the edge watching and talking. At one point, Rob and Carla jived energetically inside an admiring circle that made space for them, finding an old rhythm as they spun across the floor. Rob was an easy mover, light on his feet. Carla tried to smile to cover the concentration needed on the more ambitious steps as she whirled. They were buoyed up by the news that their old neighbours had brought with them. The planning application near the Old Manor had been turned down: Rob and Carla were back in the warm embrace of their friends.

Nina had stayed busy throughout, helping with the food during the party, a distant yet determined look on her face whenever Peter caught her eye. Now she sat holding a mug of tea, looking exhausted, her dress crumpled, the ballet pumps grubby. In a day or two she'd start packing her stuff. She'd need to clear the room above the studio and take on another girl to help her. Ideas bubbled; her own designs coming to fruition at last, bridesmaids dresses and evening gowns in jewel colours took shape as her thoughts ran on and on, making plans beneath the chatter.

Hours later, nearly midnight, tears pricked the backs of her eyelids as Rose sat with the family at the long kitchen table, finishing off the leftovers. How nearly she had blown her chances by allowing an obsession to distort her perception, utterly clouding her judgement. She'd let things get out of control, had ignored the warning signs. She swore she would never let it happen again; she'd had a wake-up call all right.

She watched Carla's expression as she took an interest in Aidan, Aidan who held Gabrielle's hand, interlacing fingers. Perhaps all along just a mother showing maternal caution; probably nothing personal against Rose.

No one wanted to be the first to go to bed. Rose was to use the spare room, her progress from observer to family a dizzying ride. All at once she felt hollow: the bitterness and rage had ebbed away. One day she might let down her guard altogether. It seemed that she was a survivor after all.

Aidan's departure set off the movement of the rest. Gabrielle went out with him to say goodbye and Carla leaned over Rob's shoulders as he remained seated, her face close to his. Peter took hold of Nina's hair, twisting it into a ponytail with which he drew her playfully to the door. Rose stood up shyly.

'Let me show you to your room,' Carla said, 'I'll lead the way.'

THE END

BROWSE OUR TITLES